Advance Praise for *Spike Unleashed*

"How do you satirize everything Woke, Dope, and Dumb in our upside-down society while making even the Wokest, Dopest, (but not dumbest) humans laugh out loud? Put the hilarious jibes into the mouth of a wonder dog like Spike and his wise-ass master Bud. OMG. I thought I'd have to be hospitalized from laughing so hard. Thank you Spike, Bud, and Boggs for doing it again. This one's screaming to be made into an animated series."

—**Linda Stasi**, bestselling author, award-winning columnist,
New York Daily News, New York Post

"The book is an absolute delight! This is an exceedingly funny inside look at the foibles of the 'business of show,' and only Spike with his hapless master Bud in hand could innocently expose his tail (tale) in such a brilliantly acerbic comic manner."

—**Brian Cox**, actor, *Succession*

"Old Dog? Not really. New Tricks? Plenty. Turns out Spike has more to say. And more encounters with the virtuous and villainous figures of our time than any person, let alone canine, I know."

—**Bob Costas**, Hall of Fame broadcaster

"Not since Voltaire has someone written such an epic, funny takedown of the world in which we live. Yes, I'm comparing Bill Boggs to Voltaire. Yes, I am. He may have spent a lifetime in entertainment just to craft this scathing, hilarious look at popular culture. Bill's written an amazing, funny book. And so hip!"

—**Mike Reiss**, writer/producer, *The Simpsons*

T0036544

"America's greatest wits like Mark Twain, James Thurber, and Dorothy Parker would've stood and applauded after reading *Spike Unleashed*, but they can't because they're dead. So, I'll do it for them—right now I'm standing and applauding because this book is great!"

—**Alan Zweibel**, original *Saturday Night Live* writer, screenwriter, and Thurber Prize–winning author for his novel *The Other Shulman*

"One of the first things that attracted me to Bill Boggs decades ago was his incredible wit and his 'enchanted sense of play.' Now, he's found a way for his alter ego, Spike, to allow the Boggs sensibility to continue to flourish. It's great fun spending time with the two of them."

—**Lucie Arnaz**, actress

"*Spike Unleashed*…is a witty, timely, no-holds-barred satirical gem, and a fun read!"

—**Joe Piscopo**, actor, entertainer, radio host

"*Spike Unleashed* is not just a canny insider's look at the wackier aspects of show business but does so with consummate humor. Spike joins Reynard the Fox, Krazy Kat, and Bugs Bunny as one of pop culture's wry commentators."

—**John Mariani**, novelist and author of *The Hound in Heaven* and *Almost Golden*

"If you're trying to make any sense of the senseless worlds of pop culture, politics, celebrity, and social media, the hilarious adventures of *Spike Unleashed* are the most entertaining way to do it."

—**Paul Provenza**, comedian

"Bill Boggs's sequel to *The Adventures of Spike the Wonder Dog*, his delightful 2020 novel based on his real-life pooch, packs a wallop from start to finish. If you liked the first one, then you are going to like this even more."

—**Tripp Whetsell**, author of *The Improv*

"A Comedic Tour-de-Farce! This book spoofs the entire zeitgeist, nothing is safe."

—**Richard Baker**, comedy manager/producer

"Spike is back—and Bill Boggs has got him. America's funniest, favoritest four-legged hero returns in a whole new set of wacky adventures, filled with another cast of crazy characters and more pithy observations from a canine point of view. Once again, Spike is up to his collar in hot water, but, as always, the wonder dog prevails."

—**Will Friedwald**, *Wall Street Journal*

"Boggs and Spike have done it again!!! They'll entertain you and make you laugh out loud in this witty and worthy satirical sequel."

—**Neil Rosen**, PBS

"The return of Spike the Wonder Dog is welcome news! *Spike Unleashed* continues the tale of Bill Boggs' tale that inverts the old saying it's a dog's world. To Spike, it's a human's world, and he lets you know. Funny, replete with comic references including the Kardashians, this is one of those rare instances where the sequel is even better than the original. Spike is an animated feature waiting to happen! Read it! You'll bark with laughter. I mean howl!"

—**Marc Eliot**, *New York Times* bestselling author

"In the burgeoning field of funny show business satires told in the voice of their canine protagonists, Bill Boggs is the undisputed master."

—**Dave Konig**, three-time Emmy-winning comedian

"Go fetch the wee-wee pads. That's how hard you'll laugh. In his second picaresque romp, the masterful Spike the Wonder Dog has lost none of his bite. Self-important celebutantes and self-deluded social influencers, beware—you're no match for Spike's silver tongue. Talk about a wag."

—**Stephen M. Silverman**, author of
Sondheim: His Life, His Shows, His Legacy

Also by Bill Boggs

*The Adventures of Spike the Wonder Dog:
As told to Bill Boggs*

SPIKE UNLEASHED

THE WONDER DOG RETURNS

— AS TOLD TO —

BILL BOGGS

POST HILL
PRESS

A POST HILL PRESS BOOK

ISBN: 978-1-63758-984-7
ISBN (eBook): 978-1-63758-985-4

Spike Unleashed:
The Wonder Dog Returns: As told to Bill Boggs
© 2023 by Bill Boggs
All Rights Reserved

Cover design by Jacob Below
Illustrations by Jacob Below
jacobbelow@webcreates.com

Post Hill Press, LLC
New York • Nashville
posthillpress.com

Published in the United States of America

*Dedicated to all those I've met somewhere along the
way who've made me laugh—this one's for you.*

Every dog must have his day.

—JONATHAN SWIFT

Never lose your sense of humor.
It's the most valued possession you have.

—HOWARD HIGMAN,
L.H.S., JANUARY 1959

Warning: I got no trigger warnings for you.

—SPIKE

CONTENTS

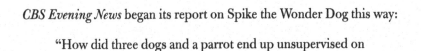

CBS Evening News began its report on Spike the Wonder Dog this way:

"How did three dogs and a parrot end up unsupervised on
a bus to East Hampton?"

Prologue

I got another big story to tell you. My first book was *The Adventures of Spike the Wonder Dog*. I did it with the help of Mr. Boggs. He's agreed to do the same with this one.

My master, Bud, and Mr. Boggs are great friends, and Mr. B., as people sometimes call him, is one of my closest pals, so I'd been missing him. Bud invited him to the world premiere of *Florida Man*. That's the movie I was lucky enough to star in last year before things broke bad for Bud and me. The premiere was in Palm Beach, where we'd shot it with Jim Carrey, Tim Allen, Lucie Arnaz, Kate McKinnon, and Prince Harry himself as the Florida Man. Quite the cast, huh? I got single title-card billing. But enough about me. Well, not quite, or that's the end of the book.

Mr. Boggs wanted to see if he could write the story of these latest adventures from my perspective, like he did with our first work. Luckily, back then, we'd found a special way to connect on a dog-human telepathic path (yes, 'shrooms were involved)—and we were able to do it again. So sit back, relax, and read all about what I was able to tell him once our psilocybin pills kicked in.

"Well, Mr. Boggs, it all began, I'm somewhat embarrassed to say…

PART ONE

HIGH POINT

CHAPTER ONE

The Parade

Because I was hoping to meet the Kardashian.
...**B**   High Point, North Carolina, a friendly town of about 115,000 people, where I'm on morning TV with Bud, was vibrating with energy on a bright Saturday morning.

Anticipation abounded that there would be a sighting of an actual Kardashian that crisp day, and maybe even an opportunity to glimpse a baby Kardashian that was rumored to be with her. They were comin' to town during Furniture Week to promote a new line of extra-comfy, wide-bottomed chairs.

"Biggest day in the history of the High Point since the Eisenhower parade after the war," a city councilman boasted on the local news, with the young anchor nodding in agreement while trying to place the name Eisenhower.

Bud's family lore has it that his great-great-grandmother as a little girl saw Abraham Lincoln at a Fourth of July parade in Philadelphia. Considering the direction our country's heading, I figured my spotting a Kardashian would be an equally prized memory for my descendants.

The city pulled out all the stops to create a parade in her honor.

That morning on the reviewing stand, I remembered the forgotten benefit of the pandemic's social distancing. Bud and me were crammed in with dozens of glad-handing, grinning, elbow-bumping business leaders and so-called dignitaries. All of them seemed to be wearing leather shoes in need of polish. Dogs will always notice your shoes.

We were standing with Mr. Lombardo, my master Bud's boss at WGHP-TV, who'd recently been drafted to be the mayor of High Point. The two North Carolina US senators and the governor had their eyes glued on their cell phones, waiting for confirmation that they'd be able to get a valuable picture with the Kardashian for social media, or, as a fallback, at least a shot of them attempting to kiss the closely guarded baby Kardashian.

"Desperate politicians," Lombardo whispered to Bud. "They figure she'll make them look hip, but if I know these guys like I do, they'll probably be leering so hard at her body that they'll be called out by the MeToo people eighteen seconds after the shot hits social media."

The Kardashian and the baby Kardashian landed with a perfect touch-down in their Zunum Agent Provocateur electric jet at the greater Greensboro airport. Bud had headed out there for an interview but turned back. "The road to the airport is so packed with people in trucks, cars, and motorcycles hoping to catch a glimpse, it looks like the traffic you see in the Woodstock documentary," he told me.

A little while later, they swooped into downtown High Point and landed at cordoned-off High Point Square in their Hermès Eurocopter EC 135, followed by the press corps in a rattling Vietnam-era Sikorsky with a couple of bullet holes in the damaged fuselage.

In order for photographers to get credentials for the event, all cameras had to be equipped with Kardashian-approved instant Photoshopping software. A woman in the press corps gave Bud an eight-by-ten she'd taken of me. Other than the fact that my head looked like Pete Davidson's, it was a fabulous shot—my tail was straighter, legs longer, waist tighter, muscles more defined. Pete's head was the only problem.

The *High Point Enterprise* described the reality star as she emerged slowly from the helicopter as "a celestial presence of voluptuous immobility in a Gucci long-sleeve tiered tulle dress holding a white wand. She was reminiscent of the Blue Fairy who grants life to Pinocchio in the classic Disney film, when she slowly pointed the wand to members of the gathered thong."

By the way, "thong," that's the word that appeared in the story—not "throng." Nobody's bothering much with copy editing these days.

For her security, she was quickly fitted with a PEF—a personal electric fence, a pink crown-like device that nestled onto her head and would emit shock waves if someone entered the defensive perimeter it created around her body. The thing's a bit like an electric dog fence, which I hate. If I'm zapped by one, the eyes cross, ears flip back, nuts vibrate, and I hafta to plunge my head into cold toilet water for relief.

The personal electric fence was designed to be a "social distancing" device to help celebrities, and was one of the many oddities invented during the pandemic. Once the PEF overcame the problem of folks electrocuting themselves by trying to power them up at Tesla Superchargers, it became wildly successful. The PEF's being hailed as an example of "America's triumph of government, science, and technology in the face of COVID-19," even though government, science, and technology haven't been able to, well…you know what happened….

The High Point Police Department struggled to restrain the onlookers straining to see the baby Kardashian, who was asleep in a lace-covered manger, handmade for the occasion at the Brothers of Nocturnal Emissions Monastery. Mother and baby were seated in a gleaming white vehicle with green stripes that resembled a cross between the Popemobile and Homer Simpson's car, "the Homer."

Inspired by "An Illustrated History of Papal Transport," printed on a souvenir placemat purchased at the Rome airport, Carolina Custom Cars created the thing on the chassis of a golf cart. The *Simpsons*-freak stoner who headed production couldn't get the idea of Homer's vehicle out of his mind, so we ended up with the irony of the Kardashianmobile being a merger of cartoon and religion.

The parade began with a roar from the crowd that rattled our reviewing stand.

The UNC marching band strode down Main Street playing the controversial new woke version of the national anthem, punched out by the unlikely collaboration of Jay-Z and James Taylor in an all-night Zoom session.

"Not quite ballad, not quite hip-hop, not quite right," the *New York Times* proclaimed in its review of the new PC anthem. "Perhaps its most relevant feature is the omission of the word 'brave' in the one remaining lyric line from Francis Scott Key's original composition into 'the land of the free and the home of the [blank],' which allows those singing to choose the word they want to commemorate in the blank."

Today the huddled masses filled in by wildly sing-screaming, "Kardashians!"

Most in the crowd were scrolling on their phones as the first float rolled by carrying local veterans of World War II. The proud old men looked like they'd rather be at home, comfortably sleeping through some black-and-white TCM movie, than squandering valuable energy waving at distracted onlookers. But wave they did, even though they weren't quite sure why they were being hauled out for a parade when it wasn't Memorial Day.

Bud had interviewed a vet that morning before the parade.

"Why the parade? Did we finally end that goddamn war in Afghanistan?" the stooped old man asked Bud.

"Rest assured it's over," Bud told him. "No, this parade's for a Kardashian."

"You know, young man, I actually saw five Civil War veterans in their blue Union Army uniforms in a parade in Newark in 1946," the old soldier recalled, "and now that's what it's like for this crowd. Here I am, eighty years after the big one, wearing my dress blues. They cheered in '46. Will they cheer today?"

"I sure hope so, but things are way different now," Bud said.

"What's a Kardashian?"

"That's what I mean," Bud answered.

I looked up at the old man and wagged the tail and smiled.

"You look like Patton's dog, Willie. Take good care of this guy," he said, gesturing to Bud.

I had no idea in that moment how challenging doing that was going to be for me.

The parade barreled on, mostly with ear-splitting music being mangled by local school bands. Because of school cutbacks, the bands had never been taught how to play and march at the same time. "I'm a Yankee Doodle Dandy" seemed to morph into Taylor Swift's "You Need to Calm Down," all in the same three-minute song.

The phonies on the reviewing stand were applauding the mishmash like aging rockers pushed to the limits of their endurance in the third hour of a Springsteen concert.

Lombardo told Bud that some businesses paid a hefty sum to advertise on electronic billboards mounted on powerful Dodge RAM 3500 trucks on loan from Marty Apple's Dodge dealership. Unfortunately, Mr. Apple forgot to fill the fuel tanks, and most of the gas-guzzling monsters ran out of gas a mile or so before the reviewing stand.

A reporter on the scene of the truck backup said, "A huge sputtering red RAM, obviously out of gas, was blocking the path of the Kardashianmobile. It seemed with a simple flick of her wrist and wave of her wand, Ms. Kardashian had the vehicle dragged out of her way by the merry men of the Ethel Merman Marching Chorus, who sang 'Everything's Coming Up Roses' as they shouldered the task."

One of the RAMs that did make it to the reviewing stand featured the latest scam of our old friend who calls himself "the Hebe named Zebe"—a former rabbi who's now a town fixture as an irredeemable but lovable con man. He was pitching his new training course. The streaming billboard on the truck was flashing:

> *Defend yourself against cancel culture.*
>
> Need apologies? We've got sniveling ones that still won't work.
>
> New identity? No problem. Just like *Better Call Saul*!
>
> Still watch Woody Allen movies? All charges dropped!
>
> Your opinions won't offend people!
>
> Why?
>
> You won't have any!
>
> Relax knowing:
>
> You won't get called out for eating ethnic food in public again! We deliver!
>
> Enroll now:
>
> *Be bland!*

I was staring at a thin man and woman holding a sign that read, "Try Veganism. Taste This Flaxseed & Chia Poster" when I smelled the High Point "Love Expert" approaching. She planted herself next to Bud, and without saying hello pulled on his arm, beg-asking, "When can I be on your show again, Bud? It's been months."

I was listening to her more intensely than I cared to, because she was standing on my right paw.

"Well…," Bud says.

"Your viewers need me. Have you ever done anything about vaginal dryness?" she wondered.

9

"Well, maybe, actually, yes, last Thursday night, yes, I think I...," Bud says.

"I mean on your show, you stupid man. By the way, you need a cougar like me to tame you."

The "Love Expert," Dr. Judith Kahill, was one of many locals ceaselessly bugging Bud to appear or reappear or have a friend appear, or have a competitor not appear, on his talk show.

She was a slight, middle-aged woman who reeked of Jungle Gardenia perfume. She had a mildly questionable French accent and oddly tinted red hair. Her clothes looked dusty, as if the perfume had deposited pollen all over them.

She proclaimed to have the power to advise people of all ages on achieving a happier, lustier love life. Her latest online certification from the Academy of Bodily Eruptions didn't enhance her credibility, or Bud's desire to have her return to the station after her last appearance, when she'd suddenly tried to masturbate live on the air. The moaning was nearing a Shakespearean crescendo when Bud threw to a break.

Unfortunately, the commercial was for Jiffy Lube.

She talks about her active sex life as if she has backbreaking sessions with a twenty-year-old bedroom mechanic six times a day. "I wonder who she's having all this sex with," Bud said to me after the show.

Years later, her diary, found in a tangle of vibrator cords, would reveal that her last major category-five orgasm had occurred back in 2003, courtesy of the singer Tom Jones in the men's room toilet stall at Elaine's restaurant in Manhattan. Apparently, only the arrival of George Plimpton and Pete Hamill entering to take leaks while gossiping about Jackie O. caused the frenzy to cease.

Her most recent recorded sexual encounter was in 2017, at the Rome airport Hilton. A flight attendant on the trip over, thinking she was Dr. Ruth and entranced by the celebrity of it all, arranged to meet her at her room.

I started barking politely to get her off my foot as she rattled on with her pitch.

"Bud, for our next TV show, we must do anal. Anal is wide open. No one's covering it. This is an historic time in the history of the human ass," she pitched him.

"Dr. Kahill, please stop. A troop of Brownies is marching this way now."

"All the more reason for a modern broadcast about the benefits of a good old-fashioned Swedish bike ride, Bud."

"Disappointing. I've always had you pegged as a tail gunner, Bud," she said.

I barked, serving notice that I'd like to regain control of my leg.

"What's wrong, Spike?" Bud asks.

"Look, Bud, back-street sessions are very popular. Just imagine those Brownies ten years from now," she bellows, pointing at the girls who'd stopped in front of our viewing platform. "Because of new restrictions on sex ed in schools, they won't have learned that what was fifth base is now the new first base."

"OK," Bud said, "in ten years you can be on the show discussing it, but for right now, you're standing on Spike's paw."

She moved her foot, didn't say, "Oh, sorry, Spike," and continued. "No, me on a show next week, Bud, me. Please, anal!" she says way too loud.

Lombardo leans over and whispers to Bud, "Get that woman to shut up about sodomy. The Brownies are staring at her, and Ms. Kardashian is coming."

Cheering—rivaled only by the roar emitted out of every window in Philadelphia when the Eagles conquered the Patriots in Super Bowl LII—greeted the sight of the Kardashianmobile.

The president of the Chamber of Commerce, walking like a man hurrying to a bathroom in the back of a restaurant, came to the microphone to introduce her.

Several minutes later, I noticed a clenching of the Kardashian's jaw stifling a yawn as the president finally finished reading the four pages of praise comparing her to Nobel Peace Prize recipients that he cobbled together as the city's tribute to her.

She floated to the microphone.

I looked at her closely. "She'll never age," I thought. "She's very beautiful, but possibly about as biodegradable as a plastic bottle."

The crowd gasped a huge "ahhhhhhhhhhhhhhhhhhhhh!" as if a tongue depressor had just been placed in fifty thousand mouths.

"Hello, High Point," she said softly.

More tongue depressor sounds.

"They wanted to give me the key to the city, and I said no. I just want to say hello to the biggest star in town."

I noticed Bud's shoulders straighten. Lombardo elbowed him like, "Wow! Bud, here you go."

"I want to meet…Mr.….Mr. Spike the Wonder Dog."

"Spike! Spike! Spike! Spike!" the crowd chanted happily.

"That dog's unbelievable," Lombardo says.

Bud wasn't disappointed. He was happy for me, for us—the Spike-and-Bud team. I was just glad to get away from the reek of Dr. Kahill's perfume.

"Well, Spike, you've done it again. This is great. Here you go," Bud says as we head to the small stage.

"Hello, Bud," she whispered into the mic. "And Spike, there you are, Spike. Come here, boy," she commanded softly.

I looked at her. She looked at me. I still looked at her, embarrassed that I didn't know exactly which Kardashian this was.

"Come here, Spike. Come here, boy. Come on."

"Put on a show," was the last thing I remember thinking.

From an all-four stance, I hopped straight into the air—one of my favorite stunts.

The crowd roared, "*Spike!*"

I ran to greet her…

The next day, I woke up at our house. Bud told me I'd been electrocuted.

The Kardashian's PEF was set to "Repel Tanks"—the maximum jolt possible. Her people hadn't had the good sense to switch the thing off before she called me to her.

I was lying on my back, four paws to the ceiling, thinking, "What the fuck?"

"Spike," Bud said, "thank God you're OK. You've been out of it for almost a day. I think you were hallucinating."

I had been. It was highly weird, and I can't remember everything, but it was intense. What I can tell you is that I was in a giant arena. Maybe the MGM Grand Garden, some big place. It was packed with thousands of people mostly wearing red hats.

It was some kind of live show.

This I remember clearly: to make money for ever-mounting legal fees, Trump had signed a deal with his friend of thirty years, Geraldo Rivera, for a live TV special called ***Uncovering the Mysteries of Donald Trump's Head.*** The concept was inspired by Geraldo's endlessly hyped but ill-fated live special where he dramatically smashed open gangster Al Capone's secret vault, and nothing turned out to be in the vault.

The one-thousand-dollar pay-per-view Trump event had been created to reap a huge profit by showing the world the bald Trump. Ringside seats in the arena went for ten thousand. Trump souvenir combs sold for a hundred bucks.

To make things as spellbinding as all of his work had been, Geraldo needed to build the drama. On the long journey to reveal DJT's scalp, he planned to use tiny scissors to cut off strands of hair in the gale-force-wind-defying concoction.

Trump was selling each hair for a thousand bucks, with the sixteen-inch locks from the back of his head, which are so crucial to the engineering of his comb-over, priced at three thousand because of their historic value in the history of the presidential head. Unfortunately, because of the three decades of accumulation of toxic elements from Gorilla Glue hair spray, sales of hair had been vetoed by the Nuclear Regulatory Commission. The whole pile of shorn hair was to be dumped into a biohazard container, to be sent to the central depository under Yucca Mountain, where much of the nation's highly radioactive waste is stored.

During his entrance, Trump appeared strangely quiet, like he'd been heavily sedated backstage or was displaying yet another version of his popular "Sleepy Joe Biden" walk to amuse the crowd.

With Senator John Fetterman flapping his long arms and soaring menacingly above the spectators like a condor in a gray hoodie, the Mike Pence Irish Dancers opened the festivities. The former VP was still not talking to Trump but was happy to showcase himself on the dance floor. He was front and center, dancing straight-backed, arms rigidly at his sides and feet flying with surprising precision as his baggy blue suit heaved up and down. His face displayed his usual no-visible-signs-of-life expression while he executed a flawless "hop jig" that segued into a rousing "Cross." You'll know a Cross if you've ever seen a PBS fundraiser. It's the one where it looks like one knee is hiding behind the other while the dancer's wooden clogs are splintering all over the floor.

Since everybody had coughed up the big bucks to see the bald Trump, the next feature was a montage of photographs of famous men without their toupees or transplants. Cardi B sang "Suicide Blonde" wearing a G-string and pasties fashioned from unused N95 face masks, as the crowd gasped at shots of Ben Affleck, Elon Musk, William Shatner, Elton John, Charlie Sheen, Nick Cage, Jeremy Piven, and on and on...

The cutting of Trump's hair, performed by Geraldo with a tone of smarmy self-satisfaction, also went on and on. Imagine about two hours of it, with breaks only for Irish dancing. No, please, spare yourself—don't. Let's just get to the end and the shocking conclusion of my hallucination.

Trump was about to rise from the table to reveal his bald pate to the world, when the plot to double-cross his pal Geraldo suddenly unfolded.

Rudy Giuliani, who hadn't been seen or heard from for months, much to the relief of the nation but to the detriment of MSNBC ratings, emerged from his lair waving his arms, screaming, "No, Donald, no!" to distract Geraldo. Ivanka and Don Jr. charged the stage, and muscle-bound Roger Stone tackled Geraldo and planted him on the canvas.

Huge banners proclaiming "Fly Trump Hair" unfurled all over the arena, revealing that the logo from failed "Trump Air" had been hastily reworked with a big "H" added to "air." The Trumps were using the spectacle to launch a business to overtake HairClub, and the former leader of the free world would serve as its bewigged pitchman.

Ivanka fitted a Trump Hair wig on Trump's head.

Thousands of phone cameras flashed as Trump rose to face the crowd.

Holding a gold mirror to his face, he said, "People are telling me I look very, very good, very good!"

Trump resembled a Viking, or maybe Mel Gibson in *Braveheart*, or maybe Will Ferrell in *Eurovision Song Contest* (Google them), or maybe any baseball player from the '80s with a mullet.

Ivanka chimed in, "Fly Trump Hair. It's real synthetic hair, factory-to-scalp fresh."

"They're telling me I look great," Trump barked. "I'm hearing I look great." "Look great...look great" echoed around the arena.

The last thing I remember was people hurling their new hundred-dollar combs at Trump in protest, while Rudy scurried around with a red MAGA shopping bag scooping them up them for resale outside at his small booth between a couple of trucks in the parking lot.

Bud was stroking me, trying to rub away the electrocution marks on my stone-like head. "And guess what?" he said. "I have a little surprise for you. It's…"

Bud's surprise announcement was drowned out by the annoying sound of my girlfriend Daisy's barking, demanding me to run out to the yard and pay attention to her, even though she knew I felt like sixty pounds of burnt bacon wrapped in a dog suit. "How much more of her can I take?" I wondered.

"A very strange thing happened yesterday when we were at the parade," Bud said.

"Yes, Bud, I know. That's why my legs feel like battery cables," I thought.

"While we were out, someone sent us a big, very talkative African grey parrot. I'll get him. He says he has a message for you."

"Why would anyone send us a parrot?" I wondered.

Daisy kept at it, with loud, insecure barks in the pattern of an SOS, which reminded me just how threatened she was going to be if I took any time away from her to give any attention to a parrot.

Bud opened the door, and in swooped a handsome bird with a dark gray body, red tail feathers, and white around his eyes that made it look like he was wearing bird-sized goggles. He flapped past me and landed on the windowsill.

"Shut the fuck up!" he squawked at Daisy through the screen.

He took off and landed on my stomach. He peered at me with his head bobbing sideways. There were yellow irises around his dark pupils.

"I'm Herbie," he yakked.

I nodded slightly, the way Marlon Brando might have done in *The Godfather* if a parrot had presented himself asking for a service.

"Where's Chicago Bob?" the parrot asked.

I raised my jaw just a touch and narrowed my eyes as if the Godfather needed more information.

"Bad news for Spike. Bad news. Spike goin' down. Spike dead dog," Herbie squawked.

While I was conjuring my most complex Godfather reaction yet, Daisy started barking again, even louder than before.

"I'm taking Daisy back to Buffy's. She's out of control," Bud told me.

"No kidding, Bud," I was thinkin'. "The dog's ruled by insecurity."

"Dump her!" Herbie commanded.

CHAPTER TWO

PILLOW TALK

The next morning, I was headed to our station, WGHP-TV, with Bud 'cause I was set for an appearance on his talk show, *Southern Exposure with Bud*.

I was shaky, not my usual confident, in-command self. Next time you get electrocuted, aim for two full days to recover.

Bud told me the setting on the Kardashian's PEF was powerful enough to overturn a Range Rover speeding into its force field at sixty miles an hour.

The *High Point Enterprise* story on the incident reported, "The Wonder Dog shot into the air and tumbled in a wide arc above the crowd. He was fortunate to be caught about forty yards away by a leaping Minnie Stokes, the center for the Tar Heels, UNC's women's basketball team, who jumped nearly three feet in the air to grab him. Ms. Stokes stated, 'Spike's body felt as hot as a turkey right out of the oven.'"

She dribbled me over to Bud, who took me home. Well, not actually dribbled me, but that's how I imagined Bud got me.

We were set for a program that would include the Bleesdales, neighbors of ours in Thomasville, who were the subject of a recent story in *TV Guide* by Matt Rousch.

"Barry and Betty Bleesdale," it stated, "are the first known American parents intentionally to raise four children to participate in reality television shows as their life profession. Their conditioning began in the crib, as each baby was indoctrinated with streaming reality shows during all waking hours of infancy.

"This year, all four children, plus Barry and Betty themselves, are set to audition for seventy-six different shows, ranging from *Swamp Families of Newark* to *Teen Hookup Nightmares*," and old favorites like, "*I'd Live with Goats to Be on TV*. Will the Bleesdales experiment in child rearing become its own reality show? Or might Barry, Betty, and the kids seem too real being unreal to seem real? Stay tuned."

I was in my little doghouse on the set, not knowing what Bud would have me do but praying it did not involve electricity.

He read a long intro of the Bleesdales, mostly culled from the Rousch column.

"OK," he said. "Here they are, with a little demonstration."

The door on our set swung open, and out first was daughter Babs. I've seen a lot of guests enter through that swinging door, but none with the enthusiasm of Babs.

She charged forward in typical over-the-top reality show style, shrieking, "Oh my God! Hello, Bud!" while waving her arms over her head. Somehow she was able to hop up and down while contorting herself in a series of shimmies, shakes, and gyrations that would have knocked Simone Biles' spine out of alignment.

"Bud," she gasped, looking at him like he was about to give her a rose on *The Bachelor*. "Bud," she whimpered, as if she'd just been voted off the island on *Survivor*, "Bud," she said, with the exact ambivalent sense of discovery she would need on *Married at First Sight* when she saw that the man she was about to marry weighed three hundred pounds and had substantial face and neck tattoos.

Babs sat down.

The rest of the family's entrances were equally surreal.

"Well, that was really something," Bud said, rubbing his eyes. "Tell us a little bit about the training that went into all of this."

"The children have any skill set that would be required on any reality show. Over the years, the thousands of hours they've absorbed have conditioned them to believe that other people are selfish, petty, and untrustworthy, a fundamental worldview required on many of these shows," Betty explained.

"How do you and Barry feel about that?" Bud asked.

"We're for anything that'll help them succeed! They speak several languages and have intimate knowledge of negotiation, deal making, and psychological manipulation and intimidation. They're able to survive without food or water for several days, and, most importantly, considering the way these shows are evolving, the kids have a complete command of every position displayed on Pornhub," their mother boasted.

"The human face," Barry added, "is capable of dozens of basic and complex expressions, which they can summon with lighting speed. Whatever the director of the reality show wants in a scene, we can deliver it on the first take."

"Please, Bud, let's have a demo," I'm thinking. "Enough with this longwinded crap. It's evident they're always performing, even when not on TV. I see this fake stuff in a lot of humans who're watching too much reality TV and not enough shows with realistic good old-fashioned family values, like *Family Guy*."

"OK," Bud said. "I'd like to see what you are talking about."

At last, the right question. Bud, I love you, but you're a step slow today 'cause once again, you were up till four in the morning joy-of-sexing it with your old friend Brenda.

I always liked Brenda, except for the fact that a while back when I wasn't quite housebroken, she wanted me neutered, and that's why she and Bud broke up.

"Love me, love my dog's balls," he told her.

These days we're proud of Brenda for lap dancing her way through law school and creating High Point's hottest new law firm, staffed exclusively by women who financed their degrees by working in the exotic services industry.

"OK, ready, Bleesdales. Neutral," Betty ordered, and the kids' faces instantly looked like *Westworld* robots with the power turned off.

"Here we go. Please show the expression fearfully angry...next, sadly surprised...and now, 'Can't find my socks.'"

As their faces were contorting into strange grimaces, a man with obviously dyed hair and clutching a pillow barged on the set yelling, "It's a conspiracy! I didn't do it. I can prove it..."

"It's Mr. Pillows!" the Bleesdales shrieked, aware he was involved in *Sleeping in Hell!*—a reality series based on people trying to fall asleep a few feet away from a blast furnace at the largest steel mill in Gary, Indiana.

Sleeping in Hell! was to be Matt Lauer's TV comeback vehicle. So as not to trigger viewers by his presence, Lauer would be unrecognizable in a beautifully tailored thirty-pound flame-resistant hazmat suit, with a massive helmet to alter his voice. He would be billed as Scott Carter, "the Hooded Host."

"I couldn't stop this pillows guy. He's crazed," Albert, the station security guard, explained. "Shall I call the cops?"

"No sense risking his being gunned down. I'll take care of this," Bud answers.

Mr. Pillows planted himself in front of a camera and screamed, "Yes, I did give my pillows to some high-ranking government officials as presents after the January sixth insurrection, but the rest is a conspiracy, a conspiracy! Won't anyone believe me?"

"Look, Mr. Pillows," Bud explained, "I told your people, for personal reasons, I did not want you on the show to discuss all the social media reports that your pillows have—"

"What reasons? What reasons?" Mr. Pillows interrupted.

"I hate your pillows, Mr. Pillows," Bud said flatly, "and as a matter of fact, so does Spike."

"Oh…no," the Bleesdales gasped.

That's the truth. Bud ordered a pillow. After one night with it, he'd needed several spine and neck adjustments at Bernie's Chiropractic down the street—not covered by insurance, by the way. Then he put the thing in my doghouse. It felt like I was lying on the stone beach in Nice.

I threw the pillow into the woods. The squirrels tossed it back.

"But it's all not true. My pillows do not automatically record conversations during sex. This is vicious fake news."

"Wow," Mr. Bleesdale said, "now there's a show idea, kids."

A wild-eyed Mr. Pillows bellowed, "Someone created those recordings of Mitch McConnell grunting and groaning like a wounded moose! Jared and Ivanka are pissed. They keep kosher. On a Friday night, after a quickie, when they should've been observing Shabbos, they're recorded sipping champagne and watching the Joy Reid show. Gavin Newsom's wife won't talk to him, even though he insists the voice on the tape praising his prowess in the sack is hers, not Senator Sinema's."

"Look, Mr. Pillows," Bud said, "from what I hear, it's not all bad."

"It *is* bad," he moaned. "All rumors."

"But how about Justice Amy Barrett, right?" Bud persisted. "First, she claimed she couldn't remember ever having an orgasm, but then she walked it all back by saying, 'Oh, silly of me, I forgot, yes, I always have them, and the four-alarm screaming on the recording is definitely me.' She's getting tons of admiring mail now, right?"

"This a conspiracy, Bud. It's terrible. It's that awful QAnon group!" Mr. Pillows says, gnawing on the corner of the pillow he was clutching. "A conspiracy!"

"But, Mr. Pillows, didn't you always kind of support their claims?"

"Yes, but this is about *me!*"

"Albert, kindly please escort Mr. Pillows out of here."

"No, let me tell my side of it," Mr. Pillows pleads.

"Enough…. Albert, he's gone."

The Bleesdales run after Mr. Pillows, hoping to audition for *Sleeping in Hell!*

"Bark us to a long commercial break, Spike," Bud orders.

After the show, Lombardo entered the studio looking unusually curious.

"Bud, fill me in, please. When I was coming back to the station from that cesspool of self-serving liars at City Hall, I saw a man running down the hall biting a pillow, chased by six people, screaming that you're an asshole."

"Quite likely," Bud says, "and by the way, that was no ordinary man bellowing that I'm an asshole. That was Mr. Pillows."

"That pillow, oh my God!" Lombardo says, painfully rotating his head. "What it did to my neck! Ugh."

"I know," Bud agrees, cracking his spine.

"Were those people chasing Mr. Pillows demanding refunds?"

"No, they're the Bleesdales, that reality TV family. They want an audition for *Sleeping in Hell!*"

"Hold it," Lombardo says, noticing the large monitor. "Let's watch. I haven't seen Brenda's new commercial."

Lombardo, Bud, and me stare at a thirty-second spot for Brenda's law firm, Wright and Wong. It was a bit like an old *Baywatch* promo, except it featured seven beautiful lawyers wearing matching Dolce & Gabbana peach silk satin pantsuits, running in slow motion with briefcases down High Point's Main Street. Brenda did the VO on the tagline: "And remember, we earned our degrees the hard way."

"You gotta love Brenda. She may end up having lap- and pole-danced herself to the Supreme Court," Lombardo says. "Aren't you dating her now that you and Buffy fizzled out?"

"Dating? Well…"

"I'll take that as a yes, Bud."

"Modern dating isn't like it was back in your day, boss. Now, it's about hooking up, texting photos, sharing apps, friends with benefits. And there are way more hazards. You can get yellow-carded, bread-crumbed, ghosted, bird-boxed, dial-toned, pillow-teared, or—"

"Are condoms in your wallet still a part of it?" the boss interrupted.

"Unfortunately, yes," Bud said.

"Then it *is* like dating back in the day."

21

At our house in Thomasville that afternoon, I was relieved Daisy wasn't in the yard. That meant she was with Buffy at their place in Walberg, exactly 19.2 miles, around 41.3 minutes, from us. When I hear Buffy on the phone happily announcing, "I'm coming with Daisy," that's all the time I have to steel myself for her arrival.

After that not-so-good year in New York City, Bud and I moved back to North Carolina. His goal was to buy the TV station with Lombardo. I was really happy that Daisy started coming over for regular visits. I was in love with her then. It had been love at first sight for us just before Bud and me departed for New York. I longed for her while I was away. When I came back and we finally could be together, it seemed too good to be true. But as I got to know her, little by little not-good stuff was happening. Now I want out.

How do you deescalate a relationship if you're a dog? Please send suggestions to Spike@Spikethewonderdog.com. Otherwise, I'm gonna have to figure this out myself.

Bud was upstairs with Brenda. Herbie was preoccupied cooing at himself and dancing in front of the mirror. I curled up and fell asleep hopin' to block my relationship woes outta my head, and I had a dream.

I think the old brain was still recovering from electrocution, 'cause it was more intense than my usual recurring dream about taking a shower with Cher.

This dream starts in a huge, very old theater, as a big red velvet curtain slowly begins to rise. Standing in the spotlight are long-dead dogs who were once big film stars—Toto, Lassie, Rin Tin Tin, Old Yeller, Beethoven, Marley, Air Bud, and my hero, Bodger, an English Bull Terrier like me, from *The Incredible Journey*.

I'm overjoyed. These are my idols.

OK, maybe I've become a little bit of a hit on TV and social media, but these are big-time movie stars—the real deal. If the ones who are still alive are living in mansions in Bev Hills, I'm way down in Orange County in a shabby two-bedroom stucco bungalow with very little landscaping, spotty Wi-Fi, and a neighbor whose biggest film credit is Dr. Joe in *Nasty Nightshift Nurses*.

The stars on the stage stare at me.

I bark hello. No response.

They're glancing at each other like, "OK, who's gonna speak?"

Very slowly, mighty Old Yeller steps forward.

"Spike, listen to us," Old Yeller barks.

The dogs part, leaving an open space in the center of their lineup.

From the rear, walking with his head high in truly commanding posture and looking freshly brushed, Rin Tin Tin strides forward.

"Pure charisma," I'm thinking.

"OK, Toto," Rin Tin Tin commands, "take it."

Little Toto scampers all the way to the edge of the stage and peers down at me.

"Don't take life too seriously, Spike. It's all a joke."

They vanish. I'm alone in the theater, like Bud was the night he got high and went to see *Hamilton* sung by the Mormon Tabernacle Choir at City Center. Thankfully, I wake up before three hundred Mormons start rapping. My head's still not right from that goddamn electrocution.

"It's all a joke, is it?" I think.

It didn't feel like a joke after Ike "I Got Money" Piles had me kidnapped, forced me into dogfights, and tried to freeze me to death back in NYC.

When I open my eyes, Herbie's staring at me. He's eyeing me warily, squawking, "Spike goin' down! Spike dead dog!"

I don't know why he's telling me that all the time. I just want Herbie to know that he's safe with me, 'cause let's face it, bird-dog relationships are not always peaceful. Think about a German short-haired pointer looking ever so happy with three birds in his mouth.

I give Herbie my biggest "hiya, pal" kind of smile and beckon him to come and stand on my head, while urging caution not to crap on the cranium.

It doesn't take long for me to learn about him. His ancestors were performing parrots in Africa. His real name is Feechi. He got stolen from a bar in Casablanca, where he worked insulting tourists. He'd achieved a big following. *World Travel Guide* said, "You haven't been to Casablanca unless you've been called a 'stupid, ugly, s-head, flip-flop-wearing, tacky American tourist' by the infamous Feechi, the African grey parrot who works the lounge at Joe's Place.

Late one night, an American, part of a team of parrot-nappers, grabbed him off his perch at the bar. He got smuggled to Greenwich, Connecticut, in 2019. "Bad stuff there. Bad dude," was all he'd say about his life in Greenwich. A couple of nights ago he fell asleep and woke up as he was being shipped here. He has no idea why. He misses a guy named Chicago Bob, who took care of him in Greenwich.

"Bob kind man, not drunk slob singin' 'As Time Goes By.' Shut up and go back to your ship, fatso," he yaks, apparently flashing back to the happier times of his lounge act.

I let him know that I'm still not quite myself 'cause of that little PEF incident. The slow-motion video from someone's phone showed that I'd spun almost three revolutions a second while going sixty miles an hour for almost forty yards.

"*Top Gun*, Spike!" Herbie says.

Bud and Brenda stagger into the living room.

"Hi, Spike. Well, our nap's over."

Folks, don't treat your dogs like children after you've had sex. First, the kids almost always know anyway, and second, we dogs are hip to it even before you start. Why? It has something to do with our noses.

"What are you two doing?" Brenda asks us.

"Buy a round for everybody! Spike goin' down!" Herbie squawks, flying to the top of the bookcase.

"We missed the first ten minutes," Bud says, "so let's put it on and have a drink."

Bud and Brenda settle in to watch their favorite new alt cooking show, *Grillin' and Pillin'*, a program promoted as "a pain-free approach to open-fire food prep, starring opioid-loving amateur cooks who'll entertain you in an Oxy-popping barbecuing frenzy."

"So what's new at the law firm, Brenda? How are your barristers in bustiers doing this week?"

"Brought in Destiny, a new woman, today. And she's terrific."

"Background?" Bud asks. "The usual?"

"Yes," she says, "worked at Edna's Foot and Rub before it closed."

"In the back room, the happy-ending room, I'm assuming?" Bud suggests.

"Quite right, Bud. She was known as the girl with the golden grip, and all the while studying at Duke Law and writing for the law review."

"Brenda, I've been wonderin,' all your lawyers were in some form of adult entertainment to finance their educations. That's cool, but what if a former client needs legal work, and he's embarrassed when he recognizes Destiny from giving him hand jobs back in the day? What does she say?"

"Good news, sir, my hourly rate's lower now."

Bud explodes in laughter.

"The release that gives you peace!" Herbie squawks, zooming around the room.

"The image problem is good and bad for us," she says, looking at me as if I'm more interested in the challenges of her legal firm than having dinner. "We're a full-service law office, but we can't help getting sex cases thrown at us."

I drift off to sleep as she's talking about how they're planning "the Alzheimer's Defense" to get immunity for the Silver Bangers Senior Sex Club members who were arrested during a group grope in front of Monkey Island at the North Carolina Zoo.

"We're going to contend they thought they were deep in the forest, not on the viewing platform of the monkey habitat," she explains.

The next morning, I see the story and picture in the *High Point Enterprise* about Mr. Pillows and the Bleesdales:

FAMILY SNOOZES ON MAIN STREET
AUDITIONING FOR *SLEEPING IN HELL!*
—NEW TV VENTURE FROM MR. PILLOWS

"The program will feature my pillows, a blast furnace, and an amazing new talent named Scott Carter," Mr. Pillows told our reporter while chewing a pillow. He claimed no knowledge of the liaison between Jake Tapper and Tucker Carlson alleged in the most recently released "Pillow Talk" recording.

"Tuck, and maybe Jake, are fine Americans, not the gay sinning type," Pillows said, before immediately walking back that statement by explaining that he loved gay people but just not in a gay-sinning-kind-of-love way."

When word of his remarks circulated on social media, shares of Mr. Pillows Class A stock plunged 80 percent. Reached for further comment on his comments, Mr. Pillows said, "I love gay people in a way that a man who makes the fine pillows gays use while sinning loves people."

After trading on his stock was halted, a spokesperson for Mr. Pillows attempted to clarify his remarks: "Mr. Pillows did not intend to imply that homosexuals were sinners. He meant to explain that he loves all gay people but just not in a perverted kind of gay way. He'd like the gay community to know that he visited Provincetown on a book tour, but quickly left afterward."

Later that day, at the station, it was time for one of Lombardo's weekly meetings to outline objectives and accomplishments. Bud took me 'cause he said Lombardo had me on the agenda.

"OK," Lombardo says, "is everyone present?"

"Yes," Buffy, the coproducer of our show, responds, "there are the four of us as usual, plus Spike today. Bark if you're awake, Spike."

"Very funny," I think, sitting there in stony silence.

"I'm going by the book here, Buffy. First order of business was attendance. Now, second, you all have your agendas. Take a few minutes and study them," Lombardo says.

"There are just three words on the page," Mike Stevens, the news director, says.

"I intend to run this meeting in an orderly fashion, Mike. I had a Zoom Vistage CEO meeting this week, and the speaker took three hours of my valuable time going over the most finite points of how to run a meeting. I have his seventy-three-page manual in front of me."

"Three hours?" Bud asks. "Wouldn't you have been better off golfing?"

"I don't see 'golfing' among the three perfectly spaced words under new or old business, Bud."

"Er, OK," Bud says. "Well, give us a few more minutes, then, to fully study the three words: 'Sale,' 'Spike,' 'Telethon.'"

"Shut up, Bud," Lombardo says, laughing. "I just wanted to have some fun trying that highly paid speaker's bullshit out on you."

He tosses the meeting training booklet at me.

"Spike, see if you can chew this organizational double-talking sophistry into a giant ball of slimy unrecognizable pulp before this meeting is over," the boss commands me.

"Easy," I think. "The old jaw muscles that kept me alive defending myself after I was abducted in New York have been gettin' daily workouts demolishing old phone books stored in the basement of our rented house."

"OK," Lombardo says. "First, the sale of the station. Bud, your funds and mine are in separate Wachovia accounts earning the current James Bond interest rate of point zero zero seven, and we will need a small loan on top of that to even attempt to buy the station. However, now I'm hearing from his lawyer that Sol "The Old Swede" Silverman, who owns WGHP, is saying he may have some big, new, exciting long-range plans for the station's future."

I'm curious about his long-range plans, because the last time I saw Sol "The Old Swede" Silverman, he was asleep with his mouth wide open, being wheeled slowly across the station's lobby by Ruth, his shapely nurse.

"But, boss, The Old Swede's a hundred and one years old," Bud says.

"A hundred and two years old, actually, and guess what? It gets worse. His daughter—"

"You mean Shoshana 'The Old Swede's Daughter' Silverman?" Buffy asks.

"That is, unfortunately, what I believe her father's insisted she be called since birth, and yes, that would be his only daughter and, importantly, sole heir," Lombardo says.

"Wait a minute, isn't she a hard-core meth addict? The *Enterprise* did a thing on her. She's supposed to live somewhere in the woods near Hagan Park," Bud says.

"Yes, and I've heard that she only has a couple of teeth and looks like she could star in *The Dead Don't Die*. They say she spends all her time taking apart TV sets she finds in dumpsters," Lombardo explains.

"Didn't she fall asleep in a dumpster and have to be dug out of the Greensboro landfill?" Mike asks.

"Excavated, Mike, excavated," Lombardo answers. "She was excavated by an extremely large backhoe. Afterwards, she refused a shower and ran off into the night singing 'The Gypsy in my Soul.'"

"One of the few songs recorded by both Doris Day and Van Morrison," Mike blurts. "Her version is—"

Lombardo interrupts, "We are all aware of your love of Doris Day, Mike. We see the ten-minute birthday tribute on our news broadcast each year, but not now, please. So to get to it, folks, her loving father, Sol 'The Old Swede' Silverman, who has already spent thousands of dollars on the finest rehab clinics for her, is suddenly convinced that her newfound passion for television in the form of dismantling TV sets means—"

"No," Bud says. "No."

"If I may finish, Bud. It means that he is convinced that maybe his daughter Shoshana 'The Old Swede's Daughter' Silverman could run this station."

The only sound in the room is that of my page-chewing, as I'm wondering, "Why, humans, why?"

"Her father wants his daughter captured—"

27

"Likely using nets," Bud interjects.

Lombardo shoots Bud his sarcastic "Be kind, or at least fake it like Ellen DeGeneres always did" look, but then remembers rumors that Ellen sometimes did use nets on her staff, and continues.

"Now, because The Old Swede is unfortunately naive enough to believe every word that ever came out of Dr. Oz's mouth, he'll put her on some nutritional program purported to cure meth addiction, insomnia, spastic colon, and make skin tags fall off on weekends."

"So?" Mike asks.

"The sale is on hold."

"Shit!" Bud yells.

"Not an inappropriate comment, Bud. So what do you think about this good news, team?" Lombardo asks.

"*Que sera, sera*," Mike sings.

"Not exactly what we were figuring," Buffy says.

"You continue to be the mistress of understatement, Buffy," Bud says. "This is complete nonsense."

As I start choking uncontrollably after swallowing a large chunk of the booklet, I see Bud's eyes close, the way they do when he's trying to formulate something.

"But," Bud asks, "how do we turn this negative into a positive?"

"That dog appears to be choking to death," Lombardo says.

"Oh…right, let me get Spike out of here before he throws up on the rug. I gotta think this over."

"OK, Bud, Buffy, Mike, fifteen-minute break," Lombardo declares.

"Want to hear 'The Gypsy in my Soul?'" Mike asks Buffy.

"Van Morrison lost me at 'Wavelength,'" she says, "I'm gonna make a couple of calls."

"Keep this quiet," Lombardo cautions.

"No one would believe me anyway," Buffy says.

Out on the sidewalk, Bud has to thrust his hand halfway down my throat to dig out the chapter I swallowed on meeting etiquette.

We're headed toward the High Point town square, the place where a couple years back, I was the star attraction in the Hebe named Zebe's illegal Christmas show. The mayor's raid closed it down. They arrested Zebe. I got shot by a tranquilizer dart but escaped. It's in the first book. I only mention it 'cause I haven't been back to the square since, and it popped into my mind.

"Thinking, Spike. I'm thinking," Bud says.

I'm thinking, too, Bud. I'm thinking you're walking way too fast for me to stop and take a much-needed emergency dump. Humans, please note, if you need digestive assistance, there's enough roughage in a seventy-five-page booklet to assure you lusty bowel movements for a week.

The park's deserted. Bud sets up and goes through some of his karate moves to get focused. He started on martial arts in third grade and kept going as a hobby.

As he's executing a run of stances, punches, and blocks, I'm relieving myself of something shaped like the thing with a tire company's name on it that hovers over stadiums.

He sits on a little bench under a tree and removes my leash, thus risking getting another thirty-five-dollar dog-fine ticket.

"What'll we do, Spike?" he asks. "What would Colbert do in a situation like this? What would Amy Schumer come up with? Chappelle? Chris Rock? Seth MacFarlane?"

I kinda know where he's heading, because of our tight dog-human connection. I'm thinking, "Give me two *e*'s for a word that starts with a *w* and ends with a *d*."

He pulls his little white one-hitter out of his jacket pocket and fires it up with a windproof lighter.

One puff. I watch as the smoke curls into a tiny cloud that disappears into the tree.

I jump up on the bench and put my stone-like head in his lap—a lap, by the way, where many female heads have also been. But I digress. He's rubbing me gently between the ears.

Quiet.

Three birds flutter by.

I see a squirrel venture cautiously toward us, maybe hoping for a peanut. I don't make a move, because I don't want to disturb Bud's concentration. Besides, have you ever seen a dog actually catch a squirrel?

Two minutes. Three. Four...

"Spike," Bud announces, "maybe I still got those crazy Bleesdales on my mind, but this is pure reality TV, except it's real. A hundred-and-two-year-old

TV station owner trying to get his toothless, meth-addict daughter to run the station that Lombardo and you and me are trying to buy. It's perfect!"

"Ownership participation?" I think. I look at him like, "Huh?"

"I've been putting money in a small account for you, Spike."

This is the first I've heard of savings for me. I always figured, God forbid something happened to Bud, I'd end up in a shelter and…no, not the needle, no! Whoops, got a little paranoid right there from that secondhand pot smoke.

"I can hardly wait to tell Lombardo," Bud says, inserting two Listerine breath strips in his mouth before spraying each of us with a squirt from one of the tiny Bleu de Chanel cologne samples he keeps with his one-hitter.

"This'll be great," he tells me. "Great."

Back at the station, Lombardo says, "Bud, you're late. We've already discussed item two on the agenda."

"Can we kill this meeting-by-the book crap?" Bud asks.

"Nah, it's OK," Lombardo says. "We were just sitting around waiting for you for twenty minutes—time when we all could have been at our desks working to build this small independent station into an even more potent global cultural force than it already is."

"Boss—"

"Excuse me, Bud, to fill you in on the final numbers. We raised almost one hundred twenty-two thousand dollars during our postpandemic-plea telethon. This will go to help the two hundred or so newly evicted homeless people living in the shantytown in Farmer Kappelhaff's field, and it's more money than state and local assistance combined."

"Boss, I got a great idea," Bud blurts.

"'Kappelhaff' is close to Doris Day's original last name," Mike interjects happily.

"Mike, one Doris Day reference a meeting is quite sufficient. Another one and you'll be singing 'Qué Sera, Sera' in the unemployment line," Lombardo warns. "Alright, Bud, what is this idea that you got in the park after likely getting high?"

"Park? High? Getting high? Whatever makes you, Mr. Two Martinis at a Friday lunch, think that I am high?" Bud asks Lombardo.

"It's well known around the station that when you return from a walk with Spike and smell like Bleu de Chanel, you have partaken of a substance that is technically still illegal in this state. But it seems to help you in some ill-gotten way, so what's the idea?"

Bud does a pitch. At first, they look at him skeptically, then nod affirmatively and applaud wildly at the end.

"Bud, you nailed it," Buffy squeals.

"Bravo!" Mike yells. "Bravo!"

"Good point on those 'bravos,' Mike," Lombardo says. "I'll be calling Bravo and Andy Cohen this afternoon. This will work, Bud. This will work. Very good idea. Maybe I'll try that stuff one day."

"But this show has to be completely ours," Bud asserts. "Sol 'The Old Swede' Silverman's limited corporation that owns the station can't have a claim on this. We need unique legal protection here."

"Absolutely," Buffy agrees.

"Bud, I suppose you'd like to use the best little law firm in the Carolinas on this, right?" Lombardo asks.

Bud, Buffy, and Mike nod in agreement at Lombardo.

"OK," Lombardo says, "give it to Brenda and the girls. But if Sol 'The Old Swede' Silverman ever gets a look at one of them in their custom-fitted Anne Fontaine white dress shirts, he might bite the big one."

"I believe the firm's recent hire, Destiny, did in fact once attempt to bite The Old Swede's big one," Bud says with a straight face.

"Stop it, Bud! You're nuts," Buffy says, laughing.

"This isn't CBS under Moonves. Enough with the big ones and the nuts," Lombardo cuts in. "Mike, Buffy, you can go. I gotta talk to Bud and Spike."

This is where I get nervous. The last time I had a private meeting with Lombardo, he told me he knew I was pissing on the big tires on his Cadillac XTS in the parking lot. I compromised and shifted to the sportscaster's Smartcar.

"Sit down, Bud, and make sure that dog is listening," Lombardo says, because he has some enemies.

"The mask?" Bud asks.

This is what I've been afraid of.

During the second half of the pandemic, when denouncing masks was at its peak and protesters were gloating 'cause they hadn't died yet, I got drafted into a Wear Your Mask campaign.

The slogan was, "Let's not have another Spike! Wear your mask."

Somehow the thing took off like Beanie Babies, Pogs, and Trolls. We made different collectible versions: some with my beady little eyes; others with my giant fangs, my nose; me smiling, sad, asleep—the works.

Kids everywhere were wearing Spike masks, many in defiance of their parents, who refused to wear masks. Mom or Dad would throw away the Spike mask, and the kids just ordered more 'cause they were free.

The craze made all three of the evening newscasts and was roundly condemned by Sean Hannity as "the sinister work of an evil dog's mind."

For months, thousands of kids refused to take off their masks. They were even going to sleep in masks. Dr. Fauci called Bud at home and told him how much we were helping. Bud put me on the line, but Fauci's voice was so raspy, I couldn't understand him. I barked like I knew what he was talking about and went back to sleep.

Eventually, with the vaccines and stuff, the Spike mask fad dropped faster than a Pet Rock. But now, trouble.

"It's 'mask ear,' isn't it?" Bud asks Lombardo.

Months of continued round-the-clock wearing of my masks had affected the growth of some younger kids' ears. When they emerged with no masks, a couple hundred of them had developed a condition known as bilateral auris oblongum, more commonly referred to as "wombat ear."

"Bud, I signed on for this mask caper with you and that dog. I even have a citation saying he saved lives, but now, we got kids who look like Alfred E. Neuman. Their hearing's improved 'cause their ears are sticking out like rearview mirrors, but we should've put a 'use at your own risk' disclaimer somewhere on the mask, and—"

"The whole point was wearing it to reduce risks," Bud interjects.

"Of course, but now we may be facing a class-action suit from those ambulance-chasing lawyers Buzz Bedol and Sons in Winston-Salem."

"Buzz Bedol and Sons sounds more like a hardware business than a law firm," Bud says.

"Yes, close. They used Costco premium cards to get law degrees right in the store, but wombat ear aside, Bud, there are still many molten-angry, anti-mask-wearing folks who need scapegoats and are pissed off at Spike for promoting masks in the first place, so watch your step with him."

"What do we do about the class-action threat?" Bud asks. "Can we call—"

"Yes, alert the sex kittens of the courtroom. And here, this is for you, registered mail. See if it's the wombat-ear suit," Lombardo says, tossing an envelope at Bud.

Bud carefully opens it and scans a letter.

"Wow! Whoa! Spike, this is absolutely great for you, if this actually happens!" he says.

"Oh boy! Is Daisy moving to India? Whatever could this be?" I wonder.

He flashes the letter at me for two seconds, forgetting that I am a notoriously slow reader for a dog.

"This might be the greatest for us yet, Spike," he tells me.

"Lemme see it," Lombardo asks. The boss scans the document. "Hard to believe, but if it happens, this is very good for all concerned."

Can someone let me in on this?

Bud shoves it in his jacket pocket and says, "OK, Spike, back to the office. We've got a show tomorrow."

Bud, the envelope, please!

CHAPTER THREE

SOL "THE OLD SWEDE" SILVERMAN

All week, I'm going nuts because the envelope is on the bureau in Bud's love grotto, generally described in floor plans as "bedroom." Bud sees me hopping next to the bureau. Little does he know; he thinks I wanna see the new photo of Daisy and me that Buffy gave him. He takes down the small framed picture and puts it in my doghouse. This, of course, creates a problem for me.

When Daisy comes over the next day and sees it, she gives me a hard time, claiming that I was hogging the camera and there should be much more of her in the shot. She's so insecure about the way she looks in the photo, I take the picture back to the house to get her to shut up. While I'm inside, a boxer runs out of the woods with a little kid chasing after. The dog stops and barks at Daisy. I come out as this is going on, and Daisy demands that I jump over the fence and bite the dog for barking at her. It happens to be Lady, a very athletic boxer that lives down the road.

First thing I'd like to point out to Daisy is that in attempting to jump over the very high fence, I could easily rip off my balls. And second, that's a dog that barked, Daisy, not an elephant. That's what dogs do. We bark at other dogs. But if I tell her this, she'll go wild sayin' I'm criticizing her. So I keep quiet.

Here's a little tip, humans: never enter a romantic relationship with somebody ruled by insecurity. Trying to make them happy or please them is like chasing a cloud that always ends up raining on you.

I had the guts to fly in a drone for boxer Ike "I Got Money" Piles' fight entrance at the MGM Grand, and I outwitted a panther when I landed, but now I can't summon the courage to tell Daisy to get out of my life because she's driving me crazy. Part of me is still trying to please her. Why?

Later that week, we were headed to a meeting with Sol "The Old Swede" Silverman to pitch the reality show idea. Lombardo had a verbal agreement with Andy Cohen at Bravo, provided that Sol "The Old Swede" Silverman would go along, and that we can somehow lure Shoshana out of the woods and see what happens with her. Would she end up running the station? Will we buy it? Or could it turn out to be something else altogether?

"You never know what you might find in the woods," Andy Cohen told Lombardo. "Look at our hit show *Swamp Families of Newark*. It originally started as a possible nature show about frogs and turtles in the wetlands near the Jersey Turnpike."

The Old Swede lives in a magnificent white mansion in a fancy development near Winston-Salem. Ruth, his nurse, meets us at the door and takes us into a large room with floor-to-ceiling windows overlooking a golf course.

After a few minutes, Sol "The Old Swede" Silverman, the man who controls so much of our destiny, shuffles toward us.

"Hello, men," he calls out in a rumbling, phlegmy voice. "And look at Spike there. He's quite the bruiser."

He appears somewhat younger than his alleged hundred and two years, because of his Robert Redford circa *The Way We Were* bright blond hair.

Bud stares at his head.

"I know, young man, you can't help noticing my hair. That's why they've been calling me 'The Old Swede' since Hebrew School—my blond locks. I've still got my original hairline," he says, pointing at what appears to be a freshly ironed polyester wig.

At this point with dogs, we'd be smelling each other's asses, but with you humans there's needless small talk that leads Sol "The Old Swede" Silverman to wonder, "Say, fellows, do you men know any frisky women?"

"Er...," Lombardo says.

"Define 'frisky,'" Bud says.

"Alive," he says. "I wanna get laid. I ordered a device to inject me with the new ED meds for guys my age that's only seven hundred dollars a dose. They tested it on corpses; that's why they say, 'It will raise you from the dead.' I want a gal around forty who doesn't mind a sixty-year age diff...diff...diff..."

The Old Swede slowly sits down. His head slumps to his chest. He begins to snore lightly.

Bud and Lombardo warily side-eye each other.

We know that Sol "The Old Swede" Silverman sometimes tricks people by pretending to fall asleep so he can hear what they actually think about him. The previous station manager was fired shortly after pronouncing him to be "a horny old man with an atrociously bad wig who should've left the TV business in 1954"—this while The Old Swede was feigning sleep in a Zoom meeting.

"What a man!" Bud whispers. "The way he walked in here, you know, it was like watching that newsreel of Douglas MacArthur wading ashore in the Philippines proclaiming, 'I have returned.'"

"Commanding presence," Lombardo agrees. "It's sad that only because of manipulative advertising directed at unwary seniors, a man like this thinks he needs that medicine. He's probably a bull under the sheets."

I bang my head against Bud's leg to let him know my dog powers are telling me that The Old Swede is actually sound asleep, not faking it.

"And that mane of healthy hair," Bud continues for the fun of it. "Who does he remind you of? Redford, Pitt, Bieber, Jon Bon Jovi?"

"Nick Carter," Lombardo whispers.

"No, Daniel Craig," Bud says. "Wouldn't you love to see Sol 'The Old Swede' Silverman in a Tom Ford white dinner jacket, standing on the patio out there squinting knowingly into the sunset, sipping a huge martini?"

"Shaken, not stirred," Lombardo adds.

The Old Swede's eyes pop open. "You have no idea what it's like to be a hundred and two years old. You're not a man, you're a novelty," he stammers. "I once had friends around every corner—they're gone. I loved dating—sex every night; in the seventies I wanted my private parts declared a World Heritage site. We'd hit the Copa, Stork Club, Studio Fifty-Four; saw the Rat Pack at the Sands; stayed up all night playing blackjack with Dean and Frank; partied with Sammy; got drunk with Liz and Burton; paid twenty thousand in cash for a week at the Hotel du Cap, where I got a blow job from…well, er, never mind…. Let's just say her initials were B. B."

Lombardo and Bud are sitting there stunned as he's rattling on about chartered jets, dinner with Sophia Loren, bridge with Omar Sharif, and yacht races with Ted Turner. They believe him, but I sense something phony around the edges of his stories.

"I can see how people could think of you just as a hundred-and-two-year-old novelty," Bud says.

"Wow," Lombardo utters softly. "What a life."

"Not now. Now I'm so desperate that I went on the Sugardaddie dating site. There was a Shaker woman who wanted to see what it would be like to get laid, but she wouldn't do it unless we made a chair together first."

"Oh my," Bud mutters.

"Let me tell you guys, I was the world's best date. Last time I had a date, you know what happened? Eighty-seven-year-old woman, friend of my nurse's mother. Ruth reports that she's quite a frisky lady. Little did I know Ruth thought frisky was playing pickleball twice a month.

"Comes here for dinner. The works. My chef cooks. I've got a jazz trio playing. I give her a wrist corsage. I'm dressed in my burgundy velvet blazer. I've got the monogrammed slippers on."

"What happened?" Lombardo asks.

"Happened? Happened? After dinner we dance. I figure this is it, maybe I'm finally gonna score. The ED stuff is working; it's pumping through me like they've opened Hoover Dam. Feels like I got a Komodo dragon lurking in my pants. As I'm trying to mambo us toward the banister to suggest we buckle up for a romantic ride up the stairs in my chair lift and hobble over to my bedroom and help each other wriggle out of our Depends, she notices the bulge."

"And?" Bud asks.

"'I'm sorry,' I tell her. 'You're so alluring, I can't help myself. So what do you think?' I ask her as politely as possible. 'Wanna maybe…us, er…upstairs?'"

"'Sorry, Sol, I closed up shop down there years ago,' she announces. This, as the trio is playing 'La Vie en Rose.' And it gets even more romantic. Likely sensing that I might suggest oral, she takes five minutes to tell me about her loose denture problems and how she's gotta change adhesive brands from original Poligrip to Fixident Ultra Max Hold."

"So disappointing for you, Mr. Silverman," Bud says gently.

"I'm not finished," he rasps. "Then she tells me that because of so much typing and scrolling on her phone, she has a condition called 'text neck' that induces violent cranial shaking. 'Even if didn't have loose dentures,' she says, laughing, 'I can't control head movement, and I could accidentally neuter you.' At this point, the Komodo dragon's asleep back in his cave.

"As I'm wondering if maybe I might be lucky enough at least to get a generic 1955-style pre-lubricant hand job, she tells me she's got carpal tunnel syndrome in both hands."

Bud says, "Ah, that's really a—"

"That was my date. I've gone from late-night dinners at Twenty-One and nights of pleasure at the Carlyle to denture-grip discussions in my living room," Sol "The Old Swede" Silverman says, shaking his head dejectedly. "Help me."

I'm thinkin' this guy needs one of those personal notices mixed in with the trucks-for-sale ads in free newspapers: "Virile centenarian with scary bad wig seeks mad night of passion with woman with stable neck and firm dentures, or at least one OK hand."

"Help you, Mr. Silverman?" Lombardo asks. "How do we help?"

"Look," he says, "I'll sign that deal memo you sent over. You'll find Shoshana. I'll put her on the Oz Miracle Cure, and—"

Bud interrupts, "Wasn't it in *Scientific American* last week that the Miracle Cure might be the same formula as the all-purpose elixirs peddled out of wagons by the W. S. Walcott Traveling Medicine Show in Arkansas in the 1870s?"

"Never doubt Oz," The Old Swede insists. "He's the man who invented the couples colonoscopy retreat. Anyway look, men, we'll do your reality show. Maybe I win and she runs the station; maybe I lose. But I want one thing in exchange."

"Yes?" Bud says.

"You guys know people. I want you to find me one last great date. One last great date, like the old days!"

"A date?" Lombardo and Bud mutter.

"Yes, but I won't pay. No dockside harlots for me. Won't pay for companionship or sex, never did. Never laid down a penny for the pleasures of the night."

Nurse Ruth shoots us a look and points to a red phone that we later find out was once The Old Swede's "hooker hotline."

"I want a woman to spend time with me," he explains, "and when the evening's over, I want her to want to crawl in bed with me, not be checking her Apple watch to see how soon she can leave me to get back to her tattooed boyfriend in some cluttered one-bedroom apartment with used needles scattered all over the floor."

"Mr. Silverman, I'm the mayor of High Point, not your partner in debauchery. I run a TV station. I am not in a position to—"

"You got it," Bud interrupts. "I will find you that date, a worthy candidate for your one last great date, but then it's all up to you to maneuver it politely, as in days of old. But I assure you we will not pay for it. There are no guarantees."

"Which is procurement," Lombardo adds, warily.

"I am simply going to set up a date, that's it. Procurement would be if I got Mr. Silverman paid companionship, boss. For all I know, I'll find The Old Swede a woman who works at the cane and walker repair shop at the Guilford Senior Citizens Center," Bud says. "But I will find somebody."

"You just let her know she'll be dealing with the John Travolta of the sack," Sol "The Old Swede" Silverman says.

"Travolta," I'm wondering. "Aren't there rumors he's supposed to be—"

"You know why I'm the Travolta of the sack? It's my reputation for stayin' alive, stayin' alive," he says, displaying a few seconds of disco movement before wincing in pain and clutching his back.

I'm figurin' with the kind of hotshot-fireball aging babe that Bud's gonna find for him, The Old Swede will be lucky to stay alive until conclusion.

"But I have my one condition," Bud says. "I'm gonna need a picture."

The Old Swede points to a black-and-white eight-by-ten photo on the piano. "There."

"Mr. Silverman, you look to be about thirty-four years old in that imitation George Hurrell headshot. I need a current photo, and forgive me, sir," Bud says, pointing at The Old Swede's wig. "What's under that?"

"This is my hair," he insists.

"Watch, Mr. Silverman. Spike will bark three times after I point to your head and ask him, 'Wig?'"

I bark three times, just like in the "Tail of the Toupee" bit we do on the show.

"Bud, I am very sensitive about this. I am Sol 'The Old Swede' Silverman, not Sol 'The Bald Guy' Silverman."

"You can wear it on the reality show, but I need pictures of you to get that date, and the wig is not gonna be a selling point for the robust, wide-eyed, hedonistic, eighty-three-year-old Nancy Pelosi type who's out there somewhere for you."

He slowly removes the wig as a moth happily flies free.

"My God," Lombardo says. "You look just like Norman Lear. Women love Norman Lear."

"Norman Lear?" The Old Swede asks.

"Yes, Mr. Silverman," Bud says, "and Norman Lear was just named the Sexiest Hundred-Year-Old Man in America by the 'Horny at a Hundred' columnist in that new *Getting On and Getting It On* magazine AARP is hawking to what they're calling the 'sensual seniors' crowd."

All he needs is a porkpie hat, and you'd believe anything he told you about sitcoms.

"OK," The Old Swede says. "I can handle it, if that makes it work. Hearing's not great. Bud, did you say you got me a date with Nancy Pelosi? My God, the body on that woman, those—"

"No," Bud answers, "but that's the standard I'll be shooting for, a ten on the Pelosi Anatomy Scale."

"That bod…bod…bo…," Sol "The Old Swede" Silverman mutters as he's dozing off, apparently lusting for Nancy Pelosi.

I let Bud know that The Old Swede is asleep, not faking. We tiptoe out of the room.

His nurse joins us in the foyer.

"He's so lonely," she says, giving The Old Swede a sad, warm glance.

"Well, we're going to try to help," Bud says.

"We also have to find Shoshana in the woods, Ruth," Lombardo tells her.

"Good luck on that one," she quips.

"No problem. Spike will be on her trail like a bloodhound. Can you give us something we can use to track her, something with her scent on it?" Bud requests.

The nurse returns with a black Jay-Z and Beyoncé OTR II tour T-shirt dangling from the tip of her middle finger.

I take a whiff, but unless they want me to lead them to the nearest box of Tide PODS, it's not gonna work.

"Too clean," Bud says.

"When they dug her out of the landfill," the nurse says, "she threw her panties at the cops, and boy did they scatter. I'll go look for them."

"We'll get it right this time, Spike," Bud says reassuringly. "Not like when we trailed Buffy for fun and you accidentally ended up at Papa John's."

Buffy had been with Daisy, so I focused on avoiding her and sampling Papa John's "half-pizza, half-sandwich," the Papadia. Gotta say, before I ate one that day, I'd actually believed the claims that it was a perfectly balanced meal.

Nurse Ruth comes back with a manila envelope. She tears open the corner. Bud and Lombardo recoil at the fumes. I bark, indicating that I could track a scent like that two miles underwater.

"Wrap it up," Lombardo gasps. "Heavy duty."

She seals it in three double-thickness freezer bags like you'd use to mail an ounce of pungent marijuana to a pal in Singapore—not that you'd actually do that; I meant "like you'd use" as a figure of speech. Of course, if you've mailed pot, then you would have known how to wrap those panties.

On the way back to the station, Lombardo's got some legitimate questions for Bud.

"How the hell did you know about that Norman Lear thing?"

"I was at the dentist, and I saw an AARP magazine with a cover article about the dangers of drooling and driving. The Norman story was inside."

"And what suddenly makes you a senior sex whisperer? How're you going to be able to find The Old Swede what he craves?"

"Watch," Bud says. "I know exactly who to call."

"Never underestimate Bud," I think, while realizing I'm having a very good day—The Old Swede called me a bruiser, and I see we're pulling into a Papa John's.

FINDING SHOSHANA

The morning of the Shoshana hunt, I'm in the living room playing with Herbie. Even though he goes on about his hero Chicago Bob all the time, he's slowly bonding with me. He rides around on my head squawking, "Spike dead dog," or "Spike goin' down." This morning he's squawking at the bed, "You one ugly pillow. No room for more tattoos," pretending the innocent pillow is a jerk he's heckling at his old bar. He stops when we hear Bud scream.

Brenda left early this morning, so I'm mildly curious as to what's happening up there while he's alone. I know he had a bit of an issue with her last night. Might as well tell you now, Brenda's always been into sex. In middle school, the girls told her she had "boner vision" 'cause she could spot an inappropriately aroused eighth-grade boy three classrooms away down a dimly lit hall. So yesterday, she and Bud had finally concluded a seismic screwing session that lasted through the new Bad Bunny album twice; Brenda was toking on the post-banging bong she keeps in a drawer with her collection of limited-edition Victoria Secret push-up bras, and had news for Bud.

"Bud," she said, "you hit a solid ninety-three just now on the SSI sensor on my new SexBit."

"What?" Bud asks.

"My Sexual Satisfaction Index. Your score was ninety-three—good work."

"Work? Score? I now get a score?" he asked defensively. I was figuring maybe he was gonna be upset about yet another intrusion of technology into our lives, 'cause a couple of weeks ago he bought a new smart speaker and didn't know it had a personal adviser component. A voice that sounded suspiciously like Laura Ingraham's was continuously correcting his behavior and criticizing his opinions.

"Bud, darling, a ninety-three is wonderful. I've only been higher than that with one other person," Brenda told him.

"That's probably Mitch, right? Your Navy SEAL?"

"OK, well, yes, so what?" she asked. "And you have your Buffy."

"No, Buffy and I are back to just working together."

I know Bud has a lot of respect for our Navy SEALs, but this SexBit thing adds a new dimension. We know Mitch is six foot four, weighs two hundred twenty pounds, can do seventy-three chin-ups, run a mile in a little over four minutes, and is being actively recruited by the WWF to wrestle as Mitch "the Mega Millennial."

"Look, Brenda, I know we have an open relationship, so it's 'Don't fence me in' right now, but making love if you're wearing that thing on your wrist to keep track of your pulse rate, among other things, it feels like pressure. Can you understand that?" Bud asked.

I can understand it. Every dog that's ever bred in the backyard has felt pressure like that. A kid sees you and your bitch havin' a little fun goin' at it, so he texts every kid in the neighborhood. Before you finish, you got nine twelve-year-old boys cheerin' you on and you're screwing live on TikTok.

"Yes, Bud, of course I can see your point," Brenda said, "but maybe you could have a session with your smart speaker about this insecurity."

"I gave that goddamn thing away. It sounded like Laura Ingram, and was constantly telling me I was too empathetic, and always calling Wolf Blitzer names," Bud told her. "But OK. Look, Brenda, just please don't wear the SexBit every time. You've got me worried about performance anxiety."

I'm feeling some performance anxiety myself.

I'm responsible for tracking Shoshana, and I've never tracked anything in my life. I'd like to be in my doghouse praying to Dog God for divine nose power on the trail, but I run upstairs to see what the screaming's about. It's my job. "That's what makes you a professional pet," my brother Billy told me. I love Bud; I'll always be there for him—hopefully that's the dullest speech I'm gonna make in the book.

Bud's sitting at his little desk, and he's got the speakerphone turned on.

"Representative! Representative! Live person! Human!" he's yelling.

I put my head on his thigh. I look up and give him my most comforting gaze, which is actually quite similar to the practiced look of concern and sensitivity you'd see on the face of a rookie local TV correspondent interviewing someone in California who's lost everything in a fire.

He slams down the phone.

"Spike, the bank is driving me crazy. There's forty-seven hundred dollars missing from my checking account, and I can't get anybody on the phone."

"Toto?" I wonder. How do I tell him it's all a joke; don't take life too seriously?

He punches the buttons again.

"Your call is very important to us. We are experiencing longer than normal wait times. Please hold…"

"No music, no!" Bud yells, as a recording of polka music fills the room.

I polka around, adding a touch of the Mike Pence Irish Dancers' footwork to keep the act fresh.

He loves it.

"That's funny, Spike. Let's do that on the show one day."

After about ten minutes of the music, we hear, "Your call is very important to us. Please stay on the line.…"

"If it's so important to you, hire some people who are desperate for work to answer the phones," Bud yells at the recorded voice.

Fifteen minutes later, the recorded voice is back, listing options for Bud to talk to other recorded voices.

"Representative! Representative!" he yells.

Finally, a fast-talking woman with a heavy Indian accent comes on the line.

After a few minutes of Bud explaining the situation, she informs him, "Forty-seven hundred and six dollars and three cents is missing from your account, Mr. Bud."

"I know!" Bud says. "That's what I just said. That's why I called. Look, I need to get to work now…"

"What is your profession?" the voice asks.

"Television. Reporting. And I'm on deadline. This afternoon we have to find a meth addict in the woods. Can you investigate this, please?"

"Did your friend in the woods take the money? Perhaps you spent forty-seven hundred dollars yourself on meth? Have you sought counseling?" the woman asks.

I give him a "sorry this is happening, pal; just speed it up so we can get the hell out of here" look.

After ten agonizing minutes with Bud pacing around, she tells him it looks like the money has gone to Thailand. He gets a reference code and instructions to call tomorrow at the same inefficient number he called forty-five minutes ago.

"Would you be able to stay on the line to answer a ten-question survey about—"

Bud hangs up. "I think that money's gone, Spike," he tells me.

In an hour we're driving to the woods near Hagan-Stone Park. With us is a woman we're meeting for the first time, Vel'vetta. Our director and camera-man, Mack Lincoln, is sitting next to me in the back seat scratching my head. I love the guy. He's always petting me, and when he's directing our show and I fall asleep lyin' on my back, he cuts away so we don't get any more letters from viewers complaining about seeing my balls on TV and demanding that I be "neutered immediately as a matter of public decency." To me, he's the quiet giant. He doesn't say much, but when he speaks, it counts. He's also way over six feet and still built like the right tackle he once was at Fayetteville State.

Vel'vetta, whose mother had gotten high and gave her new baby a name inspired by her favorite low-priced cheese spread, is the only person Bud could find who knows Shoshana. They met in Iowa when Vel'vetta was stripping in the Iowa Straw Pole Dancing Competition during the 2020 Iowa caucuses.

"Bud," Brenda said, "V is one of the most gorgeous women I've ever seen. She isn't always as good on the pole as some, but she beats them on sheer beauty."

Since Brenda spends a good part of her day gazing at herself in the mirror, and likely billing her clients for the time, Bud and I were figuring, "This we gotta see."

I may not agree with her taste in vibrators, but Brenda sure was right about Vel'vetta.

Suppose you got J.Lo behind door one; Kerry Washington, door two; and Vel'vetta, three. You're barking at three.

Vel'vetta fills us in on Shoshana during the ride.

"I met her out there in Ames. She's with a troupe of celebrity lookalikes whose big attraction was a singing and dancing one-legged Ruth Bader Ginsberg. The whole thing had kinda like a shabby, washed-up circus vibe. But this lookalike shit goes over with the political hacks. They like getting a picture with an RBG, a Streisand, or an Obama. The George Bush really resembled Bush, but he was a little cross-eyed, so he looked like even more of a simpleton than the real George has in photos recently. Anyway, Shoshana was part of it with her Carole King tribute show."

"How was she?" Bud asks.

"Earnest performer, but she's got about an average seventh grader's command of the piano and a thin voice that can go flat and sharp in the same line. If you listened to her, you wouldn't wake up in the morning with a smile on your face."

"Ha!" Mack laughs.

"Good to know you're awake back there, Mack," Bud jokes.

"I don't know what she's trying to prove," V says. "We had a couple of fun nights drinking together. By the way, the fake Hillary was drinking heavily, 'cause nobody wanted her picture. Shosh wasn't doing meth then. I'll tell you one thing: she sure as hell is angry at her father."

"Why?" Bud asks.

"If we find her, my guess is you're gonna figure it out. Mind if I vape?" she asks. "I'll blow it out the window. I gotta try this new strain from the West Coast. Wanna hit, Bud? Spike? Mike?" she asks.

"Not while driving and working—so, later for me, but blow a cloud at Spike," Bud suggests. "He's gonna need all the inspiration he can get to lead us to the promised land."

God, yes please, anything. I'm nervous. Bud's counting on me, and I got no idea how to find someone in the woods, even though the scent from the triple-wrapped panties under a blanket in the trunk has traveled through solid metal and is fouling up the inside of Bud's Lincoln. If Matthew McConaughey was shooting one of his Lincoln Aviator commercials in here, the air in his "sanctuary" wouldn't be too breathable.

We leave the car in the park's vast parking lot.

Bud doesn't need to do that thing where the hound sniffs the evidence and charges forward in pursuit, because the "scent" (really using the term loosely there) is all over our clothing.

Standing on the edge of the woods, Bud delivers a little pep talk.

"Well, team," he says, "here goes a new reality show that may reunite a father and daughter, and lead to our buying the station. Spike, you're on…"

The woods are beautiful. They're lovely, they're dark, they're deep, and I got miles to go before I peep to Bud that I'm totally lost. We follow one small trail, then another, or cut a path where I think there may be one. Like every Bitcoin player in the world, no skill—just hoping to get lucky.

Mack learned to forage in the woods as a boy, and he's getting video of the edible foods he's describing: "Here we have canary-yellow mustard flowers, wild wheat, blackberries, and these are trees with edible bark, the slippery elm and black birch."

After around an hour, I think, "Oh, thank you, Dog God. I hear voices."

I flip my tail straight up into the "Bedbugs ho!" signal beagles use when they smell bedbugs during an inspection, or maybe there are no bedbugs, but the beagle does it anyway 'cause she know her owners will give her pizza for flashing the signal and still make a lot of money pretending to eliminate nonexistent bugs. Don't doubt me here; this was revealed to me directly by a certified bedbug detection beagle, only moments before she died of obesity from too much pizza. Kind of like a deathbed confession, I suppose.

I charge toward the sound.

We're back at the parking lot. I've spent the hour going around in a big circle.

"Well, Spike, that was a nice warm-up," Bud says. "Maybe we need to sniff those panties again."

"Spare me," I'm thinking, just as Vel'vetta notices, "That's odd. There's a man who looks like President Bush. He just climbed out of that dumpster, and he's hurrying into the woods carrying an old TV set."

I'm waiting for Bud's Inspector Clouseau–like brain to put this together. Nothing. He's still transfixed by the allure of Vel'vetta's beauty.

I slowly start across the parking lot to follow the guy into the woods.

"Bud, look," Mack whispers. "Spike may be onto something with that guy."

"Oh, right," he says, snapping back to reality. "OK, Spike, go ahead and follow him. We'll stay quiet and lag a little bit behind."

I'm trotting along a narrow trail in an easy saunter, 'cause the guy's walking like he's on speed—which, in fact, he probably is. Mack's about twenty feet behind me, and Bud's stopped to wait for V, who had to take a leak behind a couple of trees.

The Bush guy has shifted into jogging while lugging what appears to be a small 1970s-era TV with sadly mangled rabbit ears. I pick up the pace and Mack calls out, "Ah shit, Spike, the goddamn knee cramped running with this camera. I'll catch up."

What I'm hoping is that I can follow the guy, spot Shoshana, then double back and lead them to her. Then we'll find out she doesn't want to run the TV station. Bud and Lombardo will buy it, and I'll get much-needed money in my retirement account. Or maybe that's not going to happen. Maybe this is just a guy who looks like George Bush and enjoys running through the woods on weekends carrying old TV sets. Or maybe this actually is George Bush, who's back on the heavy booze and runs through the woods with appliances to get rid of hangovers.

Can you see Bush doing that? It's not impossible, and you know it.

I come to a clearing. There're several small tents and a couple of lean-to buildings. It looks like one of those semi-bombed-out villages you might remember from the movie *Platoon*. It's inhabited by a grungy group of strangely familiar-looking people.

Standing on a rock preaching to no one in particular is a man who looks like Tom Cruise, wearing a robe like Charlton Heston as Moses in *The Ten*

Commandments. A woman who's singing "I feel the earth moving under my legs" grabs the TV from the Bush guy and runs off cackling happily.

"This must be the place," I figure. I walk into the open space as a cloud passes from the sun. Light streams down. They spot me and shriek, "He's here! He's here! He is among us!"

"Lo, and then immediately behold," Tom Cruise acting like Heston as Moses proclaims, "it has come to pass that the great white animal has appeared. Bow in his presence. He will lead us to what is justly ours."

I, of course, look at him like he's completely nuts.

"Let this be a sign unto you, and me, too, a sign unto me, and to you, so a sign unto all of us, may this sign be given," he continues. "And I say 'unto' like you would want to say 'unto' when you see God in the form of a great white animal."

I sense I am being worshipped even more than I usually am by my hard-core fans.

"Fire up to celebrate," a woman who looks like Hillary Clinton says, frantically trying to light a pipe. "Fire up the ice. The great white dog is among us!"

I'm frozen. I'm facing a tribe of deranged celebrity lookalikes who apparently practice canine idolatry; if you stop to think about it, maybe that's not so bad. Humans went off track when they stopped worshiping animals in search of higher heavenly comfort, and eternal lifetime guarantees. You never saw marauding crusaders killing people because they didn't worship dogs.

"Hosanna in the highest; hosanna in the highest," Tom Cruise as Moses exclaims. "The highest kind of hosanna that you can possibly hosanna at a high-hosanna-ing time like this!"

A woman who kinda resembles a two-hundred-pound Marilyn Monroe breathlessly says, "Amen. Amen," while slowly extracting a syringe from her leg.

"Yes, amen, Marilyn. Many, many, many amens, which is actually 'amen again, again,' enough 'amen agains' to lead us to more 'Unto you an animal is delivered,' and then back to more hosannas, and finally again with the amens. Right?" Tom Cruise as Moses says. "I'm ready for a whack of your blunt, Obama."

"You bad, Tom Cruise as Moses. You bad," the fake Obama says.

A wide-eyed, gaunt, unkempt, smoking-meth version of Oprah announces, "It is proclaimed that he will lead us to the fame we truly deserve in our own right, superfluous as it may be."

"So it is proclaimed," the group of a dozen or so people utter. "So it is proclaimed."

I amble over toward Shoshana. She's not in as bad a shape as we figured— just a couple of missing teeth; unwashed, stringy hair; blotchy skin; heavy BO; and needle bruises all over her arms and legs. I'd start the rehab with a light sandblasting.

"Oh my God," she says to me.

"Enough with the adulation," I think, adding bad breath to the above list.

"You look just like my Moby. I had a dog just like you when I was really little. The Old Swede took him away 'cause he thought he'd bite me, but he loved me. I cried for three days."

Note here, folks: before you give away a little kid's beloved dog out of some unfounded fear, make sure you know what you're doing. I'm gonna save Mr. Boggs a couple of pages of amusing but tedious backstory here and let you know right now that this woman's problems with her father almost certainly started the day they dragged Moby from her little clutches and dropped him off to an uncertain fate at the dog pound.

"Spike! Spike!" Mack calls as he enters the encampment.

I bark.

"Unto us the Dog God has delivered a tall, broad-shouldered man," Tom Cruise as Moses says. "And behold! Behold! Behold like you've never beholded before—as a crown, he wears a WGHP-TV hat, and carries a magic video scepter for taping us."

"Hair and makeup!" the Caitlyn and Bruce Jenner lookalikes scream. "Hair and makeup!"

Bud and Vel'vetta arrive and sit down with Shoshana. Mack circles and records the encounter while the celeb lookalikes photobomb their way into his shots.

"V, oh my God am I glad to see you," Shoshana gasps. "Get me the hell outta here."

CHAPTER FOUR

MEATBALL MENDACITY

The next evening, Lombardo makes a rare appearance at our house. Bud's invited him for a Sunday meal. He's thinking the boss is gonna be impressed with his preparation of a traditional old-world Italian Sunday meatballs-and-spaghetti dinner. He doesn't stop to think that Lombardo's mother came from Sicily. She'd sooner submit to a facial skin graft than serve Bud's made-in-Mexico "authentic Italian marinara sauce" and frozen Chinese meatballs from Costco.

Since Herbie is standing on the table staring at him, Lombardo has a few parrot-related questions that reflect his journalism training:

"Who is this Chicago Bob he keeps going on about?"

"What's this about 'Spike's a dead dog?'"

"Where did he come from?"

"When will he shut up?"

"Why is he telling me to go back to the ship and get in the buffet line?"

Lombardo is feeding me the meatballs he's hidden in a large napkin on his lap when Bud finally emerges from the kitchen to serve flaming-hot, microwave-defrosted cannoli. Vel'vetta, whose Jaguar is now in the driveway, is with him.

Using my dog powers, I sense maybe the reason it's taken Bud ten minutes to get the desserts out of the cardboard container and put them on three plates has more to do with canoodling than cannoli. I give Bud my "Bend over and scratch my head please" woof, so I can protect him from Lombardo's prying eyes and lick the lipstick imprint offa his neck.

Vel'vetta fills us in: Shoshana's staying with her in a guesthouse, and claims she can cold-turkey the meth as long as she has plenty of Martha Stewart CBD gummies, frequent nicotine enemas, and a small bottle of chilled vodka each morning.

Sol "The Old Swede" Silverman was getting a massage when Shoshana called him. He said he'd talk to her later. That pissed her off, but when they finally connected, he committed to wire twenty thousand for her dental, send over a hairdresser, and give her an Amex black card "strictly for emergencies only." He also arranged for an overnight shipment of Miracle Cure, including an autographed photo of Oz, which he bragged cost him an extra hundred bucks. She said she wanted another dog like Moby, the one he'd taken away. He didn't remember taking away a dog when she was a little kid, so she slammed down the phone.

See, folks, told ya.

Vel'vetta continues. "He called back," she explains, "and he wants Bud to get her an English Bull Terrier dog like Spike."

"Easy. I'll contact Mrs. Erdrick, Spike's breeder," he says.

I'm hopin' with all my might that my bother Oswald's still available. Last I heard nobody ever bought him, likely because he's always seemed too wacky. My brother Billy and me theorize he's somewhat nuts 'cause he accidentally exposed himself to an all-night quadruple feature of Gary Busey movies on TCM as a puppy. Our whole litter fell asleep ten minutes into *Carny*, but Oswald stayed up watching it, then *The Gingerdead Man*, *Surviving the Game*, and *Hider in the House*. He was different, somehow, in the morning, and it wasn't just because his teeth had grown during the night.

"But V," Bud asks, "where do you think we stand with her on the purchase? Might she have any interest in running a TV station?"

"Who knows? But start with this: she claims her father's living proof that the good die young, so ya gotta figure they need some kind of a rapprochement before she signs on to do anything that's gonna please him. Plus, all she really wants is to perform her Carole King tribute at cabaret festivals around the world, but lots of luck with that unless The Old Swede pays for some vocal lessons," Vel'vetta explains.

"Meanwhile," Lombardo says, "I saw what Mack shot. We've got ample good video for the first show. We'll record all of her makeover—dentist, dermatologist—and her other progress. I think maybe we decide right now we'll be skipping video of the tobacco enemas. But a big part of this is also the sexy date we promised The Old Swede. That's maybe the third show in the series if you can pull it off, Bud, and actually find a living, breathing viable woman for The Old Swede to wine and dine."

"Watch," Bud says. Then he speaks to his phone, "Call Dr. Judith Kahill."

We listen. *Ring, ring, ring…* Then a booming male voice speaks, "You've reached the office of world-famous sex therapist, love expert, and everyone's favorite all-around hot female, Dr. Judith Kahill. For advice for what to do in the sack tonight, hang on. If you're calling to order Jungle Gardenia perfume, press two, otherwise—"

"Hello, hello!" Dr. Kahill shouts, picking up. "I'm here. I'm here ready to help you."

"Dr. Kahill, it's Bud here from *Southern Exposure.*"

"Finally ready for anal, Bud?" she asks. "I've got to warn teens that whiplash can result from rear-end collisions."

Vel'vetta looks at Bud and lets out an "eww!" Lombardo buries his head in his hands.

Folks, remember this warning from your old friend Spike. If you're thinkin' about bein' a rump ranger tonight, check with a vet first, or maybe even your doctor. It might be a little painful for one of the people involved.

"Dr. Kahill," Bud says, going into his master pitch-meister mode, "how would you like a blind date with a worldly gentleman, a little bit older but virile fellow, a very impressive media-savvy guy. And the date would be recorded to be included in our new reality TV show series?"

Silence.

"Are you there?" Bud asks. "Dr. Kahill…Judy…Dr. Ka—"

"Yes," a stunned Dr. Kahill gasps. "I'll do it."

We hear a thud. The offer of an appearance on a TV series apparently induced a fainting spell.

A little while later, Lombardo is sipping milk to soothe his tongue after he bit into a molten cannoli.

"These things are normally served cold," he says.

"Sorry, boss," Bud says. "But the tongue heals very quickly, I've heard."

Bud's phone pings. His bank's on the line about the missing forty-seven hundred dollars. He goes into the kitchen to take the call.

Lombardo and Vel'vetta are looking at each other across the table. I'm wondering what level of human small talk they'll initiate to fill the silence. Face it, folks, in a situation like this, no more than twenty seconds of quiet can pass before it's likely that some form of meaningless chatter erupts and words pour forth from your mouths faster than chipmunks running out of a hole in the ground.

To amuse myself in situations like this, I've created my one-to-ten Phil the Neighbor Small-Talk Score, based on the sheer stupidity of the comments the potbellied Phil makes to Bud to initiate oxygen-wasting chitchat every time he sees Bud.

"I see you're standing on some leaves, Bud," is your basic Phil the Neighbor Small-Talk Score of one, and it rockets all the way to a ten with "Hot enough for you?"—which he always asks when it's snowing.

"What's the most difficult challenge of being both mayor of High Point and general manager of WGHP-TV?" Vel'vetta asks the boss, a question that is obviously beyond measurement on my scale.

Lombardo explains that he got drafted into the mayoral job after Mayor Gordon went to jail on the corruption charges that Bud and me had uncovered, but that when his current term's up, he's quitting.

"City Hall's filled with self-serving phonies who'll do or say anything to retain power," he complains. "And you?" he asks. "Bud tells me you're quite the entrepreneurial businesswoman, and if I might add, at the risk of going to jail for harassment, or at least losing my job, and then being trash-talked out of town and forced into a downward spiral of guilt and alcoholic despair, I'd like to take the risk of complimenting you—and I'd say this if my wife were here—you are also a very beautiful woman."

"Ha, no, no! You're great to say that. Thank you, I love it. It makes me feel so good, like the old days. About two years ago, nice compliments suddenly stopped, but the staring at me seems to have increased," she says.

The boss wants to know about her business, and Vel'vetta explains that aside from the pole-dancing competitions, which are purely a hobby for exercise, she has an agency for all manner of men and woman who're exotic performers. "I call my business The House That Silicone Built," she says.

"Topless dancers, bikini models, lingerie fashion models, male strippers—if they want someone to get onstage or show up somewhere and act sexy, I've got it for them. I'm thinking of adding a canine division with just one client: Spike. Think you'd like that, my big handsome Pooh Bear?" she asks, scratching my head.

"Shit!" Bud yells, walking through the swinging door from the kitchen. "I've lost the forty-seven hundred, and it looks like way more's been spent on the Mastercard on that account."

He's upset, and even though I'm fantasizing about the cash I might be raking in with the gigs from Vel'vetta, I run to him and start barking. It's something we dogs do to let our owners know we're there for them in a crisis. Of course, normally it would be more like barking 'cause the house is on fire, or barking 'cause the basement's flooding, than making a lot of noise over credit card fraud.

"I'll know more in the morning. This is bad," he says, smashing his fist into his palm over and over.

"Alright," Lombardo commands. "Let's calm down, take three breaths, and deal with it on Monday, 'cause I've got an idea, and we might make that forty-seven hundred back and a lot more, if I can get a coexecutive-producing fee for us."

He gives Bud an "anything you can do, I can do better" look, pulls out his phone, and says, "Call Andy Cohen cell."

Andy picks up fast. "Well, it's Mr. L on a Sunday night. How lucky, lucky are we, Anderson? It's the one and only Lombardo. If only he could have been here to judge our collaboration on the fabulous Italian Sunday night spaghetti-and-meatballs dinner we've just enjoyed."

Andy explains that every once in a while, his pal Anderson Cooper swings by for a Sunday night meal. "Tonight," he explains, "Anderson told me he made the marinara sauce from a secret recipe his mother, Gloria, got from Frank Sinatra when she was dating him. Sinatra told her the recipe came from Sicily when his father, Martin Sinatra, emigrated to American in 1902."

As Lombardo's explaining his views on the finer points of marinara sauce, a ping on his phone indicates that Andy is texting him:

> in truth there's no way anderson made the sinatra marinara. I had the real deal at nancy sinatra's. tonight's sauce was the made-in-china stuff you get in the big container from walmart.

"I'm not much of a cook like Anderson," Andy continues on the phone, "so I got Sal at Patsy's to deliver a dozen of their beef-pork-and-veal balls made from the recipe that came from Naples with Sal's grandmother."

Lombardo's phone pings again. This time a text from Anderson:

> don't believe him I know these meatballs. There was a barely defrosted vat of them from Costco at last years CNN labor day picnic.

"Sounds like you two went overboard tonight. Just watch out for any blistering-hot cannoli," Lombardo warns. "Now listen. Andy, you said, 'You never know what you're going to find in the woods.' Well, we found your next Bravo partially scripted—but still like you're watching a train wreck—reality show. Think *Celebrity Lookalike Big Brother* meets *Celebrity Lookalike Survivor* meets *Celebrity Lookalike Rehab with Dr. Drew* meets *Celebrity Lookalike Recovery Road* meets—"

"Lookalikes, so fun," Andy interrupts, loving it. Is the Wonder Dog involved?"

Andy, pal, my dog bowl is full. I got forthcoming sexy modeling gigs from Vel'vetta, a daily show to do with Bud, a possible project sealed in the mystery envelope, plus the show with The Old Swede. And don't forget my main job as professional pet for Bud, and I gotta deal with the major problems with Daisy, plus I need to work out two hours a day so I can be as buff a dog as Anderson Cooper is a human.

"And by the way, before I sign off on this, what the heck are you talking about, Mr. L?" Andy asks the boss.

Lombardo tells the story of the lookalikes living in the woods. "Put cameras everywhere, *Big Brother* it, throw in some actual D-list celebs, stage some arguments, have Moses fall in love with Oprah, make the Obama guy gay with a crush on Bush—you've got endless potential here," he pitches.

"Why are they living in the woods?" Andy asks. "So many ticks and stuff."

He explains that they spiraled into drugs and booze during the pandemic 'cause no one would hire lookalikes wearing masks. The Caitlyn Jenner lookalike's mother now tours the country making big bucks singing, dancing, and reading phony legal briefs in her Ruth Bader Ginsburg show, and she sends them money.

"Their leader is a dead ringer for Tom Cruise, except much shorter. The fake Cruise is in full costume as Charlton Heston playing Moses, and he never breaks character."

"That's new. I mean Moses is old, sadly—very low TV Q for Moses these days—but a tiny Tom Cruise playing Moses, that's refreshingly new," Andy says enthusiastically.

Bud gets on the line. "Hi, Andy, and if you want Spike, he can appear every now and then because they practice canine idolatry."

"What?" Andy Cohen asks.

"They believe Spike is a god who will lead them to the fame they deserve in their own right, and if you do this show, the Wonder Dog will actually have done it for them."

"Wow, all of our research indicates that a significant percentage of people who compulsively watch reality shows are also inclined to secretly practice some form of animal idolatry," Andy explains. "Thank you, Spike."

OK, I've done it again, and I didn't even try. And now it's time for...

CHAPTER FIVE

A Date With Judy

Monday morning, Bud's tense, and there's not much I can do to help him 'cept lick his ankle while he waits to speak to a human on the phone. He's on hold with his credit card company about the thousands of dollars of charges made on the card in Thailand.

He learns that someone using his name and a complete fake set of his IDs enjoyed a seven-night Your Angels in Sex Paradise erotic holiday VIP package in Phuket, Thailand, thanks to his Mastercard.

"They took the premium option with three girls," he's told.

"Are you sure you weren't in Thailand for a week last month? Please double-check your calendar," the representative instructs Bud repeatedly before Bud calmly tells the guy that he can prove he was on television.

"Perhaps to jog your memory, look in your phone to see if there are photos from last month of you, looking somewhat tired and drained, standing on a beach with multiple Asian women drinking large frozen beverages through colorful plastic straws. Or, Mr. Bud, maybe you've been treated for STDs recently and you've forgotten why."

"As I said, I was on TV last month. In fact, we had a telethon to raise money for people made homeless in the pandemic."

"Can you access some of that money immediately to pay this substantial bill? I see your checking account is overdrawn from a hacking."

"Stop it," Bud demands. "I was not in Thailand last month. Please dispute these charges."

"Sometimes the husband goes over for a sex vacation, and the wife sees the charges on the bill, so he calls to try to dispute them just like you are doing now," the guy says suspiciously.

"Look, I'm a bachelor, I live alone, and my roommate is Spike, a dog. He wouldn't care if I went on a vacation to Thailand as long as I took him," Bud says flatly.

"Good thing you didn't take him," the rep says, laughing. "They eat dogs over there."

Yeah, I know we're delectable menu items in Thailand. Repulsive. The low point of my life was when Ike "I Got Money" Piles was freezin' me to death and planning to ship me to Bangkok for a banquet. Bud saved me. I covered it all with Mr. Boggs in the first book. That title is likely referenced on the back cover of this book. If not, somebody has really screwed up.

Bud says, "Sir, I want to see surveillance video of the guy at the desk checking in, if they have it."

"These places are usually very discreet, but we will investigate that, thank you. We'll be back in touch."

"OK," Bud tells the rep. "Thanks."

"Enjoy your dog," he says, like a waiter in Phuket serving a steaming bowl of collie casserole.

"Whoever did this," Bud tells me, "I hope he ends up marrying one of these girls and has a messy divorce when she doesn't want to screw him anymore once they get back here and she's maxed out his credit card at Louis Vuitton."

A few nights later, we're set to cover Sol "The Old Swede" Silverman's big date with love expert Dr. Judith Kahill.

Bud and me are front and center when Dr. Kahill pulls up at The Old Swede's mansion at the wheel of a cute little red electric Chevy Volt. She's got a giant stuffed panda next to her in the front seat wearing a "Phew! I survived 2020" T-shirt.

Using the little GoPro camera on my head, I scan the bumper stickers plastered on the back of the car. I'm impressed—Defenders of Wildlife, Jane Goodall Institute, Be Happy Have Sex Today, Green New Deal, So Make Me Happy, Ocean Conservancy, Save the Spotted Owl, I'm Still Not Happy. The license plate is L84ANL, which seems to have hidden comedic meaning to Bud and Mack.

She's dressed in the same dusty-looking red dress from the parade. She's slathered on enough makeup for a Kabuki dance audition, and as usual, she reeks of the oily smell of Jungle Gardenia perfume. Judging by the signs on the doors of her car, in addition to advising as a love expert, she's a franchise rep for the fragrance.

The Old Swede is eagerly waiting inside. When she appears in the doorway, trailed by a camera, he says, "You must be Dr. Judith Kahill."

Take a moment to note what a stupid way that is to greet somebody when you already know who they are, and you've been waiting for them all day. Got it? Sure you won't utter something dumb like that in the future? Good. Let's move on.

Ah, but first, you gotta know this.

Central to the success he craves for this one last great date are the timed doses of Viagra Plus that will be injected into The Old Swede's wrist at crucial junctures during the evening by his just-delivered new Erecto-Watch, a joint venture of Apple and Pfizer.

His hope is that if Dr. Kahill is as attracted to him as he's certain she will be, and by dint of that attraction, she's desirous of a little horizontal refreshment at the end of the evening, he'll be at the peak of arousal in the nick of time because of the watch's many new features.

Mack has the room rigged with tiny cameras.

While Sol "The Old Swede" Silverman's eying Dr. Kahill's body like it's a vein of gold he's just discovered in a wall of his home, she's scanning the living room looking for cameras and smiling and posing seductively each time she spots one. He's balancing precariously on an ebony cane with a gold handle. Real ebony, real gold, not the lightweight imitations they sell in New York shoe stores. I position myself next to him, figuring in case he succumbs to sleep, he'll bounce off me and maybe avoid breaking every brittle bone in his body.

"Whaddaya think, Judy, Robert Redford?" he asks, pointing to his wig. "Or," he says, yanking it off, "Norman Lear?"

"I'll risk it with the Norman now, and if I come back, maybe I'll want Redford for the way we were tonight," she says, confusing him.

I see that Bud's thinking, "That was quick. She's good."

The Old Swede is in full feather. He's wearing an expensive old blue blazer that's now too big on him. He's adjusted a blue ascot at the throat of his crisp white shirt. He's got a gold American Institute of Certified Public

Accountants lapel pin. He's sporting a circa-1974 tan, flared slacks, and in an effort to be as hip as possible, huge, bright yellow Yeezy sneakers. The bottom half of his body looks like the Donald Duck character that greets you at Disney World. The top resembles just about any man his age you'd see in a casket.

Dr. Kahill sits next to him, which provokes a violent sneezing fit that seems to be an allergic reaction to her heavy perfume.

He puts on a COVID mask. Doesn't help. Pops a couple of Benadryl. Doesn't help. Uses several squirts of a twenty-four-hour-relief nasal spray to dim his sense of smell. Doesn't help. Takes a couple of drags from a steroid inhaler. Doesn't help.

Dr. Kahill heads to the bathroom to "maybe splash a little of my perfume off."

"She's no Pelosi, Bud, but she's cute," Sol "The Old Swede" Silverman confides. "But, dammit, she smells like a cheap French whorehouse. Not that I've ever been to one, or ever spent a dime for sex in my life—not me, guys."

Nurse Ruth glances at me, rolling her eyes.

I wish I could properly respond, but evolution has yet to allow us dogs to display sarcasm. The best we can do is tilt our head and look at you like, "What the fuck?"

The staging area for the first phase of the date is the middle of the living room.

Sol's in a straight-backed chair, sitting on an inflatable sciatica pillow, and Dr. Kahill's next to him.

Rather than asking her a single question about her life, The Old Swede plows ahead talking about himself.

"I love dating, and I always like to have a major overarching important theme to my dates," he says, as his arm flies up at a steep angle.

He warned Bud that something like this could happen. Sudden rigidity of limbs can be a rare side effect of Viagra Plus being injected directly into a vein in the wrist by the Erecto-Watch.

"How charming," Dr. Kahill responds. "Is the theme tonight a celebration of the Proud Boys? You appear to be offering me the Nazi salute."

"Sorry, just a muscle twitch. Must have done too many one-armed push-ups this morning," he lies, frantically tugging on his sleeve to reposition the arm.

"Can I help you at all there, Ruth?" Dr. Kahill asks, as the nurse struggles to force the arm back into his lap.

"No, I'm OK with this," she says, grunting at the effort to lower it.

"OK, good luck there," Dr. Kahill tells her, speaking directly into the camera.

"No, Judy," Bud instructs. "Don't look into the camera, just at The Old Swede."

"So shall I say that again?" Dr. Kahill asks.

"No, Judy, no second takes or faking it here," Bud explains.

"Hear that, Judy?" The Old Swede says. "No faking it tonight."

"Did you know, Sol, nearly one hundred percent of all women fake an orgasm at some point during the course of their sex lives?" she says.

"The 'Little Old Swede' and I wouldn't know anything about that," he boasts. "It's a subject I'm not the least bit familiar with."

"Funny, all my male clients say the same thing," she says.

"To continue, Judy, to continue—now, about my plans for our evening together. I've based tonight's date on a song I discovered by a promising young singer named Billy Joel. I think the fellow is really headed somewhere. Maybe he's even the next Mel Tormé, "the Velvet Frog.""

"Actually, no," Dr. Kahill corrects him. "Mel Tormé was known as 'the Velvet Fog,' not 'Frog,'" she says.

"I was hoping to take you to see the Frog tonight," he responds. "I once had the chance to try to shake his hand while we were both standing at urinals in the men's room at the Desert Inn, so I'm disappointed my pal Mel's not touring in the area."

Bud and I exchange knowing glances, since it's common knowledge that Mel Tormé died at 1:45 a.m., June 5, 1999, at the Los Angeles Medical Center. We figure she'll break the bad news to him.

"Well, Mel was a little bit more of a pure jazz singer with perfect pitch, while Billy Joel is a rock-and-roll icon, and of course Mel Tormé played the drums, not the piano, like Billy Joel, and incidentally, your pal Mel died at one forty-five a.m., June fifth, 1999, at the Los Angeles Medical Center," she says.

Completely ignoring the fast-breaking news that his old pissing buddy Mel is dead, The Old Swede continues. "So, Judy, the Billy Joel song I picked as our theme for our night together is—"

"Oh please, Sol, you flatter me. Let me guess. 'Uptown Girl?'"

"No."

"'Just the Way You Are?'"

"Never heard of it."

"'She's Always a Woman?'"

"No, isn't that Helen Redeye's—what's-her-name's—song?"

"Is it 'She's Got a Way?'"

"No, and no more quizzes, please. The song I picked to celebrate tonight is—"

"Maybe it's 'Tell Her About It?'" she suggests, giggling.

"Close," he responds. "It's 'My Life'! The theme for our date tonight is young Billy Joel's spirited composition 'My Life.' I've got eleven of my scrapbooks out, the trophies dusted, dozens of other tributes, so get ready for me to hit all the high points of the last hundred-plus years."

Dr. Judith Kahill's looking at Bud like, "If television exposure weren't more important to me than losing my sanity, I'd be out of here."

"To start, let's do something I've never done in all those years!" he announces.

"Anal?" she asks.

"Huh? Amal, Clooney's wife? Never touched her, but I was quite close to George's aunt Rosemary Clooney during both of her marriages to José. He once caught Rosie and me having chocolate malts together on their front porch."

"What are we going to do?" she asks.

"Chair dance! We are going to—play it, Ruth," he instructs. "Play 'My Life' on the Victrola over there, and we'll dance sitting right here in our chairs. Why bother to try to get up? We'd only have to try to sit down again."

The music overtakes him. Judy's wriggling a bit, trying to be a good sport. He's bouncing up and down on his sciatica pillow. He's got the self-satisfied look of a man who'd dare to vault through the air on a trampoline on top of a ninety-story building.

As Mr. Joel's singin' not to worry about him 'cause he's alright, the sciatica pillow explodes, tumbling Sol "The Old Swede" Silverman headfirst to the floor.

"Pain! Pain!" he screams. The sciatica's on fire. "Hydrocodone, Ruth!" he orders. "Pain! Pain!"

The nurse whispers in his ear, something only I, with my dog hearing, can detect.

"Mr. Silverman," she says. "You haven't had a bowel movement in two weeks and—"

"Pills!" he yells. "Three pills now! Pain, pain!"

The Old Swede swallows three pills, and Bud and the nurse get him back into his chair. He opens a thick scrapbook, and his bartender serves two large, glistening martinis.

"Sorry, Judy. I guess I got a little excited, like when I used to do the reverse four-and-a-half-somersault high dive in the pike position into the pool at The Beverly Hills Hotel," he says, taking a giant gulp of his drink.

This is likely a lie, which I detect because we dogs can pick up a subtle scent when you humans tell a whopper of that magnitude. I sensed it before during his Omar Sharif bridge-playing yarn and a lot of his other boasts.

"That's odd," Dr. Kahill counters. "When I was eighteen, I briefly dated Swen, the pool manager at The Beverly Hills Hotel. I was there almost every day. I don't remember a ten-meter platform anywhere, just a simple little springboard at the deep end."

"Well, er…ah," he fumfers, "I get confused sometimes after the steroid inhaler. Maybe it was just a perfect jackknife off that little springboard. Anyway, take a look here at my scrapbook. By the way, the TV station I own with no debt is really just a hobby for me. I earned my fortune in the action-packed world of accounting. I led my own company for sixty years. Look at this. Here I am with all of my employees in 1957, the year I founded The Old Swede and His Vikings."

He shows her a black-and-white picture of thirty identical-looking Caucasian men with one-inch crew cuts, each wearing a dark suit, white shirt, and narrow dark tie with a small silver tie clip.

"Fascinating," she says, forcing a smile.

"Glad you like it. Now here we all are a year later," he says, turning a page and finishing his drink. "And here we all are the next year"—he turns another page—"and look at us a year later!"

Apparently, he plans to continue showing her the annual employee group shot for the next forty-seven years, but he pauses at page thirteen with a question.

"Now," he says with his mouth hanging a little more open than usual, "have you been observing anything changing about Sol "The Old Swede" Silverman as the years are passing? And please, Ruth, another martini from Joe."

I notice The Old Swede's watch flashing the word "dosing" in red. Nurse Ruth looks at me and raises her hand to her mouth and rotates her wrist with the international signal that tells one person at a bar that another person at the bar has already had too much to drink.

"Well, Sol 'The Old Swede' appears to be losing hair faster than Lake Mead's losing water," Kahill observes.

"I thought you'd miss it, but I took action, so here on the next page, who do I look like after a little refurbishment topside?"

"Eddie Van Halen," she says, with Bud and Mack stifling laughs.

"Who? Who? Van who? Johnson? *No*! Wait! Oh my, oh no, not the leg now, no, no," he says, as his right leg begins to elevate.

"Down, leg! Down, leg!" he screams. "Bad leg!"

The leg continues to rise.

To me, it appears to be going up with the same certainty as the two-thousand-ton section of the fabled London Tower Bridge. By the way, you pick up these international facts watching PBS documentaries on Wednesday nights instead of *The Masked Singer*.

"Why is your leg elevating like that, Mr. Silverman? What can I do?" Dr Kahill asks.

"Thanks. Oh, so sorry, Judy. It's just the old rugby injury. Could you and Bud just ease me down to the carpet? Ruth, get me muscle relaxer, maybe the thirty-milligram cyclo."

By the time he's settled on the floor, his leg appears to be in a fully erect position—pointing straight at the ceiling.

"I can try to force it down," Bud tells him, "but it seems ossified, like cement."

"I'm sorry, everyone. Dammit, this is what I get for still playing senior rugby."

He swallows a big white cyclobenzaprine tablet.

"Let's see what I can do," Ruth the nurse says.

She pushes the leg down as forcefully as she can, but as she does, his body pops up.

"I'll try again," she says.

But it's the same thing—leg down, body up; leg down, body up; leg down, body up.

"Are you OK there, Sol?" Dr, Kahill asks. "You're moving like a seesaw."

"Enough!" he yells. "Down, leg!" Down!"

He takes a swig of his second martini and swallows another big white pill.

"Maybe Spike and I can help," Bud says.

Bud plants his foot on The Old Swede's shoulder, and I climb onto his chest. As Ruth and Dr. Kahill slowly force the leg back to the floor, it makes the sound of a door hinge that hasn't been oiled since the Revolutionary War.

"I'll just lie here in the supine position and rest for a minute," he gasps. "No more rugby for me; finally time to retire, promise."

Dr. Kahill mouths the question "Rugby?" to Ruth, who smiles calmly and shakes her head, saying, "No way."

Ruth whispers to Bud off camera and explains that before Judy arrived, The Old Swede had gone to his safe and taken out one of the last of his Dexamyl pills. He's been hoarding a small stash given to him by his diet doctor in 1969 before amphetamine sadly became illegal.

"That was to keep him awake," she explains.

She continues with the news flash that the mix of the Dexi, martinis, Benadryl, steroid spray, opioids, and muscle relaxer, plus "whatever the hell is in that watch," has clearly rendered Sol "The Old Swede" Silverman incapable of movement.

"The date's over for him. Let's just talk him down for a couple of minutes until he passes out. And by the way, I've seen him bombed like this before," Ruth explains. "Right now, Mr. Silverman's probably got no filter and will tell you…"

It doesn't take long for us to discover that the real Sol "The Old Swede" Silverman is a man broken on the wheels of living, who's become pathetic in his own eyes. He's haunted by the boring life he lived as an accountant. While friends from school were living the high life of the 1960s, he was under bright fluorescent lights in an office filled with guys who looked like they were in the Apollo program—men who brought lunches to work in carefully folded, crisp brown paper bags and left the office exactly at five p.m. each day, announcing it was quitting time.

He'd constructed an alternate reality that he came to believe. Rat Pack? He saw them in the parking lot at the Sands as they were getting out of a limo. Joey Bishop pointed to The Old Swede's head and hollered, "Nice rug!"

Drunk with Liz and Dick? No, just home alone and bombed on martinis watching *Cleopatra*. Romantic nights at the Carlyle hotel turned out to be standing behind a pillar struggling to see Bobby Short perform.

Lunch with Sophia Loren? His chef made a recipe from her cookbook. Played bridge with Omar Sharif? Not quite, but he did watch Omar on a closed-circuit bridge tournament at an accounting business expo in Milwaukee.

"One last thing before you rest now, Sol," Dr. Kahill says. "Tell us about you and your daughter, Shoshana. What went wrong there?"

The Old Swede's eyes are closed. He's drifting off. "I…never…should have taken…away…the…dog."

If only he could have known that at that moment my brother Oswald was asleep in his crate in Devon, Pennsylvania, likely dreaming of Gary Busey and not knowing that soon he'd be on his way to meet Shoshana, so her father could make good on her long-lost dog, Moby.

A MEETING

I'm lyin' on the floor of Lombardo's office waiting for the start of a meeting about Saturday night's Old Swede mess. But my mind's elsewhere—I'm imaginin' the ear-flapping pleasure in store for me in a few days when I'm in Bud's old convertible as part of the classic-car cruise on High Point Heritage Day.

If you're a dog, or extremely lucky enough to be a protruding-eared human, nothing short of, say, multiple you-know-whats compares to the joy of the wind flapping your ears. That's why you'd sometimes see Obama sticking his head out of the window of the speeding presidential limo.

Buffy, Bud, and news director Mike Stevens are waiting for Lombardo. Mike is singing "Secret Love," while Buffy is surfing her phone lookin' for material for one of Bud's monologues on the show.

"Here's a new actual advertising pitch in this tech magazine we can do something funny with in a monologue," she says. "'Tired of the same old boring hanky-panky with your sex robot? All is not lost! Ship your sex robot to sex robot school at SORAPT, School of Robotic Advanced Pleasure Training, in Las Vegas.'"

I'm wonderin' if that's so your sex robot can be the envy of all your friends' sex robots?

"Shit!" Lombardo yells, storming in. "I'm late, and I'm never late, but I'm late because of this goddamn arm, those goddamn jerks at City Hall, and the damn doctor who kept me waiting while she was probably rolling around on the exam table with her nurse."

"What's happened? Are you OK?" they ask, genuinely concerned about Lombardo, so it's not the phony distress of employees who'd ask their boss the same questions while being clearly disappointed that the guy hadn't dropped dead at the doctor's office.

"Fuck being mayor of High Point," he says. "Now I got machine-gun elbow."

"What the hell?" Bud says.

"Yeah, the latest of our postpandemic medical problems. And I got it from having to elbow bump every time one of those yahoos at City Hall sees me. They don't wanna shake hands anymore; they think it's more fun to bump elbows and give me this big stupid smile like they just executed the Rubik's Cube of personal greetings."

The boss reads the new American Medical Association explanation of his condition.

"Splitting pain at the bony tip of the elbow. The throbbing spasms resemble the rat-a-tat of a machine gun. Treatment: ice, Aleve, or Advil and refraining from elbow bumping to avoid looking like an asshole.... OK, I added the last part there," he says.

"Sorry about that," everyone murmurs.

The bump might be more dangerous than everyone figured, but it's still a way faster greeting than having to sniff the ass of every dog you meet—not that you would do that when you meet a dog, no, not you literally. That ass-sniffing reference was intended for the dogs who might be reading this page. By the way, I'm able to get more factual information from one sniff than watchin' an hour of CNN.

"OK," Lombardo says, snapping into focus. "Sol 'The Old Swede' Silverman—what happened? Is Dr. Kahill OK? Is he still alive? If so, was he charming? Do we have a show?"

Bud explains that Dr. Kahill was a really good sport, and The Old Swede passed out with a mammoth erection about a half hour into the proceedings.

"The guy checks off a lot of boxes for offending people, places, and things," Bud explains. "Old people, honest people, Jewish people, Swedish people, accountants, dirty old men, really dirty old men, rugby players, platform divers, Apple watches, plus Norman Lear, Billy Joel, and Mel Tormé."

"God," Lombardo says with a faraway look in his eyes. "I remember exactly where I was when I heard that Mel Tormé had died at one forty-five a.m. on June fifth at the Los Angeles Medical Center."

"The Old Swede thinks Mel's still alive," Bud says.

"That's hip," Lombardo adds. "So anyway, whadda we do, Bud?"

"Thankfully, we have no more obligation to get The Old Swede a date, and if we did, we wouldn't do it anyway. I got a dog coming down for Shoshana—actually it's Spike's brother Oswald—and we'll see if that helps heal the father-daughter rift. But from what I hear, she'd rather be singing 'You've Got a Friend' in a dimly lit lounge in the Poconos than running a brightly lit TV station in High Point."

"Bravo basically wants us to produce a 'miracle meth-addict makeover' show with her," Lombardo says, "and the dog angle's a good thing."

"Hopefully, if it works," Bud explains, "but Mrs. Erdrick, Spike's breeder, was reluctant to let us have Oswald. She says he's maybe, to use her term, 'a little too unpredictable.' When I asked her to elaborate, she was honest enough to say she thought Oswald might be full-blown crazy."

Oh, no. I hope Oswald's not even more nuts than I remember, but every family has a secret because there's someone somewhere in their bloodline who's wacky. You're probably thinking about that person in your family right now, and you're remembering how their life has played out.

Hey, maybe it's you. Maybe you're the nut, and that's why you're reading a story narrated by a dog? There's a crazy part of everybody, only some of us control it better than others. At least that's what Mr. Boggs told me it would be wise to mention here.

"OK, let's move on to coverage of Heritage Day and the Parade of Heroes," the boss directs. "The good news is, you can leave the earplugs at home. There'll be no leaf blower demos."

What a very bad memory for my very good dog hearing.

Last year at Heritage Day, one of the many crafts, products, and services on display was the new locally manufactured Bazooka Power Jet 10,000 leaf blower. It was showcased with an array of other loud, polluting, gasoline-powered, lawn care products.

The Jet 10,000 can effortlessly remove the heaviest mounds of wet leaves and scatter stones and rocks, and if you're not careful, knock over the sculpture in your garden. Its thunderous roar during demos drove crowds indoors, but the sound easily traveled through brick walls.

Bud told me that the fine print on the instructions says, "Your new Bazooka Power Jet 10,000 can be heard within a two-mile radius. Do not operate blower before seven a.m." Sad fact it is that you humans have evolved beyond the ability to use a good old-fashioned rake.

"Is it true we have the Oscar Meyer Wienermobile this year, but with a safe-space tent next to it?" Mike asks. "How could that adorable rolling pantheon of processed meat offend anyone? It's so cute. So many memories. Makes me want to sing 'Sentimental Journey.'"

"Yes, but objections to it came pouring into City Hall," Lombardo explains. "Apparently the somewhat crooked shape of the hot dog on the Wienermobile offends a small subset of our male population with Peyronie's disease."

"My God," Bud says, "what's next?"

"Next," Lombardo says, "the next is simple. We also had a subset of objections from church groups who thought the hot dog looked too much like a normal-shaped, but very large, penis that just happened to be mounted on a yellow car. They labeled it 'stealth porn.' Then we had fourteen people who didn't care that the hot dog looked like a giant penis; they just wanted it circumcised. And of course, the vegans complained, and the Dildo Appreciation Society of Thomasville bombarded me with emails.... I could go on."

"And so we need dozens of safe-space tents all over the grounds this year," Bud says.

"Yes, and we need extra security, because a lot of the angry anti-mask fanatics from the pandemic are turning their wrath on the safe spaces, complaining that the tents are violating their right to have a better view of what's behind the tents," Lombardo explains.

"So it's theoretically possible that you could be hiding from a giant penis and get beaten up for it?" Bud asks.

"Let's see what happens on Saturday," Lombardo says. "By the way, now that I'm mayor, they asked me to make remarks from the reviewing stand. I got an email from the producer saying, 'You'll make remarks between one and one fifteen.' What the hell are 'remarks'? Shall I remark that Heritage Day attendance is skewing so old, the main sponsor this year is Our Lady of the Perpetual Nap Cemetery?"

CHAPTER SIX

HERITAGE DAY

On Friday, our *Southern Exposure* show is dedicated to promoting Saturday's High Point Heritage Day.

First up, Bud introduces a local woman who'll be in the library tent plugging her new self-help book, *The Other End of the Q-Tip: How to Compromise in a Relationship*. Couples with heavy earwax problems are certain to rocket this little gem up the bestseller lists. She drones on about how all of life is a negotiation. Read the book, Daisy!

She lists ten techniques for peaceful compromise. Ever notice how these self-help lists are always an even number? There might be only nine techniques, or even seven, but she had to round it out to ten. So which of the ten are ringers?

Up next is Ms. App, a local inventor of niche apps. She dazzled me last time with her two small contributions to saving Western civilization. She demonstrated an app to automatically erase man buns from photos sent to you, and another one to retroactively put a complete Lululemon outfit in naked pictures of you shared by former girlfriends.

"So, Ms. App," Bud asks, "what will you be showing at the Heritage Day festival tomorrow?"

"Thanks, Bud. And hi, Spike—I got a little gift for you in a minute. But first, our research shows that the ubiquitous use of 'LOL' letters in emails, texts, Facebook posts, and so forth is finally annoying people. So our new multifunction app will not only return all robocalls from a universal number and tell whoever's calling, 'Shut up and go to hell!' It will also delete every 'LOL' written in anything coming your way, plus there's an algorithm to remove any reference you might see anywhere on social media wishing 'happy birthday in heaven' to a dead person."

I'm figurin', "You're really taking a risk by pissing off a lot of dead people, who're already pissed off 'cause they're dead, with that one."

"And finally," she says, "there's been phenomenal demand from mothers and fathers for this app, which we expect will be on millions of kids' phones in a few weeks. As we know, the trophy business for children has exploded. The latest is getting a trophy for not getting a trophy."

"Must be something to have a bedroom full of trophies for not getting a trophy by the time you're twelve," Bud says, laughing.

"That's right. That's why I've created, for all of the overpraising parents out there, the Tony the Talking Trophy app. Tony will enable them to bombard their kids with kudos and validation from anywhere on the globe.

"There are a hundred different accolades that parents themselves will record, from 'high five,' 'good job,' and 'you're so smart!' to 'way to go,' 'I'm so proud,' 'standing ovation,' and on and on. Tony the Talking Trophy will randomly communicate to a child as many times a day as the parents might need to make them feel they're being great parents, even though, let's say, they could be off for a week away from their kids at a swingers retreat."

The closest I came to winning a trophy was at a dog show where I finished second to a Yorkshire terrier, which was like losing to a hair dryer.

Ms. App gives me a gift that I think I'm gonna love. It's an AI talking dog collar with a powerful little Bose speaker that can make it seem like I'm happily spieling all manner of sharp ripostes at startled humans. There's a lot for me to learn to work it, but I figure this talking collar's gonna be a lot of fun.

During the final segment, I'm waiting in my doghouse on the set to help Bud with a food demo. This is my specialty. I eat and then react based on my careful study of how TV chefs sample food. I can channel all the way from an enraged Gordon Ramsay heaving a plate of steaming lasagna at an unwitting chef, down to Guy Fieri, smiling while extolling the exquisite taste of Pennsylvania scrapple even though he sees clumps of hair sticking out of the piece he's sampling.

The food guest is a fifty-year-old man named Todd Corker, who once was a Chevrolet dealer in Winston-Salem. By the way, has there ever been a better name for a car dealer than 'Todd Corker'? You'd see Todd Corker on TV, smiling and doing his commercials nattily dressed in a suit and tie. His business was strong. He'd been able to make a solid comeback after being arrested for illegal airbag manipulation. His shop had been making cash by converting the passenger-side airbags into inflatable people to enable solo drivers to commute in the HOV two-or-more-passenger lanes during rush hour.

He'd been a respected member of the community. But his anger at the results of the 2020 election somehow forced him off the rails. He sprouted a bushy white beard, wears a red baseball hat and a tight black T-shirt pulled over a bulked-up body, and sports a load of painfully fresh tattoos on his arms.

He tried to drive his Harley-Davidson Green Monster motorcycle through the front door of our station and up the stairs to the studio, which might be a bit of a hint about his newfound aggressiveness.

His new product, Angry Man Meals, offers edible proof that our culture is becoming more and more engineered to create menace.

Todd Corker yells, "Great to be on this great show, Bud! You and Spike are terrific! Love your work; it's beyond great. You're going places in TV for sure."

"Thanks, Todd, we appreciate that. Now I see we have an array of products here on the table with your big red AMM logo. What's up?"

"Well, many men like me around the country are angry today because of what's going on, and we've realized we enjoy being angry and want to stay angry. So I'm meeting the burgeoning needs of the emerging anger market with an array of ultra-high-sodium meal kits of bad-tasting food made with terrible ingredients. Of course, to give the meals an extra wallop, I've infused everything with a pinch of testosterone and a dash of anabolic steroids."

"Well," Bud says, "I don't think this is really—"

Corker cuts him off. "My popular Meth Malt Shakes will have you pissed off that it's four a.m. and you're wide awake cleaning the baseboards in your kitchen."

"Sort of like discomfort food," Bud quips. "And you—"

"Hold it there, pal," Todd Corker interrupts aggressively. "My products have the distinction of being the official breakfast of those great patriots on the morning of January 6, 2020. Here's how the meals work. If a guy kicks off the day with one of our wake-me-up specials, it'll jump-start his temper by getting his resentment, bitterness, and hostility flowing just the way he wants it. Our steroid-laced lunches assure a full afternoon of chest-pounding fury over even the slightest of grievances, and with one of our testosterone-glazed raw chuck steak dinners, a man's temper will hover at the brink of a violent tantrum for hours until he collapses in bed vowing to hit somebody in the face first thing in the morning."

Bud's not happy with this guy and is about to toss him off the show, so I'm saved from having to sample a peanut butter, pastrami, and Prednisone hoagie.

Todd Corker cheerfully explains that "all Angry Man Meals are packaged in bright red plastic containers with large bags, suitable for tossing out a car window. Everything is made of extra-flimsy plastic, so the slightest breeze will scatter the trash, making it ideal for disposal near peaceful protests or while driving through any neighborhood where you think elites might reside."

"Well, I want to thank you, Todd. That's all the time we have for this right now," Bud says, backing away from the demo table and cutting the segment short.

"No way in hell!" Todd Corker screams. "My people said I'd have a full eight minutes! I haven't even showed my Road Rage Snacking Balls or cooked the Impossibly Angry Burger."

"No, that's it. Sorry, Mr. Corker, I don't like the way this is going. We were not told Angry Man Meals are designed to create violence and scatter litter."

"This is complete bullshit!" he yells in Bud's face. "You're gonna have to make me leave." Bud looks into the camera and says, "We'll take a break right now—"

"Fuck you, Bud, you asshole!" he interrupts. "You and that stupid dog are losers. Your career's in the toilet. You got a lower IQ than that dumb Don Lemon…"

"I think you might have eaten too many of those snacking balls," Bud jokes.

"Don't make fun of my balls!" he yells.

The veins in Todd Corker's red face are bulging like caterpillars as he swings a wild right at Bud, who neatly blocks it with his palm. One long leap from my doghouse and I land between them. I'm growling at Corker, showing fangs. He backs off.

"You fuckin' sissy, Spike. My dogs would finish you in ten seconds. Your wimpy wear-a-mask campaign sucked. I wouldn't let anybody in my family wear a goddamn Spike mask, and most of us are still alive."

Big Mack, who's been operating a camera, steps in.

"Good job, Spike," Mack says as he picks up a squirming Todd Corker, wraps his massive arms around him, and carries him away.

"And your studio's a shithole, and I'm hearing your loser show is about to be canceled. Sad, so sad!" Todd Corker screams as the door slams behind him.

I get a strong urge to run after him and take a chunk outta his leg, but not having sampled any of his food, I'm able to suppress the desire.

"Well," Bud says, looking into the camera, "there's a man who obviously uses his own product. Thanks for watching. Spike and I will see you all at the WGHP booth tomorrow at Heritage Day."

The next morning, Herbie and me are havin' a great time playin' around in the living room while Bud's crankin' up his old Mercury convertible.

Herbie's favorite movie is *Top Gun: Maverick*, 'cause he likes to copy the fighter jet maneuvers of the pilots—he can fly changing angles and pitch, do multiple rolls, and execute a full-body air brake. "Watch this, Chicago Bob!" he's squawking as he swirls like a pinwheel, then dives straight at me. "*Bam-bam-bam-bam-bam*, Spike goin' down."

I've got a good thing going in the dog-bird relationship and communication departments with Herbie. He's great company, so I devised a plan to take him with us to Heritage Day. We've been practicing: he attaches himself to my stomach, and I'm able to walk around with him there, and unless you're lying on the floor, you can't see him. And if you do, you'll just think, "Oh look, a big white dog with wings on his tummy. What'll they think of next when creating these exotic new breeds?"

When Bud rolls up outside, I get into the car with little Herbie clinging to me. The sun's streaming down, and Bud drives off, saying, "Beautiful day. No worries about rain, which is good, 'cause the convertible-top motor is broken."

I guess Herbie kinda shocks Bud when he lands on the seat next to him singing his version of a Jimmy Cliff favorite: "…bright, bright, extra-bright, oh so bright, sun-shining, sun-shining day."

"I'm taking Herbie back!" Bud yells at me.

"I goin' nowhere, Top Gun Bud," Herbie squawks. "Top Gun Bud, Top Gun Bud."

Good old Bud gives me his familiar "You win again, Spike" glance, and we zoom along—my ears flapping, Herbie singing, and Bud smiling at the wheel of his beloved old car.

At the fairground, we're makin' our way through the friendly crowd to the WGHP-TV booth, where we'll take pictures with our fans. A lot them will attempt to feed me. Last year I ate so much food, I got disoriented, wandered off, and threw up in the middle of a square dance.

This year Bud ordered a "Please Don't Feed Spike" poster that never arrived. So he took a "Please Don't Feed Squirrels" sign, crossed off "Squirrels," and printed "Spike" under it. I'm a million-dollar act but get second billing to squirrels.

Herbie's standing on my head and spewing all manner of insults at people walking by. We tell him to shut up after a trifecta of "You don't need that ice cream!" "Two ugly children." "You fattest man here."

Performing on the main stage under the music direction of "Big Walnuts" Willie are local music legends "Junkyard" Joe, "Crowbar" Crawford, and "Flophouse" Fred, formerly known as the Shut Up and Cuddle Up Boys but now billed as The Sophisticated Gentlemen of the Blues. Most of their songs have to do with things that happened down by the river or how bad they felt when they woke up one morning.

I'm curious to see the exhibition of the latest exercise gimmick, full-contact yoga, scheduled onstage after the music. Following that, there's a demo of the new Atomic Weed Whacker, which can clear anything from stubborn weeds to the annoying heritage elm tree blocking your view of the street. Lombardo is in the enviable position of making his "remarks" following a weed whacker demo.

Our old friend "the Hebe named Zebe" is frantically waving us over to his area. He's the former rabbi whose synagogue went out of business after he sold its naming rights to the Rodney Dangerfield estate.

"My main man, Bud, my main dog, my parrot, the Zeeb's cancellation-culture-prep course is breaking big, but get over here to see what I've got for you today," he calls out.

As we're about to absorb one of Zeeb's rhyming sales pitches, Bud's phone vibrates. It's our Channel 8 newsroom. There's a big fire nearby; he's gotta get to it as fast as possible and do a live report.

We arrive to discover that Big Woody's Gentlemen's Club, home of the notorious Dance of the Seven Oils, is on fire.

The club was created by Big Randy Woody, an atheist and a former basketball star at Duke who became a controversial figure in town when he converted the former Tabernacle of the Immaculate Misconception into Big

Woody's Nudie Club. There was substantial outrage that he'd positioned the club's dance pole exactly where Reverend White's pulpit had been.

He tried to redeem himself at the start of the pandemic, when protective gear was low, by ordering his strippers to forge their pasties into masks. In spite of the lives saved by that noble effort, his club is famously off-limits to churchgoing gents in town.

On Heritage Day, there was meant to be a gala reopening of the club, after it was shuttered for two weeks due to an outbreak of creeping thong syndrome among the dancers.

It was also set to be a popular day because of the offer of "Big Randy Woody's Stimulus Package" to new customers. Heritage Day always attracts first-time visitors, because guys who're normally afraid of getting caught in a jiggle joint convince themselves that nothing could possibly go wrong on Heritage Day if they simply tell their wives or girlfriends they're playing in the annual Thomasville-versus–High Point two-hand touch football game.

About fifty or so guys go to the football field, with only a few intending to play. The rest rub a little dirt on their pants as if they'd been in the game, and then rush to Big Woody's for some two-hand-but-no-touch playing.

When we got to the club, dozens of those men were covering their faces and racing from the building like the English soldiers running into the sea fleeing the Germans at Dunkirk.

Two fire trucks are in front, so Bud parks in a vacant area behind the place. He grabs his reporting gear, orders me and Herbie to stay in the car, runs toward the smoke pouring out of the front door, and gets set for a live report.

I'm sitting in the Merc following orders. Herbie happily takes off for a flight in the open air. He's zooming toward the wall of the club, veering off, flying straight up and looping and looping. He circles back and hovers by a second-floor window. He's listening.

"Girls! Girls!" he squawks.

I see a woman unsuccessfully trying to punch a hole in the heavy double-pane window using a broken-off stiletto heel. Smoke is curling around her.

She looks to be screaming. I read her lips: "Open the downstairs door! Open the back door!" she's yelling, hoping someone will hear. She glances down, sees only a dog in a big convertible, and bursts into tears.

This would be a most appropriate time to gently hum the *Rocky* theme.

Go ahead: "Ta da da da da da da da da da...ta ta da da, da, da da, da da da..."

I jump out of the Merc.

The big old back door is locked. I bump it to gauge how strong it is. I back up twenty feet and charge straight at it. My brick-like head cracks part of the lower half. I charge again and again and again at full speed.

"You Wonder-Doggin', Wonder-Doggin'!" Herbie cackles.

After five smashes, I've got a headache that's a ten-plus on the Johnny Depp Hangover Scale, and I've rammed through the bottom half of the door.

Smoke is pouring out.

A couple minutes later the door slowly opens. Staggering out are four women. They have exceptionally large breasts and are completely naked, except for their new USDA-approved non-creeping thongs. Their skin is glistening with oil. I don't like to jump to conclusions about anyone's profession, particularly someone possibly serving in the exotic services industry, but I sense they may be strippers.

"Oh my God, you saved us," possible stripper number one says. "The big hole you made in the door cleared enough smoke out so we could come down the stairs."

I bark my version of "you're welcome," which I prefer to "no problem," which seems to have replaced "you're welcome," but anyway, back to the possible strippers.

"He's so funny-looking and cute," possible stripper number two says.

"Wait, I think he's Spike the Wonder Dog," another chimes in.

"Wow! Yeah! It *is* Spike," number two says. "My kids love Spike. They wore his masks every day."

"My girls have three pictures of him on the refrigerator," number four says. "And they have every mask in his collection."

What were the odds when I woke up this morning that I'd have four naked women drippin' oil all over me, explaining that their kids are fans? Ya really never know what the day's going to bring, do ya?

"Tell him what happened," possible stripper three says to possible stripper one, who's probably the spokeswoman for the group 'cause she has the largest breasts.

"We were just getting ready for the Dance of the Seven Oils when the room started to fill with vegetable oil smoke, and we couldn't open the window."

That's it, confirmation: strippers.

"I thought we were finished," she continues. "I was so scared, I almost gave myself a golden shower."

I give her my Tom Hanks–like nod of empathy, but with a trace of disdain for the mention of a golden shower in the presence of Tom Hanks.

"He's so handsome and strong," stripper three says. "And look at these wounds. Let's kiss the boo-boos on Spikey-Wikey's big head that just bashed in that door, and make him all better."

Herbie watches them kiss me over and over. My head, which is throbbing on the inside, is getting covered with loving lip prints on the outside.

"Strippers goin' down on Spike," he squawks.

And, of course, this is the moment when Bud returns. Our eyes lock. For an instant, I sense he might be mildly jealous of me, his loyal dog, since it's reasonable to assume that I'm experiencing some unfulfilled fantasy of his.

"What happened?" he asks.

"It's Bud from television," they squeal, abandoning me to surround him. They describe how I demolished the lower part of the door, and how enough smoke cleared for them to escape.

"I'm really sorry. Thank God for Spike," Bud says.

"Can we all be on your show on Monday, please?" stripper one asks.

"Yeah, maybe we can even do a regular segment, 'Strippers Are People, Too.' Nobody ever interviews strippers," stripper four says.

This is yet another confirmation of how much you humans want to be on television. Four nude women are standing in the blazing sun and inhaling smoke from a burning building. They'll probably never see their clothes, money, IDs, or phones again, but their immediate desire is to get on TV on Monday morning.

It doesn't take Bud long to recognize that he's got the responsibility of driving these four in-the-buff babes to their apartments across town.

"OK, into the car, and don't worry about the oil on the seats. It'll probably help the vinyl," he jokes, already knowing it'll be at least a thousand bucks to replace the upholstery. "Let's get outta here."

They pile in. Bud's at the wheel, I'm next to him with Herbie on my head, stripper one is on the passenger side, and the others are reclining on the big back seat.

They're telling Bud how they love being in convertibles with the top down.

"That's good," Bud says, "because I can't…"

He hesitates, either because he didn't want to say the words "I can't get it up," or because he just realized he'll be chauffeuring four naked women in an open convertible.

"Should have gotten top fixed, Spike," he mutters.

His safest option is to drive across the baseball field behind Big Woody's. That'll take him to the country road he figures will be the most discreet way to get where he needs to go.

We head across the field. My ears are flip-flip-flapping, the girls in the back are cooing about how good the air feels on their breasts, and Herbie's singing his crazy version of the AC/DC classic "Cover You in Oil."

I'm thinkin', "Ain't life grand!"

We hit a small junction and Bud takes a right, but the road where he needed to turn is blocked by the fire department, so he's forced to continue on what's now a one-way route.

In the rearview mirror, I notice other convertibles following us.

"Oh my God, no! This is bad," Bud says.

"No, the sun feels so good," stripper one says, stretching out.

"But I can't back up. We're now driving in the Heritage Day Parade of Heroes," he blurts.

"I was in a parade when I was in the Brownies," a stripper tells Bud.

"What are your names?" he asks.

"Crystal, Amber, Angel, and Cherry, but after my next implants I'm changing to Bambi," Cherry says.

"Well, Crystal, Amber, Angel, and Cherry name-transitioning to Bambi, for the next few minutes, please try to be as incognito as possible," he says.

"You mean like when Governor Warnock comes to the club, and everyone knows he's there because he wears sunglasses, a raincoat, and a snap-brim hat trying not to draw attention to himself?" one of the girls asks.

"That's close," Bud says.

We're approaching people packed along both sides of the narrow street who're watching the parade pass by.

The first two minutes unfold like a nightmare: Children happy to see me are dragged off by parents screaming, "Evil women!" College boys are trying to snap selfies with boobs in the background. Wives are forcing husbands to turn away. Mothers are covering the eyes of their preteen sons, not realizing this is nothing compared to what the kid watches on his computer for three hours a day, seven days a week, fifty-two weeks a year.

"There's Mr. Lewis," Amber calls out, spotting a regular lap dance client in the crowd. "Hi, Mr. Lewis. It's Amber."

So much for incognito.

I'm hurtin' for Bud. He's trapped, breathing hard; sweat's running down his face. He's biting his lower lip.

I look at Herbie, wonderin' how we let Bud know, "Hey, don't take life too seriously. It's all supposed to be a joke."

Herbie tilts his head to the side, has a thought, and launches into the air. He flies up about ten feet, squawking at the crowd, "Dig those melons on the top shelf. Look at the jugs—six outta eight natural!"

I get a flash of fear that maybe Bud's gonna be roasting Herbie for dinner, but instead, he lets out a big laugh.

"You are one fuckin'-A funny bird, Herbie." Then Bud addresses the crowd: "The truth can always set you free, so why not give a look, folks?" he calls out. "Here's what happened: Spike saved their lives. They were cornered in the fire at Big Woody's."

"We love you, Spike!" a couple of people holler.

"I got trapped in this parade tryin' to drive them home from the fire. I don't think you'll see this next year," Bud explains.

"Unfortunately not," a guy yells back.

"You're right," Bud answers. "Like I said, enjoy the view."

"But they're naked!" a man screams back at Bud.

"It's nature, and with the exception of global warming, don't be afraid of nature," Amber retorts.

"In this case, nature's been somewhat enhanced," a lady calls out, laughing.

We roll to a stop at the reviewing stand. It's crowded with dignitaries, sweating in the heat.

Bud's smile disappears as his boss Lombardo steps to the microphone. He's glaring down at us.

"I've been asked to make a few remarks. First, I'd like to remark that somehow my station employee Bud, that dog of his, and their foul-mouth parrot appear to be surrounded by four well-bosomed but modestly clothed women."

As Bud's nervously explaining to Lombardo what happened, the sweaty dignitaries on the reviewing stand are outraged. They're demanding Bud's immediate arrest, followed by a quick trial and a jail sentence for him in a filthy prison filled with menacing sex offenders.

North Carolina governor Warnock is makin' a quick exit from the front row as Cherry stands up in the back of the car and yells, "Guv, I'll see you for your regular Wednesday special if the club's open by then!"

The very pious Reverend Jordan from the Church of the Perpetual Collection steps to the microphone.

"Lust not," he intones, "lest the sins of Jerry Falwell Jr. rain down upon you!"

"Amen!" a few believers in the crowd respond.

Reverend Jordan continues, "You are a witness to a growing and virulent danger in the city. I have evidence that there are now twenty-seven card-carrying nudists in High Point who have infiltrated our schools to groom our young people to follow in their evil ways."

"Oh my God," a few of the faithful murmur.

"So bow your heads," he says, "and let us pray. Dear God, we beg your forgiveness for all here today who, unlike yours truly, stared wide-eyed, gaping at the prurience before them. May the money they place in our collection plate this Sunday absolve them of their visual sinning. And we pray to you, please, to grant your eternal strength to our servant, Police Chief Bendix. Command him now, by all that is holy, to rid us of these blasphemous creatures."

Several men in the crowd chant "amen" while gazing at Crystal, Amber, Angel, and Cherry through slits between their fingers as Reverend Jordan continues, "And now, Officer Bendix, even though one of these women is claiming to be your beloved niece, please arrest them immediately."

"Not so fast," Lombardo says, grabbing the mic from Reverend Jordan. "I am the mayor of High Point, and nothing here is illegal."

The boss immediately explains that at the height of the pandemic, because of pressure from activists, an anti-mask-wearing mandate was rushed through state legislature on the basis that having to wear a mask was an infringement of individual freedom of expression.

"Yes," a man in the crowd yells, "that's why Spike and Bud are assholes! They liked masks!"

Bud and me shoot the guy a set of glances that shut him up.

The boss explains that when the anti-mask legislation was rushed through late on a hot Friday afternoon, Representative Betty MacQueen slipped in a provision applicable to the small part of the county she represents, which includes the vast park area where Heritage Day is held.

"It states in article two, paragraph four *a*, 'In the Forsyth County section of High Point, a woman may not be required to cover her breasts in public, on the same basis of freedom of expression as an individual may not be required to wear a mask here.' So, folks," Lombardo explains with a coy smile, "although it may be a little embarrassing and shocking to some, the big news is that from now on, toplessness is perfectly legal here in this area of the city."

The crowd gasps.

"I'll strip to that!" a woman yells, yanking off her tank top. "Me, too!" another screams, throwing her T-shirt at the stage.

As we slowly drive away, Reverend Jordan is on his knees praying for divine intervention, or at least some cold weather, while women all over the park are peeling off their tops, enjoying a particularly bright, bright, really bright, sunshiny day.

CHAPTER SEVEN

THE CANINE KING OF ALL MEDIA

Howard Stern said I was the "Canine King of All Media," and I guess for a little while I may have been.

We got lucky.

Or maybe it had just been a slow news weekend. Or maybe we were exactly the kind of sexy human-interest hot-weather story that people were craving. Or maybe it was simply the very large breasts, but…

The *High Point Enterprise* printed the headlines, and it all broke big:

WONDER DOG SAVES FOUR DANCERS
Spike's head destroys door. Strippers flee fire at Big Woody's

TV'S BUD DRIVES NAKED WOMEN IN PARADE
"All things considered, I'm glad the
car's top was broken," he says

BARE BREASTS LEGAL!
Topless clause tucked into 2020 anti-mask legislation

REVEREND JORDAN HOSPITALIZED
Cites "overpraying"

It didn't hurt the appeal of the story that the dancers saw opportunity in their newfound fame, and planned to quit stripping and sign with Vel'vetta's agency to launch a travel service to make High Point a unique destination in the country for topless tourism.

It also helped that the security camera video of my head smashing the door was shot at a perfect angle. That video had more than a million views in one day.

BMBD (Follow)   (•••)

1:03   -1:06

58,072,530 views   ♡8K ⬤2K ◪1K

We went to New York. All the shows wanted us: Bud. The dancers. Me.

Stephen Colbert had us on first, then Stern, the *Today* show, and Joe Rogan. On *Jay Leno's Garage*, we drove around with Jay in Bud's 1968 convertible. The dancers wore monokinis, the kind of bathing suit that was the fad in the summer of '68, and Jay had the strippers laughing hysterically with some very good motor oil jokes about their Dance of the Seven Oils.

Speaking of fads, when I bashed in that door, I did what any dog with a brick for a head would've done, but that doesn't mean you humans should try it. Why would anyone attempt to destroy a door with their head just 'cause they saw me do it?

But that's what happened. For a brief period of time, door bashing became as trendy as eating Tide PODS or shuffle dancing on TikTok. Only a massive public service campaign by an organization called Friends of the Cranium ended the mania the week before ESPN 2 was set to broadcast The Excedrin National Door Bashing Championship.

The thing Bud was most excited about was me getting booked on *Saturday Night Live*.

All I had to do was appear on "Weekend Update," sitting next to Colin Jost doing my yawning routine while he read his material. Then I'd bark and run off when smoke covered his set. I'd also appear in a sketch with Maya Rudolph, Tina Fey, and Kate McKinnon, back on *SNL* as the guest host, about women arguing over a dog in a pet store. I was just happy that Bud had gotten me a Screen Actors Guild card when I was a puppy, and I'd be making SAG minimum for the appearance, 'cause I think ya work just a little harder when you're getting some coin at the end of the gig.

At rehearsals that day, Kate tells Bud that maybe I should audition to be the dog in a movie she's making, called *Florida Man*. She'll costar with Jim Carrey. The premise is that Kate has been cast as Vicky Ventura, the daughter of Ace Ventura, the wacky-pet-detective character Jim made famous in a couple of '90s movies.

The film is inspired by an actual incident that occurred in Palm Beach at an animal charity luncheon at the Colony hotel. A wealthy society couple attended the luncheon with their beloved dog Gatsby, who was abducted that afternoon by one of those weird "Florida Men."

You know what a Florida Man is, right?

In the news, you'll see the words "Florida Man" starting a sentence reporting something weird a man who lives in Florida did that day. The headline is followed by some mind-bogglingly true story about what happened. (There are hundreds of examples on the internet, but in case your Wi-Fi is down, here're a couple of the actual headlines.)

FLORIDA MAN CAUGHT ON CAMERA LICKING DOORBELL

FLORIDA MAN DIES AFTER WINNING ROACH-EATING CONTEST

**FLORIDA MAN USES PRIVATE PLANE TO
DRAW GIANT PENIS ON RADAR**

The Florida Man who kidnapped the dog is obsessed with alligators. His body is covered with fifty-seven tattoos of the Lacoste logo, which is a crocodile that Florida Man thinks is an alligator. Anyway, his plan is to use the dog Gatsby as bait to trap the Everglades' largest alligator.

The society couple who owned the dog are Rambi and Eva von Whipper-Snapper, who'll be played by Tim Allen and Lucie Arnaz. The von Whipper-Snappers will spare no expense to find their dog. Kate's character, Vicky, is at the luncheon receiving an award from the International Hamster Society for her work reviving the popularity of the hamster. Vicky helps in the search for Gatsby but gets nowhere.

Out of desperation, Vicky's father, Ace Ventura himself, is coaxed out of retirement. It's a choice role for Jim, because he'll portray multiple Florida Men. The plot has Ace realizing the best way to track down a wacky Florida Man is to become a wacky Florida Man himself.

Bud and me are huge Jim Carrey fans, and we want to do it. I'm still young enough to launch a career in movies as a leading dog, and it's probably better pay and a lot less tension than dealing with jerks like Todd Corker on TV.

Kate McKinnon explains that producers are suddenly in a panic to find a dog to play Gatsby, the kidnapped dog.

The original dog cast was Spots, an unneutered Dalmatian who tried to bite Tim Allen three times during their first rehearsal. Somehow that got him fired. You gotta figure a Dalmatian who's called Spots dozens of times a day might develop an anger issue toward humans.

All we have to do is stay over in New York till Monday, when they'll audition dogs. If I get the part, we'll go to Palm Beach as soon as possible.

Bud makes a call from my *SNL* dressing room and sets me up for the tryout. Since there's the little matter of his job, he crosses his fingers and calls Lombardo to see if we can take even more time away from the show, which Buffy's been hosting while we've been away.

"Boss, another opportunity's come up for us," Bud says.

"Don't tell me," Lombardo says. "Spike and you will be honored at the Kennedy Center awards. No, wait, is it a human rights award for saving strippers, or—"

Bud interrupts, "A movie with Jim Carrey and Kate McKinnon called *Florida Man*. Spike can audition on Monday, with shooting in Palm Beach immediately if he gets it."

"That dog will end up supporting all of us. Do it if you can, and don't worry, Buffy's fine on the show; ratings are steady. By the way, that's brilliant casting of Carrey and McKinnon."

Bud agrees but tells the boss he's concerned about all the other stuff they've got going on: Shoshana, Sol "The Old Swede" Silverman, the celebrity lookalikes.

"Everything's progressing; they don't need you or that dog yet," he tells us. "Word is, The Old Swede is in the hospital being treated for a dangerous condition. The doctors won't say what it is, just that it's something that's lasted way longer than three hours. Anyway, I got enough trouble with half the town protesting toplessness. They act like I personally should race over to the fairgrounds and cover all the naked women basking in the sun with itchy wool blankets. Good luck at the audition."

THE CASTING CALL

On Monday we go to a big-deal casting agency down in SoHo. From what we've heard, The Leslie Davis Agency has a vaunted position in the insular world of animal casting. We enter the building and make our way through a hallway filled with some of the oldest actors I've ever seen. They're trying out for the final installment of the long-running *Walking Dead* movie franchise, *Walking Dead on Walkers*.

We head upstairs to The Leslie Davis Agency. Bud settles me next to him in the waiting area. We're sitting outside the room where they're going to record our audition. There's a sign on the door that reads, "Casting: 'Dog,' Florida Man."

I study the faces of the dogs' owners. They're smiling, happy, and reacting to each other in the most friendly, encouraging way. They're making small talk about feeding schedules, grooming, and nail clipping, all pretending to be the least competitive people in the world, even though what they really want is for everyone else's dog to have a seizure and be dragged off in a coma before he's called in.

Looks like I'm up against seven other dogs.

There's a very confident Wheaten terrier, fresh off a national tour playing Sandy in *Annie*. She's the only one who seems to know what's going on. The others are nervously eyeing the audition room door like they're at the animal clinic about to get an emergency worming from the vet's heavy-handed assistant.

I size up the competition. Joe is an overweight brindle bulldog who, of course, is drooling all over the floor. The only time you won't see your bulldog drooling is the day you pick him out of the litter. By the time you get the puppy home, the secretion glands have been officially activated. You might as well throw a tarp over your living room furniture for the next twelve years.

There's another white English Bull Terrier here, but he's a miniature named Little Louie Jr. He's a mini-me, except no eye spot. His owner tells us he's weighing in at only twenty-two pounds and is eleven inches tall. I'm twenty-three inches, and sixty-eight pounds first thing in the morning, always afraid to get weighed later in the day, when I might be lookin' at seventy-five. I'm conversing with Little Louie Jr. about the pros and cons of being eleven inches tall when he gets called in to audition.

There's a perfectly coiffed light gray standard poodle with a beautiful Louis Vuitton collar. If they need a dog that looks like she has a perfect credit rating, the poodle's in.

The basset hound's their pick if the part only requires the expression "I'm sad and about to fall asleep."

There's a guy with no dog, but he's holding a long leash attached to a thumb drive. It's for a CGI-generated dog, so I'm up against software as well as a major canine star that's also auditioning, Benji.

Yes, *that* beloved Benji. He's had an obvious eyelift, and that's got him thinkin' he might be cast again as a young leading dog. I wish I could tell him, "Benji, old-timer, ya got nothing to prove. Maybe just accept there's an end to everything, and you gotta face it, and face it well." But that's not my place, and besides, one day if my career's in the toilet, it might not be so easy to accept that it's over. My hero Muhammad Ali had to get beaten to a pulp before he knew he had to hang 'em up.

Good to be thinking about the champ as a young man opens the door. All the owners lean forward with forced nonchalance, beaming at the sight of the assistant to the person who could control years and years of residual checks.

In unison, their chins drop to their chests and eyes return to phone screens when he calls, "Spike the Wonder Dog, please."

"I'm an animal casting agent, not a zookeeper," a casually dressed, heavy blonde woman is barking into her phone as we enter the room. "You hired a gerbil wrangler, and that's what the gerbil wrangler does, not me! He'll be there any minute and straighten this out, and in the future do not let gerbils out of the cage if you have a cat on the premises."

She slams down the phone, takes a deep drag on her unfiltered Camel cigarette, and looks up at one of her assistants, saying, "Those idiots have no idea what they're doing."

"Hello, Bud. Hello, Spike," she says, changing gears rather sweetly. "You're a lot bigger than Little Louie, Spike, but then, you know that because you're the Wonder Dog."

I nod in agreement.

She raises her eyebrows, a bit surprised that I understood what she said.

"I'm Leslie Davis, Bud," she says. "Sorry for yelling just then, but I cast twelve gerbils this morning, and the director's cat is chasing them all over the set."

I like this lady. It's easy for me to tell if a person I meet loves animals. She does, and she's hung pictures of some of her most beloved clients on the wall behind her: the Geico gecko, the chihuahua from the *Beverly Hills Chihuahua* movies, the Aflac duck, and Bullseye, the Bull Terrier with the red circle around his eye in the Target commercials.

"I think you do interesting work," Bud says. "I'm just wondering—"

"It's a tough business, Bud. No room for sentiment, ever, but a sad day here in the office nevertheless," she says, pointing toward a framed photo of a camel surrounded by what looks like fans taking his picture.

"That's Titus, the actual camel that was the model for the Joe Camel cartoon figure. His funeral was this morning. R. J. Reynolds once used Titus for personal appearances at conventions and events to promote their cigarettes. Titus loved it. But after that vicious campaign to get rid of the Joe Camel figure, they got rid of Titus, too. Never worked again. Lived off of the fumes of fame. The service was at the Actors' Chapel in Saint Malachy's. Closed casket. He died a very unhappy camel."

"Oh, gee," Bud says. "Sorry for your loss…. I was just wondering, what are the gerbils for? Some kind of new campaign?"

"Really want to know?" she asks sarcastically. "They're somehow involved in Megan Thee Stallion's next music video, 'WAP—G12.' No one's exactly certain what those poor little things will have to do."

This might not be pretty, I'm figurin'.

"Who's the mouse?" Bud asks, gesturing at a framed photograph of a large, happy-looking rodent.

"That little fellow lives in London. He's Harry A. Mouse from season four of *The Crown*. Remember? He scampered over the rug in a scene in Buckingham Palace in front of the Queen Mother."

"I do, and I think he came across better in season four than Prince Charles," Bud quips.

"Ha, Bud," she laughs. "True! Alright, let's get down to work."

This is it, and I'm focused, I'm centered, I'm grounded, and I'm hungry, figuring the large dog biscuits in the fishbowl on her desk might be what she gives ya when you're finished. If not, she's made an odd choice for personal snacking, and must have very strong teeth.

"The dog in this movie is named Gatsby," she explains, "and Spike as Gatsby has to do three things, actually four, the first being not to attack Tim

Allen. Gatsby's initial scene would be walking with Tim and Lucie through a crowd of their ritzy Palm Beach friends when they enter the ballroom for the luncheon. For scene one, I want you two to walk toward the camera very slowly, no leash on him. We want to tape Spike's expressions, as if he's moving through the crowd and spotting the many people he knows."

I can tell Bud's wondering just what the hell I'm gonna do, but this is simple. I got a whole arsenal of ways to play this based on my observations of the politicians I see on TV. They're always performing in one exaggerated way or another when they wade through crowds.

I'm gonna play this three ways: my Ronnie, my modified Hillary, and my Mitch.

"OK, *action*," Leslie's assistant says softly.

I stride forward in a most genial manner, the way Ronald Reagan did. I nod. I smile knowingly, pretending I can actually hear a question someone just asked. I tilt my head. I wink. Like Reagan, I look like the happiest guy in the world, even though nobody has a clue as to what's actually going on in my head, including me.

For my Hillary, it's a way bigger facial performance. Unfortunately, this is a modified Hillary, 'cause I'm a dog. I don't have an arm and a hand to use to point zealously at someone as I tilt my head back and gaze at them wide-eyed, with my mouth wide open in a frozen smile as I pretend to be sincere.

My Mitch involves shuffling along, more like I'm on a conveyor belt than actually moving my legs and walking. I show no feelings, but my eyes transmit the sense that I'm plotting a sinister scheme. I rotate my head slowly from side to side, as if my neck's the turret of an M1 Abrams battle tank. The big fun for me is pretending I have several chins that follow the head wherever it goes.

"My, my," Leslie Davis says. "I rarely see a dog do a scene three different ways. Good work. You've got my vote on that, Spike."

I eye the Milk-Bones, so she tosses one to me.

I catch it, sit down, and get it sticking outta my mouth like it's a seven-hundred-dollar Gurkha Black Dragon cigar. I want this part for Bud and me so much that I'm posing for the casting director like I'm puffing away on the cover of *Cigar Aficionado* magazine with the caption "Wonder Dog Lights Up Screen in 'Florida Man.'"

"Now, Bud," she says. "If Spike gets the part, you'll be handling him. In the kidnapping scene, the Florida Man jams a needle into Spike's leg to knock him out, and stuffs him into a duffel bag and wheels him out the service entrance of the hotel."

Sounds like fun as long as it's a prop needle and Bud remembers to get me outta the bag, instead of chatting up Lucie and Tim all afternoon.

"Have any idea how you'll get him to appear passed out?" she asks. "He always looks so full of energy."

"Spike," Bud says, "remember how you got shot with the tranquilizer dart when they were trying to capture you during the raid at the Zeeb's illegal Christmas show? What was that like?"

I collapse on my back, four paws up.

"Remarkable, Spike," Leslie says, reaching down and scratching my tummy with the kind of beautiful nails New York women always seem to have.

"Now, Bud, in the alligator scene, we'll need a big jump. Can—"

Bud interrupts, "He did a vertical leap of six feet that probably saved his life in the—"

"Oh right. He'd been forced into a dog-fighting ring. Other than that Money Piles character, did they capture the other guys behind it yet? I saw the *Dateline* piece and the video of Spike outwitting the two dogs with his big jump."

Yeah, I faced two very tough dogs, Monstro and Little Tiger. If you read *The Adventures of Spike the Wonder Dog*, now a cult classic just a notch below *Reefer Madness*, you know exactly what she's taking about. If not, you really took a chance buyin' my second book. I hope you're enjoying it and you'll stay with me even if I don't get the part in the movie. If not, pass this copy along to someone who'll have the good sense to finish reading it.

We have the rest of the audition day free. We walk through Central Park back toward our hotel, the Lowell, in our old neighborhood at Sixty-Third and Madison.

Mayor Eric Adams has only recently declared the most recent wave of the pandemic officially over, and the city's murder rate has dropped a full 1 percent, so there's a jubilant feeling in the air. In the tough year I spent in New York with Bud doing his *Noonday* show, I never felt this much unpretentious energy from Manhattanites.

People are jogging and playing Frisbee so rapturously in Sheep Meadow, it looks like a live version of that TV laxative commercial—the one where a constipated, worried-looking couple takes laxative pills at bedtime. At breakfast, they hug and kiss, affirming with discreet slow-motion nods that the pills worked. Next, they're magically jogging in ultraslow motion on the beach in what looks like Malibu. They're smiling gaily, wide-eyed at how wondrous nature can look after you've had the most monumental bowel movement in the history of your large intestine.

That night we go for the special lasagna dinner at one of Bud's favorite haunts, Patsy's. I've got special fake IDs that Bud has made for me, so I can go with him anywhere. One ID says I'm a food critic for *Dog World* magazine, so I know my way around restaurants.

Patsy's is buzzing. Bud shakes hands with a couple of other regulars, who are happy to see us.

The marinara sauce drenching the lasagna smells as good as I remember, but I'm not concentrating on food. I'm off in my own world. I can't stop thinkin' about the possibility of the movie part, and how happy we'd both be with the adventure of heading to Palm Beach and working with comedy greats Jim, Tim, Kate, and Lucie.

The way I'm figuring it, the basset hound and the bulldog won't make the cut, 'cause neither can jump high enough. The Wheaten terrier from *Annie* is a pro, but also a constant reminder of a cloying little girl in a red dress singing about the sun coming out. Little Louie Jr. is smart and really cute, just the kind of dog you'd be freaked out about if an alligator snatched him, but maybe he's so small, the alligator would toss him back. Benji should retreat to the Hollywood Old Dogs Home. Producers won't spend the money for the CGI dog in the software. That leaves one dog—the poodle. Yeah, the poodle is the tough one.

As Bud's opening his mouth to insert a forkful of steaming lasagna, I spot a woman heading toward us. She's got that "I'm coming to talk to you while you're having dinner" look on her face. She's a well-dressed middle-aged lady whose face looks like it's a landing strip for bimonthly deliveries of cosmetic fillers.

We're accustomed to people hovering over our table during meals. We've been interrupted by everything from high praise for our work to people begging to get a relative on the show, to angry complaints about a kid's wombat ear, to autographs, and on and on. Bud says, "You never get a second chance to make a first impression," so even if they babble while his dinner's turning into a block of ice, he'll be polite. Bud also knows that at a certain point, I'll growl menacingly enough to get them the hell outta there. We're a team.

"I don't mean to interrupt," she says.

This is the usual opening line, which is a bit of a paradox, since, "Lady!" as Jerry Lewis would yell, it's obvious you mean to interrupt, or you wouldn't be interrupting, thus causing my beloved master Bud to swallow a forkful of molten lasagna whole.

"Didn't you used to be Bud?" she asks him.

This is a new one. Perhaps she's one of those unfortunate people who got the partially defrosted Pfizer vaccine, and it's led to a partial melting of her brain.

Bud points to his mouth, indicating that he's chewing.

"What happened to you?"

He's still chewing, but more quickly than usual.

"I'm sure you used to be Bud, and this dog was…. What was his name?"

"I'm still Bud," he gasps, after slugging some wine.

"What happened to you? Are you OK? Are you sitting all the way back here at this corner table 'cause you're embarrassed that you're not on TV now?"

Bud launches into a quick explanation that he quit the *Noonday* show in New York because he wasn't happy there, and he's returned to North Carolina to his old show, which is syndicated all over the South, and that he and his boss are trying to buy the station.

"Humph," she scoffs. "I don't care if the pandemic closed a third of the stores on Madison, and that Thirty-Fourth Street is now a tent city for homeless people, and that we've got daily stabbings on the subway. Why in God's name would anyone leave New York for North Carolina?" she says, sneering. "You must have gotten fired."

Bud's got his "OK, let's fuck the politeness" look on his face. "Ma'am," he says slowly, "let me repeat: I...just...said...I quit. I did not get fired. Got it?"

Sal the chef and owner steps in. "Can I help you, Mrs. Snide...er...I mean, Snyder?"

"This man used to be Bud from TV. You sat him back here 'cause he got fired, right, Sal?" she asks.

Bud's phone rings. It's Leslie, the casting agent.

"I have to take this. I need privacy," he signals Mrs. Snyder.

"I'm sorry for you, Bud. I really am," she says, turning away and muttering, "Humph, North Carolina."

OK, this is it: part or no part?

Yogi Bob once told Bud that "a person is limited according to his attachments," so I know I shouldn't be so attached to getting cast. I am, but I'm bracing for disappointment.

"Hi, Leslie, how are things looking? Ah, the poodle..."

Nuts!

Bud pulls the phone from his ear, which means it's sending way less radiation into his brain and, even better, so I can hear all the bad news from Leslie Davis, casting agent to the animal stars.

"The young director, Christie Leigh Ingalls-Thomas, wanted the poodle. She thought the elegance of the poodle fit the Palm Beach scene."

"That's some set of initials to monogram on your luggage, Christie Leigh Ingalls-Thomas," I'm thinkin'. "And OK, have big fun groomin' that goddamn poodle every morning, Christie Leigh." I'm feelin' mean 'cause I'm disappointed—that ever happen to you?

"But," Leslie Davis continues, "I told her Spike has a different kind of elegance, the raw animal magnetism of a Jason Momoa combined with the graceful athleticism of young tennis whiz Carlos Alcaraz."

"And what did she say?" he asks.

Probing questions like that are what makes Bud such a notable talk show host.

"She didn't buy the Momoa angle, but I made her watch Spike's takes over and over, and you know what happened?"

Christie probably indicated that I should keep my day job.

"She said, 'Any dog that can channel both Mitch McConnell and Hillary Clinton in the same audition is in my movie.' He's got the part! So, Bud, a big congratulations to Spike the Wonder Dog."

With this, I start glee barking uncontrollably, the kind of barking you hear when you finally come home to your lonely dog after twelve hours at work. Unfortunately, the glee barking cues two other dogs in the place, turning Patsy's into a growling, yapping, snarling, woofing madhouse, which somehow brings a big smile to Bud's face. I lick his cheek.

"Hey, partner, we're going to Florida!" he says.

PART TWO

PALM BEACH

CHAPTER EIGHT

MAKIN' A MOVIE

I'm crammed into a middle seat on United Airlines, but at least I'm not trapped in my crate, which would mean three hours without bein' able to turn my head. The worst part in the crate is the last half hour of the flight, when I'm always suppressing the panic of a psychologically induced urge to take a leak.

Has that ever happened to you as a male human? They announce, "Fasten seatbelt for landing." Instantly, you feel a tingling sensation in your lower stomach that combines with the alarming realization that you suddenly have to go the bathroom real bad. The tingling sensation morphs into paranoia that the only way you could relieve yourself is in your small plastic water cup, except you're sitting between two morbidly obese people whose bodies have flopped over their armrests, partially covering you, so you can't move your arms to get the cup. Even if you could, they'd see what's happening and shoot a video. You'll be arrested, dragged off the plane in handcuffs, and thrown into a smelly cell with other public urination offenders; but far worse, you'd suffer a lifetime of humiliation on social media over how your penis was able to fit in the little plastic cup.

Your only hope is to race to the bathroom while ignoring multiple pleas of "Sir, please return to your seat!" You lock the door, trying not to be distracted by the two flight attendants pounding on it to get you out of there. As you're standing over the toilet waiting for a stream that you figure is gonna be like something shot outta a New York City fireboat on the Fourth of July, you realize that you actually didn't have to go after all.

You slink back to your seat hearing whispers of "Look at that asshole."

I'm glad to be in the Economy Plus section with Bud. I'm hoping my pal little Herbie is gettin' along OK down with the luggage. Bud bought him an expensive traveling cage for the trip. The thing is climate-controlled and has filtered water, a daily-reminder calendar, and every modern convenience a parrot could want except for a miniature flat-screen TV with nature films of bird life in the Amazon rainforest.

News director Mike took care of Herbie while we were on the publicity tour, but after days of enduring his foul-mouthed insults, Mike was ready to slide squawkin' Herbie into the microwave.

"I can't take any more of him," Mike told Bud. "He screams 'Chicago Bob!' first thing in the morning for five endless minutes; he hates Doris Day. Who hates Doris Day? He's always telling me I'll get six months to three years in jail for same-sex activity in Casablanca. How does a parrot know I'm gay? Doesn't he see I've got pictures of beautiful, sexy women all over my apartment—Streisand, Midler, Gaga, Whitney? How does a parrot figure this out? Did you tell him, Bud?"

"So far, I've never discussed your, or anyone else's, sexual identity with him," Bud said. "But Herbie's just having fun, and he's had a rough life. Thanks for taking care of him."

Snuggled into the window seat next to me is Brenda. She's with us for a couple of days at the start of our trip because Gwyneth Paltrow invited her to a special Palm Beach candlelight reading of *The Vagina Monologues* lit by Gwyneth's This Smells Like My Vagina candles. After that, Brenda will head to Lauderdale for a legal case she's handling, representing five women in their lawsuit against the makers of the Self-Waxing Bikini. She told Bud it has something to do with boils, blisters, and welts on the inner thighs.

When they open the airplane door, I smell the warm, moist Florida air and know I'm gonna like it here; but leaving the plane, I'm alarmed. There're so many wheelchairs lined up on the ramp, I'm thinkin' maybe the pilot made a left turn and we're in Lourdes for healing services.

As we're headed to the baggage claim, I'm hungry, and I notice a couple of places to get food: a "doughnutery," a "sandwich carvery," a "tartinery"—I guess adding "ery" makes airport food seem more food-like.

While he's waiting at the luggage carousel, Bud presses a button under a big screen to watch highlights of Palm Beach's history. There's JFK smoking a cigar and sneaking Marilyn Monroe onto his yacht. There's Mickey Mouse and Donald Duck parading onstage and disrupting Governor Ron DeSantis' State of the State address. Next up, angry parents are protesting to remove Gay Talese's books from schools because…well, look at his name. The film ends with the happy sight of Jeffrey Epstein's Palm Beach mansion imploding in slow motion as Louis Armstrong sings "It's a Wonderful World." The ashes and debris from Epstein's place are being scattered at sea over the Bermuda Triangle. As the stuff sinks into the ocean, a woman's voice proclaims, "Palm Beach is safe for young girls again!"

Bud had hoped we could stay in the new cannabis-themed hotel, Bowl Bath and Beyond, in funky Lake Worth Beach, but that somehow got nixed by one of the suits, so we're on the top floor of the Ridgefield Suites facing the Intracoastal Waterway. A careful investigation would reveal there are no suites in the place, only rooms. We're on South Ocean Boulevard in Palm Beach, which you may know is an island. The man at the desk gave Bud serious trouble about a dog staying in our suite—I mean room. To get me checked in, first Bud tried my fake ID stating that I'm a robot dog you get when you buy the newest Tesla, but they saw the Chevy Cruze the production company rented for us and turned me down. That forced Bud to pull out my phony canine Treasury agent badge, which has large print reading, "Question this dog's identification, and you *will* be audited."

There's a basket of fruit from the production company with a note saying that filming will be a little delayed because of a tattooing problem on Prince Harry, who's playing the *Florida Man* culprit. He needs to have fifty-seven henna tattoos of crocodiles all over his body. Unfortunately, because of a major ingestion of cocaine by the make-up artist, the seven-inch ear-to-ear menacing crocodile on Harry's face ended up looking like Bob from *Bob's Burgers*.

What's Prince Harry doin' here? First, let me tell you he's a great guy, easy to work with, and we bonded immediately 'cause he's English and, let's face facts, I'm an English Bull Terrier. It seems his Netflix deal includes a clause for Harry to take a small role each year "against type" in a film. When the sheet with a couple of available parts came through, he and his wife just loved the idea of Palm Beach. The exiled Duke and Duchess of Sussex had spent time in Palm Beach, so, "Hey, why not us?" they figured.

Aware that he might also finally gain some sympathy from his father by being swallowed by an alligator at the end of the film, Harry quickly signed on.

But back to the afternoon of the day we arrive at the hotel. I'm with Herbie looking at the beautiful vista of the water, the Lake Worth Bridge, boats gliding by with seagulls and hawks sailing overhead. There's even an ibis strutting around on the tiny beach. We can't help wondering what's gonna happen on this Florida adventure. Judging by the screams coming from the bedroom, Bud's gotta be wondering what his latest score on Brenda's SexBit's gonna be.

On our schedule for that night is cocktails and dinner at Swifty's by the Pool, a couple of miles away at the Colony hotel. The actual von Whipper-Snappers whose dog was snatched by the actual Florida Man are hosting a party for their well-oiled Palm Beach pals. When they heard we were in town for the film, they invited us.

Since it's our kickoff evening in Florida, I can't leave my little feathered friend behind, so Herbie's tucked under me as we walk into Swifty's on a crowded terrace at the Colony. The women are dressed beautifully, and the Palm Beach men equally so. Not like the guys in LA, who seem to think that if their wife's decked out in head-to-toe Valentino for a dinner party, a yellow Hawaiian shirt sporting five large palm trees along with jeans and white sneakers is the fashion equivalent.

"Well, there you are, Bud. Glad you could come, and this young fellow must be Spike the Wonder Dog," Mrs. von Whipper-Snapper says.

She's the kind of handsome woman who gets described as being "of a certain age," so I'll be more specific: she's about seventy, beautiful, with no apparent signs of having massive work done. She's wearing a pink-and-green dress that's either straight out of the Lilly Pulitzer resort collection or a maid's uniform from The Beverly Hills Hotel. The best part is her scent. I'm sniffing her, and she smells like warm meatloaf.

"Ah, Spike," she says, "I think you're smelling the Swifty's Mike Wallace Meat Loaf that I've chosen for our menu. You'll get an extra slice if you're a good dog."

Meat loaf is a favorite of Herbie's. He crawls out from under me, stands on my head, looks up at her, and says, "I love you, Mrs. von Whipper-Snapper."

"Oh, please just call me Eva," she tells him.

That's when we realize we really like Mrs. von Whipper-Snapper. She's cool—no shrieking, no screaming. No "Oh my God a parrot!"-ing. Simply, "Oh, please call me Eva."

"Now, Bud, you must say hello to my beloved husband, Rambi. He's particularly delighted that Spike will be playing the part of our late, great dog, Gatsby," she explains.

Rambi von Whipper-Snapper commands notice because he's a sixty-five-year-old man wearin' a gold lamé jacket and pegged pants, and sporting a jet-black Elvis ducktail hairstyle that looks like it would encourage a horny mallard to make a pass at his head. I'm expecting Rambi to greet me croaking, "You ain't nothin' but a hound dog," but no...

"Spike, the *Palm Beach Post*'s headline about that fire at some gentlemen's club was, 'Dog uses head to usher in topless mania in North Carolina.' See if you can do the same thing here, kiddo."

"We love nudity," Mrs. von Whipper-Snapper quips.

"Well then, you'll feel very comfortable talking to my friend Brenda here," Bud says.

Brenda has Mr. and Mrs. von Whipper-Snapper mesmerized with the story of how the daughter of a poor pastor from Boone, North Carolina, saved her childhood Christmas gift money for the breast implants that enabled her to strip and pole-dance her way through college and law school.

"Plastics!" Mr. von Whipper-Snapper blurts, making a dated reference to a notable line in the movie *The Graduate* regarding Brenda's boob job.

"Now let me tell you why we like nudity," Mrs. von Whipper-Snapper says. "It all started—"

"Excuse me," the manager interrupts. "Mrs. von Whipper-Snapper, it's time to ring the dinner chime."

"Thank you, Robert," she says. "You're at table twelve, Bud, and there's a place set for Spike. I'll get a little meatloaf for that bird. There's an invitation under your plate; if you're free tomorrow, please come to our Dining with the Dogs charity luncheon right here in the Colony ballroom, where you'll be shooting your first movie scene. I think Spike will love the latest Palm Beach dog breed we'll be introducing."

"Greenwich man! Greenwich man!" Herbie squawks, flying to the floor.

"Sure, ah, thanks, Eva," Bud says. "I'll see what's up for tomorrow. What was that, Herbie?"

Glancing at us as he hustles toward the exit on the other side of the pool is a bulky fellow in a blue suit and red tie, whose neck is ballooning out of a too-tight white collar. He looks like the kind of fat, rich man who always heaps extra sour cream onto the baked potato next to his big steak.

"Odd for Herbie to be afraid," Bud says.

"Greenwich man," he peeps from below.

That night back at the hotel, we discover we don't have a maid, only a Roomba that somehow can elevate itself to fold the toilet paper into a point.

Bud's got the results of the deep research that Buffy's done for us on the von Whipper-Snappers.

Eva Whipper comes from authentic old Palm Beach money. The old money was found in a chest buried under the small bungalow that her Cuban grandfather purchased in Lake Worth. On the advice of Irish tenor Morton Downey, a Palm Beach celebrity, the grandfather invested most of it in the IPO of Coca-Cola. One original forty-dollar Coke share would be worth around four hundred thousand dollars today, so do the math and figure how the von Whipper-Snappers made it to the top of Palm Beach society.

Rambi's father, Rambi Snapper Jr., was a gambler who came to Florida from Germany in 1920. He won a hundred acres of land in Central Florida in a two-day poker game and turned most of it into the internationally acclaimed Sunshine State Naturalist Center. Basically, folks, it was a nudist colony.

In the mid-1960s, Rambi Snapper's father made a fortune selling the land to Walt Disney, who paid top dollar to avoid having hundreds of deliriously happy naked people romping around next to Disney World. The sale to Disney also spared all the nude men at the camp from hearing the recording of "It's a Small World (After All)" wafting over Disney World's wall all day.

Young Rambi's happiest teen memories were of how he impressed fellow naked teens with his spot-on imitations of his idol, Elvis Presley.

Rambi met Eva at the nudist resort when she spiked a volleyball at his genitals during a mixed doubles game. At first, he had no romantic interest, since Eva was a few years his senior and a far cry from the young Priscilla Presley type he was currently wooing. All that changed when he saw one of her bank statements. They married and purchased the German preposition "von" from Nobility Titles to Go, which still operates out of a basement in Boynton Beach.

Florida Man wasn't shooting the next morning, so Bud was eager to go to the Dining with the Dogs luncheon. Brenda opted out of getting dressed again. Her plans were to catch some rays by the hotel's coffee table–size pool and rest up for another SexBit session that night with Bud.

Driving on South Ocean Boulevard toward downtown Palm Beach, I'm looking at the beauty of the surroundings with eyes that are seeing everything for the first time: palm trees, bushes with exotic flowers, fat iguanas lounging in the sun. The ocean's on one side, and on the other, we're passing mansions with nattily dressed illegal immigrants maintaining exotic landscaping. Some hard-core New Yorkers we knew were always goin' on about how much they hated Florida. Is this what they were talking about?

We cruise past Mar-a-Lago. Hanging in the air over the estate is the musty scent of Xanadu, the palatial setting for *Citizen Kane*.

In the town, I notice that the fireplugs in the sidewalks are carefully painted a Palm Beach pink.

At the swanky Colony hotel, it doesn't take us long to realize that nothing feels quite like waiting in the valet line behind a gold Bentley SUV, a bright lime Aston Martin Vantage, and a silver Porsche Taycan 4S in your dusty brown Chevy Cruze.

"Be careful with this thing," Bud tells the valet attendant. "I've got to get it back to Alamo in one piece."

The ballroom floor is set up with large round banquet tables. I'm happy to see many dogs in attendance.

By the way, you know the kind of big tables I mean? You'll see people scattered around them at the poshest, most expensive occasions, like fancy weddings and bar mitzvahs, or even at dismal catered events under way-too-bright fluorescent lights. The tables seat twelve and are so large that the guests can only scream back and forth in conversation. Once the music starts, all you can to do is yell in the ear of the lucky person next to you.

A waiter comes over with something special for us. He serves me a large chopped-meat dish that he says is ground Japanese Wagyu strip loin. "This is a 'Welcome to Palm Beach' gift from one of your fans," he tells me. Bud's handed a red Baccarat flute filled with Cristal champagne. As he takes a drink, he squints and notices a woman across the room waving at him, so he waves back mouthing, "Thank you, thank you."

Wrong there, Bud. I could tell she didn't send us anything; she was simply waving a "Hi, I've seen you and Spike on TV" kind of wave, not an "I've just sent you a five-hundred-dollar gift; enjoy it and maybe let's slip up to my room if this luncheon turns out to be as boring as last year's" kind of wave.

I'm seated in a comfortable chair between Bud and Rambi von Whipper-Snapper. Bud thanks him for inviting us, and Rambi retorts, "Bud, you and Spike are more than welcome to be here." Appreciate the thought, sir, but please send us the memo on how anyone can be "more than welcome" for anything.

We can't help staring at Rambi's gray bolero-style suit, with its ruffled white shirt and short lapel-less jacket snuggly fitted at his waist.

"All of my clothes are designed from the actual patterns that were used for costumes that Elvis wore in his movies. This is from *King Creole*," he explains to Bud. "I stopped wearing the black-and-white striped *Jailhouse Rock* suit after I was mistaken for an escaped con and got thrown to the floor and handcuffed in the cereal aisle at Publix. I always perform Elvis songs at our parties at home."

Before Bud can ask him if he still does the Elvis shows naked and maybe sings "My Ding-a-Ling" as part of the set, two doctors across from us from start hyping Bud about their work. This burst of friendliness is, of course, in hopes of getting—what else?—TV exposure from him.

"Here's my pamphlet," one yells to Bud. "I'll pass it over. I'm sure you're aware of me..."

People always say this to Bud—"I'm sure you're aware of me"—when what they really mean is, "I'm completely unknown, so let me talk about myself."

"I'm the inventor of the new do-it-yourself Palm Beach Prostate Exam. It's a revolutionary new self-exam technique. Most of the men here today have tried it."

That gets me realizing how I've never really wondered how many guys at a charity luncheon might have recently stuck their fingers up their ass. I hope—I truly hope—that I'll never have this thought in my brain again. And God forbid, now that I've mentioned it, that I've accidentally caused you to contemplate it the next time you're at a charity lunch. Please, completely forget about the possibility that men you see anywhere have ever tried this guy's prostate self-exam.

Bud politely leafs through the brochure, eyes widening with each page. From what I see, it looks like you'd have to have an extremely flexible thumb and middle finger to execute the procedure on yourself. It must be successful, though, or there wouldn't be so many "Do Not Examine Daily" warnings plastered all over the cover.

"Hello, Bud and Spike, I'm Dr. Randy Loomis," the other doctor screams across the table at us. "Bud, when I look around the room, you know what I see?"

"Well, I see a lot of dogs sitting in white high chairs," Bud responds, "and well-dressed guests who seem to be rejecting the appetizer because it's Everglades python sushi served with a mercury detox pill. Is that what you see?"

"No, Bud, but to quote Johnny Carson greeting the Academy Awards audience in 1979, "'I see a lot of new faces—especially on the old faces.'"

"Ha!" Bud laughs. "Carson was the best at the Oscars, even better than the guaranteed-not-to-offend-anyone asexual hologram that was the compromise host choice this year."

"Yes, but listen carefully, Bud. What you hear coming out of those new faces are raspy old voices," the doctor explains. "You may have seen me on Dr. Drew's show. I'm the creator of the new—patented term here—Feather-Light voice lift."

"Voice lift?" Bud asks.

"Yes. Why should these women sound like Sam Elliot first thing in the morning, or speak with the grinding resonance of a Port Authority bus announcer who's been smoking and drinking since third grade? Listen," he says, turning to the woman next to him. "Joy, please demonstrate your new—patented term here—Feather-Light voice."

"We're all so excited to have you here for the *Florida Man* movie," Joy murmurs breathlessly.

I think I may be feelin' a little odd. The bloody four-hundred-dollars-a-pound meat with the amusing chemical aftertaste may not be agreeing with me. My acute hearing might be a little off, but that woman sounded like six-year-old Jodie Foster talking to Goober in *Mayberry R.F.D.*

The voice of Mrs. Von Whipper-Snapper blasts through an overamped sound system and rattles the glasses on our table. "We will now formally commence our program here on the ballroom stage. All of the money today raised at our Dining with the Dogs luncheon will go to help eliminate Amish puppy mills in Wisconsin."

The audience applauds politely, and since I know a couple of dogs who came from puppy mills and how hard it was for them, I offer a warm, subtle bark of appreciation.

Except the sound I'm making is not soft, warm, or subtle. It's a series of loud, snarling barks and growls like I'd give to an intruder breaking into the house in the middle of the night. I was gonna say, "Like I'd give Ted Cruz if he tried to pet me," but didn't, 'cause I realized if he tried to pet me, I'd run away.

The room is silent. All eyes on me. I don't know what just happened, but I'm feelin' disconnected from myself. Bud covers for me. "The Wonder Dog just hates puppy mills," he announces.

The line gets laughs and big applause. Bud looks at me like, "What the hell was that barking about, Spike?"

Mrs. von Whipper-Snapper continues, "Well, we've just heard from one of the dignitaries here today. That was the famous Spike the Wonder Dog, who'll be playing our beloved dog Gatsby in the *Florida Man* film. Spike is in town with his master, Bud, from *Southern Exposure*. Please stand up, Bud."

Bud pushes back his chair, waves, and flashes a big, authentic Bud smile. I look up at him, and he seems like he's stretched twelve feet above me, and his mouth is a foot wide. "Spike and I thank you for having us today, Mrs. von Whipper-Snapper," Bud says. "This is a worthy cause."

"You're more than welcome, Bud," she says. "More than welcome. Now, folks, please say hello to the great comedian, actor, and peerless TV star Tim Allen, who'll be playing my beloved Rambi. He's also with us."

The place erupts with applause. Tim stands up, beaming. He thanks everyone and knocks out a couple of terrific one-liners about his stay so far in Palm Beach.

Why are the laughs booming around the ceiling and exploding inside my head? I'm feeling weird, so I slurp up the water from Bud's finger bowl.

"I'd like to introduce another guest in town for the film," Mrs. von Whipper-Snapper announces. "The talented young director Christie Leigh Ingalls-Thomas is here."

A small young woman with curly blonde hair and granny glasses stands up and waves. She's obviously an animal lover, since she's holding a "Save the Spider Mites" tote bag, but to me, the spider mite in the logo is growing and looks like a tarantula that's about to jump off the bag, come over here, and slither up my tail.

"Like all of us, our featured speaker today is a dog lover. He's well known as the town's most noted flaneur," she continues, "who's dedicated to helping the troubled among us as head counselor at the Palm Beach Social Climbers Anonymous meetings each week. And of course, he just happens to be the town's favorite self-published author. Please welcome Donald 'Ducky' Plugsworth."

"There's a smattering of embalmed applause that's somehow indicating these people are likely thinking, "Oh, no, not this fuckin' guy.""

"Yes, yes," she continues, "and Ducky's done it again. He's just self-published what the *New York Times* described as 'the grand ho-hum finale to the trilogy that Mr. Plugsworth began five years ago with *Valley of the Dull*, followed by *The Other Side of Dull*. He finally puts it all to sleep with his latest, *Dull Takes a Holiday*.'"

A short, stocky man who looks like a well-dressed owl rises from his seat. He seems to be waddling toward the stage in ultraslow motion.

"Let me continue with more encomiums," Mrs. von Whipper-Snapper says. "The *Palm Beach Post* describes Mr. Plugsworth as 'a writer unencumbered by linguistic charm who has cornered the niche market in dull fiction.' Of his latest work, the *Miami Herald* wrote, 'Once again, Ducky delivers the dull,' and *USA Today* proclaimed, 'Plugsworth is the absolute master of the dull form.' Ladies and gentlemen, our own Ducky Plugsworth."

The cover of his new book, *Dull Takes a Holiday*, snaps onto the big screen above the podium. It's a photograph of a man sitting on a beach, relaxing and smoking a cigar while reading the first Plugsworth book, *Valley of the Dull*.

Nothin's dull to me. My head feels like it's twice its size. I've either been teleported to a space station or I'm hallucinating, 'cause I see dishes, knives, and forks lifting off tables and floating around with bits of food dropping onto people's heads. My left paw is burning; my right one, freezin'. Tongue is throbbing. How do I tell Bud I feel like I'm this week's guest on the new Netflix series *Have a Bad Trip!*?

Ducky Plugsworth's droning on and on about what constitutes good dull writing. I got an idea, Ducky. How 'bout your next book is *Profiles in Dull*. The first chapter is about you, and you work all the way up to "Barhopping with Mitt Romney."

After what seems like three hours, Ducky's off, and Mrs. von Whipper-Snapper returns to reveal the latest in the specialty line of crossbred dogs engineered by Palm Beach Concierge Dog Sciences to raise money to fight puppy mills.

"Several years ago, our breeders created a new lap dog, the now-very-popular nonshedding, nonbarking, mostly immobile Cavaspanapoo," she explains. "Then, on a lucrative commission from Her Majesty, Queen Elizabeth, we created the Gasless Corgi. The queen wrote us reporting that 'even when driving on a cold day with the windows up in my Range Rover filled with your Corgis, there's not a hint of digestive flatulence emanating from our new royal pets. Thank you, Palm Beach Concierge Dog Sciences.'"

Bud leans over and whispers, "Hey, Spike, the next time there're no offensive vapors from you after two bags of pork rinds, you'll get a standing ovation like this."

The "whisper" sounds like any track on a Metallica CD.

"Notably," Mrs. von Whipper-Snapper explains, "a few years later came our next amazing creation, the Bag Pointer. A dog that wags her tail and points when she spots an authentic designer bag, and snarls at a fake one. We know the Bag Pointer has ended some relationships, but honestly, what could be more useful in determining the true merit of your friends than the authenticity of their handbags?"

The burst of applause explodes in my head like fourteen howitzers firing at a target range in Delray Beach.

My mouth is hanging open, and my eyes are closed, like the ninety-year-old man's sitting across from me. Bud whispers, "Hey, Spike, wake up. You're almost on."

On? I'm on? What?

Mrs. von Whipper-Snapper says, "I'd like to call Spike the Wonder Dog to the stage with Bud, so that Spike can be the first dog to greet our newest canine creation."

Bud slips my red leash on, and as I'm walking through the narrow spaces between the tables, people are looking down at me with the same diabolical eyes as the humanoid White Walkers in *Game of Thrones*. My heart's pounding from whatever the hell is tripping me out.

I barely make it onto the stage, but like a spaced-out lead singer in any rock group, a certain amount of professionalism clicks in once I'm up there. I figure I'll bark hello, be polite, and head straight to the door, pulling Bud behind me the instant this is over.

In front of me, covered by a blue wool tarp like a tiny new truck that's about to be unveiled at an auto show, is a dog. Holding the sides of the tarp, wearing white lab coats, Palm Beach–style plaid pants, and white buck shoes, are the scientists who've created whatever the hell kind of ill-purposed canine monstrosity they're about to uncover.

"Our scientists, Drs. Leo and Larry Levering, have combined several breeds of hunting dog with, yes, the DNA of a koala to create the first dog able to climb trees."

The guests in the crowd nod in approval, imagining cocktail parties on their lawn watching their new dog building a nest in the outstretched branches of the highest tree on their massive property.

"We now unveil—are you ready, folks?—the new…"

Drumroll…

"The Palm Beach Iguana Hound, bred to chase the iguanas from your mansion's lawn to the mansion next door," Mrs. von Whipper-Snapper proudly announces.

Later, when I see the video of this moment, I realize the dog's jaws are not open two feet and he isn't trying to swallow me like I'm a sixty-five-pound white iguana. The poor thing is just yawning and overheated from the wool tarp. He doesn't really resemble the ugly Therizinosaurus that seems to smile while chewing people in *Jurassic World: Dominion*. Seeing the replay, you couldn't tell I was tripping, only that after they yanked the cover off him, I collapsed.

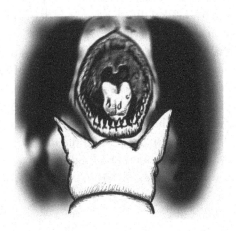

"Spike the Wonder Dog fainted at the unveiling of the new Palm Beach Iguana Hound, and was rushed to Island Animal Hospital today," is how the story begins that night on the local Channel 29 news. It ends with the line, "If this new breed can scare the Wonder Dog, the iguanas on your property are already swimming to Nassau."

Of course, there is no follow-up the next night to report that I passed out 'cause the meat I'd been given was spiked with a version of acid created by drug guru Timothy Leary to freak himself out while watching a double feature of the French horror films *Repulsion* and *Diabolique* at the Paris Theater in New York over a Labor Day weekend in the early '70s.

I'm embarrassed that the fainting video goes viral. When I look at it, I see that this new breed, while obviously confused about his identity, is actually a friendly dog. Before I collapsed, I looked into his eyes and thought I was seeing a humanoid monster about to devour me. When I study the video, it's apparent he has deeply expressive, empathic, warm brown eyes—probably from the koala DNA—and what he seemed to be telling me was, "I'm think I'm gay. As long as we're in Florida, let's do the Keys."

Why was I slipped the LSD mickey? The bad trip amplified some of the suspicions I've had since Herbie showed up squawking about Chicago Bob. A Chicago Bob character was talked about at the dogfight center. What I'm fearin' is even though he's in prison, maybe the sleazy boxer Ike "I Got Money" Piles is after us. Bud saw the video of the person who checked into the Thailand sex resort using the fake ID. Slouching off to the side was a guy who coulda been James Three, one of Money's henchmen. Bud didn't notice him, and even using all of the powers of our dog-human connection, I couldn't let him in on my hunch.

The other night, Herbie was screamin' in fear about a Greenwich man. There's always been a rumor that the international part of Money's dogfight operation is financed by some rich sicko guy in Greenwich.

Or maybe the antimask people drugged me, or the wombat ear crazies? Someone once threw a brick through our front window back home. Attached to it was a mask filled with termites. I saved the day by eating the termites before they spread all over the house. Bud didn't see me do it, so he never could link my heroic action to the splinters in my stool the next day.

I may just be Captain Paranoia reporting for conspiracy-theory duty here, and be way off base. But someone purposely drugged me, unless I got the meat from Japan's only psychedelic steer.

At the Island Animal Hospital, I started to calm down 'cause the kindly vet gave me some heavy-duty tranquilizer for dogs. It helped, and because Bud and I support each other in times of crisis and otherwise, he made sure to get extra pills and give me a horse-size dose. I'm all for euphoria.

That night, Bud laughed at Brenda's story about how she dealt with the guys gazing at her as she lounged topless by the pool.

"OK, OK, guys, come over here and get your pictures of them if you must," she told them, "and then leave me alone."

Bud gallantly canceled his opportunity to advance his lifetime SexBit score with her, because he felt he had to tend to me that evening. Actually, I'd never felt better in my life. To get even higher, I was scheming a way to pry the rest of the pills outta Bud's pockets even though he was still wearin' the pants.

As I was savoring the complete bliss of my altered state (try about seven dog tranquilizers to know what I mean), Bud and Brenda decided to have some fun and get high, instead of having a martini at cocktail hour like everyone else was doing in Palm Beach at that time.

As I was falling asleep, they were on the edge of their seats in the grasp of the new Apple TV show *Shit! I Lost My Phone!* It was packed with horror stories about people trying to cope for several days without their phone.

During the show, Bud's own phone rang.

It was his mother.

"Get me out of here," she says.

CHAPTER NINE

THE SILVER SINGLES HYPERACTIVE COMMUNITY

The next morning, Brenda leaves for Lauderdale to work on behalf of clients wounded by the self-waxing bikinis. Bud goes jogging, so I have a chance to recount the bad trip and my joyous recovery with Herbie.

"No big deal," Herbie tells me. He lets me know he did a tab of acid in Casablanca. A guy left it to tip the bartender. He stole it to save the bartender the embarrassment of getting arrested again, like the other time he'd been tripping and walked around the huge Hassan II Mosque blasting "Stairway to Heaven" over his portable PA system while a thousand men were kneeling down to face Mecca for afternoon prayers.

"The four-chamber heart handles all drugs well, except coke—makes me feel like the motor's running too fast," Herbie claims.

Personally, I don't know what kind of chambers I got in my dog heart, but I got no interest in ever hallucinating like that again. But it did provide clarity on one thing: the Daisy dilemma. I'm ending it once we're back. Telling her the truth will set us free, and the truth is, we can't stand each other.

While the *Florida Man* team continues to tattoo Harry for our scenes together, the plan for our day is to rescue Bud's mother. She came down from Philadelphia to enjoy a couple of winter months in Florida visiting her friend Bernardine at her ranch house in the Silver Singles Hyperactive Community in Wellington.

Seems that Bernie recently published a book, *Lindsey, Judy, and Me*, describing her experiences one summer while babysitting for Lindsey Graham. The memoir is loaded with touching pictures and sentimental stories about the backyard musicals Bernie helped young Lindsey create and perform with his beloved Judy Garland marionette.

Unexpectedly, Bernie had to go on a speaking tour promoting the book, so Bud's mother ended up alone in the house and was not happy with her situation.

We crank up the brown Chevy Cruze and drive toward Wellington. There's a small encampment under busy Interstate 95, where about a dozen die-hard protesters are waving tattered signs demanding that all 1,908 miles of Interstate 95 be renamed Donald Trump Drive. Originally, they wanted Donald Trump Artery, but after the alarming headlines about DJT's heart scan, they changed it.

I love car rides. It's educational to observe the little details as the neighborhoods change. For instance, the quantity and size of tattoos on people increase in direct proportion to the number of miles you drive west in Florida from Palm Beach.

I'm eager to make this trip, 'cause I like Bud's mother. She heats my dog food, and there's a wise, calm way about her that older people have, as long as they're not worried about bladder leakage in their underwear.

Even more important, her dog Pip is with her. Pip's a friend—like family to me and quite a character. He's a macho black and tan seventeen-pound wire-haired Dachshund. Pip's about ten years old, and is now paranoid about aging.

"The back—I think my back's going out," he's always complaining. "I can't end up like one of those embarrassed dogs you see pulling themselves around with two wheels for hind legs."

He considers himself a fearless hunter of squirrels, even though he's never caught one. I only see him on holidays, so I'm looking forward to the chance to catch up, as you humans say.

Bud's mother told us she's bored and needs to head back to Philadelphia but wants to see Bud before she leaves.

"It was fun here with Bernardine, having conversations and listening to music together, but she's gone. I don't golf; I don't play cards; I don't like to talk politics with people who don't deal with actual facts. I can't bear to watch morbidly stiff seniors trying to do the hustle wearing neuropathy shoes, so I don't go to Friday-afternoon disco. Unless I can find satisfaction in complaining about how salty the food is at dinner, like everyone else does, I'm out of here," she explains.

"But the place is advertised as a hyperactive community, isn't it?" Bud asks.

"Ah," she says, laughing. "Anytime you see the word 'hyperactive' in an ad for a singles community, be careful; it's a code," she explains.

"Code?"

"Yes. Bernie didn't know it when she moved in, but the 'hyperactive' label applies to the enclave of people living on the north side of the development, which we call the cheating side of town."

"Good line from the Eagles," Bud comments.

"Thanks, Bud. We love the Eagles, don't we? 'Hyperactive' is code for the over-sixty international swingers' retirement residences supposedly financed by Dominique Strauss-Kahn, the fat French biggie they let off the hook for sexual assault in New York. You might notice that some of the men who live over there have a small alarm device around their neck. It's promoted as a 'Help, I've fallen down and can't reach my orgy' wellness tool."

"Are any of these swingers hitting on your friend Bernie?" Bud asks.

"Just the creepy guy across the street who wishes he was a swinger. He's over there on his front lawn now staring blankly into space with his mouth hanging open, which is generally his recreation for the day."

I look out the window. He's standing in the middle of his property, slightly stooped, with his head jutting forward and glasses perched low on his nose, looking about as lifelike as Chuck Schumer does droning away to an empty Senate chamber on C-SPAN. If there's a woman somewhere in the world that gets off on men with bushels of ear and nose hair—which unfortunately, there probably is—I've got a match for her in this guy.

"He's a harmless, boring pest," Bud's mother continues, "but recently I noticed the guy's dog might be starting to give our Pip a little trouble."

Pip shoots me an ashamed glance.

"What's up?" I wonder.

Pip nods, like, "No problem, no problem."

I let him know I want the truth.

The guy across the street, whose nose seems to have produced its own nostril beard, has a Doberman named Luke. Luke's big. He probably outweighs Pip by around seventy pounds. Recently, the Doberman's been coming over when Pip's on the grass out back. He bullies him bad—real bad. Pip tried to bite him on the leg the first time it happened, and Luke just picked him up and threw him across the yard. "I think I hurt my back again," he lets me know.

"Enough with the back, Pip, please," I'm thinkin'.

Bud's mother continues to explain. "So it was great being here with Bernie. We had fun. But she's gone for a while, and I'm headed home."

"Wait a minute, Mother. The weather's so beautiful here—no way for you to stay? What about singing?" Bud asks. "You always loved singing. They must have a singing program you'd enjoy."

"Ha, ha, no way," she says. "But I'll tell you what. The group sing-along is just about to start. Drive me over there, and you'll have in-person proof as to why I'm out of here on Jet Blue tomorrow at the ungodly hour of seven a.m."

"OK," Bud says. "I wanna see this."

While they're off on the musical fact-finding mission, Pip heads out to take a leak, and I hang back to sniff around the kitchen floor for dropped food. As I'm crunching a hard, dusty cheese cube that's probably been under the counter since construction on the kitchen was finished, I hear barking blasting from the backyard. It sounds like a bark that's likely coming from that big Doberman. I wriggle through Pip's dog port to get outside.

Luke is towering over Pip, barking and snarling. Pip's trying to be brave, but I can tell by his tail that he's intimidated.

Put yourself in Pip's spot. Figure what it would be like for you if someone five times your size were looming over you and screaming in your face just as you were urinating on your favorite rosebush. OK, forget the rosebush part; just focus on the menacing.

I walk over.

Luke gives me an ugly growl that's saying, "Stay out of this."

I growl long and low at him, "Leave."

He growls at me and his mouth curls, revealing yellowed fangs.

I move a touch closer.

"This is between me and stupid Pee Wee here," he indicates.

"Yeah, I don't think ya'd enjoy pickin' on someone your own size, would you?"

Pip's agitated. "I don't need you to fight my battles, Spike."

Then it happens in a flash, or a blink, or whatever best describes something so fast that you really don't see it.

Pip springs at Luke using a power in his little legs he probably hasn't felt in years.

Before I tell you the dramatic and satisfying details of what Pip did, you gotta know that Dachshunds are routinely described as fearless dogs. They were bred with extra-large lungs for underground air supply, and they have hinged knees to help them crawl deep into burrows to exterminate fierce badgers. Usually, the Dachshund will stage a surprise attack just as the badger is settling down for dinner, courtesy of the nearest chicken coup.

Fighting badgers underground is a tough gig for a dog. It takes a little more courage than pointing at birds in a field, chasing a fox with ten other dogs, or even sitting on the king's lap all day while he's ordering the beheadings of large numbers of his subjects to get him in the mood for dinner with his new wench.

Pip latches onto Luke's neck. His long fangs enable him to clamp down as tightly as he needs. Luke tries to shake Pip off by jumping and rolling and bucking all over the yard.

After two action-packed minutes that recall the end of any *Fast and Furious* movie without the special effects, Luke surrenders and retreats to his house.

Luke's tail would be between his legs if it wasn't clipped off. They do that to Dobermans, and the reason is never fully explained to the unwitting dog. One day, the Doberman goes to the vet for what he figures is gonna be another annoying checkup. Surprise! On the way home, he's got a stub for a tail. For years, he's plagued with a serious case of phantom tail syndrome and haunted by the existential question, "Where's my tail?"

Maybe that's why Dobermans are so damned mean and cranky-looking all the time—they're pissed that someone chopped off their tail.

"I won," Pip tells me. "I won, and my back feels better now, too."

On the way to the music session, Bud's mother shows him some sights.

"It's a vast property," she explains. "In addition to having twenty-seven bagel stores, it's full-service for everything a senior could need, from an Instant Hips! facility to a shaman who'll administer a mélange of last rites options. Plus, they just built a state-of-the-art crematorium. It's all here."

"Oh my," Bud says. "Very upbeat to drive by a crematorium on your way to play tennis in ninety-nine-degree heat."

"Ha!" she laughs. "Bernie got lucky with the crematorium. Her house isn't usually downwind. But yesterday, the breeze shifted and a puff of smoke drifted through the backyard. 'Say goodbye to George Jacoby,' she said. 'I smell his Polo aftershave.'

"Oh, see that?" she says, pointing to a house with the shades pulled down and six pickup trucks in the driveway. "The big rumor is that QAnon people moved in. What's up with this QAnon? What is it?"

"I figure it's like a religion, except the computer is the church, and they worship conspiracy theories on it," he says. "Actually, there's big news about them today. According to the *Washington Post*, the mysterious identity of the founder, 'Q,' has been revealed as a voice that speaks through the semi-defrosted head of baseball slugger Ted Williams."

"Oh, well, there you go. That explains it," his mother says dryly. "By the way, the community also has a small cryonics center. But it hasn't been successful. Not a lot of residents want to have their body or head in the deep freeze like Ted or Disney, so the place makes money selling frozen yogurt."

The singing room is filled with people ranging in age from late seventies to mid-nineties. Each has a book of songs on their lap and a tired, bored expression on their face.

Dr. Sharon Rogers is the director of the singing. She's a twenty-five-year-old with a Ph.D. in senior citizens' musical entertainment. She waves at Bud and his mother warmly.

"Well, everybody, isn't this wonderful, now?" Dr. Rogers says very slowly, talking to the old folks like she's reading from a first-grade storybook. "This is Bud. Bud is in show business. Bud is on television. Bud has a white dog named Spike. Spike is famous, too. Bud is here with his mother. Let's welcome them."

They're rewarded with a polite smattering of applause.

"Bud has sung professionally onstage, right, Bud?"

"Yes, it all started when I was in a fully clothed high school production of the musical *Hair*," he jokes.

"Well, *Hair*. I'm not sure we all know much about newer shows like *Hair* at all now, do we folks?" she says with a laugh.

"Let the Sunshine In!" a man in the back calls out.

"Got it, George. I'll pull up the shade in a moment," she says.

"Easy to Be Hard!" the old guy next to him volunteers.

"Ralph, I think that information is confidential and should be kept strictly between you and your doctor," she tells him.

"I'm Black!" a woman in the first row chimes in.

"No, Ming Lee. You're not Black; you're Asian American," Dr. Rogers gently explains.

"Sodomy!" a woman yells. "Sodomy!"

"Lucy, please, let's not go there today. Just keep your mind on the music, in spite of what Ralph just said about being hard," a flustered Dr. Rogers instructs.

Bud whispers to her that they were simply calling out songs they know from the score of *Hair*.

"Well, oh my gracious," Dr. Rogers says, recovering. "How surprising. Well, thank you, everyone. Now, Bud, with your background, you're more than qualified to lead us in our next song, and you'd be more than welcome to do so. Please select a peppy number from my book."

She hands Bud *The Official Book of Songs for Seniors: PhD Thesis of Dr. Sharon Rogers*. Bud's mom shoots him a glance like, "OK, now you'll see what I mean."

He thumbs through a couple of the pages:

SUNG WITH ENTHUSIASM!!!!!
"Down by the Old Mill Stream"

DOES THIS RECALL YOUR FIRST KISS???
"Let Me Call You Sweetheart"

REMEMBER THOSE LIVELY TIMES OF MOON, JUNE, AND SPOONING!!!!!
"By the Light of the Silvery Moon"

"Hi, everyone," Bud says. "I couldn't quite find it here in Sharon's book, but what do you say to singing this with me—ready? One, two, three, together: "Desperado..."

The group responds enthusiastically by singing the next line.

Dr. Rogers is looking at Bud like he's staging an insurrection.

Bud's mother joins him, and for the next couple of minutes, the group belts out a medley of the Eagles' greatest hits.

Afterward, Dr. Rogers says, "I figured these people are really old, so they would only know really old songs."

"Well, 'Desperado' isn't something Nicki Minaj wrote last night; it's almost fifty years old itself," Bud tells her.

"Bud, excuse me, but the idea of seniors singing a borderline heavy-metal rock song like that with tawdry lyrics was never broached at Pocono Mountains Bible College, where I studied. And besides, I think they were more challenged trying to understand the complex rhyming metrics of 'moon,' 'spoon,' 'tune,' 'June,' and 'soon' in 'By the Light of the Silvery Moon,'" she says, in the unapologetically defensive way humans do when they can't admit they're completely wrong about something.

"With all due respect to your alma mater, Dr. Rogers, maybe you oughta revise the song list to take into account that the only light of the silvery moon most seniors remember is seeing it reflected in a pond filled with naked people in the Woodstock documentary."

"Woodstock?" she asks.

LOCAL NEWS

Later that afternoon, we zip over to Palm Beach's WPTV for an appearance on the five o'clock news, hosted by ace newswoman Shannon Cake.

Shannon produces a segment about what's hot and happening around town, which she combines with oddities in the news to give the viewer a little levity between the weather forecasts, reports of shark sightings, and other compelling local headlines of the day.

We're watching the show, waiting in the green room with her other guests, Rambi von Whipper-Snapper and the chef who's catering the food for our movie's crew.

Just before the commercial, Shannon has a Skype with Barry Morton, a Harvard Business School graduate and QAnon member. Morton is confirming the revelation that a voice speaking through the partially defrosted head of Ted Williams is, in fact, the identity of the mysterious "Q" when Shannon interrupts him.

"Excuse me, sir, just a moment," she says. "We're told that there's an official update on this story just now. Earlier today, the head of Ted Williams was removed from the tank at the Scottsdale cryonics facility where it's been housed since 2003. The report indicates that the head was taken outside and warmed in the afternoon sun. Once defrosted, Ted's head chatted with Hall of Fame broadcaster Bob Costas about changes in the game today, after which it released a statement indicating—"

"And yes and…and so," Mr. Morton interrupts.

"…Indicating a desire to be reunited with its body, following which Ted's head categorically denied any involvement with Q and concluded by saying, 'The key to hitting is just plain working at it.' Your response to this, Mr. Morton?"

"There are plenty of other Ted Williams heads out there!" he yells.

"Frozen heads are not like autographed baseballs," Shannon shoots back.

"Well, I read about them this morning on my computer and—"

"Thank you very much. We'll break now, and after, meet some of the people involved in the *Florida Man* movie that resumes shooting tomorrow."

"I'm not finished, Shannon!" Barry Morton yells. "A big shout-out to Anna Wintour, who, according to QAnon's reporting, became the nation's first artificial heart donor yesterday—"

"That's enough. Thank you and goodbye, Mr. Morton," she says.

"And remember," Barry Morton screams, "Bill de Blasio is not six feet five inches tall! The height you see on your TVs is an effect generated by the Hollywood elite. He's actually five foot three, the same size as his wife—"

"Here's that commercial," Shannon Cake says.

We hustle onto the set, and the segment kicks off with Shannon talking to Chef Tyler Gore, who'll be catering the food for the crew.

"Chef Gore," Shannon asks, "how do you face the challenge of dealing with the fickle food requirements of world-class stars, animals, and all manner of crew, stuntmen, drivers, grips, extras, the works? *Florida Man* is a major Netflix production."

"These days," Chef Gore explains, "no matter where you actually get the food—you could even be serving Bubba Burgers—you go very far by assertively stating you're using only the finest, freshest, locally sourced, farm-to-table, certified-organic ingredients, and that you're avoiding recipes from anything ever seen on Guy Fieri's *Diners, Drive-Ins and Dives* on the Food Network. Those words seem to inspire confidence in your cuisine."

"No unusual requests?"

"Eggs," the chef says.

"Can you elaborate a touch there, Chef Gore?"

"Well, Kate McKinnon's people talked to the production people, who talked to the on-location services manager, who talked to a nutritionist, who talked to my people, who talked to a local egg farmer, who talked to me, and apparently Kate wants the name of the chicken that laid any egg she consumes to begin with the letter e. Now, it's quite possible something from Kate got lost in translation here, but I'm taking no chances. After an exhaustive search, I've located two hens named Ethel and Edna, who'll be living in my home for the duration of production."

"Thank you, Chef Gore, and welcome, Spike the Wonder Dog—who'll be portraying the kidnapped dog, Gatsby, in the film—and his owner, Bud, from the syndicated talk show *Southern Exposure*," Shannon says.

"Good to be here, Shannon. You do wonderful work; thanks for having us," Bud says politely.

"You're more than welcome, Bud," Shannon says, glancing at me. "And good to have you with us here in Palm Beach, too, Spike."

"Er…ah, thank you, ah, thank you very much," I say, employing for the first time the Elvis voice on my now fully programed talking dog collar. Remember? The gift Ms. App gave me back on our show. It's huge! I can emit all manner of bon mots and pithy quotes from famous people. This is the first time we're trying it in public.

"Bud, did Spike just speak?" Shannon Cake asks. "Did he talk?"

"What I heard sounded just like Elvis Presley," Rambi says.

I look at Mr. von Whipper-Snapper and say, "I'm not tryin' to be sexy, sir. It's just my way of expressing myself when I move around."

"Oh my God!" he screams, reaching for a nitroglycerin pill in his shirt pocket for his heart. "Forget that Ted Williams thing. Elvis is speaking through this dog. Call Priscilla. He's back! He's back!"

Bud quickly explains that the voice is coming from a small speaker in my collar, and we're using the collar for the first time in public after weeks of practice. He lets them know that it's taken me quite a while to get full command of the tiny control lever under my chin to operate the voices.

"We thought you'd get a kick out of it," Bud says. "Right, Spike?"

"I'm a hunka hunk burning love," I respond.

"We've had a bit of a meltdown of our telephone system with calls," Shannon says. "Some viewers think Spike's actually talking or they're hallucinating."

Bud whispers in my ear, "That was awesome, Spike. Really awesome, awesome."

"Awesome," Bud? Apparently he's been in Florida too long. He's starting to use "awesome" multiple times in one sentence, like everybody else does down here.

CHAPTER TEN

FLORIDA MAN

The next morning, we're up at the crack of dawn to get to the Colony hotel to shoot the ballroom scene. Not sure why everything always starts so early in the morning on movie sets, but our call time is six a.m. and Bud gets us there at six sharp.

We're directed to my dressing room, which is one of several small rooms in a silver trailer parked next to the hotel. A sign on a door indicates "Spike/ Gatsby." This is a reminder that I've got to start getting in character to play Gatsby, even though no one, including Bud, has imparted any information about Gatsby's life to me, the star entrusted with the role.

For my acting prep, I go "method" and create a backstory on Gatsby.

Eva von Whipper-Snapper and Rambi find an abandoned puppy on their doorstep. Eva names the lonely pup Carraway, in honor of Nick Carraway, her favorite character in the novel *The Great Gatsby*. After enduring months of ridicule from friends telling her Carraway is a ridiculous name for a dog, let alone a tiny seed, Eva and Rambi relent and rename him Gatsby. This creates a lifelong insecurity in Gatsby. Is he really Gatsby? Or is he still Carraway, insecure of himself because of his fixation on Gatsby?

After I spend a bleary-eyed hour cramped with Bud in my tiny dressing room, a lovely young woman comes to tell us that hair and makeup are ready for me. Turns out the reason we had to be here at six is hair and makeup. She leads me to another trailer and puts me in a chair next to Tim Allen, who's funny even this early. I get brushed for about a minute while Tim watches, somewhat transfixed by the fact that a dog had to show up before dawn for hair and makeup.

After I hop off the chair, he slips me the rest of his breakfast sandwich. I recognize it as a Jimmy Dean croissant with bacon, egg, and cheese. I nod thanks to Tim and swallow it in two gulps, to avoid the aftertaste of possible preservatives that could keep the thing fresh until the dawn of the twenty-second century.

The lovely young woman takes me back to my dressing room and reminds us that craft services is serving breakfast.

Tyler Gore is in full chef regalia, including an obviously fake International Gastronomic Society Chaîne des Rôtisseurs medallion on a long gold ribbon hanging from his neck. He's chatting up as many people as he can, hoping that one of them is a savvy show business pro who'll see his screen potential and create another urgently needed celebrity-chef TV show.

He tells Bud what happened with Kate McKinnon and the eggs.

"So Kate didn't say that the only eggs she'd eat had to be from chickens whose names started with *e*. She told her people, who talked to the production people, et cetera, et cetera, that she loved eggs. She 'loves eggs with a capital *e*,' is what she actually said, to emphasize how much she loved eggs," he explained. "Now I've got two hens named Edna and Ethel laying eggs all over my house, and the chicken farmer won't drive down over from Tampa to pick them up."

We survey the large breakfast selection he's created.

"You'll love my sausage," Chef Gore says. "It's hand-processed from a recipe recently discovered in a Bavarian farmer's wife's journal. The sausage won the Munich International Sausage-Tasting Competition in 1914. It arrived last night by special courier from Düsseldorf. By the way," he continues, "please try the croissant sandwich. It's identical to the version served at the Sunday champagne brunch at the Hôtel de Crillon in Paris. It took me weeks to perfect the flaky croissant."

"Well, thank you, Ch—" Bud starts to say, but Chef Gore races off, calling, "Miss Arnaz, Miss Arnaz, you must try my mini omelets with imported white Stilton Gold cheese and Tennessee wild boar bacon."

As Bud's loading a plate for each of us, I slip around to the kitchen. The plastic containers in the trash and the ones scattered on the floor confirm my suspicions that Chef Gore's actually serving a world-class array of very tasty, locally sourced (read: purchased at a bodega two miles away) popular Jimmy Dean sausage and breakfast products. Jimmy's Hearty Sausage Quiche seems to be getting the most play. I notice that the packages of the egg sandwiches claim they're made with real eggs. That's the kind of authenticity I always look for when I'm shopping for an egg sandwich.

(Note to reader: Congratulate yourself. You've just read the most ever written in an American novel about Jimmy Dean sausage. For more extensive prose on the subject, please reference the book *Thirty Years of Sausage, Fifty Years of Ham* by the country music icon himself, Jimmy Dean.)

While Bud's standing at the table scarfing down a Jimmy Dean Egg'Wich, described by Chef Gore as "inspired by the spa cuisine at the exclusive Ventana resort in Big Sur," we're greeted by the diminutive Christie Leigh Ingalls-Thomas, the film's director.

I like her. You've probably known someone like Christie Leigh. She's one of those people where you have to look beyond their odd appearance and quirky habits to see the true individual, and the talent within.

With Christie Leigh, you'd need to disregard her somewhat dated clothing style—the 1973 John Lennon–style granny glasses, the modest ankle-length cotton dresses, and the blue sunbonnet that all combine to make her look like she should be working at the Dutch Country Soft Pretzel stand in Blue Ball, Pennsylvania—not directing a major comedy film.

You shouldn't be distracted by Christie's two hobbies either—she's collecting all twelve hundred species of spider mite, and she plays the fife in the country's only R&B fife and drum corps.

She's also one of those people who pronounce the word "poem" as "poi-" (rhymes with "koi") "-em." But beyond those oddities, she was first in her class at the University of Southern California and had an internship with Martin Scorsese, who brought her on as a second assistant director on *Killers of the Flower Moon.* He recommended her for the *Florida Man* assignment.

"The kid's got it," Scorsese proclaimed in *Variety.*

"Hi, fellows," she says. "All set for your first day?"

"We are, but how about you?" Bud asks. "The way that lighting director guy was talking to you at the meeting the other day really pissed me off. Are you OK? How ya gonna handle that jerk?"

"Well, I don't know. I don't like confrontation, and it's sad. Obviously, Goldfarb's an insecure fellow," she says. "I'm twenty-four and directing, and he's forty-two years old and still hasn't helmed a film, except for a thirty-min-ute documentary on grass seed that never got released."

That's his problem; it shouldn't be hers. I don't like this guy. So the other day at the meeting, while he was verbally assaulting her about her camera angle choices, I quietly crawled under his chair and passed enough gas to inflate a Macy's balloon. People were moving away from Goldfarb like he was wearing a sign saying, "Hi, I'm Frank Goldfarb. I've got a new incurable strain of COVID."

"When I first got into television," Bud tells her, "a veteran comedian at the Friars Club took me under his wing. 'You seem a nice guy, Bud, so let me tell you one thing. In this business, you gotta be able to cultivate the ability to tell somebody "fuck you" with clarity and precision.' Keep that in mind going forward, Christie Leigh."

"I will, Bud. I will," she says. "I won't forget that."

The ballroom of the Colony hotel is filled with Palm Beach luminaries. The others scattered around the banquet tables are professional movie extras. Sadly "extra" is one of the lowest rankings in the intricate but rarely discussed caste system in show business, where being an extra is just a touch above working as a bathing suit caddy in a Michael Phelps commercial. The extras are portraying hamster enthusiasts who've traveled to Palm Beach for the luncheon where Vicky Ventura will receive the award as the person who's done the most to further the popularity of hamsters in the past decade.

"I've got four extras who actually look a little bit like hamsters," the casting director bragged.

The "International Hamster Society Lifetime Achievement Award" banner is stretched across the top of the ballroom's stage. There's a picture of a hamster at each end of the thing. Unfortunately, the FedEx employee in West Palm Beach who printed the banner failed to enlarge the little hamster pictures as directed, so the hamsters on the banner are actual size, and look like tiny smudges of dirt when viewed from the audience.

Christie Leigh's done a good job re-creating the atmosphere of an actual Palm Beach charity luncheon. The emcee is the popular Dick Robinson of Legends Radio. The musician Bob Merrill has a quartet on stage. They're discreetly playing classics from the Great American Songbook while Christie Leigh finalizes the shooting details.

Unfortunately, to get into the ballroom, Dick and Bob and the band had to wade through several protesters who're demanding changes to some song titles and the elimination of other songs altogether.

The protesters are part of the latest craze—niche protesting. The movement sprang from the nation's first WokeFest, at Barclays Center in Brooklyn, New York. It made big headlines by featuring a rare musical performance by Alexandria Ocasio-Cortez and "the Squad" rapping a peppy version of the Kurtis Blow classic "If I Ruled the World," with lyrics modified to reflect both political correctness and political ambitions.

Some of the protesters' signs outside the Colony that morning read, "Cancel songs offensive to Alzheimer's patients: 'Try to Remember,' 'I Remember You,' 'Thanks for the Memory.'"

Other protesters chanted that "I've Got You Under My Skin" upsets scleroderma victims.

A few screamed that the "The Tender Trap" is about perverted bondage.

"It all started with 'Baby It's Cold Outside,'" Dick Robinson told Bud.

This Robinson guy is a media veteran in his eighties. He's lived through the golden age of radio, the golden age of television, and the golden age of theater, and now has the distinct privilege of living through the golden age of sensitivity.

A while back on our show, Bud did an interview with Jim Abrams, one of the organizers of WokeFest. To me, the guy came off like a klieg light of virtue signaling.

"Sorry to hear you had to cancel the Woke Comedy Afternoon at the festival," Bud told him.

"Yes, we didn't realize that we'd be unable to find any material from any comic anywhere in the country that didn't contain objectionable material," Abrams explained.

"Yeah, I knew you were in trouble when Carrot Top got pulled. So, what was your main accomplishment at WokeFest?" Bud asked.

"Well, we tied an ailing Mel Brooks to a chair and made him watch as we burned the last remaining thirty-five-millimeter prints of *Blazing Saddles*."

SHOOTING SCENE ONE, PAGE TWELVE, OF FLORIDA MAN

Script: "Rambi, Eva, and Gatsby will enter the ballroom and find their places at the VIP table in the front."

I'm in the back of the ballroom with Tim and Lucie, who're portraying my owners, the von Whipper-Snappers.

The real Rambi von Whipper-Snapper had to be escorted off the set because he was in nonstop complaint mode with Tim Allen and Christie Leigh about Tim's costume, which was a very cool Palm Beach look: a blue blazer with gold buttons, a white open-collar shirt, and white linen slacks. The costume designer even got a pair of ridiculously expensive maroon velvet slippers with the initials *RvS* on them.

"Tim must change clothes, Christie Leigh," Rambi insisted. "At the luncheon on that dreadful day when Gatsby was abducted, I was not dressed like Mr. Allen is today, in a blue blazer."

"What were you wearing?" Christie Leigh asks politely.

"I was wearing what I have on now, which is an exact replica of the bright red one-piece jumpsuit that Elvis wore in the hotel lobby scene in the film *Clambake*. I'm sure you remember it."

"Elvis actually made a movie called *Clambake*?" she asks, wrinkling her nose so much that she has to adjust her granny glasses. "Ewww!"

"Mr. von Whipper-Snapper, I don't remember much about the movie," Tim Allen says, "except that the song 'Clambake' may be the worst thing Elvis ever recorded."

"Tim, how can you overlook him singing 'Fort Lauderdale Chamber of Commerce' in *Girl Happy*?" Bud quips.

"Do not defame the King, Bud," Rambi von Whipper-Snapper snaps. "Now, Tim, let's go into the men's room so you can change into my jumpsuit, although it's going to be several inches short on your arms and legs."

"Go ahead and do it, Tim," the surly lighting director, Goldfarb, demands. "But hurry."

Christie Leigh shakes her head no.

Tim thanks Christie Leigh.

"You're wrong again, Christie Leigh," Goldfarb tells her, wagging a stubby finger in her face.

Two guards pick up Mr. von Whipper-Snapper and whisk him away. "The Colonel wouldn't have let this happen!" he screams.

Christie Leigh's just about ready to clap the board for the start of the shot. The morning's been tough for her. Goldfarb's been hounding her every decision. He's also been mocking her appearance, calling her "Sister Wife."

"OK," Christie Leigh says though a small megaphone. "Places…and… quiet please, and…*action*."

The crowd murmurs small talk as Tim, Lucie, and I start a slow walk toward the stage, winding our way through the extras and guests at the tables.

"There he is!" a beautifully deep, mellifluous voice calls out, interrupting the scene.

"Who the heck is that?" Lucie asks.

"That sounded like Darth Vader. Is James Earl Jones here?" Tim wonders.

What I heard was a slightly higher-pitched and more honey-touched version of Sam Elliott's voice.

"Cut! Cut!" Christie Leigh instructs. What is…"

Standing at a table in the back of the ballroom is a beautifully dressed statuesque Palm Beach lady who's maybe fifty years old.

"Malpractice! Malpractice!" she yells, her voice sounding deeper and more resonant than Morgan Freeman's when he has a head cold. "That's plastic surgeon Randy Loomis, the doctor who gave me his so-called Feather-Light voice lift three weeks ago."

"That's a patented term there, folks," Dr. Loomis says, getting up. "Now just calm down for a moment, Mrs. Kramer."

"Calm down? Calm down? My voice dropped overnight. I woke up yesterday, said, 'Good morning, darling' to my husband, and he thought Vin Diesel was in our bed."

"Get her out of here now, you fool!" Goldfarb screams in Christie Leigh's face. "She's slowing things down and wasting time, just like you were doing while placing the extras. And why the fuck are you reading a text on the phone right now, Sister Wife?"

"Look at me, folks," Mrs. Kramer says. "He did my face. Youthful, right? My neck is beautiful, right? My breasts…"

"Perfect Salma Hayek's," one of the extras tells her.

"Exactly," she says.

The crowd looks at Dr. Loomis and murmurs approval.

"I must say, Hayek's are my specialty," he boasts.

"And now, the voice? If I want to, I can sound like Brad Garrett or—"

"Dr. Loomis, Mrs. Kramer, excuse me," Christie Leigh says. "I don't know how you two will work this out, but we have to continue the production."

"Of course you do, honey," Mrs. Kramer says with a resonance that rattles the forks on her table. "But when I spotted him over there, I snapped. I'm sorry; you were very sweet to us explaining the movie before."

"But wait, Mrs. Kramer," Christie Leigh says, "maybe good news for you in this text. My mentor, Martin Scorsese in New York, has been watching a live feed from the set for the past half hour with his friend Fran Lebowitz.

Fran heard you and thinks that you should be the narrator on *Florida Man* instead of Liev Schreiber."

In short order, little Christie Leigh Ingalls-Thomas straightens things out. She books a recording session with Mrs. Kramer, whose unusual voice will guarantee enormous PR for the film, and she fires Goldfarb.

"Scorsese has been watching?" Goldfarb asks her, incredulously. "I bet he'll love my grass seed film."

"Yes, Goldfarb," she says. "Marty's been online off and on observing us all morning. And you know, Goldfarb, Marty likes a happy set."

"Of course. He's the wizard, a genius. I want to work with him. Scorsese's great."

"And I texted him about your behavior. He's seen you in action, and he agrees with me," Christie Leigh tells him. "You're a decent lighting man but a poisonous presence. Marty has someone on the way to replace you. You're fired, and on a personal note, fuck you, Goldfarb."

"You can't be saying this," a red-faced, shaking Goldfarb yells.

"I believe I just said it with clarity and precision," Christie Leigh tells him.

Watching this, I'm motivated to give her the highest accolade I can award someone.

"Oh my God, Spike, that was hard for me to do," she tells me, "but you're making it all the more worthwhile by licking my ankles like that."

SHOOTING SCENE FOUR, PAGE FOURTEEN, OF FLORIDA MAN

Script: "Vicky Ventura will receive the Golden Hamster trophy from Higgins, president of the International Hamster Appreciation Society."

It's slow work doing a movie, not like being with Bud on live TV back home. We shoot different angles and reverse shots of me with Tim and Lucie, until finally we're up there with Kate McKinnon as Vicky Ventura, receiving the Golden Hamster trophy.

Comedian Tom Cotter is playing Higgins, president of the International Hamster Appreciation Society. He has some great lines packed with tongue-in-cheek double entendre hamster jokes, and he concludes by linking hamster ownership to achieving world peace. He cracks up Lucie on camera a couple of times. You'll see that in the film's credits, which I'll explain in a second.

I'm not at liberty to put any of the excellent script from *Florida Man* in the book, due to a very long and boring letter Mr. Boggs got about copyright infringement issues and a potential $14 million lawsuit against him, and threats of harassment in the press if we failed to comply.

But I can tell you this:

After Tom hands Kate the trophy, she hammers out a very funny thank-you speech. It kills, so she decides on a quick improvisation. She bends over and holds the trophy in front of me, figuring I'd lick it and we'd get a big "awww" from the crowd to end the scene.

Licking's silly, I thought. But to get a laugh, I opened my mouth real wide, closed my mighty jaws on the trophy, and lifted it up like I've just won Wimbledon. Unfortunately, I bite the hamster's head off, since the thing is made of gold metallic paper on cardboard. We then have to reshoot with the backup hamster trophy.

Christie Leigh thinks the head bite is hysterical and immediately says, "Mark it for credits." So the film ends up including the scene with the outtakes they sometimes show during credits in comedies. You know what I mean? You see stars having laughing fits with each other in an exaggerated way when one of them blows a line.

SHOOTING SCENE SIX, PAGE FOURTEEN, OF FLORIDA MAN

Script: Vicky, Rambi, Eva, Higgins, and assorted guests dance the association's traditional Hamster Hop, which replicates indigenous people's powwow dance, in celebration of the award.

(Note: the Hamster Hop has been approved for use in the film by tribal elders for 3 percent of net.)

During the dancing, Gatsby is taken backstage by an attendant. Prince Harry, as the Florida Man, is revealed—one tattoo at a time—as he slowly steps out of the shadows. He chloroforms both the attendant and Gatsby. Gatsby is shoved into a suitcase and wheeled away.

We shoot the scene from several angles. It takes a while. Harry is unrecognizable. He's covered with henna crocodile tattoos and wearing the long, scraggly wig last seen in the 1958 Roger Corman movie *Teenage Caveman*.

Backstage, the last shot of the day is the Florida Man shoving unconscious me as Gatsby into a duffel bag.

I don't know who's supposed to get me out of the duffel bag. Maybe it's Harry, or the intern, or Christie Leigh, or the grip, or the best boy, or the driver, or the costume designer, or the nice lady from makeup, or any one of those other people whose titles you see at the end of a film. By the way, "best boy"? What the hell is that, actually?

Immediately after Christie Leigh yells "cut," bandleader Bob Merrill makes an announcement. "We at the Legends family love music and encourage young talent to perform, and we've done a bit of research. Turns out, one of the stars of the film has a great voice but has been too shy to sing much in public. In addition to charitable causes, and polo, he's a fan of the Great American Songbook, and we should get him out here and make him do a number."

"Oh, no," Prince Harry says, looking at the ceiling. "I can't."

"Like his grandmother was, the prince is a big fan of Bobby Darin, so let's welcome him to the stage—the one and only Prince Harry. Come on out and let's hear you rock your late grandmother's all-time favorite song, 'Queen of the Hop.'"

The band vamps the intro.

Merrill continues, "Let's coax His Royal Highness to sing, please, folks. Come on, let's hear it."

The news coverage the next day includes lines like:

> "A heavily tattooed Prince Harry wearing a Neanderthal man wig wowed a stunned crowd at the Colony hotel singing a couple of popular songs."

> "Angry protesters outside the ballroom screamed that 'Queen of the Hop' should be 'Person of the Hop.'"

> "Spike the Wonder Dog, trapped in a bag backstage, chewed his way out in time to join Prince Harry to bark at end of "Bad, Bad Leroy Brown."

OK, I just made the chewing-himself-out-of-the-bag part up to see if you'd believe it and/or remember that Frank Sinatra actually did bark after singing the line "meaner than a junkyard dog" when he recorded "Bad, Bad Leroy Brown." (Insert *womp, womp, womp* cartoon sound effect to give that sentence the intended impact.)

I got out of the bag 'cause Bud and me are wordlessly in sync. We've got that unique dog-human communication they report about at the end of the nightly news when producers are desperate for a human-interest feature but can't find one about a seven-year-old running a food bank. I sent Bud the "find me" vibes, and when he was finally finished dancing with Lucie, he managed to unzip the bag moments before I turned blue.

Later that afternoon, back at our room, Bud is going over business with Buffy on the phone for the show back home.

"Lombardo wants you back soon," Buffy tells him. "I'm holding down the program, but the daily numbers are slipping slightly. People want you and Spike. Plus, we'll be getting some unexpected morning competition from the new Podcast Network."

"What?" he asks.

"Listen," Buffy says, "here's one of the audio promo kits Lombardo got."

She opens a file, and the voice of New York radio personality Mark Simone announces a new morning program.

"If you loved following him under house arrest or in prison, you'll love him even more inches away from you on TV. It's time for the charming new morning show *Wake Up with Julian*. Start your day the Julian way, with the kind of warm and fuzzy feel-good stories only Julian Assange can report. Get ready to wake up with Julian. Brought to you by Fresh Start bedroom spray. Coming soon on the Podcast Network."

"Somehow, I think we'll prevail," Bud says. "Anyway, we miss you, the show, everybody; so please just hold on, only a couple more days here. What's up with The Old Swede, the lookalikes in the woods, Shoshana?"

"Lombardo's sending you an update tonight. But tell Spike his brother Oswald arrived and that Shoshana's crazy about him, but Oswald keeps escaping from the yard and running over to play with Phil, the neighbor's goat. Remember Phil the goat? He was on YouTube drinking thirteen Pepsis, then burping for two straight minutes? Got millions of views."

"Fortunately no, I somehow missed that one," Bud says.

"OK, we're all ready to record the two spots for tomorrow's show. Let's start with the 'Ask Herbie' bit," she instructs.

This is a segment Bud dreamed up: Herbie stands on my head, peers into the camera, and insults viewers asking for personal advice about their love life.

"Three questions for you today, Herbie," Bud says.

"Shoot," he squawks.

"I'm Gloria. I'm twenty-nine years old, I live with my parents, and I'm looking for a satisfying romantic holiday. What should I do, Herbie?"

"Got a vibrator?"

"Er, no, all I want is an idea for romance while traveling, Herbie."

"Driving with vibrator. Next."

"Hi, I'm Phil. How are you?"

"Bored...next."

"I'm Justin. I wrote Oprah about my love life, and she's recommending—"

"No Oprah!" he squawks.

"But Herbie, I'm having trouble satisfying a woman, and—"

"Get vibrator. Call Gloria. Done."

"Very funny again, Herbie." Bud laughs. "Your answers work every time."

"Just like vibrator," he cackles.

"Great," Buffy says. "Now for Digital Dan and the Obama thing, if you and Spike are ready?"

Digital Dan is an in-demand national guest who loves to come on our show because he has a Bull Terrier like me, named Chloe. I like Chloe. She's a sweet older dog who always sits next to Dan when he's with us. We bark at each other. Digital Dan, who's a special effects genius, loves it.

Dan bills himself as "the world's greatest CGI special effects political prankster." His goal is to embarrass notable politicians of both parties. He hacks into visual media and inserts embarrassing images live. To date, his greatest success was creating the illusion of a bright red leather bondage set with handcuffs, collar, whip, and leash hanging on the door behind Senator Susan Collins of Maine during an interview on CNN.

Dan comes on. Chloe and I bark, and Bud gets right to it.

"OK, Dan, we have a tape of your latest spoof with Michelle and Barack Obama, at home in their den, talking to Chuck Todd on *Meet the Press*. You surely made headlines with this. Almost a billion views," Bud says. "Let's watch."

Michelle and the former president are seated next to each other. Over their shoulders, on a mantel, originally were figures of Martin Luther King Jr. and Rosa Parks, but Digital Dan has replaced each statuette with an image of a large bong. The way Dan works is that somehow only viewers at home—not in the network control room—can see the bongs. That's why the greatest hackers in the world call him "the FX Wizard."

What he does is like a digital version of 1980s craze "Pie Kill Anonymous"—you'd hire a pie thrower to embarrass a person by pushing a pie in their face. Mr. Boggs told me once he got "pied" on live TV while interviewing Lord Snowden. Could it be that things were so simple then?

"Now watch closely," Digital Dan says.

In the friendly, formal style he uses on *Meet the Press*, Chuck Todd observes: "I see you have statuettes of two great civil rights leaders on your fireplace. Can each of you talk about their significance? What it means to you when you look at Rosa Parks and Martin Luther King Jr. each day."

"Certainly," Barack says. "Let me get them."

He gets up and brings the two statuettes back to the couch. He hands Rosa Parks to Michelle and gazes at Martin Luther King Jr. in his hand.

At home, however, viewers see him clutching a twenty-inch blue-and-red triple-barrel glass bong, which appears packed and has smoke floating from the mouthpiece.

"I get inspiration, revelations, and vision from this," the former president says softly. "Sometimes at the end of the day, when I'm tired, I find this can be a great source of energy and renewal."

"Well stated, and I think our viewers will agree with you about the inspiration you derive there," Chuck Todd says. "And Mrs. Obama, tell us of the importance of the statuette of Rosa Parks cradled in your lap right now, please."

"Sure, Chuck, I'd love to," she says.

Viewers see Michelle Obama pick up a similar bong and thrust it directly at the camera. "Everyone in America should have one of these to stimulate their mind and open their awareness about what they can do to move America forward. I draw from this every day. That's all I can say, Chuck—I draw from it every day."

Hard-hitting segments like this are what makes our show, *Southern Exposure*, the go-to program throughout the South for morning enlightenment.

And both Bud and me are anxious to get back home to the studio. Plus, I'll be reunited with my loopy brother Oswald.

During the next two days, I knock out some shots with the Florida Man staking me out as bait for him to catch the biggest alligator in the Everglades. We shoot in a couple of locations around Palm Beach that look enough like the Everglades to work in a comedy—except for a woman in the background zooming by on a Segway a couple of times.

My final scene is with the giant alligator that will ultimately eat the Florida Man. The producers are still waiting for more poll results to come in to determine how to end the film, so we shoot Jim Carrey carrying me off, Kate McKinnon carrying me off, Jim and Kate saving me together, and also me swimming into the sunset with the alligator. Bud protests that last ending, claiming that my falling in love with a reptile is not in the contract. Anyway, when we all see the movie, we'll know how the poll respondents wanted it to end.

Before we shot anything with the alligator, Christie Leigh, Bud, and me went over to Mike's Mechanical Alligator Showroom in West Palm Beach to inspect the creature. The gator's listed in the cast notes as "Big Mel the Alligator." Who knew that Florida is the country's largest producer of motorized mechanical alligators?

Mario Messasalma, the old man who founded the business, told us Big Mel is the largest and oldest mechanical alligator in his fleet.

"Young lady," he said to Christie Leigh, "you can't find a better motorized mechanical alligator in the world than Big Mel. He was built during the fifties, when they really made things right—like the Corvette, black-and-white TVs, and pointy bullet bras. Mel's capable of making every conceivable move that a real alligator can make, like climbing over a fence and running at thirty-five miles an hour."

"He's a very impressive specimen," Christie Leigh agreed, gazing at Big Mel, who seemed to be peering through her long skirt at her thighs.

"Best mechanical alligator I've ever seen for sure," Bud lied, to make the old man feel good. When he woke up this morning, Bud didn't even know that motorized alligators existed. He thought Big Mel would be a made of rubber, like the one Johnny Weissmuller somehow killed successfully in the movie *Tarzan and His Mate*. Their battle is on YouTube, FYI.

"Sometimes it seems like Big Mel's got a mind of his own, but you know, he's like a son to me, and he's done it all," Mr. Messasalma continues. "He worked for Clyde Beatty's Jungleland in 1960, and no one ever knew he was mechanical. One season, he chased little horses around the ring at the World of Miniature Horses show in Pompano Beach. Remember the movie *Where the Boys Are*? Well, Big Mel had a great scene chasing George Hamilton and Connie Francis down the beach in Fort Lauderdale, but the scene was cut."

"That's a loss for Big Mel. How come?" Bud asked.

During this mechanical alligator chitchat, I studied Big Mel. Whoever crafted his eyes back in the '50s did an outstanding job. I would have sworn, by the look in those big alligator eyes, he was recalling the sight of Connie Francis' ass as he was chasing her down that beach.

"Why did Big Mel get cut, my young friends? I'll tell you why. They cut the goddamn scene because Big Mel was chasing Connie and George at ten miles an hour, and Hamilton was pouring sweat every time they did a take. George had a 'no sweating on screen' clause in his contract, and they had to burn the film."

"Oh my. Sorry, Big Mel," Christie Leigh said softly, patting his huge head. And there he went again—staring at her thighs.

As we were leaving his alligator showroom, the old man got a little misty and sentimental.

I could tell he needed to talk about something that was bothering him. A dog can look at a human and know they'll be moaning and groaning at him for hours.

"I'm the last of a kind. This is a family business," he told us. "In Italy, our little village was Mosciano Sant'Angelo. For the tourists, we made Pinocchios with tiny motors. Our Pinocchio could do anything—dance the tarantella at weddings, twirl pasta, pretend to masturbate; he could even swim the back-stroke in the ocean on a calm day—anything. When I came to America in the fifties, I figured anyone with guts, a gun, and a decent mechanical Pinocchio could achieve the American dream."

Seems like a perfectly reasonable outlook, I was thinkin'.

"I moved here for the hot weather like at home and quickly learned, to my surprise, that the Pinocchio market in Florida was quite limited. Alligators were always in the papers, so I started making them. But I'm left with this—my only child, Angelo, won't follow me into the business. He doesn't see a future in it."

"That must be disturbing for you," Bud said.

"It's worse; it's bleak," he said. "Angelo decided he wants to be a scientist. The only school he can get into is Old Shep College in Raleigh."

"Oh my," Christie Leigh said.

"I know," Mr. Messasalma murmured. "Ranked around seventeen hundred and seventy out of out of the seventeen hundred and seventy-nine schools in the country. With the help of highly paid tutors, he somehow graduated in six years, but of course he can't get a job as a scientist, so now he works for Cologuard. My son spends eight hours a day examining stool samples, when he could be here renting alligators. Oh yeah, and try to find a wife on Match. com when you type in 'stoolologist' as your profession."

Not a bright outlook for a relationship, I was thinkin'. A lotta female dogs don't want to mate up with bloodhounds, 'cause on the job, they spend the whole day sniffing things. They come home. The bitch asks, "So how was your day today?" All the bloodhound can do is describe eight hours of inhaling revolting smells along some fusty trail.

"I tried sending to the village back in Italy to get a wife for Angelo, but even the women with the mustaches won't come over to marry him. I tell them, 'He's studying stool samples all day. You'll look like Sophia Loren to him when he comes home.'"

I know Sophia Loren has been accorded the highest of accolades in her life as a sex goddess, but nothing quite like that, I was figurin'.

"They don't care," Mr. Messasalma said sadly. "I'll die without descendants."

"Maybe it's time for Big Mel to have children. I think a little nest swarming with thirty motorized baby mechanical alligators would make you very happy, Mr. Messasalma," Bud said.

"My God, that's great, young man. Great. Come back in two months to meet my new family, and if you ever want a motorized mechanical version of that formidable dog of yours, consider it done. He'd have a double to play with."

Wow! Don't get me started on how much I'd enjoy playing with myself.

Whoa…I know there's a joke in there somewhere, but I'm gonna pass.

SHOOTING A SCENE INSERT FOR FLORIDA MAN:
BIG MEL IN ACTION

Maybe it's the way Mel seems to be admiring her legs, but after Christie Leigh meets him, she decides he needs more screen time.

"Don't you think we need to make Mel a more sympathetic creature, Spike?" she asks me, in the way humans question dogs. "I think Marty would like that."

"The kid's got it," I say, using the Scorsese setting on the talking collar.

"Yeah, maybe just a touch of the good old Frankenstein monster simpatico, or maybe Mel could recall that weird fish thing that somehow manages to have sex with Sally Hawkins in *The Shape of Water*," she says.

She decides we'll add an early morning shoot at the Palm Beach par-three golf course on the Intracoastal, on South Ocean Boulevard, to our schedule.

Her plan is to have Big Mel swim up to the little beach on the edge of the course and crawl across the green of the ninth hole. She'll film this undercover to capture the actual reactions of golfers spotting a massive alligator approaching them during their morning round. If it works, she'll ask each one to sign a release.

"Marty did something realistic like this in *Mean Streets*," she claims.

The morning sun is casting long palm tree shadows over hole nine at the course. A slight breeze is rippling the Intracoastal as Big Mel's ready to emerge.

Mr. Messasalma is seated at Big Mel's master control panel, which he's created to replicate the cockpit of flying ace Chuck Yeager's 1952 F-86 Sabre jet, complete with a framed picture on the console of Chuck Yeager and Big Mel hugging each other.

"I don't know," he cautions Christie Leigh. "Ya got eight golfers out there. What if somebody has a heart attack when they see Big Mel?"

"I'll take the risk. Plus, we paid big-time for insurance on all Big Mel scenes in case he ends up accidentally swallowing Prince Harry," she says.

"You're a fearless director, like John Ford. Now there was a man who knew how to direct a movie. They don't make movies like they did in the fifties," he says.

She's looking at him like, "Yeah, there's never been anything quite like *Bedtime for Bonzo* since the fifties," but she simply whispers, "OK, action."

With the sun reflecting off of his massive wet head, Mel comes ambling out of the water in a friendly sort of a way. He starts plodding slowly across a putting green. He looks like the happiest motorized mechanical alligator in the world.

"Not good," Christie Leigh says. "They've got their backs turned to Mel, and he's getting too close to them. They have to see him right now, or he'll end up knocking them over like bowling pins."

"No problem," Mr. Messasalma says. "Listen."

He presses the number-three switch, then holds down a button that says "Gentle Nonthreatening Mating Bellows," and Mel emits three soft mating calls.

The golfers whirl around, see Big Mel, and like you'd expect, stampede away screaming.

"Perfect," Christie Leigh says.

"Now I think this will be exactly what you wanted," Mr. Messasalma says, indicating a big red switch. He pulls it down, and Big Mel somehow looks sad. You get the impression that all Big Mel wanted to do was make contact with people.

"Oh, wow, Mel," Christie Leigh says. "I love you."

After the golfers have sprinted about twenty yards, I notice that they stop and are rooting around in their golf bags. Christie Leigh didn't anticipate this, so I guess she forgot she was filming in the state of Florida, where people carry guns and shoot each other on a regular basis while arguing over the closest parking space to the supermarket. One golfer pulls out a small sawed-off shotgun. A woman is cocking her mini Glock 42, and two men have heavy, standard army-issue forty-five-caliber pistols. They look like nothing could make them happier than pumping thirty rounds of lead into Big Mel before they return to the tranquility of their game.

They charge toward Mel, whooping and waving their guns.

"Oh my God!" Mr. Messasalma shrieks. "They can't shoot him!"

"Yes," Christie Leigh mutters to Bud, "they're attacking Big Mel, just like John Ford did in the fifties with white men pretending to be Indians in his westerns."

A couple of shots ring out but are way off target—bark flies offa the trees behind Mel. No one ever said you need training on firearms down here.

Mr. Messasalma grabs Christie Leigh's bullhorn. "Hold your fire, please! Hold your fire. That's Big Mel, the world-famous motorized mechanical alligator. He was on *The Tonight Show* with Steve Allen back in the fifties, when TV hosts were TV hosts. He won't hurt you. He can dance, see?"

The four people stop about twenty feet from Big Mel with weapons pointed directly at him. "Oh, yeah?" one snarls, cocking his pistol. "Who's Steve Allen?"

Out of a tiny speaker in Big Mel's left ear comes the pulsating sound of the 1958 rock hit "At the Hop."

"They don't write songs like this anymore," Mr. Messasalma says to Christie Leigh, as the four people lower their weapons and stand mesmerized as Big Mel begins bouncing along perfectly on each beat of "at the hop, hop, hop…"

As much as I've done in my short life, I've never danced with a motorized mechanical alligator, so I join Big Mel and the whole group for Mel's next selection, "The Twist."

You'll see it all in the rapidly expanding outtake reel during the credits.

BIG MEL AND SPIKE'S ODDLY EXCELLENT ADVENTURE

Later that day, we're on location a little farther south on the Intracoastal, across the road from a big fancy apartment building that faces the beach. There's an open grassy area and a patch of woods that the set decorator has again been able to transform into something that vaguely resembles the wilds of the Everglades.

My scene is simple. Prince Harry as the Florida Man has me staked down as bait to lure the alligator from the water, and he's hiding behind some potted plants the set designer borrowed from the building across the street. His plan is to use an alligator rifle to shoot Big Mel, and a net to ensnare him.

But in the planned sequence, the alligator rifle jams, and in a dramatic turn just as Mel's about to bite off my head, he stops and charges over to gobble up Prince Harry. All Christie Leigh directs me to do is bark, look brave, and give Mel a nod in the direction of the Florida Man.

Big Mel eating the Florida Man is Hollywood filmmaking at its best. Although it looks like Prince Harry's screaming as he's being devoured, what you're seeing is Mel eating a mannequin. They bought one right outta the window of the Saks men's store in Palm Beach, and dressed it and tattooed it as a double for the Florida Man.

Christie Leigh carefully inserts half of the Florida Man mannequin into Big Mel's mouth. Mr. Messasalma presses the "Chew, Savor, and Swallow" lever on the controls—a lever he once used mistakenly, causing Mel to pulverize a thirty-pound gingerbread house on Martha Stewart's popular *Christmas in the Everglades* special—and voilà, you think you're seeing the Florida Man being eaten alive. It's realistic, except maybe for the way one plastic arm breaks off and rolls away, followed by the mannequin's plastic head. Look closely in the movie, and you'll spot that the head doesn't have a nose. When Saks switched mannequin production to China in 1989, noses on mannequins were eliminated, and no one has ever really known why.

"Back in the fifties, when they knew how to make things, the mannequins had noses," Mr. Messasalma is quick to point out.

Big Mel was programmed to turn around and head for the water, and that's it.

Prince Harry graciously autographs a couple of the mannequin's bitten-off fingers for kids who are watching, then races back to his hotel and attempts to scrub off the tattoos.

While Bud, the crew, and Mr. Messasalma go for a boat ride and shoot the next sequence, I stay on shore with Big Mel as he cools down in his idle setting. Christie Leigh is shooting several angles of the Florida Man's body parts floating in the water. She needs them for one of the three possible feel-good endings the test audiences reviewed:

1. An actor playing California congressman Kevin McCarthy hoping for a campaign contribution returns Gatsby.
2. Jim Carrey, now playing his *Cable Guy* character, makes the return.
3. Body parts sink slowly into the water as the *Palm Beach Daily News* floats to the surface with headline "Dog Returned. Whipper-Snappers Arrested at Nude Street Party Celebration."

I'm glad mosta my work is done.

I'm relaxin' on the grass, daydreaming about returning to High Point, when Big Mel seems to get affectionate. He grabs me, shakes me a little, and locks me in his jaws. "If they'd hired the canine-and-robot intimacy coordinator Christie Leigh wanted, this wouldn't be happening" is my first thought.

Nothing was programmed on the talking collar I'm wearing for me to say, "Hey, thanks, Big Mel. A pleasure working with you, too, but can you please put me down? 'Cause your teeth are a little pointy, and I don't want to get any of my messy dog blood on your rubber tongue."

My head's sticking out one side of his mouth; my tail's protruding out the other. Mel scampers to the bottom of the ramp of the flatbed truck parked in front of us. The driver has just loaded the Bentley that was used in an earlier scene onto the truck. Big Mel quickly crawls up the ramp and under the car. The ramp slides back in place, and the flatbed truck, the Bentley, Big Mel, and me drive off.

I try to flick my tail to hit one of the little control buttons near his ear but can't reach it. I got no idea where I'm headed, or if he'll suddenly go into the "Chew, Savor, and Swallow" action again. I'm hanging outta Big Mel's mouth lookin' like a wild albino pig he's just snatched outta some swamp. I can't believe it's possible that after all I've been through, my demise might be in the jaws of a mechanical alligator that was on the Steve Allen show.

You're probably wondering, "What does being trapped in a mechanical alligator's huge jaws actually feel like for Spike?" Are you? No? Well, if you're not even the least bit curious, you might consider developing more empathy with the new Oz Empathy Now! app. The subscription also includes a year's supply of specially formulated one-a-day empathy-enhancing lozenges. (The previous sentences are a paid advertisement from The Wizard of Oz Promotions Inc.; Spike the Wonder Dog does not endorse this product.)

OK, well, I'll tell you what it feels like. It's like I'm lying on a bed of nails with another bed of nails on top of me. It's most painful when the truck hits the occasional small bump and Big Mel's mouth clamps harder on me for an instant. Fortunately, South Ocean Boulevard in Palm Beach is pretty smooth, and for that, we gotta commend the hardworking chain gangs from Florida State Prison that the government uses to keep the Gold Coast pothole-free. Good work, guys, and I want you to know that Bud and the whole film crew signed the petition to make the town give you more than one six-ounce bottle of water for every eight hours you work in the blazing sun.

Odd where your mind goes at a time like this, but the way Mel has me clutched in his jaws recalls a distant memory of my mother carrying me around when I was a tiny pup. In some ways, none of us is ever really that far from our childhood, are we?

Except maybe for George Will. There's a man who seems like he's never actually been a child. His first sentence as a baby was probably, "Tell me more about Tocqueville." If he had Play-Doh, little George likely constructed a scale model of the Acropolis, with tiny Play-Doh figures of Socrates and Plato challenging Aristotle about his views on the function of politics.

The trip with Big Mel is uneventful until the flatbed stops at the corner of Peruvian Avenue and County Road, in the middle of swanky downtown Palm Beach. The Bentley is quickly unloaded. Big Mel's self-driving system goes into reverse, and he backs off the flatbed onto the road when the driver is getting back into the truck.

Across the street I see the striped awnings of BrickTop's restaurant, where Bud had parted with so much time and money during our stay. A few people are lounging on the patio. They start screaming that an alligator's on the loose and killing a dog. A couple of conscientious Floridians spring into action and fire their handguns at Mel, but, like before, they're off by about ten feet and only shatter the window of the post office behind us.

Big Mel seems spooked by the sound of gunfire. He scampers across the street, lumbers through a little park, and comes to a small area behind some shops and restaurants. His navigation system steers him toward the light coming from an open door. It happens to be Ta-boo, the restaurant where Bud took Brenda to celebrate their new all-time-high SexBit scores on a day she was back here from Lauderdale.

Mel strolls through the back door of Ta-boo and navigates around the tables in the empty rear dining room. I spot several women and a couple of men at the bar who're deep into their lush lives. When they notice us, a couple of them hoist themselves on top of the bar; others scramble to run for their lives. One really drunk old guy in a tan blazer and pink pants tries to feed Big Mel a half-eaten piece of avocado toast.

Outside, in the bright afternoon sun on pricey Worth Avenue, Big Mel turns right and ambles along the sidewalk past some really fine stores. I spot three thin, well-dressed blonde ladies walking toward us with their heads buried in their phones.

They finally eye Big Mel directly in front of them, burst into high-pitched screeches, and charge into oncoming traffic. The screaming must have affected his self-driving system the way an approaching ambulance warns a car, so Big Mel swerves to the right and runs down a long entrance pathway with a colonnade leading to the exclusive restaurant Le Bilboquet.

Derek, the maître d', is tapping away on his computer, and without looking up asks, "Reservation?"

Big Mel slowly takes three steps forward. I hear his system shutting down. The battery light clicks off. His jaws open. I tumble onto the floor.

"Spike! Spike! Spike the Wonder Dog, welcome to our party!"

It's the bandleader Bob Merrill, who's at a big table with his friends celebrating the radio station's anniversary. Bob drags over a chair so I can join their table. Everybody piles a little food on a plate for me. Bob says, "Now Spike, I know from reading your book you drink Bloody Bull shots, so I've ordered one for you."

"Mighty nice of you," I'm thinkin'. "I can use a drink."

I have a couple of gulps of my Bloody Bull shot, feel the buzz, and pause to be grateful—surviving the jaws of Big Mel, making the *Florida Man* movie, and looking forward to returning to my beloved orange doghouse, ending things with Daisy, seeing the results of the makeover on Shoshana, playing with Oswald, and finding out if the effects of The Old Swede's OD of Viagra Plus ever wore off so he could get outta the hospital, or at least put on his pants.

After a while (technically, two Bloody Bull shots later), Bud, Mr. Messasalma, Christie Leigh, Tim, Lucie, Jim, and Kate track us down, and we party the evening away.

At one point Mr. Messasalma lifts the cover off Big Mel's control compartment to make some adjustments and recharge him. I have a look at the inner workings, which are bristling with more wires, antennas, cameras, sensors, titanium fittings, and probing devices than the Mars *Perseverance* rover.

Just before it's time to go, Bob sits down at the piano and plays "Some Other Time," the classic song from *On the Town*. Its lyrics are about people sadly saying goodbye after a wonderful short adventure together. Bud gets up and sings it. The song ends with a part about how everyone's time together is all gone, but maybe, hopefully, they'll all catch up "some other time."

I could swear I see a tear in Big Mel's eye.

HERBIE

When we get back to our room that night, it's strangely quiet. It hits us at the same time—Bud and I look at each other and realize Herbie is missing.

"Spike, I'm sorry," Bud says. "I swear I put him in his cage before we left this morning. This is terrible."

My heart is pounding. Bud gets frantic. He calls the front desk hoping that Herbie somehow has been flying around the hallways and the desk knows where he is.

The housekeeper has no recollection of him makin' any noise like he usually does when she's in the room. "It was kind of a relief," she says. "Normally the parrot's telling me I look like I eat too many tacos. But it generally only takes me three minutes to reset the Roomba to do the cleaning, so maybe your parrot was sleeping."

Herbie loves Palm Beach. "This is Herbie country," he'd cackle. We had plenty of happy moments with Bud on the little beach on the Intracoastal behind the hotel. He'd be out there flyin' and swoopin' all over the place, sometimes makin' friends with other birds, sometimes cackling insults at people on boats passing by, but always immediately comin' back and landing on my head when we were set to return to the room.

I never figured he'd bolt without tellin' me his plans. Maybe he somehow got out of the room to have a breedin' session with another parrot. He was embarrassed about still bein' a virgin. Even if he did somehow sneak out to have a hookup, he would've made it back. He knew we were leaving. While Bud was cleaning his cage for the trip home, Herbie was squawking that he wanted "a first-class seat, not steerage like last time."

Bud changes our flight reservation so we can mount a search. He calls the fire department, which really doesn't do much for you in tropical climates when you report a missing parrot, even when you tell them the bird has had significant TV exposure.

We put "lost parrot" notices on trees all over the place, offering a five-hundred-dollar reward. We get a call from a guy over in Lake Worth who says he found him perched on a bench, and he'll head over with him to collect the reward.

Suddenly the world is right again. Except the parrot isn't Herbie. The guy went to a bird store, bought a parrot for eighty-nine bucks, and used cheap makeup on its face tryin' to match the picture of Herbie.

After two days, Bud says, "He's gone, Spike. He's gone. We have to go home now."

That's it. I have to adjust—no more Herbie. No more best pal. He'll never know that I was able to break up with Daisy like he said I should. He'll never get to go to the premiere of *Florida Man*. I vow to think of him every morning while I'm takin' my leak, and just hope my little pal is OK, and safe and happy somewhere.

On the flight home to North Carolina the next morning, I'm sad thinkin' about Herbie's empty cage down with the luggage. I'm takin' deep breaths to help myself relax, and I spread out in my aisle seat in Economy Plus. Bud is next to me having fun reading about Big Mel's caper in the Palm Beach Post.

Florida's most famous motorized mechanical alligator, Big Mel, terrified downtown Palm Beach this week as he strolled through Taboo restaurant and along Worth Avenue with Spike the Wonder Dog from the *Florida Man* film locked in his jaws.

Worth Avenue's sidewalk was littered with Manolo Blahnik shoes discarded by women who ran for their lives, believing that the seventeen-foot Big Mel was a real gator. At Taboo, a moment before they scattered, some alarmed patrons at the bar reported hearing Winston Churchill's voice coming from the dog urging them to "keep calm and carry on."

The creature's new electric motor ran out of battery life just as he and the Wonder Dog appeared to be trying for a hard-to-get reservation at Le Bilboquet. Big Mel's creator, Mario Messasalma, was embarrassed by the incident, explaining that Mel snatched Spike the Wonder Dog after something accidentally activated his "Grab and Go" setting, which is generally only used when Mel is sent to pick up a pizza.

Although Bud is chuckling at the *Post* writeup, I can tell he's a little nervous about getting back to High Point and the show and all that we have going on; so he isn't in the best of moods when the flight attendant comes over and says, "Excuse me, sir, the man and woman across the aisle from you two said they are unsettled at the sight of your dog's testicles."

"Testicle touchiness"—this is a new one for me. People are always urging Bud to "get Spike fixed!" Animal Control in High Point even offered to neuter me live on our show as a public service—not an appealing demo on an early morning show, particularly for viewers munching away on hard-boiled eggs.

Bud leans over me, looks at them, and says, "Unsettled?"

"Yes," the man across the aisle complains. "We couldn't help noticing the big white balls on your dog there. They unsettled us."

"Unsettled?" Bud asks. "How unsettled are you? Like on a one-to-ten scale, with one being your fifteen-year-old daughter is secretly dating Matt Gaetz, and ten being your Wi-Fi's down for an hour, how unsettled are you?"

"Sir," the attendant says to Bud, "there is no need to start trouble."

"We just feel unsettled," the woman chimes in, as she gives me a disgusting look. "That's all I can say. Does he have pants?"

"No pants, sorry," Bud tells her. "The tailor always has a problem measuring his inseam."

At this point, I decide I gotta try to raise their "unsettled" status to "flat-out alarmed," so I slowly roll over on my back, offering an unobstructed view of the glory of my mature self. I feign sleeping by making soft yelping noises, like I'm having a pleasant dream of running across a sunny field with my balls gently swinging from side to side.

"Oh my God, not that!" they shriek. "A penis!"

I hit the Eastwood sensor on my collar. "Go ahead, make my day."

"What? What? Is your dog threatening us?" the man yells.

"Attendant, protect us!" the woman calls.

Bud looks at both of them and says, with clarity and precision, "Ah, now that's a more apparent example of being unsettled. OK, Spike. One, two, three—showtime."

I snap into the upright sitting position I always use when Bud introduces me at the top of our show.

"Thank God," the woman mutters. "Please schedule an emergency neutering as soon as you can make a call."

"Good work, Spike," Bud whispers to me. "Now let's get home."

An hour later, walking through the terminal of the Piedmont Triad International Airport, Bud stops to check a CNBC monitor to see what the stock market's doing, only to learn that a trio of his childhood favorites, the iconic cartoon characters the Three Little Pigs, are in trouble.

Scott Wapner is reporting, "Today, in a sure loss of fourth-quarter revenue, Disney Plus responded to the seventy-four-million-dollar class-action suit against the company initiated by seventy-four parents of five hundred and twenty-two obese triplets. Disney agreed to cancel its popular new series, *Kitchen Capers with the Three Little Pigs*, effective immediately. A spokeswoman stated, 'We fully sympathize and apologize to the parents of the overweight triplets who've been bullied at school because of their resemblance to the Three Little Pigs. We will be retooling the program, and future shows will feature beloved Disney characters Chip and Dale as vegan chipmunks.'"

I pray my favorite Disney character, Donald Duck, doesn't get canceled for never wearing pants, but I can't focus on this sudden career setback for the Three Little Pigs. I only got three things on my mind: get home, get back to work, and end it for good with Daisy.

CHAPTER ELEVEN

BACK ON THE BLOCK

Does love's young dream ever come true?

You know the facts. Fools rush in, right? It was love at first sight with Daisy when I saw her as a puppy.

I never thought we'd be together, 'cause right after I met her, I moved to NYC and she stayed in North Carolina with Buffy. When I made it back down South with Bud a year later, it seemed like love's young dream was gonna come true. But when I actually got to know her, it was bad. No peace, no fun, just constant demands on me to pay attention to her—and oh yeah, no love.

Not sure why, but I couldn't end it, couldn't pull the plug. Maybe I was still in love with the idea of being in love. Did I hear someone singing that falling in love with love is like falling for make-believe?

Now I'm over at Buffy's walking slowly toward Daisy's doghouse, planning to break up.

She wants to hear all about my trip. This is unexpected, 'cause generally when I see her, the conversation is focused entirely either on her or on what's wrong with me.

Now I'm being told she missed me, she's proud of me, and she's had a profound psychological awakening because of something she learned on TV. Whose program? What else? The new Dr. Phil weekend show, *For Dogs Only*, sponsored by Phil Chow.

During the "Canine Cupid" segment, a dog psychologist was explaining how insecurity from early puppyhood could ruin a relationship. And Daisy says that's when it hit her: she had been the runt of the litter, and nobody had paid her much attention; she'd always been trying to replace what was missing.

Honestly, I had major insights like that doing 'shrooms with Mr. Boggs, and even after being severely electrocuted, and I'm sure it was a lot more fun than watching that show.

Well, I let her know I've had an insight, too: the truth will set me free, and the truth is, we can't stand each other and we should call it quits. I'm prepared to see a flood of tears—but no, now she wants to work on it together.

Work on it? Isn't that just going to prolong the agony for me? My head is saying, "Go now while the going's easy, not after months of working on it," which likely would mean blocking out valuable weekend time to watch *For Dogs Only*.

"I don't know," I tell her, which isn't exactly the truth, 'cause a lot of times when you say you don't know, you do know, right?

"I think we should work on it," she urges.

If I want to do a little tap dancing here, like a human might, I could respond that I'll think about it, which really means, "The answer is no, but I don't have the guts to tell you right now."

"Come here, Spike," Bud yells. "Lombardo called, and we gotta get to the station as soon as possible.

"Please don't disappoint me, Spike," Daisy says. "You were always my prince."

I was your prince? But why were you demanding that your prince throw away his beloved orange doghouse and get a junior one-bedroom doghouse to impress your friends? By the way, what the hell is a junior one-bedroom doghouse anyway?

"Spike! Come! Say goodbye to Daisy," Bud yells.

"I gotta go. The best I can say is, let's just try to get to know each other, but see if this Dr. Phil guy makes doghouse calls."

"You're funny, Spike."

Wow, she just handed me a second compliment in less than two minutes— a record.

"Then the pilot light's still on? There's a chance?" Daisy asks.

Maybe it's just self-deception—never an ally in solving relationship problems—but I say yes and then hedge, "The pilot light might still be on."

BIG PLANS FROM "BIG WOODY"

"You're not going to believe this," Lombardo says. "Oh, and by the way, Bud, please tell that dog to avoid any giant mechanical reptiles for the duration of his contract here at the station."

"We're glad to be back," Bud says. "A lot to do."

"A lot? Oh really? Maybe you dimly recall that before that dog became a movie star, we were attempting to try to buy the station from Sol "The Old Swede" Silverman. Well, now there's a new wrinkle."

"Three guesses," Bud says. "One, Shoshana wants in. Two, Sol 'The Old—"

"Would that it were that simple," Lombardo interrupts. "Big Randy Woody's now in the picture."

I'm lookin' forward to maybe meeting Big Woody when I'm in New York on the World Animal Awards show with him and the strippers. The strippers have described Woody as an enigmatic character, so I'm figurin' maybe he's a Howard Hughes type, with long fingernails good for scratchin' my head.

"Woody hit it huge," Lombardo explains, "like millions and millions huge, on crypto. After the fire, he was so pissed at his insurance company for spending hundreds of thousands of dollars a day on TV commercials featuring an emu but not wanting to pay him for all the damage at his strip joint, that he decided to roll the dice—take all the cash he got paid under the table while playing college ball and buy cryptocurrency on a tip he got from Bambi the stripper that—"

"She had the operation then," Bud points out.

"What?"

"Yeah, boss, she used to be Cherry but said she'd change her name to Bambi after her implant operation," Bud explains.

I gotta give Bud credit. I totally forgot Cherry said that, but he seems to have amazing recall about some subjects.

"Bud," Lombardo barks, "try to spend more brain cells retaining information for your interviews on the show, and less time recalling trivial facts about certain elective medical procedures."

"Got it, but I thought Cherry was a better name," Bud says, to egg Lombardo on.

"Shut up! Well, actually, yeah, Cherry probably *is* a better name for a stripper…. Anyway," the boss continues, "the headline here is, Big Woody saw the nationwide economic possibilities in sex tourism, because you, Bud, chose to drive naked women through the parade and I was compelled to reveal that toplessness is completely legal in that part of town."

"How could I forget?" Bud says.

"You'll wish you could," he continues. "So Big Woody wants to buy the station, have WGHP converted into WT&A, featuring the nation's first completely NC-17-rated twenty-four-hours-a-day smolderingly sexy programming, and tie it in with his creation of a new national chain of Throbbing Member massage joints, and he wants to have a monthly Release for Peace Day at the parlors."

"Phallic service centers? You're jerking my chain," Bud quips.

"I hope you said that on purpose, Bud, 'cause if not, I'm gonna rip your face off," Lombardo snarls through a laugh.

"Can he do all that? I mean, is that legal?"

"Bud, Big Woody has enough money to bribe all nine of the Supreme Court justices into retirement and replace them with Lil' Kim, Andrew Weiner, Stormy Daniels, George Santos, and five holograms of Herschel Walker if he wants to. Furthermore, Big Woody is a libertarian who believes sex work should be legal, and—"

"We're in agreement there," Bud adds.

"Yes, right, agreed. Well, not to go into the minute details now, but when the White House was frantic to rush through legislation preventing mandatory wearing of masks—"

Bud interrupts, "The thing that led to Representative MacQueen tucking the topless clause into the legislation in her district here, and—"

"Yes, of course you remember that, Bud, because it's about strippers, and when Big Woody learned what MacQueen did, he found out that low-level politicians all over the country who were closet libertarians also took advantage of the fact that no one was reading the clauses in the legislation, so the bottom line is, there are now about thirty districts in the US where sex work is legal—it will not be seen as prostitution. The women and the men working at sex parlors will be seen as medical workers satisfying a health need."

I watch as Bud contemplates his own "health needs." It's been nearly a week without Brenda, who's been texting him, shall we say, "saucy" pictures of herself to get his need level as needy as possible for when she returns from Florida. The so-called underboob has been her photo theme for the week.

"Big Woody's Throbbing Member massage spas everywhere?" Bud asks.

"Yes," Lombardo says, "and they'll look like those clean and cheerful walk-in urgent care facilities, not some mysterious massage parlor storefront with a flashing red sign and a few cheap-looking neon lotus petals to suggest exotic faraway places even though you're in a generic strip mall."

"But back to the sale. Only The Old Swede can sell the station, correct?" Bud asks.

"Bud, Big Woody can send Bambi, Candy, Jade, Crystal, Amber—an entire squadron of oiled-up babes—over to The Old Swede's place, and the old man would likely pay Woody to take the station in exchange for a couple of free feels."

"Whadda we do?" Bud asks.

"When you and that dog appear on the World Animal Awards show, we'll figure what you'll say when you talk to Woody, and meanwhile, we're shooting the big reunion with Shoshana and The Old Swede tomorrow. Let's see what happens, and make sure you bring that dog; his brother Oswald will be there. Shoshana's happy with him, but the dog appears completely demented on camera. He mostly stares blankly into the monitor," Lombardo informs Bud.

If only I could bark in Morse code to Lombardo that Oswald is looking for Gary Busey in the monitor, and that he needs a steady diet of Busey to maintain mental balance. Which, even though he's my brother, I admit is a bit unusual. But anyway, wow! Tomorrow I'll see Oswald for the first time since Bud lifted me out of the big box and took me with him to start our adventures together.

"OK," Lombardo says, "Buffy's on Zoom now to read the research she's pulled together on Big Woody, so we'll get a—'scuse the expression—grasp on the driving force behind the Throbbing Member men's spas and his TV ideas."

"Hello, Buffy," Bud says.

I bark.

"Hi, Bud. Hi, boss. Hi, Spike. Oh, Spike, is that a mechanical alligator tooth mark on your head, or are you just happy to see me?" she asks.

"No, the tooth marks are on his body," Bud explains. "The head is still healing from bashing in the door at Big Woody's, and yes, he's happy to see you—notice the tail."

"Can we get to the point, rather than discussing that dog's combat injuries?" Lombardo asks.

While they're jabberin' on, I'm imagining some of the small-print disclaimers on the ads for Big Woody's Throbbing Member spas, like:

> Do not use spa services if your body is not strong enough for eruptive convulsions. Do not drive into the spa's parking lot if you're happily married and prone to guilt. Do not use spa services if you're too shy to have an intimate experience with total stranger in a less-than-soundproof room serenaded by Yanni music...

"OK, guys," Buffy says. "This is not a particularly happy background story I have for you on Randy Woody, so, not to get morose, I'm going to read it like I'm doing a perky audition for *Entertainment Tonight*."

"Go," Lombardo orders.

"Woody's parents were only eighteen years old when baby Randolph was born," she reads with forced glee. "They were part of a strict evangelical community in Georgia that strove for a purity culture and preached that women's bodies were the source of evil temptation. Men were commanded to have nothing in the house to tempt them sexually, with the exception, of course, of their drably clothed wife..."

"Perk it up way more," Lombardo directs. "You're channeling a mildly sedated Margaret Brennan reporting on the NXIVM sex cult."

"OK, perkin' up more. And so, get this: the young couple naively name their son Randolph, in honor of their favorite star of TCM cowboy movies, Randolph Scott, not realizing they'd be horrified to know Randolph Scott was gay and had once dated Cary Grant. Nor were they aware that the name Randy can mean 'sexually desirous' and that 'woody' has a double meaning as 'an erection.'"

"Buffy," Lombardo says, "I think your perky reading plateaued at Deborah Norville. There's still way more bubbly and overwrought cheerfulness out there, so as a last resort, break out your dimples and reach for a wildly excited Mario Lopez for the rest of this."

"OK, brilliant direction," she says. "You should be in television, so…get this: apparently, Woody's fascination with naked breasts can be traced to the fact that his mother breastfed him into advanced childhood, meaning he had to come home from school for lunch. Randy was always the tallest among his peers, and it wasn't long before he acquired the nickname "Big Randy Woody," which appears to have been a source of humiliation for him, particularly when heckled by Bible-toting classmates during sermons on virgin worship at vesper services."

"No kidding," Lombardo says.

"Randolph's mother adhered to the strictest of the strict church rules to the extent that a few times a year, she would turn their home inside out searching for evidence that her husband was lusting for evil by having sexually arousing material hidden somewhere in the home.

"Randolph's father's blasphemy was discovered when his wife noticed a strange gleam coming from the eyes of the huge moose head hanging over the family's fireplace. With a chainsaw, a ladder, and help from two husky neighborhood women, she removed the head from its mounting and found a March 1992 *Playboy* magazine centerfold of Anna Nicole Smith lodged in the moose's snout."

"Ingenious," Lombardo says. "I was figuring maybe he'd hide something under his ammo and grenades."

"Their pastor ordered the couple into intense Christian sexuality indoctrination, hoping that during the ten minutes each month they were permitted to have intimacy, they'd get in the sack and have an authentic 'come to Jesus' moment.

"The training didn't work, primarily because the twenty-four hours a day of lute music employed as part of the reprogramming didn't have the desired effect of squashing the husband's raging libido. Facing the shame of it all, the mother fled with young Randy and hastily relocated to an even more pious evangelical community sixty miles away—you'll like this, Spike—so strict that the family dog had to be baptized. Research is unclear, but the Joel Osteen Canine Christian Ministry may have dunked young Randy's bewildered pet for a not-insignificant fee, thus anointing him a certified Christian Tick Hound.

"For days, Randy was enraged that his mother had destroyed the Anna Nicole Smith centerfold before he could get a good look. The father worked day and night painstakingly Scotch-taping the shredded nude photograph together. Once that was completed, he abducted his son and moved to North Carolina. Thus began Big Randy Woody's transition from a horny teenager with a tree house as his personal masturbation sanctuary to a strip club operator and outspoken libertarian libertine."

I gotta figure that if Woody becomes a rock star of the exotic services industry like I predict he will, that little tree house will be visited like Graceland.

"And the only other things we know," Buffy says, wrapping it up, "are that he was a major basketball star at Duke, then joined the Marines, became a first lieutenant, and saw some seriously bad action in Afghanistan and Iraq, which he never discusses."

"OK, good job as usual, Buffy," Lombardo says. "Don't be late to The Old Swede's tomorrow, Bud. Somehow he's taken a liking to you and that dog. Oh, and by the way, some fan named Mel in West Palm Beach has sent that dog a case of frozen alligator meat."

RAMPAGE AT THE OLD SWEDE'S

The Old Swede is happy to see us, chatting away about his hospital stay while restless for filming to start so he can finally see his daughter and attempt to restore some kind of relationship with her. "Will she take on the job of running the station? I hope so," he mutters.

He's outfitted in his blue blazer with the gold buttons. Under his pleated 1940s-style tan slacks belted high above the waist, he's wearing the same incontinence designer underwear Jeff Bezos and his guests employ on trips to space. The Old Swede has taken care to have the long-haired blond rug on his head dry-cleaned, and the shag carpet on his floor looks spotless as well.

"Guys," he says, "sorry about the last time. I musta gone a touch overboard with dosage from the V Plus watch. I went kicking and screaming to the hospital. Turned out to be no big deal; in fact, I had fun askin' the nurses to help me by pleading that a boner like mine was a terrible thing to waste. On the third straight day of my tumescence, I heard them say they were flying in a woman named Lola from Las Vegas who was a specialist in ending erections. 'Finally,' I say to myself, 'Lola's going to give me exactly what I need.'"

Nurse Ruth starts with the "here we go again" eye rolls to me.

"And what happened?" Bud wonders.

"Lola turned out to be a goddammed doctor. She gave me five different pills and a pamphlet to use in the future, titled *The Bluffer's Guide to Erections*. Then she yanked the sheet offa me, took a 'before' picture of the rigid glory of my condition, and a little later she snapped an 'after' picture. She told me that very soon I'd be in every urology textbook in the world. This, plus my toupee and a couple of accounting awards, will be the proud legacy I'll be leaving my descendants."

"Have you been in touch with—" Lombardo starts to ask.

"Yeah, I sent Dr. Kahill a dozen of those new seamless nylon stockings, and I've been calling," he answers. "Lovely woman, bit of a name-dropper. She always brings up Amal, George's wife, and how much she loves her. I just listen. You know, Kahill's cute, but she's no Pelosi physically. Who could be? What a dame!" He leers, trying to channel some Rat Pack cred.

I'm thinkin' that from what I see of her on TV, the esteemed former House Speaker is impressive in the way she gingerly minces through the marble halls of the Capitol in those ultrahigh heels and hardly ever topples over.

The Old Swede continues, "I wrote to her office from the hospital for an autographed Pelosi photo. All I get is a stupid headshot stamped, 'Get well, Nancy, LOL, xo, xo,' with a smiley face and a heart. Why didn't someone on her staff send me a picture of her in a bathing suit like I asked? You know, guys, there have to be shots of Pelosi in a string bikini out there somewhere in the world."

"Try the Freedom of Information Act to get them released," Bud jokes.

"Yeah, good idea, young man," he says. "At least her assistant could have included a shot of her wearing one of those pantsuits with the tight jackets buttoned right under her bulging—"

"And I think we're almost ready to go," Bud quickly interrupts.

"Nancy," The Old Swede says, sighing longingly. He takes a gulp of his icy martini and watches the crew finish setting up for his long-awaited reunion with his daughter.

Nurse Ruth corners Lombardo and tells him she'd like to get paid for her appearances, and flashes an expired Actors' Equity card she got for her work playing the blonde bimbo Ulla in a 2003 regional production of *The Producers* with Lee Roy Reams and Tony Danza.

"Good part, and good for you," Lombardo says graciously. "But first, let's just see how this goes."

Even though we're shooting digital, Mack yells, "Roll tape," the instant he spots Shoshana's new black Porsche Panamera pulling up in front.

I've got a knot in my stomach. Oswald's been out of control with Shoshana. At one point, I heard she might be considering zapping him with a transcranial magnet. I'm worried. He's coming with Shoshana, so the viewers can meet the dog The Old Swede kindly bought her to help heal the rift over taking away her childhood puppy. Good production idea, but ya got one potential problem. Nobody, not even Bud, has taken into consideration that my highly excitable brother hasn't seen me since we were eight weeks old. Maybe first, Oswald and I should have a little "meet, greet, and go" reunion by the fireplug outside.

Sol "The Old Swede" Silverman stands up, and in they come.

The Amex black card he gave Shoshana, demanding that it was strictly for emergency use, has been generously employed. Cosmetic surgery to make her look like Carole King is healing perfectly. Her pink silk Pucci dress and matching Manolo Blahnik Lurum crystal-embellished cocktail mules are sizzling on the monitor. The only slight flaw in her ensemble appears to be Oswald's chew marks on her eleven-thousand-dollar dyed-pink calfskin Birkin bag.

Unfortunately, I can't say the same about Oswald, 'cause for a muscle-bound English Bull Terrier like him, he's a little overdressed—decked out in your basic black seven-hundred-dollar Versace collar and leash with matching Versace gold-embroidered Barocco dog vest. Dangling from the vest on a red-and-white ribbon is something Shoshana really splurged on with her dad's money—the rare solid-gold medal awarded to Winston Churchill's bulldog Dodo for service in World War I. Oswald's annoyed by it and is stretching his neck trying to rip the medal offa the vest.

"Dad, oh my God, there you are!" Shoshana shrieks from across the living room. "Oh, Dad, finally! Here we are!"

"My lovely daughter Shoshana, how I've missed you," he says, doddering toward her at what for him must feel like warp speed.

"And you, look at you," he says. "How wonderful, but strangely different, you look now. Who's that singer Dr. Parker made you resemble? Is it…Ben E. King, who sang 'Stand by Your Man'?"

"Ha, ha. No, it's Carole, Dad. Carole—"

Oswald spots me. He charges forward, jerking Shoshana, who's holding his leash. The left heel of her delicate shoe catches the leg of a chair and cracks. She spins and crashes to the floor.

"Aaagh!" she cries. "My ankle!"

Mack whispers to Lombardo, "Cut?"

"Keep rolling," he signals.

Oswald hurries toward me, stopping briefly to peer into a monitor, hoping against hope to catch a glance of Gary Busey. No luck, so he leaps away, accidentally smacking his rock-like head into The Old Swede's kneecap.

The Old Swede loses his balance, yells, "Goddamn ugly dog," and grabs a light stand by one of the cameras. He can't stabilize himself and twists headfirst into a swan dive toward the glass coffee table. Nurse Ruth is able to catch him, and lowers him gently to the floor.

"My leg," he moans.

Ruth starts to rub the knee and glances toward Lombardo. "Payday?"

"Affirmative," Lombardo mouths back.

Oswald comes face-to-face with me and starts hopping up and down.

"Calm yourself. You'll get in trouble," I indicate.

He jumps higher.

I let him know that Dad would not like this. But the thought of Dad only launches him into booming nonstop barking.

The Old Swede is crawling toward Shoshana, as she inches her way across the gleaming hardwood floor toward him.

"That dog's crazy, Shoshana," The Old Swede yells over the barking. "Ruth, get him out of here. Take that dog to the farm, where he can live out his life and be happy."

I realize this is not good, 'cause studies reveal that when a parent tells a kid that their dog's a problem and it's being "sent to a farm to be happy," 92 percent of the time the dog is headed straight downtown to be gassed. The other 8 percent of the time, the dog ends up in another state getting thrown over a fence and landing in a backyard behind the darkened house of an unsuspecting stranger.

"You're not sending Oswald to a farm, like you did with my Moby and Mom's two parakeets," she says, still slithering toward him. "Sure, he's a little rambunctious, but I love Oswald, and he's mine and I'm keeping him. By the way, Dad, where is that farm? I just realized you never knew anyone who had a farm, and why would parakeets be happier on a farm?"

"OK, sure, OK, keep the stupid thing," he says, inching closer. "Now I'm coming to kiss you."

"I want to hug you," she tells him.

Mack whispers to Bud, "Ya want to scrap this and start all over?"

"Are you nuts?" Bud whispers. "Two people actually so desperate to see each other that they're crawling across the floor in agonizing pain is a lot more compelling than all those dimwits on the beach in the opening credits of *Love Island* running toward each other in slow-mo, tryin' to figure out who's gonna bang who in the new season."

"But…," Mack says, pointing to Oswald.

"Spike, do something about that barking," Bud commands softly. "Stop him."

I can't stop him. Once he starts woofing like this, no one can. When we were puppies, Mrs. Erdrick shut off the TV during the series *Gary Busey: Pet Judge*. Oswald was so upset that he barked all night, and the neighbors called the police on him. By the way, if you haven't seen *Gary Busey: Pet Judge*, it's like the *Judge Judy* for animal problems with Gary in the Judy role. In the unlikely event that it's still available on demand when this book is published, be sure to check it out. As you're already imagining, it's a true cultural milestone.

"Last week, I discovered by accident that Oswald calmed down listening to the Buddy Holly music they were playing on Sirius. Try that," Shoshana tells us.

"Siri, play Buddy and the Crickets," Nurse Ruth instructs.

"I love Greco," The Old Swede says, confusing everyone but Lombardo, whose parents knew the singer Buddy Greco.

Oswald hears the first notes of "Maybe Baby," shuts up, and stares off into space.

The Old Swede and Shoshana reach each other and are lying on the floor holding hands.

"You're beautiful," he says.

"No, Dad. No, you," she says quietly. "You, for a ninety-six-year-old man...look at you."

"Shh," he whispers. "I'm trying to pass for at least a hundred and two these days. They say once you reach a hundred, the eighty-five-year-old babes flock around you like it's 1962 and you're French movie star Alain Delon in a tiny blue bathing suit, glistening in the sun on the beach in Saint-Tropez."

"And your hair, Dad, it's perfect. Is that the official Andre Agassi mullet wig they sell on Amazon Prime?" (Just a note here, folks, in case you think we're making stuff up: search for "Andre Agassi wig" on Amazon, order it, and see what comes in the box.)

"Never let anyone tell you this isn't the actual hair of Sol 'The Old Swede' Silverman," he says. "But, at least temporarily, let's forget about my appearance if possible and focus on each other. I've missed you."

"Thank you, Dad. I've missed you and I love you."

"I love you," he says, "even in spite of the fact that it's cost me seven hundred and six thousand dollars in goods and services to get you back. By the way, the lifetime supply of quick-on-and-off prosthetic Carole King noses and the wig that you had Lucas Films' special effects makeup artists create for you were twenty-two thousand and change alone. But still, I love you, and here we are."

"I'll pay you back for it with the money I make with my new Carole King act."

"I want nothing from you but your love, Shoshana."

"Dad, I think we should go to temple to sanctify our reunion and have a rabbi bless our restored love as father and daughter," she suggests.

"Sure, temple's free. Why not? Even though I haven't been inside one since 1960 in the Marais district in Paris, when I sat in the Synagogue de la rue Pavée for three hours every day, hoping to pick up a grieving older widow and lure her back to the youth hostel for a quickie."

Shoshana asks her dad if he'll come hear her sing in a couple of days when she'll be decked out in her full Carole King ensemble at the reunion with her former lookalike troupe in the woods. He begs off, saying he's pretty certain he'll be having a bad back that afternoon and will need an emergency erotic massage.

She sighs a "Dad will be Dad" sigh and smiles weakly at him.

Bud and Lombardo signal that the shoot's over. Oswald curls up while Buddy's singing "It Doesn't Matter Anymore."

As we're packing up to go, Nurse Ruth passes a note to Lombardo: "It's important I talk to you or Bud confidentially about Mr. Silverman. I'll call this week."

MEANWHILE, BACK IN THE WOODS

Bravo's done quite the job upgrading the production values of the lookalike show's campsite to make it conform to the slick style demanded these days for reality TV.

The encampment, which originally resembled a bombed-out village in the Mekong Delta circa 1968 now looks like a three-thousand-bucks-a-night Four Seasons Safari Lodge complex in Tanzania. The show is largely scripted. A local dentist is working as fast as he can to replace the missing teeth of the original cast. Other than the Hillary impersonator, who is still toking frantically on her worn pipe, all the stars have been weaned off the ice and are happily getting as high as possible on merchandise from the show's latest embedded sponsor—Bill Maher's pot product, New Rules.

Maher appeared on an episode but claimed he was someone impersonating Bill Maher to explain that the unique cannabis strain he created was specifically designed to stimulate the brain and help the smoker understand complicated issues more clearly.

"We tested this for eighteen weeks on people who usually read David Brooks' column on Friday morning in the *New York Times*. Each group read the column three times," he explained. "The control group that did not smoke the New Rules pot could not, as usual, come close to comprehending what Brooks was talking about, but the users of our New Rules marijuana thought they might be able to have a vague idea of what he was getting at if they could read it one more time while looking up several strange words in the dictionary."

There have been a couple of additions to the cast, including a ghost of Anthony Bourdain character as the cook. The guy looks cranky enough to be Bourdain. Unfortunately, his only culinary experience was as a busboy at Chickie's & Pete's restaurant in Wildwood, New Jersey. Most important, a

Steve Harvey impersonator now creates storyline conflict with Tom Cruise as Moses, over which one of them is the true on-camera spokesperson for the tribe.

I'm waiting a little off the set with Bud, Shoshana, and Oswald, who appears mildly sedated. I'm in the cast, 'cause Andy Cohen really wants the original dog-worship idea to be a central aspect of the plot. He loves that I walked into their camp looking for Shoshana, and in their spaced-out state they thought I was the Great White Dog God who would bring them fame; which, in fact, Bud and I did—at least in their minds. To play off the canine-idolatry point in the narrative, Bravo has hired a Kanye West character whose only role on the series is to prepare a new convoluted two-hour sermon about dogs for a Sunday service each week that no one will attend.

There's a gleaming new miniature electric chariot the Tom Cruise looka-like can use to channel more Charlton Heston-as-Moses schtick. The big hit on the last episode was the touching duet sung by the Bruce and Caitlyn characters. Arm in arm, they offered alluring harmonies on a medley that included "The Man That Got Away," "Oh! Look at Me Now," and "I Get Along Without You Very Well."

Today, the Bravo people had run through two rehearsals. Everyone nailed their lines, all was set, the director yelled, "Three, two, one..."

Carrying his small plastic scepter and sporting a new long white beard from the David Letterman Signature Beard Collection (available wherever fine beards are sold), Tom Cruise as Moses mounts the stage.

"Behold! Behold with all your beholding powers! Today, the two newest impersonators who'll join our wandering tribe of celebrity clones will be delivered unto us as a gift from the all-powerful gods of reality show casting," he announces solemnly.

"Ohhhh...I bet it's Jay Pharoah!" a voice calls out.

"You're shot down on that, oh dynamic diva sort-of-still-hippie-look-ing Cher with the early-1970s-era Cher face, not the ever-changing one we started to see in *Moonstruck*. We must wait, and wait we will, until the Great White Dog God reveals our fate unto us," Tom Cruise as Moses says.

The Steve Harvey character storms the stage.

"Not so fast, miniature Moses," he says. "Hand me the microphone."

"When you pry it from my cold, dead hand," Tom Cruise as Moses retorts.

"Let us not have a family feud. Verily, I say unto you that you're a two-inch-shorter version of the already tiny Tom Cruise. Hand me the mic, please."

Tom Cruise as Moses fires back, "You imposter Steve Harvey, who cannot talk and smile while showing all teeth like the real Steve Harvey can—may your underwear be plagued by locusts!"

"Let thy people groan, bantam Moses. Survey says: the microphone, please."

"We want Moses! Moses! Moses!" the crowd chants.

"Begone, you snively wretch," Tom Cruise as Moses proclaims, waving his arm, "and while you're begone-ing, may your fake Steve Harvey moustache become a burning bush on your upper lip."

The Harvey impersonator stalks off, and the Bravo team high-five each other over how well the scene played.

"OK, Spike, you're on," Bud says.

All I gotta do is walk forward, be worshipped (believe me, I'll milk that for all it's worth), and play the message in my talking dog collar that Andy Cohen got Al Pacino to record. This will resolve a plot point from last week's show, which featured a gathering in the woods of the heads of the Five Families of Celebrity Tribute Acts: the Vegas family, the Branson family, the Orlando family, the Atlantic City family, and the reclusive Addams family.

The light hits me.

"Lo!" Cruise as Moses proclaims, pointing at me. "Let us all 'lo again,' quickly followed by much beholding again, for the Great White Dog God has returned to reveal our fate. We bid him good tidings. What does the head of the Five Families say? Will the Vegas family take over our territory and play the Gilroy Garlic Festival this year?"

I realize I'm in big trouble. Last night, I didn't feel like working to find the new Pacino voice setting on the collar. So this morning, I went outside to practice cueing Pacino but got overheated chasing the Canadian geese outta our pool, and jumped in for a swim. Now I'm as tense as I ever get, frantically trying to locate Al's voice.

"Pronounce unto us," Tom Cruise as Moses asks again.

Silence—and you know how TV hates a lull. Bud's givin' me the "Let's go, pal, let's go" arm waves.

I hit a button. No Pacino. Big mistake; it's the voice of Mike Tyson.

"I don't understand why people would want to get rid of pigeons. They don't bother no one," Tyson says.

"Ahhh," the lookalikes gasp, pretending to know what the hell that means.

The Bravo people are conferring. I figure they're sayin', "Fire him, but first neuter him on camera in a pagan ceremony that might get a ratings bump."

I try again, but unfortunately, it's more Mike Tyson: "I ain't the same person I was when I bit off that guy's ear."

"Our ears hear you, oh Great White Dog God, but what about our last episode? The Five Families, our fate, may we please know?" Tom Cruise as Moses nervously improvises. "I bid you to speak."

Another search for Pacino…but again with the Tyson: "It's good to know how to read," he says.

Just as the director is about to yell "cut," I locate the Pacino frequency.

I bark three times to let them know this is it.

Pacino speaks: "There are some negotiations being made right now to answer your questions and solve your problems. This year, you'll split the garlic festival with the Atlantic City family. You'll work the cooked-garlic stands; they'll work the raw-garlic stands."

"So it is written, so it shall be done," Moses proclaims.

The lookalikes applaud. I slowly step back into the darkness of the woods, embarrassed and vowing never to be underprepared again.

The Steve Harvey impersonator takes over.

"Thank you, Dog God and miniature Moses. Now, the newest member of our troupe of strolling players, Joe Biden, joins us direct from his zero-gravity sleep chair. Let's make some noise, and pretend you mean it, folks, ha, ha, ha. He's here to prove he's not as dotty as most of the Dems secretly think he is… so…please welcome Joe Biden, the forty-sixth president of the United States."

Over a thunderous version of "Hail to the Chief" recorded by the Roots, the Biden impersonator shuffles onstage, perfectly nailing the stiff, short strides of the president. It's a very hot day, and he's sweating heavily under his blue suit, white shirt, and red tie as he lifts the microphone from its stand and looks around.

"How did all these people get into my room?" he asks, aiming for a laugh with a line from an ancient *Dean Martin Live from Las Vegas* album.

"Ha, ha, and welcome, Mr. President," the fake Steve Harvey says.

The Biden character delivers another one from Dino: "How long have I been on?" he asks.

"Mr. President," Harvey says, "no pun intended, but let's face it—the world agrees, the plastic surgery you've had makes you look days younger than your actual age. And importantly, our newest sponsor, which you're about to announce, is the miracle product you've been using to keep the skin on your face as soft, unlined, and smooth as frozen Lake Michigan would be if it weren't for global warming and people falling through the ice."

"I love Michigan, and we're gonna fish those people out someday. What was the question again, Lee Harvey?"

"Your skin, sir—what do you use?" Steve Harvey asks.

"It's simple. Here's the deal, folks: no need to spend all the money from your child tax credit on costly Botox, or scrub your face with gentle Twenty Mule Team Borax, like my son Hunter does when he's high. That's no malarkey. You get paint on you when you're a struggling artist like Hunter. That's no malarkey either; the poor guy only sells in the low six figures. Hunter takes commissions. Look, here's what happened. He painted a big nude of Kamala, 'cause Mitch said he'd vote for my infrastructure package if he could hang it in his office. The painting turned out great, although Mitch thought it looked too much like a Tina Turner album cover—"

"Er, ah, please, Mr. President," the Harvey impersonator says, following the script, which has him trying to interrupt to get the Biden character back on track, "let's get back to—"

"Thanks, Lee Harvey. I'm sorry, right, back to Hunter. I can get discounts on his paintings for anyone."

"Please, sir, please. Your skin, sir. Your skin care regimen—tell us," Harvey says.

"Oh, sure, thanks for asking. So, here's the secret of my ultrasmooth skin. I use…"

A camera cuts to Caitlyn Jenner with a pad and pen poised to jot down Biden's beauty secrets.

"…Downy Wrinkle Guard. Three times a day for forty-five minutes, I plunge my head into an icy vat of Wrinkle Guard. But don't forget to wear a snorkel. I forgot once and ended up in intensive care at Walter Reed. I use the scented WrinkleGuard to cut my monthly Old Spice aftershave bills, and Putin, who's a hair sniffer like me, told me I smelled like the roses in the garden outside his villa at Mar-a-Lago."

"Thank you, Mr. President. There's a laundry tub of WrinkleGuard waiting for you offstage. Joining us now is our main attraction, a man who's a legend in our business. In the shabby world of tribute acts, lookalikes, and celebrity impersonators, he's known as "the Man of a Thousand Paychecks" for the sheer volume of the bookings he gets with his wide range of impersonations."

The stage lights dim as the slow tapping on a snare drum and some guitar chords signal an upcoming entrance.

The Steve Harvey impersonator continues, "One night he can be destroying eardrums channeling Brian Johnson of AC/DC, and the next crooning as the silky-voiced singer Sam Smith. On the convention circuit, he's been known to perform at a Conservative Political Action Conference morning session as cute-as-can-be Pete Buttigieg dressed in a chipmunk costume talking about global warming, only to be pelted with nonbiodegradable plastic bottles and booed offstage. But he'll return minutes later as a wild-eyed Marjorie Taylor Greene and receive a standing ovation for blasting the ballroom's chandeliers to smithereens with an assault weapon.

"Today, we'll witness the ingenious impressions that launched the career of the Man of a Thousand Paychecks. Return with us now to both April 1958 and April 1978, and the Buddy Holly hit 'That'll Be the Day,' as performed by both Buddy on record and simultaneously as sung in the movie of Buddy's life staring Gary Busey. So welcome, Busey, Holly, Busey, Holly, Busey!"

Oswald's ears fly up. In a few seconds, he's standing onstage transfixed by the Man of a Thousand Paychecks, who's rocking "Maybe Baby."

Shoshana later explained what happened next on that hot afternoon. "It was a bolt out of the blue," she said. "I went onstage to get Oswald but fell in love with Paychecks in the middle of 'It's So Easy.' I saw our future together, so I slapped on my Carole King nose and wig, which of course I have with me at all times, just like the EpiPen I used to carry. I sat down at the piano and started 'You've Got a Friend,' he joined me, and, well, the rest is…"

Yep, folks, the rest is history. If you haven't experienced their act, head to Vegas and venture out to the Orleans casino off the Strip, where they work the lounge in "Buddy and Carole Rave On!" Please give my regards to the dog with the fifteen-inch mallet in his mouth, bangin' away on the big drum, 'cause that's my extremely happy brother Oswald.

BUD'S TURMOIL

Bud and me have been getting along really great, as usual, but just because we're happy doesn't mean that my dog powers can't detect trouble in his mind.

Herbie once told me—and boy do I miss Herbie—that some guy who wrote a novel that had a parrot in it said, "Keep your fears to yourself and share your courage with others."

That's Bud. He holds his emotion around me, like maybe he doesn't want to upset me, so here's a heads-up on his head, and if you think this might be a little too psychologically astute for a dog to comprehend about his owner, you're wrong. Trust me, your pet—your dog, your cat, your horse, and even your pet pig—has a far greater insight into what's goin' on with you emotionally than you probably do.

We read you.

Of course, not all pets can do detailed readings. Guppies, for example, are woefully deficient in that area.

For months Bud's been plagued by bank and credit card problems caused by somebody hacking his accounts. Also upsetting him is ugly fake news on social media, like that his mother's a bag lady living in a tree. "TV star Bud won't give hungry mother food money. She eats bark and leaves" was a post that drew a lot of notice.

Another one had him vacationing on his private island and bangin' multiple interns who work on our show, even though we don't have any interns, and the only private island the guy has is the pink flamingo float in the middle of our pool.

A couple of times, outta nowhere, crazy stories about both of us have landed on the front page of some supermarket tabloid:

I've got my own strong suspicions about this stuff, starting with the guy who looked like one of Ike "I Got Money" Piles' henchmen on the video of the check-in counter at the sex resort in Thailand. Piles, who snatched me off the street and ended up gettin' busted for his dogfighting ring, is probably behind this even though he's in prison. Or maybe it's the fat rich guy from Greenwich we heard was bankrolling their international racket?

Bud's money hassles mean constant calls to banks and credit card companies, and hours bein' on hold most every month. He's personally upping the statistic that the typical American spends forty-three days of their life on hold. By the way, research indicates that when that voice with the heavy accent says, "Please hold for a second," the average "second" lasts four minutes.

Trouble in mind.

I know he's gettin' more and more fed up with horny old Sol "The Old Swede" Silverman and his obsession with Nancy Pelosi's body, not to mention the general fact that The Old Swede is so out of step with the times that he thinks that references to STDs in the news concern Sigma Tau Delta, his old college fraternity.

Bud is being stretched too thin—dealing with the offers coming to me, the station sale, two reality shows, and on top of that tryin' to get to the studio every day for his own show, which is his priority.

That's why, in a snap decision one night when he and Brenda had just gotten high breakin' in the latest bong she'd added to her museum-quality collection, he decided to temporarily convert our studio show, *Southern Exposure*, into a virtual one that he could do anywhere in the world.

"Colbert's the best of late night," he said, pitching the idea to Lombardo, "and he was never better than when he was shooting remotely from home at the height of the pandemic. It was a brilliantly intimate, funny show, and Steve's interviews were better when he didn't have to play them more for laughs like he does with a live audience. I'm going to do the same thing. Let me shoot completely remote for a while."

"Good idea," Lombardo said. "Was wondering when you'd figure that out, and then two days ago, I knew very soon you'd be in here to pitch me on remote shows."

"Really?" Bud says. "Whadda you mean? How'd you know that?"

"Well," the boss says, "the other day, when I was in the head shop for jasmine and sandalwood incense to get rid of the foul cat litter smell in our basement, I ran into Brenda, who was buying a knockoff of Miley Cyrus' seventy-thousand-dollar salvia bong. I thought, 'This will be it; he'll get the idea any day now.'"

A stunned Bud left Lombardo to report the incident to Brenda.

Bud's mental trouble and new plan for a remote show aside, I have to appear on the World Animal Awards with Big Woody and the strippers, so we're planning to go up to New York City for an extended period. The day before we're set to leave, Bud gets an invitation from Andy, the kid who was a lowly production assistant on Bud's New York show, *Noonday with Bud*.

"Hey, you guys," Andy says on the phone. "Oh wait, sorry, I shouldn't be saying 'you guys'—it's the latest outlawed term, even though you two are, in fact, guys."

"We'll let that little lapse slide for right now, Andy," Bud says. "Tell us, what's up? Why the call, my friend?"

"Not much, except that I left my four-flight walk-up studio in Hell's Kitchen and bought a brand-new condo. It's a five-bedroom penthouse apartment with a wraparound terrace at Fifty-Fifth and Eighth Avenue. Come up and stay as long as you want; I miss you gu—er, you and Spike. You'll be my first guests, except for the girl who came up because I called a number on one of the back pages of the free paper the *Neighborhood Voice*."

How does a guy who was making the New York TV station's standard wage for PAs—$12.14 an hour—end up buying a multimillion-dollar condo in the heart of Manhattan?

Andy explains that he's been raking in dough on business concepts. He didn't get much traction on his Mood Ring Toilet Seat idea, but has a solid deal for revolutionary self-driving golf clubs that enable anyone to play golf like a pro without ever practicing. The holdup is the distributor wants Tiger Woods to endorse them, but Andy says with Tiger's record behind the wheel, he'd be better of selling self-driving cars.

Substantial money came rolling in at the start of the pandemic. He saw a big opportunity in the manufacture of masks when he realized no one was printing any form of humor on the masks as an incentive to get men, in particular, to buy and wear them.

"I somehow got the CEO of Trojan condoms on the phone," he says, "and gave him my one-sentence pitch: 'Sir, immediately manufacture masks with the line "I'm finally happy wearing a Trojan!"' The boss loved it. It's just a shame so many guys ended up not using the mask 'cause when they looked in the mirror and saw the word 'Trojan' on their face, it reminded them of high school and the stress of fumbling for a rubber in their wallet in the back seat of a friend's car while their hard-on was disappearing faster than their weekly allowance."

"I'm getting stress at the very thought," Bud says. "So where did the other big bucks come from?"

"I also started Out Toks. A friend of mine sent me outtakes he'd saved when he was soundman on a crew that spent days unsuccessfully trying to shoot those memory commercials—you know, the ones about how the product helps to improve your memory. You'd be amazed how many people are happy to send me money so they can watch people not being able to remember the name of the memory product they're endorsing."

Bud makes the arrangements to stay at Andy's place, but just as he's hanging up, Andy says, "Oh, by the way, is Spike still OK with other dogs? I adopted a rescue dog during the pandemic."

At this news, my ears flick to attention.

"Good move for all concerned. That was a lonely time for a lot of people, and dogs really helped. I'm sure glad I had my buddy Spike as company," Bud says.

"No, no, I wasn't lonely," he explains. "There was always the back pages of the *Neighborhood Voice*. I adopted Jane to give myself a bit of relief from editing hundreds of outtakes from those commercials. You can only watch an older man who's identified as an empowerment coach not be able to recall the word 'empowerment' on fourteen straight takes, and at one point claiming he worked as a power tool."

"Ha, that's how I functioned after a couple nights closing the clubs back in the New York days. Don't worry, Andy. You know Spike; he gets along with all creatures, including mechanical alligators. I'm sure the Wonder Dog and Jane will have a great time," Bud answers, speaking for me with great certitude.

Thanks, Bud, but how do I know if we'll get along? Jane's a female? I need to be washed with the good shampoo the night before we leave. Where will I sleep? What if she's got the sofa? How about her walking pattern? Will I have to orchestrate my every excretion to her every walk? Will I be dragged out into the rain if she has to go, when I'd be perfectly content to take a quick leak on Andy's terrace and keep watching *The Hidden Lives of Pets* for the twelfth time? What if she thinks I look like Shrek? It's possible!

Imagined outcomes. There I go again, worrying about things I can't control. It's hard for me not to take life so seriously. Maybe that's why Toto told me it's all a joke.

PART THREE

NEW YORK

CHAPTER TWELVE

The City That Never Sweeps

How hot was it? By the day we arrived, the heat dome that had been punishing the Midwest in July had settled squarely over New York City. Andy and Jane were away someplace, and we couldn't get into his apartment because he forgot to inform the staff we were coming, or he didn't fill out the eight-page inquisition about us and provide our DNA samples that his swanky building demanded. This by way of telling you that we couldn't get past the doorman, so we went for a walk in the blistering sun on the sidewalk of litter-strewn Eighth Avenue toward Central Park.

While on this stroll, I imagined, like I sometimes do, that I'm in a major TV commercial—this one for designer dog shoes. Try walking in your bare feet like a
dog over molten-hot cement and scalding tar on sidewalks and streets. With global warming cooking our continent like it's a giant slab of chicken parm in a microwave, your basic dog feet need protection.

The dog shoe market is gonna be vast. Since we were walking by the Stuart Weitzman store on Columbus Circle, I was pretending that I could be part of his sales pitch:

"Hi, I'm shoe designer Stuart Weitzman here with Spike the Wonder Dog. For years, millions of you supported my efforts to bring humans the finest in footwear. But times have changed. Last week, in this continued intense heat, we saw the antennae on top of the Empire State Building melt into the mountain of lead now covering the observation deck. That's hot, right, Spike?"

I decide to respond with the same kind of practiced shallow nod that local TV news anchors give to each other. I look at Stuart Weitzman, which gets me wondering if anybody has ever called this guy Stewie, and nod the anchor nod twice.

"Today," he continues, "the real-feel temperature on the blistering sidewalk in Times Square is so hot...well, hey, why not show the folks, celebrity chef Marcus Samuelsson."

"Well thank you, Stuart Weitzman," Chef Samuelsson says, being careful not to call him Stewie, like I can tell he wants to. "Watch this."

Chef Samuelsson throws a small New York strip steak on the pavement. It sizzles for a few seconds. He flips it over. "Seared to perfection in a matter of seconds, right, Spike?" he says, tossing it to me.

I catch it and chew, doing my imitation of Al Roker sampling food on the Today show.

"So, Spike," Stuart Weitzman says, "the air temperature is at a record hundred and fourteen degrees and far, far hotter on the sidewalk, as we just saw. Folks might be wondering: Spike, how are those Wonder Feet of yours?"

I shrug a "non ti preoccupare," like DeNiro's shrugged in half a dozen mob movies.

"Of course, folks, Spike's not concerned. He's got nothing to worry about in this heat, 'cause he's wearing my new Paw Pumps from the Stu Goes to the Dogs Collection—they're a neat treat for canine feet to beat street heat."

I bark. Chef Samuelsson waves. Stuart Weitzman smiles as sweat runs down his face. The camera cuts to my feet. I jump straight up and deftly click all four paws.

"Great quadruple Leprechaun kick there, Spike. And that's a cut and print," the director says, pretending he's shooting on seventy-millimeter film and not an old BlackBerry.

"Stewie, great job!" his wife, Jane Gershon, says, walking onto the set.

"'Stewie'? I knew it, I knew it," I'm thinkin'.

"I knew it, I knew it," Bud says, rousing me out of my daydream. "Andy called, and we can get in. He apologized; he forgot we were coming, and he got tied up across town dealing with an issue with some vocal group he's promoting that's working in Provincetown."

We head back to his pad. I'm looking forward to meeting Jane and getting settled in.

Crossing Columbus Circle and heading down Eighth Avenue, I notice one of the things that has changed in town since Bud and I spent that tough year here a while back—marijuana smoke. There was a little on the streets then, but now pot is for sale in stores and it's OK to smoke it in public. Its strong scent is coming from playgrounds and bicyclists and old hippies on walkers arguing about bogarting a joint.

Forget the heat dome. Once cannabis is fully legal, the Weather Channel's gonna be tracking the pot dome—a massive pressure system of very high-quality cannabis smoke locked over the country. Can't you see the new tourism slogan? "Come to America. We're happy again!"

Andy's apartment is even bigger and better than I pictured. Andy left a message that he's on an errand, and we're kind of shocked to be greeted by the hologram/android/avatar/robot that Andy commissioned to be created as his virtual self. He uses it as a personal assistant and as a companion for Jane while he's running around town making deals and making a fortune pitching his crazy ideas.

"Hello, Bud. Hello, Spike the Wonder Dog. Glad you are here. I see you're nervous in my presence; unfortunately, many people are. Please relax and call me Virtual Andy," he drones in a voice powered by ChatGPT that sounds like a cross between Andy's and the one on the navigation system in your car.

"When Actual Andy's not here," he continues, "think of me as his stand-in. I have the advanced intelligence of IBM's Deep Blue computer, plus several luxury options that are combined with the mensch-like qualities of your friend and my boss, whom I call Actual Andy."

Bud and I are staring bug-eyed at this cyber thing. Hafta admit, they did a great job. It's a bigger, stronger-looking, and more handsome version of Andy, except it/he has a fixed smile; flat, expressionless brown eyes with no pupils; and plastic hair.

"By the way," he drones, "as a sideline, I sell virtual real estate. I represent the new RE/MAX virtual properties market. Right now I'm offering some prime lots on Snooptown Island, the latest Snoop Dogg development. Don't be shy if you're interested."

When we first met Actual Andy, he was a friendly kid who was starting as an intern on the New York show. Now he's rich enough to have his own digital double. The fact that he got this virtual android Andy character, which seems quite friendly, as a companion for his dog, Jane, would make me like the metaverse even more, if I could ever figure out what the metaverse actually is.

Virtual Andy suggests we look around.

The huge terrace is phenomenal, with a view of the Hudson River that's gonna mesmerize Bud if he's ever stoned around sunset time, as I suspect he will be. To decorate all this, Andy shrewdly got the apartment booked on *Extreme Makeover: Home Edition.* They transformed it from a stuffy, dusty dwelling crowded with the doily-laden, gold, fake Rococo furniture favored by its previous occupant, a very old woman who died on the terrace choking on a grape, into a showcase for the kind of midcentury-modern furniture Andy had fallen in love with as a child when his family spent a week at the Fontainebleau hotel in Miami Beach.

"All that's missing for my boss," Virtual Andy tells us, "is an old Jewish comedian kibitzing around the hotel pool."

The other thing missing is his dog, Jane, who's been taken for a shampoo and blow-dry at a nearby full-service organic beauty parlor for dogs. I still don't know what kind of dog Andy adopted. He could have a pocket dog that's so small, the poor thing can't even jump up in a chair, or a Great Dane that's gonna tower over me.

The apartment door swings open and Andy comes in slurping a Pineapple Upside-Down-Cake Frappuccino from the Starbucks across the street.

"Andy, my boy," Bud says, "I'm so proud of you. Look at this place. I always knew you had that entrepreneurial talent, the way you made money for us with Spike on his YouTube channel back on the old show."

"Ah...thanks, Bud. Wow, you're here. Great to see you and, yeah, er, thanks again. I'm doin' OK, and onward and upward together. Hey there, Spike, you're looking as cool as ever."

I wish I could say the same for our pal Andy, but his dark hair is noticeably weird—the left side is a jagged mess, with some clumps of three-inch hair and the rest about a quarter of an inch. There's a narrow, slightly bald strip on his scalp, as if a tiny lawn mower shaved partway down the back of his head.

As Bud and me are gazin' in wide-eyed wonderment at this cranium chaos, Andy explains what happened. He saw George Clooney on the CBS *Sunday Morning* show talking about how he's been cutting his own hair for thirty years with something called a Flowbee, an electric-powered vacuum gadget that people use to trim and style their hair at home.

We know young Andy to be a rabid George Clooney fan who once spent an entire weekend watching a loop of *The Men Who Stare at Goats.*

"I love Clooney's hair, so I got a Flowbee," Andy says, "and it was really easy to work, so I started to give myself a light trim, but I took a phone call about contract problems while I was Flowbeein' away and had to do computer research at the same time about some issues. I was never too mechanical to begin with, and I musta pressed too hard or something and, er, well, now..."

"Don't worry," Bud says. "By coincidence, I brought you a hat with the latest headshot of Spike on it. Just wear it night and day for the next couple of weeks."

"Ha," he laughs. "Let me get you guys something."

He gives Bud a frosty ginger ale and puts down some cold water for me. It's great to see him again. When he started as our intern at Channel 5, he was a twenty-year-old kid fresh from Loyola University in Chicago. He was kinda shy but honest enough to confess to Bud—after he'd downed thirteen Jell-O shots in ten minutes at a party—that he was a virgin. Based on the upside-down pile of "personal ads" by the phone, I'm reasoning that's no longer the case for young Andy.

"Fill us in," Bud says. "What's with the vocal group? And tell us about the new idea you have for Spike."

Andy explains that he's put together a small management company for emerging music acts. The hottest performers he's booking this summer are a quartet playing the gay cabaret circuit called the Four Bottoms, who are working Provincetown, Fire Island, Key West, and the Rainbow Lounge at the Bears on Bikes motorcycle rally in Sturgis, South Dakota.

"Great voices, great harmonies," he says, "and the Four Bottoms have some wonderful novelty numbers. Their special lyrics to 'How Deep Is Your Love?' get a standing ovation every show."

"I'm sure," Bud says, "and the thing, maybe, for Spike?"

"Right," Andy asks. "So, remember how we'd always joke about the colossal size of Spike's mouth, and how extremely wide his jaws open when he yawns?"

This praise was greatly appreciated. It's a well-known fact that I got a trap on me that springs wide open like an alligator's. Even Big Mel in Palm Beach seemed to take notice.

"Here's my pitch to use that mouth of his," Andy says. "I want to corner the market in over-the-top, mouth-wide-open victory gloating in sports."

"Gloating?"

"Yeah, gloating—those displays of triumph you see from athletes in all sports now except maybe croquet."

Andy explains he's making deals with networks and cable carriers for a special camera that will only record gloating.

"You're creating a gloat cam?"

"Yes, an isolation camera covering the wide world of smug bragging in sports."

"Things have really changed for sure," Bud says. "Remember the old days in tennis, when the winner would smile, shake hands with the loser, wave to the crowd, and walk off the court, or when Jim Brown would just throw down the ball and smile after a ninety-yard TD? Wilt Chamberlain scored a hundred points in a game once. Did he run around the court waving his arms and pounding his chest? No."

"Of course not, Bud. He just wanted to get off the court and get laid."

"He did gloat over having slept with at least twenty thousand women," Bud points out.

"Any man or woman gets a pass for bragging once they're beyond the fifteen thousand mark," Andy jokes. "Right now, personally, I'm at a solid two. But anyway, these days, whether it's Djokovic screaming with his eyes closed and mouth wide open while waving his clenched fist, or NFL players show-boating in the end zone with better choreography than on *Dancing with the*

Stars, or a soccer player running down the field after a goal with her arms spread wide and screaming madly, all of these displays of exultation involve having the human jaw spread as far apart as nature allows."

"And that's where Spike comes in, right?" Bud says.

"Yeah, I figure he can kind of be like the old MGM lion used to be when he'd roar at the top of the movie credits."

The doorbell rings, thus interrupting Bud and me from looking at each other and agreeing that using my mouth with its gleaming white fangs as the official symbol of Gloat Vision might have the effect of driving people away. When I toss a giant yawn, people tend to run for help.

Wanita, the dog walker, comes in with Jane, who at first glance is a lovely, quite beautiful, seemingly very happy golden retriever—a breed, by the way, that really benefits from a full day at a high-priced canine grooming salon featuring a shampoo, organic oats-and-barley conditioning treatment, and back massage, followed by a two-handed blow-dry of her coat, topped off with an oxygen facial, followed by an hour in a darkened room listening to soft Hawaiian chanting and surf sounds. They do this stuff to dogs, folks. I've seen it.

Jane seems happy having a dog visitor, instead of the various human media types who fawn all over her hoping it'll get them a better deal with Andy if he thinks they like her, when in fact they can hardly wait to get home and vacuum her hair offa their pants.

Jane and I display enough of the mandatory dog sniffing and chasing each other around the living room to entertain the humans for a minute. We then adjourn to her area in the apartment, which is a nice-size space with a big pile of dog toys.

Andy spared no expense. She's got a custom-made green-and-white number-seven-setting Tempur-Pedic dog bed. It's inside an actual junior one-bedroom doghouse. I can see why Daisy was demanding one. This thing's almost three times as large as my beloved orange doghouse, plus it features one little window, just enough to qualify it as "light-drenched" in the real estate listings of the *New York Times*.

Following in the tradition of the hard-hitting line of questions Bud would be firing at a guest on TV, I query, "So what happened that you became an abandoned dog that Andy rescued?"

I learn that it all started on a beautiful sunny day in East Hampton.

Jane came from one of the top AKC breeders of golden retrievers in the country and was purchased online by Manny and Walter, a wealthy couple who live on an estate at Georgica Pond in East Hampton.

Manny, who is more like the husband in the marriage, makes a wad of cash managing and marketing specific parts of celebrity bodies.

Jane tells me she heard him saying that he put J.Lo's backside on the map, and that prior to when he took over managing it, "its popularity was flattening out."

Apparently, the guy has exclusive rights to the images of things like the shadow in Katy Perry's cleavage, the top of Shaquille O'Neal's head, Kate Upton's eyebrows, most of Mariah Carey's body except for the upper arms, Justin Timberlake's left foot in a Croc, and hundreds of others.

Manny's husband, Walter, founded the OkStupid dating site. He did it by creating an algorithm that collected info on thousands of men and women who failed miserably on dating sites 'cause the people they went out with gave feedback indicating they notched high scores on the stupidity index.

Jane indicates that he's locked in a major lawsuit with OkCupid over the name, but he's really raking in the cash and making a lot of unusually stupid people happy in the meantime.

The couple adopted a young Mexican boy, who even at age three refused to have his name changed from Pedro to Chad. The little kid and Jane were getting along great until one day Pedro, while aiming for her mouth, accidentally shoved a small Tootsie Roll up her left nostril. Jane reflexively barked and growled at Pedro. What would you expect?

Anyway, Manny and Walter rushed in. They yelled at Jane and dragged her outside and lashed her to a tree, not knowing she had a Tootsie Roll in her nose and was barking in pain. As the Tootsie Roll was slowly melting and unexpectedly inducing a wonderful sense of elation, which she realized could be a new revenue stream for the product—particularly for people with large nostrils—Jane heard Manny telling little Pedro that in the morning a nice man was going to come and take Jane to a farm, where she'd be happier and never bark and growl at him again.

At dawn, knowing that her life was in mortal danger, she managed to slip out of her collar. She crept down the lawn and swam off into the mist of Georgica Pond, which is a vast tidal lagoon at the beach between East Hampton and Wainscott. Her plan was to get as far away as possible and throw her fate to the kindness of strangers.

By the time she got across, she was really hungry. She saw a beautiful couple having an elegant-looking brunch on a deck by their private beach. Serving the duo was a guy who wasn't Sean Combs but really resembled him. She realized, "Oh my God, that's Jay-Z and Beyoncé's estate! That's the place Manny and Walter always wanted to visit but never got asked to, even though Manny once got down on his knees and begged and pleaded with Jay-Z for an invitation when he spotted the couple dining at the Almond restaurant in Bridgehampton.

"You're cool, man," Jay-Z had said to him, "but get off your knees. You'll make knee marks in those Botany 500 slacks a' yours. We'll get you into one of Bey's fundraisers. Bring your checkbook. OK? All good? Now let me finish my risotto."

Jane swam toward them and staggered out of the water.

"Even though they've got kids and pets all over the place, Bey and Jay welcomed me," she says, "so I gave them the classic look of an abandoned dog who's starving to death and needs to join you for brunch. The next thing I knew, the P. Diddy type was serving me a large egg-white frittata, fiber muffin, and steaming bowl of Paleo grits on white Dalton china."

She relaxed and spent the day recovering from the stress of her escape and the big swim.

By the way, she informs me: "Who knew those two would be listening to John Denver music all day?"

Jane was served a little sushi for lunch, and was hoping maybe this just might be her new home. But before dinner she heard Beyoncé on the phone talking to the East Hampton animal control warden (that would be your basic dogcatcher, folks), telling him that a beautiful golden retriever was lost and surely someone was searching for her. The warden left skid marks driving off to meet Jay-Z and Beyoncé.

Not wanting to be captured and returned to Walter and Manny, and thus "the farm," she dove off the dock into the water and swam away while Jay-Z and Bey were in the kitchen harmonizing with Denver on "Rocky Mountain High."

At this point, even though I'm desperate to take a leak, I'm sticking with listening to her, and I'm glad I do 'cause she tells me...

Pretty quickly, she was in trouble in the water 'cause of a tidal pull. While fighting the current, she was being dragged toward a bevy of swans. The closer she gets, the more tense she becomes, knowing that a while back the headline "Donna Karan Jack Russell Terrier Killed by Swan" knocked the story about Alec and Hilaria Baldwin's newest baby off the front page of the *East Hampton Star*.

The largest swan swam toward her, arching its long neck to attack. She dove as far down as she could manage, swam up, breeched, and barked. The thing flew away. The current was pulling her along the southern rim of the pond. She saw all manner of celebs relaxing after dinner. She noticed Steven Spielberg on his deck shooting video of her just as a big snapping turtle stuck his ugly head out of the water. The snapper spotted Jane and dove. She imagined he was heading toward her.

"Who wouldn't think about the opening scene of *Jaws* in a situation like this?" she says.

"And?"

No turtle attack. Just panic, but a moment later a handsome young guy named Harvey came floating up behind her on a long teak paddleboard. He had kind eyes, a big white smile, and sunny blond hair. Harvey could tell she was struggling in the water, but she had enough strength to get up on the board.

He said, "I'm taking you home."

Gliding to the place where he lived and worked, Harvey told Jane all about himself and how he'd ended up working for a Mrs. Tishman on her waterfront estate on Georgica Pond.

At this point, I hate to interrupt the narrative, as much as you probably hate that I'm doing it now, but I need to take a leak. Jane is fine, so Bud takes me out for a quickie.

Brutal hot afternoon.

I could use a pair of dog shoes from the new Stuart Weitzman line I was fantasizing about earlier.

A couple of seconds after my paws have adjusted to the pavement, I see a motorized wide-tire bike whizzing in the wrong direction in the narrow bike lane inches from the curb on Eighth Avenue. The bike hits a texting teenager who just stepped offa the sidewalk, and knocks him for a loop. It isn't the metaphorical loop, as in "knocked him for a...," it was an actual loop. He lands on the hood of a parked car. Miraculously, the kid hasn't dropped his phone, for which he seems quite relieved in spite of two severely dislocated shoulders.

This is the first example we will see of the thousands of people around New York who get injured by speeding motorized vehicles. All kinds of things with wheels and propulsion—short of full-fledged Harley-Davidson Screamin' Eagle motorcycles—now barrel at high speeds in two directions down one-way streets and on the narrow bike lanes all over town. It's a post-pandemic phenomenon. It started 'cause the overworked food delivery guys needed to move faster.

A gruesome project being run by two girls for their physics class at the Bronx High School of Science measured the bike speed times victim's weight times cheering bystanders divided by humidity and air pollution to calculate the distance that someone can be hurled by a motorized bike.

When I get back to the apartment after takin' a leak, I learn about what happened to Harvey, and how Jane ended up getting adopted by Andy one hot summer night at the Southampton Animal Shelter's Unconditional Love Gala.

On the paddleboard trip heading back to Mrs. Tishman's house, Jane found out that Harvey was a true outdoorsman. Because of the glow of his natural bronze suntan, he'd gotten involved in the tanning salon business. He'd somehow ended up as the managing director of indoor tanning operations at Mar-a-Lago. He had the skills to calibrate Trump's custom-built extra-wide tanning bed to the exact "pumpkin orange on a crisp October morning" color setting that produces the skin tone the former president demands, so Harvey became DJT's personal tanning clinician.

One morning before work, he got way too high sitting in his car in the parking lot at Mar-a-Lago smoking a couple bowls of the Mexican weed the grounds crew secretly sold guests and Secret Service agents to supplement their punishingly low wage of $74.12 a day for ten hours of labor on the estate.

The cannabis gave him a sharper understanding of just how truly unfulfilled by his job he was. He trudged off to work feeling unusually pissed off at what was going on.

Melania was always snapping at him in that brittle accent of hers that the "Sophia Loren after a sunny weekend on Capri" skin tone she expected was never quite right, even though Harvey was using the exact calibration Sophia herself endorsed in the tanning bed's brochure.

And Trump was constantly sending Harvey to Palm Beach for the cheeseburgers he'd eat during his tanning sessions. Harvey was sick of scraping all that congealed Vermont cheddar cheese and those smelly grilled onions and crushed French fries from around the indentation made by Trump's ass on the bottom of the tanning bed. Furthermore, Trump was always shortchanging him by a couple of bucks, claiming the burgers were a little cold or light on the cheese, so why should he pay full price?

Out of anger and frustration, Harvey switched their tanning bed settings.

There was a dinner-and-a-movie party that evening for Franklin Graham and evangelical Christian leaders. Trump himself selected the film *The Aristocrats*, because he liked the classy title and thought that it would reflect well on him.

When Melania and Donald arrived at the ballroom for dinner, Trump was fuming.

Standing in front of the ballroom behind a podium embossed with his special "I'm Still the President!" plastic seal, he immediately commanded his followers to "put down your mai tais, get off your chairs, and kneel and pray as hard as it's possible to pray."

"Get directly to God now!" he demanded. "Tell Him I said I think He's terrific, a real winner, and order Him to help us recover!" he yelled, pointing at his face, now the tone of an olive. Melania, standing beside him, looked like a pumpkin head in Prada. "And while you're at it, demand that God have the flesh of Harvey, the former director of our indoor tanning operations, burn in hell before he cashes last week's paycheck."

"Amen," the assembled murmured.

Harvey left Florida that night and headed back to his hometown of Wainscott, Long Island. He found a job helping Mrs. Tishman as estate manager at her place on Georgica Pond. Her former estate manager had been fired for using the new Bazooka Power Jet 10,000 leaf blower and waking up Ron Perlman a mile away.

Jane became adept at balancing on the paddleboard while she was with Harvey, but her new beloved master met his fate on one of their oceangoing excursions.

At the outset, they were enjoying a blue-sky day with just a couple of puffy clouds. By the time they were about a mile out in the ocean, the sky was overcast and the sea was getting too choppy for a safe ride on the board. Harvey was a confident athlete, and he started toward shore. "Don't worry," he told Jane. "I'll get us back."

Things got rough. Balancing was difficult. They were hit from behind by a rogue wave. Harvey toppled headfirst into the water into a smack of jellyfish. He screamed. Dozens of the large, ugly creatures were stinging him repeatedly. Jane crouched to leap in to help, but he yelled, "No! Stop!"

The paddleboard was skimming away from him. Again Jane set herself to jump in to help. Again he warned her, "*No*! Stay, Jane, no, they'll…kill…y—"

She watched him sink. Saw bubbles, but in a few more seconds she was swept too far away to see anything else.

She spent that day and all night, and all of the next day, drifting and not caring if she lived or died. She was mostly out of sight of land, but in the middle of the third afternoon, the currents shifted and she came in close enough to shore to jump off the board and let the waves wash her up on Gin Lane Beach in Southampton.

The lifeguards spotted her coughing up water and took her to the Southampton Animal Shelter. After days of treatment, she was well enough to be placed in an adoption unit.

Jane was lucky enough to be one of several dogs being walked around the grounds for adoption at Southampton's Unconditional Love Gala, a posh event filled with well-dressed people and two guys in Hawaiian shirts. Everyone coughed up a lot of money to be there, hoping to get their picture in *Dan's Papers* and oh, yeah, also raise funds to help abandoned animals. Maybe they'd even adopt one? If so, *wham*—just like that, an orphaned canine has a new home.

Andy was staying in Sagaponack that week, doing promotion for one of his latest ventures, the Hampton Restaurant Reservation Crisis Hotline. To get a reservation in the high-demand restaurant environment of the Hamptons, all a client had to do was pay the hotline double the exact amount of their meal check, including wine, tips, and valet charges, as a fee, and they'd get a table.

Jane spotted Andy. There was something about him she liked immediately, in spite of the fact that he looked like the kind of guy who'd always tuck a long white napkin in his collar when he'd sit down to eat, even if for just a piece of toast.

He was standing near the bar, dressed in a red, blue, and orange madras blazer and rumpled khakis, talking to a young couple who'd just adopted a small Wheaten terrier. Jane tugged on her leash and made her way over to him.

"Hi there, blondie," he said with a kind smile.

She rubbed against his leg, looked up at him, took a deep breath, and gave it everything she had.

She'd seen enough of the dogs in the horrifying ASPCA commercials on TV to know what to do. It was crucial that she appear as desperate as possible, yet without seeming permanently needy, or vicious, or deranged, and especially not the kind of dog who would ever need to be walked in the rain.

Jane knew she had one chance that night. Thousands of years of evolution of dogs learning to manipulate humans went into the emotion her sad brown eyes conveyed to Andy:

"You really need me, pal!"

"Have you ever seen a tail wag faster?"

"I know, you're not sure what to do about me yet."

"Well…"

"Think of those lonely nights after the escort leaves!"

They've been together ever since.

I gotta say I'm mighty impressed with her story. She played Andy like Mozart played the harpsichord.

This is not a non sequitur. I mention the harpsichord because we've learned that Andy converted his fourth bedroom into a man cave where he could watch OnlyFans while practicing Goldberg Variations and other baroque keyboard concertos on his beloved harpsichord. His parents had given him the instrument in tenth grade at New Trier High School to console him after the principal cut his oboe section from the marching band because music funding had been diverted to hire yet another diversity consultant.

We have a couple of free days before things will get hectic with the World Animal Awards. Andy gave us our own wing in the place, and Bud's done a couple of top-notch interviews for *Southern Exposure* from a Zoom space that Andy set up. On the Zoom calls, I basically try to look engaged during the segments, even though I was mostly counting the minutes till the dog walker would ring the bell and take Jane and me to the park.

For two dogs that have just met, we're completely relaxed with each other, and it's good to have a new friend. She's my first one since my little pal Benny the Chihuahua, who belonged to my neighbor back at our old pad on Sixty-Third Street.

"You're doing my job for me, Spike," Virtual Andy said. "I'm happy to see you and Jane are friends. I'll go sit in the corner."

I'm really impressed with Jane. She's brave, smart, secure—a long way from Daisy's insecurity. Don't get me wrong here; I'm not makin' any moves on Jane. She's a new friend with a capital *f* who just happens to be a female. Gettin' involved in a so-called relationship's not my agenda—or hers, I can tell.

"Andy talked about Spike the Wonder Dog all the time," she told me, "and the crazy stuff you did on your TV show here, and what happened to you, and how you saved your life by fighting your way out of that horrible situation. We've seen you on TV; that stuff with Colbert was hysterical. I figured you'd be really full of yourself—big star and all that, your own line of pandemic masks, saving women from a burning building—but you're basically a nice dog, and a little shy."

Shy? That's a new one. But maybe I do seem a little shy because I'm so impressed with her. As hearty and sporting and powerful as the golden retriever breed is, they're really beautiful, and a way more popular breed than English Bull Terriers. I think our low popularity is due primarily to our resemblance to baby dinosaurs.

When I'm out on the street with Jane, I feel like I'm strolling along with a real beauty. I'm not saying she's "leash candy"; Jane's very smart. But I feel like I'm walking next to the Jennifer Lawrence of dogs. The only difference is Jennifer's not headed to the park three times a day to take care of…well, you know what I'm talking about.

CHAPTER THIRTEEN

The World Animal Awards

We head to Madison Square Garden for the World Animal Awards rehearsal. Apparently, I'm one of the many animals that have saved humans in the past year. The show will celebrate some of our daring rescues with reenactments, interviews, and videos. Three large, middle-aged turtles were somehow able to save a little girl, and that's part of the overhyped promo airing all week.

I've never been in the Garden before; just saw the place on TV when Bud and me watched the Westminster Kennel Club Dog Show the night my beloved brother Billy was competing. If you're intellectually advanced enough to have read our first book, you might remember that Billy was a puppy prodigy, a deep thinker, and the real brains in our family. (By the way, he would've just written "Bud and I watched" correctly, using "I" as a subject pronoun, of course.) Billy made it to the finals but didn't win Best in Show. Got beat out by a Shih Tzu that looked like a little gray mop waddling around the ring. There's a breed that couldn't win a prize against a flea-ridden street dog without first enduring fourteen hours of intense grooming using an entire can of hair spray.

We're assigned a handler named Louie.

Bud has to fill out a legal form indicating that he'll be responsible for damages if I hump the host. Apparently, the show's host has recently been humiliated on social media by an angry underpaid call girl who claimed the guy could achieve a state of arousal with her only if his fourteen-year-old beagle was humping his calf.

"Would you like Spike to have a few subtle Nike promo swooshes?" Louie asks. "The company's offering three thousand dollars to have a fifteen-inch Nike swoosh stenciled on both of Spike's sides, and a couple of tiny golf-ball-size swooshes lettered on the gonads."

"Does Nike really need gonad promo?" Bud asks.

"They believe the swoosh should be everywhere," Louie says. "Their research reveals that the typical American under the age of eighty-five sees only about seventy-two of the logos in a sixteen-hour waking period. Sightings plunge to a meager four during REM sleep. They want more! Again, three thousand dollars and, OK, because he's still got them, we'll round it out—no pun intended, Bud—with another two fifty for each of his testicles."

"I don't know," Bud says.

"Most of the dogs are doing it—not so much with the cats," Louie adds eagerly.

Bud is tempted, 'cause as usual, his personal cash situation continues to be disrupted by illegal charges on all his cards, and he keeps forgetting the complicated new passwords he has to create each time a new set of cards come in the mail.

"I think I can easily remember 'FlaT@#%*=%ulence!'" he said recently. "No reason to take the risk of writing a password down, hiding it in the bureau with the underwear, and having someone discover it."

Mainly, though, Bud nixes the stenciling idea 'cause the artist who's doing them turns out to be a fan of our old New York show. She whispers that the ink she's using probably wouldn't fade from my white coat until the early 2030s, if at all.

We have our own large dressing room, which, to my acute sense of smell, has the aroma of jock straps and Jamaican Mango & Lime Locking Firm Wax.

The strippers I saved from the fire at Big Woody's are in a large dressing room next to ours, and stop by to say hello before rehearsal.

"There he is," Bambi says, rushing over and leaving one of her big lipstick prints on my head, "the dog that made it all possible."

"Hello, Bud. Hello, Spike," Crystal, Amber, and Angel chime in.

It's nice to see them dressed this time. They're still smokin' hot, but not the kind of smoking hot like they were at the fire.

They're really looking forward to staging the reenactment of the rescue on the show.

It's unfortunate, Bud and I think, that they can't be portrayed on the program as the strippers they were. There was just too much pushback from the title sponsor, a very conservative fried chicken company that didn't want to be paying big bucks for an association with the Dance of the Seven Oils, etc. So the women have to dress in ballet rehearsal gear, as if Big Woody's burning strip joint was a rehearsal space for a national tour of *The Nutcracker*.

"Fill us in on what all's been happening with the four of you?" Bud asks, again demonstrating the penetrating and probing questioning style that makes him the Emmy-winning—well, maybe someday—talk show host that he is.

"It's been unbelievable," Amber explains, "No more stripping—just endorsement offers and political work and product repping. The first offer we got was..."

Folks, would you like to hear about all of the good fortune that has come their way since I saved them from the fiery inferno by bashing in that door with my rock-like head?

I thought so.

Angel teaches a course in public nudity studies at Georgetown's School of Public Policy.

Crystal and Bambi are global ambassadors for national Go Topless Day. They'll be addressing the UN General Assembly about the expected pushback in the Middle East on the worldwide Free the Nipple movement. Amber is working in the hastily formed Office of Topless Intelligence in the Department of Homeland Security.

And all of them are scheduled for a promo tour for the newest dolls in the Barbie collection: Topless Wedding Night Barbie and Wildly Aroused Ken.

The follow-up set is Insatiable Barbie and Entering Priesthood Ken.

Amber keeps checking her phone for a text. "We're worried about Woody," she says. "He's supposed to be here now. Haven't heard from him for days— in the past few months, his post-traumatic stress syndrome has gotten really bad. He's become erratic."

The door swings open, and a young man barges in. He's wild-eyed, trembling, breathing heavily, sweaty, and panicky over something.

"You're Spike the Wonder Dog, right?" he asks me.

I start toward him with my all-access pass in my mouth, but Crystal says, "Yes, he's Spike, and now that we've confirmed that, who the hell are you?" Apparently, strippers have a thing about men barging into dressing rooms.

"Oh, sorry, I'm Arnold Kauffman, the associate producer. Look, girls, Bud, we've got a problem. The first segment of the show, the re-creation of that rescue with Elaine, the cocker spaniel who ran across ten yards of burning coals with a cell phone in her mouth to give to trapped people so they could call for help…well, Elaine went haywire at rehearsals. Had a panic attack when she faced the coals and was so scared, she humped the host. Things got ugly."

"I'm sure," Bambi says.

"The host has it in his contract that any dog who humps him is fired on the spot, no matter what. Elaine can't go on, and we can't cut the segment because Kingsford charcoal and the Inconceivable Burger, the new after-sex contraceptive meal, are the segment sponsors."

"So?" Bud asks.

"The producer Rune Scott's angry at me because of this."

"That fat jerk hit on all four of us before we even made it to our dressing room, the creep," Amber says. "I have the feeling he'd make Harvey Weinstein look like just a clumsy romantic."

"Why is Rune Scott angry at you?" Bambi asks.

"Because that's the kind of boss he is. If something goes wrong, he has to scream and blame somebody, even if there's no way it's their fault. Says he's going to make me run across the burning coals unless I can solve the problem—and he's not kidding."

"So," Bud asks, "whaddaya want?"

"Someone said this is a job for Spike the Wonder Dog, so I—"

"He'll do it," Bud says.

I love Bud, but perhaps further inquiry would be appropriate—like, what's the risk? How about money? Will Spike's SAG-AFTRA minimum be raised? Or simply, what's involved? If we asked those questions, we would have found out that once Bud said yes, the costume department over at Leslie Davis' animal casting agency clicked into high gear to create an anatomically correct female cocker spaniel outfit to disguise me.

This is not a stunt I'm eager to perform.

If I could just get to that host's leg, I'd give it a couple of big you-know-what's, and we'd be back at Andy's. I'd be playing with Jane, Virtual Andy would be sitting in the corner, Bud would be looking at the sunset, Actual

Andy would be hatching another deal, and young, sweaty Arnold Kauffman would be running across the coals.

After a boring day of rehearsing, we're set for the live broadcast.

Big Woody is still MIA. The strippers have crafted a statement about his gratitude for the rescue that they'll read in case he doesn't show up. I have concerns. I still haven't been fitted with the Elaine the cocker spaniel costume, and haven't rehearsed running over the hot coals because their fumes have been setting off the sprinkler system in the control room. Rune Scott is so pissed that he fired the first person he saw after eating lunch, because the rye bread on his Reuben sandwich was soggy.

Again, I really don't want to do the stunt. This is the crap that happens when you get this "Wonder Dog" title slapped on you.

But Bud, as usual, knew what he was doing for me when he OK'd the walk. He's done a couple of shows with a professional speaker who gets people to walk across burning coals barefoot to overcome their fears. If there's ample ash on top of the coals and the feet move fast, the people are OK.

"Just run as fast as you can, and it won't be nearly as bad as walking on the sidewalks was last week," he tells me.

Leslie Davis comes to the dressing room with her fitter and my costumes.

Yeah, little did I know I have two getups. Under the cocker spaniel suit, I've got to wear a blue cape with a yellow WD logo. At first you think, "Nice, that's 'WD' for 'Wonder Dog.'" But it's actually the logo for the WD-40 lube product. Typical of the crap the money-grubbing king of embedded advertising and over-the top productions, the producer Rune Scott, does for his shows.

He's planned explosions of fireworks after each stunt. Ribbons of confetti and booming drums and trumpets will accompany the animal introductions. A choir of twelve runners-up from the past couple seasons of *The Voice* will sing songs about animals—be sure to listen to how they turn "Octopus's Garden" into something that sounds like the Naval Academy's "Anchors Away."

It's sad that the heroic deeds of so many beasts are reduced to a sideshow floating in a sea of television glitz.

"Gotta keep the viewer," Rune Scott has been quoted as saying on *Entertainment Tonight*. "Energy, explosions, spectacle. The more outrageous and more exaggerated the production, the bigger the costumes, the more they'll keep watching. That's why music booms between innings at baseball games now, and they blast rock on the changeovers at the US Open. They have to make it more exciting than just plain old Major League Baseball or World Championship Tennis. These days the viewers and fans need nonstop stimulation if they're going to enjoy themselves at all."

Just wondering, folks, do you require that stuff as part of the entertainment package?

Please send your opinion on the state of American culture as seen through the prism of glitz on network TV to Spike@Spikethewonderdog.com for a chance to be a judge on the latest Food Network show, *Fruits Vs. Vegetables*—people outfitted in elaborate food costumes tag-team wrestle each other while racing to cook a five-course dinner eaten by people on stilts.

"Hi, fellows," Leslie Davis says. "First, thank you. I've heard nothing but good reports on your work on *Florida Man*, Spike. And Bud, little Christie Leigh Ingalls-Thomas has been singing your praises for helping her as much as you did. She's got her eye on both of you for parts in her next project, tentatively titled *Buffy the Karen Slayer*."

"Timely and terrific entertainment," Bud says. "We're ready. Oh, Spike and I were wondering, how are the gerbils? Did they survive Megan Thee Stallion's video shoot?"

"Just a few minor back injuries. What happened was Megan herself used them. Nothing salacious, but you can bet on one thing: look for a surge of gerbil juggling once the video drops."

"Juggling gerbils?" Bud says. "What the...?"

"Yeah, Bud," she explains. "Who knew Megan taught herself to how to juggle with her three pet gerbils when she was ten years old? Now, she sings, dances, twerks, and does splits all while juggling multiple gerbils. It's fabulous. But now, Spike, business—and quickly. Please put your head down; I want to get this cape on you, then we'll fit you with the spaniel body and hope we've gotten the head just right. No time to waste here."

Bud, Leslie, and her fitter, Louise, grunt and groan through ten minutes of getting the stupid costume on my massive body. As tight as it feels, the thing fits. The good news is, the legs are closed at the bottom, so my feet are inserted into the paws—I've got protection from the burning coals.

But the problem is the cocker's head. It's a molded, full-head mask. Forcing it on me is like a New York Knick trying to put on one of those Junior G-Man miniature condoms they'd give to seventh-grade boys in sex-ed classes at Montessori schools back when you were still allowed to teach kids about reproduction.

My head's shaped like a football. It's not small and round like a cocker spaniel's. Louise opens up her tool kit, hammers the sides wider, and drills two additional eyeholes. This time it slips on too easily, and it's crooked and loose. I can only see by looking out of the original eyehole with one eye and the new one with the other. I glance at myself in the mirror. Not pretty.

Bud hurries me to the stage and my spot.

The opening credits are just starting. Our old friend, the Man of a Thousand Paychecks, made up to look like Eddie Murphy in the *Doctor Dolittle* movie, is singing "Talk to the Animals." Gyrating down the aisles are the World Animal Award Dancers in grotesque *Lion King*-style costumes, saluting the animals featured in the show.

Some of the so-called heroes include your pal Spike the Wonder Dog, a baby zebra, six beavers, a seagull, a porpoise, and the three mysterious turtles.

I'm standing on a smelly, damp rug. In front of me are ten yards of hot coals that look like they could grill a Peter Luger porterhouse faster than the cook could grab a plate. Special effects lasers are shooting from the coals to make them appear as menacing as possible.

I need to carry a cell phone across the coals. The stage manager tries to put the thing in my mouth, but I can't clamp down and hold it because the jaws on the head don't move. The phone keeps falling on the rug.

"You idiot! Do your fuckin' job," Rune Scott screams at the stage manager. "He needs that phone in his mouth."

"The plastic cocker head can't hold the phone. The jaws don't work, sir," the frightened stage manager says. "Sorry."

"Sorry? There is no 'sorry' in this business. Give it to me. I don't care if I have to shove the goddamn thing down the dog's throat," Rune Scott yells.

"I care," Bud says, stepping forward.

"Who the hell are you?" Scott barks at Bud.

"I'm Bud. I'm with Spike; that's my dog."

He moves into Bud's face, hisses, and shoves him away hard. "Get the fuck outta here!"

This little confrontation has taken my mind off of the flaming challenge ahead of me. "Well, Mr. Scott," I'm thinkin', "you've messed with the wrong dog owner."

Rune Scott is yankin' my head back, literally trying to shove the phone though the mouth on the mask.

"That's it," Bud says. "Stop it now, Scott!"

"Shut up," Rune Scott says.

I once heard Bud tell someone that he never really had to employ any of his karate skills outside of classes. He reached black belt in tenth grade and always kept at it—even goes to the dojo in High Point on Saturdays, if there's no babe hanging around the house that weekend.

Bud grabs Rune Scott by the collar of his suit jacket and yanks him off me.

"You asshole!" Scott screams.

Bud spots a stagehand with a phone shooting video and thinks, "Let this jerk take a few swings at me so it's self-defense."

Red-faced, with veins bulging on his forehead, the stiff and bulky Rune Scott throws a roundhouse at Bud.

He blocks it.

"No one hurts my dog," Bud says in a preternaturally calm tone.

Please mention that to the vet, Bud, before your faithful dog Spike's next anal-gland releasing.

Rune Scott swings wildly twice and misses.

"Aren't we the angry bully boy today," Bud says.

Rune Scott charges. Before he can grapple with Bud, he's on the floor. Bud has a foot on his shoulder. He grabs the phone and tosses it on the coals. Oddly, the phone bursts into flames.

"Hot call from the unemployment office waiting for you over there," Bud says.

The announcer, stage crew, costume woman, production assistant, and prop master looking on give Bud a thumbs-up as a booming sound effect rocks the Garden. More smoke and lasers swirl around the stage. The announcer speaks, setting up my stunt and giving a sample of the kind of embedded product plugs Rune Scott has in store for unsuspecting viewers of the World Animal Awards:

"It was just a normal day for Elaine the cocker spaniel. She was asleep on her Orvis memory foam dog bed after a lunch of two Chick-fil-A Deluxe Sandwiches. When she awakened, she saw a problem: her family, who had dressed in matching gray AG Jeans sweat suits that morning, was trapped, and they didn't have their ultrathin iPhone 17 Pro to call or text for help.

Elaine removed the iPhone from its Pro Max dual charging dock. That's when she saw that the only way to reach them was across a path of smoldering hot Kingsford charcoal, the kind of charcoal you can light with a match. With disregard for the grave danger she faced, and ignoring the juicy Inconceivable Burgers cooking on the charcoal, Elaine dashed across the blazing embers carrying the phone."

The audience is cued to scream and applaud wildly, even though half of them are coughing from the smoke, while others all over the vast Garden are ashamed to be using a bulky iPhone 5 instead of the appealing new ultrathin iPhone 17.

"And so," the announcer intones, "let's begin our show and watch as the valiant cocker re-creates that dangerous dash across the burning coals. Heeeeere's Elaine the cocker spaniel."

"Go, Spike," the stage manager cues me.

I'm off. As soon as I hit the charcoal, I see that the four paws of my costume are on fire. I figure this'll burn through to my feet. I hear Bud yell, "What the hell's going on?"

A second later, the legs of the costume are catching fire. I'm running as fast as I can run, and I'm fast, but it's burning agony.

At the end of the charcoal path, I spot the large round pool that's set up to demonstrate how the three turtles somehow rescued the little girl who was about to be sucked down a storm drain. In one mighty leap, I vault into the vat and plunge into the water. Never felt better to go for a swim.

I shake off the loose plastic head and climb outta the tub with the head in my mouth. A couple of people in the crowd scream, "That dog has two heads!" The rest are applauding wildly and yelling, "Bravo!" My legs have some minor burns—not serious.

"Spike, I'm sorry," Bud says. "I have no idea why the paws on that costume caught fire as soon as you hit the coals."

"No, I'm sorry," Arnold Kauffman says. "Mr. Scott had me soak the little rug Spike was standing on with some flammable fluid. He said it'd be way more exciting for the viewers to see some flames coming off the dog, rather than just watch a dog effortlessly running across the coals. He was concerned that the feet in the costume would make it too easy for Spike."

Bud and I pull outta the show on the spot, and I don't have to hump the host's leg to make it happen. The strippers are happy to take a pass, 'cause Rune Scott never stopped harassing them about coming to his penthouse to "party" with him.

"When you invite four strippers to 'party with me,' you're speaking the international code for, 'Let's have an orgy, and oh yeah, do you take the Amex black card?'" Amber explains.

Bud tells the other participants what Rune Scott did. Most immediately refuse to go on. The live broadcast only runs twelve minutes and Scott will later get sued by the network. Al Roker has to be rushed on camera to fill in with a forty-seven-minute weather report. Rune Scott is disgraced and ends up as a traveling tire salesman in the Outback of Australia. He died being mauled by kangaroos while taking a leak in the underbrush. We animals know.

Some would say that it all ended well with the World Animal Awards, except personally, I'm disappointed we never found out how the three turtles saved the girl. Mr. Boggs is doin' some research into it; maybe it'll be in the back of the book.

CHAPTER FOURTEEN
Let's Do Some Business

I'm back at Andy's and having fun with Jane, in spite of the fact that I smell like a camphor ball with legs from all the Unguentine ointment Andy's slathered over the minor burns. Bein' laid up recovering, I'm finding that I'm missing Herbie's satirical squawking even more…and oh, by the way (mental drumroll, please)…let's have a round of exit applause for Bambi, Amber, Crystal, and Angel.

As far as I know, they've made their final appearance in the story. I thought they might be able to join us over here for a lunch with Andy, who's never met a stripper he wouldn't want to have lunch with. Well, technically, he's never actually met a stripper, but Jane's certain that if he ever did meet one, he'd want them over for lunch.

Be on the lookout for their new series, *Strippers Are People Too*, this fall on FX.

Bud's been busy with *Southern Exposure from NYC* shows. Guess what? He caught the ultrasavvy Buffy, whose nickname is "Little Ms. Mensa," making a mistake with the guest she scheduled for a Zoom interview.

She thought she'd struck talk show gold when she booked the first ever appearance of an unhooded Scott Carter—the new TV personality who's become quite popular as the hooded host of the *Sleeping in Hell!* reality show. Remember? The one where the contestants try to sleep through the night in front of a roaring blast furnace on fire-retardant mattresses using Mr. Pillows' pillows. Bud knew, of course, that Scott Carter is actually Matt Lauer, attempting his television comeback disguised as the hooded host.

He had gotten the inside word on what Lauer was up to from a friend of Lauer's. If you're reading this, so-called friend of Matt Lauer's, you know who you are.

"*Sleeping in Hell!* is now a big hit," the "friend" explained, "so everybody wants to see what the hooded host looks like."

He said that Lauer rationalizes, "Sure I gotta wear a thirty-pound asbestos suit, and I need two hours to be rehydrated by that awful male nurse after tapings—why they wouldn't get me a female nurse like I asked for, I don't know. And, yes, a couple of the contestants are in the hospital recovering from burns, so I get that it's not quite a home safety segment on the *Today* show, but I'm finally back, I'm back! I'm back!"

The "friend" told Bud that Lauer's given himself a complete makeover for his big reveal as Scott Carter. "It's like he's put himself in the witness protection program of the MeToo movement," he joked.

The guy explained that Lauer likely has had a little cosmetic work done, has procured a blond wig, and is planning to use one of those official Tom Selleck glue-on big black mustaches anytime he appears in public.

"But his biggest challenge," he told us, "was the voice. He solved that by going to some celebrity plastic surgeon in Palm Beach for a new procedure called the Feather-Light voice lift. But he's not happy that when he opens his mouth, it's like Joe Biden's talking. He can't seem to raise the new voice above a somewhat raspy, aged whisper."

Buffy is extremely embarrassed when Bud tells her the true identity of Scott Carter.

"Have him on anyway," Buffy says, "and expose who he really is. It won't be long before someone figures it out. Break the story. That's major press for us there."

"Nah, can't do it," Bud says. "Not my style. And anyway, Spike and I met Lauer a couple of years ago at a Joy Behar party in New York. He really was nice with Spike, and any friend of Spike's—"

"Is a friend of yours, I know," Buffy says.

Later that day, Bud gets a call from Lombardo.

"Let's do some business," Lombardo says. "Big Woody's finally resurfaced and wants to meet with you at his New York office. Set it up. I think he's on the verge of deciding if he's gonna buy the station from Sol "The Old

Swede" Silverman. And, oh yeah, call Ruth, Sol's nurse. She's got an idea that might help us. She started to tell me, and I said, 'Please talk to Bud.' I'm so sick of The Old Swede. The guy's a wedge of iceberg lettuce in a world of mixed field greens and baby kale."

"Do not speak ill of the dull," Bud says.

"Call Ruth."

A couple of seconds later, Andy says, "Bud, let's do some business."

Is anyone even paying attention that Jane and I both have some business we'd like to do in the park—called playing Frisbee? Maybe it's time for you guys to take your two loyal pets out for a romp together. She's ahead of me 106 to 97 in Frisbee catches, and the Wonder Dog must have complete and utter victory.

But no!

Bud walks over to Andy's office, and Jane and I follow so we can sit on the floor. Our plan is to stare at them, acting as bored as possible, to make them feel guilty for keeping us indoors—a technique we dogs first perfected while living in caves with humans during the Stone Age.

"OK, Bud," Andy says. "A few ideas I've had, want to bounce offa you. You wanna get involved, just let me know."

"Andy, you're the genius entrepreneur here. I'm just a humble talk show host with a dog who's a superstar and Bravo breathing down my back to finish a reality show about buying a TV station. My boss is pissed off that the reality show focused on trying to find a woman for a date with a dirty old man living in the past while battling ED. I regret that we got involved."

"But, Bud," I'm thinkin', "how could you possibly have misgivings about this show concept? It was one of your many 'stoned ideas,' when you get high and think you've come up with the greatest idea in the world—like the trampoline in our backyard that's never been used, or that five-day vacation you booked for us in Newark that we had to cut short because, well, on the second day, you said, 'Spike, how did we get stuck in Newark?' or..."

"Well," Andy says, "maybe you'll like this. After you told me about Megan Thee Stallion and her gerbil juggling, I figure when the video is released, there's no question that people, a lot of people, are going to try juggling gerbils. Look what happened to sales of lube gel after she released 'WAP.'"

"I actually don't want to know," Bud says.

"So I'm making a big play in gerbil futures," he announces.

"I'll pass on buying rodents. What else?" Bud asks.

"The big idea I have is in what I see as a whole new market in human breath."

"Breath?" Bud asks. "Like meditation breathing?"

"No, celebrity breath. Listen. During the long, controversial, mask-wearing phase of the pandemic, millions of people who've always had bad breath finally realized how offensive their breath actually was, 'cause it was torture smelling it every day with their masks on."

"Good point. But there's all kinds of breath products out there, like breath strips," Bud says.

"Of course, but not...but not my idea. Are you ready?"

"Yes," Bud says, leaning forward. "Celebrity breath strips?"

If this is headed where I think it's headed, send me a six-pack set of Lassie's breath. I think Jane would find that alluring—not that I'm gettin' any romantic notions about Jane.

"Yes, Bud, Celebrity Breath Strips. Now anyone's breath can smell like their favorite celebrity's breath. I've found the equipment that can to do this. It's actually simple. The celeb breathes a sample through a small straw and mails it back to us."

A far more pleasant collection and mailing process than what poor Mr. Messasalma's son has to deal with at Cologuard, I surmise.

"The technology can reproduce the breath samples and print the scent on a small strip. Each little dissolvable strip will have the celebrity's face on it," Andy explains. "The alluring softness of Katy Perry's breath will melt in your mouth, or the husky masculinity of Ving Rhames' will build your confidence with each exhalation. The Beeb's, Harry Styles'...there's no limit to the completely untapped celebrity-breath-scent market."

"Andy, you're gonna make a fortune with that; the lower-tier celebs are doing those Cameo recordings, but the really big ones will go for the breath strips. It's a pure ego stroke for them, having people all over the world exhaling their breath aroma."

I'm planning to sniff around Andy's massive apartment to search out his pot. I just want confirmation, 'cause this whole thing is starting to sound like...

BUSINESS WITH BIG WOODY

Big Woody's New York office is in Carnegie Hall Tower. Bud says he thinks it's the same giant Midtown space Bill Clinton was planning to lease for his postpresidential offices, until he got rocked by massive criticism about the high rent and immediately "walked back" his preferred choice and went to Harlem.

What is it with all these politicians constantly walking back their decisions and opinions? How come no one ever has the balls to say something like, "Whoops, sorry, ya caught me. I had my heart set on that gorgeous, convenient office, but since everybody criticized me for wanting it, now I suddenly don't want it, and in fact, I hate the damn thing, and what has dawned on me is that I've always craved a completely inconvenient place way, way uptown in Harlem."

Bud had never met Big Randy Woody. Strolling over to the meeting at Carnegie Hall Tower, I can tell he's a little nervous. That goes away when we walk into Woody's corner office with a view of Central Park. Bud instantly is comfortable, 'cause Woody smells like Bay Rum aftershave. At a whopping eight dollars a bottle, the aftershave has a pungent aroma that doesn't usually enable new social connections; but Bud keeps a sample in his medicine cabinet to remind him of his father, who apparently swore by the stuff.

"Welcome, gentlemen," Woody says, towering over us. "Good that you're here. Much to discuss, but first, let me show you around. This place kinda tells my life story."

Woody's a handsome guy, about six foot seven, still in reasonably good shape. Dressed in a black blazer and light gray slacks with a sharp crease. He's got a head of thick, perfectly coiffed, dyed-black hair and wears brown Oliver Peoples glasses. He looks you straight in the eye when he speaks.

He shows us some of the trophies he won playing college basketball. He's especially proud of the photos of his units from Afghanistan and Iraq. The large white pulpit that he replaced with a pole when he converted the church into his topless club has been refigured as a wet bar and liquor cabinet. A small glass display case houses vials of the seven oils used in the club's infamous dance routine. A cover of the *National Enquirer* shows the pastor from the South's largest megachurch, The Holy Leg of Lamb of God, enjoying a lap dance from Amber. The headline reads, "Cleric Stripped of Duties."

Behind his desk, framed in gold and the focus of a pin spotlight, is the Anna Nicole Smith centerfold that young Woody's faithful dad painstakingly restored after Woody's mom had torn it to shreds after she found it in the moose head. Next to Nicole is a large blue sign "TM spas…relief you need when you need it."

"Gentlemen, where to begin?" he asks as he sits down.

"Well," Bud says, fidgeting a bit, "wherever you'd like to start."

"OK, let me give you a piece of advice. If you see your Bitcoin investment's made you thirty million dollars on paper, sell! A guy I know who bought in when I did, of course he wanted even more profits, so he let it ride and rode it all the way back down to a couple of million and change. I didn't—I sold, thankfully, and I'm sitting on big bucks."

"I know," Bud says. "Can't help wondering if you feel different being a really wealthy guy now. I mean, I know a little about your kinda hardscrabble background; what's the money done for you psychologically?"

Good question, Bud.

"Good question, Bud," Woody says, apparently reading my mind, "and I have a simple answer. I've spent my whole life worrying about money, and now I'm not worried anymore. Huge relief, and I intend to do something big with the big bucks."

"And that's why we're here? To find out…er…ah…about the station?" Bud says.

"Yes, I've talked to Sol 'The Old Swede' Silverman."

"Oh," Bud says, "and…"

OK, here we go. Is Woody buying Sol out? Are Lombardo and Bud finished?

"I spent an afternoon with him—"

"And?" Bud interrupts.

"The Old Swede is a man who has never suffered from an absence of preoccupation, and he's like a wedge of iceberg lettuce in a world of tossed organic field greens and baby arugula," he says, laughing.

"Exactly. A wedge of iceberg dripping with bright orange Russian dressing," Bud says. "So?"

"Ha! And relax, my friend—and you too, Wonder Dog. I'm not buying the station, and I'm not starting a chain of Throbbing Member spas either," he says, gesturing at the TM sign, "but I was pretty far along. As part of getting some instant brand identification, I was on the verge of a major deal with the BJ's Wholesale Club chain. Was going to wall in the mattress department in each BJ's store and create beautiful, relaxing, palm-tree-lined, luxurious TM relief spas. I had ideas for converting other locations—like making spas out of comedy clubs that closed 'cause stand-up comedians couldn't work in them outta fear of being videoed and canceled."

I like the guy, and not just because as he's going on and on about his plans, he's lobbing lightly seasoned miniature chicken meatballs at me as thanks for saving the strippers. He arches each little ball high in the air, like he's shooting a three-pointer into my vast, drooling mouth.

"But last weekend, my mind was changed, and changed big time."

"What happened?" Bud queries, and I gotta say, it's a completely appropriate question from a TV pro like Bud, if not just a touch predictable.

"I flew with some of my men to a facility in Upstate New York that treats PTSD in vets using hallucinogens and virtual reality. It was a beautiful location on a lake."

Bud leans back in his chair to listen.

"It all traces back to the mental anguish of war," he explains, tossing the little chicken balls at me with the smooth rhythm of a metronome. After ingesting about twenty or so of them, I'm ready to stop, but of course keep goin', not wanting to be an impolite guest. At one point, when Bud's mouth is hangin' open listening, Woody pops one right on his tongue.

"All of us were pushed beyond our limits. Not a man or woman came back without some kind of problem," he says. "The stuff we had to do. The things we saw and heard. The situations you never read about, my God, stuff like…"

He pauses, puts the few remaining little chicken balls in the fridge. He sits down and shakes his head, like he's asking himself if he should really let us in on something.

"One intelligence unit had a rather sadistic captain. The captain needed crucial information and was pissed at Obama 'cause waterboarding had been forbidden. Stateside, the guy's wife worked in a waxing spa. This is not a non sequitur, by the way," he says with a laugh.

"So the captain gets the bright idea that he's going to try waxing the hair offa the backs and chests of detainees to get information."

"That's never been reported," Bud says.

"Yeah, it involved ripping strip by painful strip of thick black hair from prisoners' backs and chests. A corporal waxed the prisoners while the captain asked questions. Hate to generalize, but a lot of these Iraqi men were really hairy. At night, lying in the dark, I can still hear the screaming. The captain reported to Washington that waxing worked better than waterboarding, but the Pentagon issued a 'cease waxing' order immediately."

"The brass said stop because waxing could be classified as torture?" Bud asks.

"Ha! Er, no, Bud. Not at all. The exact order read, 'Waxing? Sorry, too gay.'"

Woody tells us that starting in 2021 after the withdrawal from Afghanistan was botched, more and more of his men have been contacting him. "Somehow, once we finally pulled the troops out, as messy as it was, it hit them like a sledgehammer that all we did, all we saw—the blood, the wounds, the sounds, all of it—was for what?

"One guy rings me at three in the morning. Woke me up, and all he said was, 'For what? For fuckin' what?' and hung up," he says.

"The word going around was that the upstate place was working under the radar and proving to be effective in helping vets. I got my own problems—I feel like the world has gone crazy with hate—so I took the treatment. After about an hour or so, I'm on this trip. It's a great trip—sometimes I'm walking, sometimes I'm flying. At one point, the top of a lake is talking to me about classical music. I put on the VR and I'm in a little town; everyone is smiling and happy and nice and polite. I feel like I'm strolling down Main Street in a cross between a Ken Burns documentary on manners and a forties Disney feature."

"Ha! I'd like to see that," Bud says.

"Everyone in town, everyone around me, is so civil! Suddenly, that's it—civil!…civil!….civil! I can't put the word away. For like an hour, the word 'civil' is screaming at me or whispering to me or taunting me. It's like there's a little speaker that only broadcasts one word on the inside of my brain."

Woody gets up. He walks over to a table and flips over a big card with a large red, white, and blue logo with "NCP" in it.

"That's why I've decided to take every dime I've got and launch the National Civility Project."

"That's brilliant," Bud says with a big smile.

"I don't know if it actually is. I don't know if I can impose any kind of civility truce on the culture wars, or tamp down the menace and anger I see everywhere that upsets me. I don't know if this can help prevent minor disputes from turning into violent confrontations; I don't know if we can lessen the shaming on social media or stop people from shooting each other over perceived insults; I don't know what kind of results might be produced for my thirty million dollars. But I'm gonna try."

"God bless you," Bud says.

"I'd accept that if I believed in God—and speaking of God, play devil's advocate for me here, Bud. Tell me what you think, please. See a downside?" he asks.

I got no idea what Bud's gonna say to Woody, but here's a polite, well-informed dog's opinion: I think, on the extreme end, this'll be seen as an antigun movement, since, as best I can figure, shooting someone isn't a particularly civil thing to do. And I also see a lot of possible "civility surfers"—grifters and bums that'll be tryin' to shame people into helping them. An opportunistic guy on the corner will spot the red, white, and blue Civility Now button on your jacket and expect immediate access to your Amex card for the day.

"Well, even though JFK in his inaugural address said, "Civility is not a sign of weakness,' it's possible that a lot of angry folks are gonna say you're just a woke pansy tryin' to take the balls outta the country and turn the nation into a bunch of mannered wimps," Bud suggests.

"Well, I'm hoping to get some dynamic figures—sports, news, films, TV, boxing, MMA…real hard-nosed-image types—to get behind this with an endless stream of short PSAs. I wanna talk to LeBron James. I've got a lot of ideas for men and women on all sides of the political field."

"Good," Bud says, "but I'd focus on kids. Like that old 'Don't Be a Litterbug' campaign in schools in the fifties that the social historians say worked so well."

The meeting goes on for almost an hour, as Bud and Woody brainstorm about all the gimmicks that could be used for the NCP. I'm grateful that at no point do they mention the deployment of mimes. Dogs hate mimes—figure out why yourself.

Sadly, here's what ended up happening: the civility project and Woody's money went down the tubes. He never came close to achieving any unity of purpose.

He faced immediate opposition from an angry countermovement—the "My Body, My Behavior" anti-mask-and-vaccine fanatics were delighted to become anti-civility protesters. Their demonstrations ranting about not wanting to be told to be polite got massive media coverage and dwarfed the occasional feel-good stories about newfound acts of kindness and civility.

Woody thought parents would love his idea, and he cringed watching videos of moms and dads in school board meetings screaming that no one had the right to teach their kids manners. "If my son doesn't like his teacher, he has a constitutional right to call that teacher an asshole," an enraged mother shrieked to a reporter, while small specks of foam formed at the corners of her snarling mouth.

Shortly after the initiative was announced, Americans began projecting all kinds of potential scenarios about how their freedoms would be limited in a far more civil society.

"Will I be arrested by the politeness police for using my car horn to get some damn old lady on a walker to hurry up as she's hobbling across the street in front of me?" one driver railed. Thousands of others protested, "My horn, my choice," saying, "If that asshole in the car in front of me doesn't accelerate the instant the light turns green, nobody's going to stop me from blastin' my horn at him a fraction of a second later to get the hell moving." Bumper stickers that read, "Honk If You Love Honking" became wildly popular.

People were fearful that they wouldn't be allowed to yell into their cell phones in public, particularly in elevators. Thousands more were annoyed at the prospect of having to take their shopping carts all the way back to the supermarket instead of leaving them scattered around the parking lot after loading groceries into their cars.

One Big Pharma company profited from Woody's idea by creating a very expensive tranquilizer guaranteed to provide "civility sedation." The drug firm lobbied lawmakers to try the pills on free vacations. As a result, deeply entrenched political partisanship stopped. Bridges, roads, and tunnels suddenly were being repaired all over the country. Unfortunately, once the politicians ran out of free pills, they realized they'd made the mistake of actually working together across the aisle, and issued orders to stop repairs immediately.

Woody lost it all. He was dead broke. But Crystal, Amber, Angel, and Bambi came to the rescue. They never forgot what a good boss he was. As we write this, thanks to their investment and belief in him, they're on the verge of launching the first Woody's Throbbing Member Relief Spa, and this time, the My Body, My Behavior men are solidly behind his effort.

IKE "I GOT MONEY" PILES IN THE NEWS

A couple of days later, I'm with Bud and Jane at Andy's. Virtual Andy is sitting quietly in the corner in his usual ultraerect posture, while Actual Andy is down on Wall Street making a pitch to backers to raise funds for his latest scheme.

"Gluten-free is wildly popular," Andy told us before he left. "Everybody from Gaga to Katy Perry to Billy Bob Thornton and Jessica Simpson and, of course, Gwyneth—and way more—are on record talking about the gluten-free lifestyle. There's more than ten brands of gluten-free dog food, Spike and Jane. I'll get you some."

We shook our heads like, "No thanks, pal. Just flip open the Friskies and keep talking."

His plan is to create a big yellow sticker that will go on all manner of products that obviously don't include gluten, but will reassure gluten fanatics that the item is gluten-free and supports a gluten-free lifestyle.

"Who wouldn't want a gluten-free dishwasher?" he claims. "Then there's your GF flashlights and your…anyway, whattaya think, Bud? It'll cost nothing to increase sales to the—"

"No," Bud interrupts. "No."

"No?" Andy asks nervously.

"No."

"No, well then, so what about my other—"

"Yeah, OK," Bud says. "I like your idea that, because of his name, the old TV talking horse Mr. Ed could be resurrected as the advertising voice of ED medicine. I thought about it."

"You do? You did?" Andy says.

"Yeah, call that animal casting agent Leslie Davis; she's terrific. Did you see that picture of her at Joe Camel's funeral on the *Post*'s website? I believe she attended the service with her longtime client, a horse that's a direct descendant of the original Mr. Ed, the sitcom star."

"Wow, great! Thanks, Bud. Glad you agree."

Yeah, Andy, I agree with Bud. Mr. Ed makes sense in this role, and not just because the horse's name is spelled "E-D." The boys who watched that show in the early '60s now have a growing (no pun intended here, my faithful readers) need for ED products, and their trusted old favorite Mr. Ed would be a source of comfort as a wise and friendly adviser. I'm also confident some advertising writer will figure a way to work "straight from the horse's mouth" into Mr. Ed's pitch.

The sun is blazing into the apartment a little later that day when Bud pours himself a glass of his favorite white burgundy wine and feeds Jane and me, and we settle in to watch the nightly news.

What Lester Holt reports shakes us.

"After two years of incarceration, the nation's most infamous athlete, the former world champion boxer Ike 'I Got Money' Piles, was released today from Clinton Correctional Facility in Dannemora, New York."

"Oh God," Bud says. "Spike, there he is!"

The video shows Ike "I Got Money" Piles limping away from the prison as he tosses hundred-dollar bills at reporters and die-hard fans. "I still got piles a' money. I still the greatest. I never hurt no dog. This all frame-up, fake news, media out to get me, and I got scores to settle."

Holt continues, "In late 2019, the boxer was arrested inside his secret dogfighting operation in Brooklyn."

We see video of then police commissioner James O' Neill speaking. Behind him, animal rescue people are trying to get the twenty or so vicious, drugged-up dogs out of their cages and off to shelters.

"This is the largest operation of its kind we've ever uncovered," O'Neill announces. "Trainers, exercise equipment, state-of-the-art closed-circuit facilities for secret round-the-world broadcasts, steroid-laced food for the dogs. We're still looking for the person or the people behind Ike Piles—the ones who bankrolled this whole thing and some of the international connections involved, and that work goes to the FBI.

"The discovery of the operation came about because the canine television personality Spike the Wonder Dog had been kidnapped by Piles' crew. Fortunately, a chip in Spike's collar led the police to the scene of the crime."

The report goes on, "Video recordings later indicated boxer Piles lost a finger in a confrontation with Spike moments before Piles was about to use a white-hot branding iron to brand the kidnapped canine as his property. Piles himself fell victim to his own devices when he was attacked and mauled by a giant dog he'd imported from South America. Piles lost a leg, which he claimed would not end his boxing career."

Cut to video of Ike "I Got Money" Piles moments after he was sentenced to jail. "I never knew nothin' about no dogs fightin'. I gonna come outta prison even richer than I am now. Jail fulla chumps. Give me a week, I runnin' the place. I get out, maybe I even fight again—there be plenty of great one-legged, nine-fingered champs over the years—and if not, my business empire pouring in cash. For example, my sky-divin' sex tour be like you havin' intercourse in outer space. For info, call seven-oh-two-six-five-five—"

Holt cuts him off. "In further news tonight…," he reads. Bud hits the mute button.

Jane, Bud, and I sit there looking at each other.

"Horrible," Virtual Andy says from his perch.

I'm reliving my abduction—my dog walker getting smashed over the head, my getting dragged into a car, the smelly cage they put me in, the fights, the freezer.

The apartment door swings open. Before we see him, Andy announces, "I met Mr. Ed—actually, he's known as Ed the Sixth—and he's all in. Leslie Davis is terrific and loves the idea. She also took a tip from me to buy gerbil futures. One thing, though: right before I left, Leslie Davis told me to keep it quiet, but that Ed the Sixth is a gelding. What does that mean, Bud?" he asks.

"Not good," Virtual Andy volunteers. "Not good, boss."

"What? What?" Andy asks. "What's he mean, Bud?"

"We're headed out now," Bud tells him, "but Virtual Andy will explain everything."

As we're closing the door, Virtual Andy's saying, "And another thing, boss: launch your campaign in November, which is National Impotency Awareness Month…"

That gets me wondering, aren't guys with the condition already aware they got it?

CHAPTER FIFTEEN

THE WONDER DOG IN DC

Bud's phone call with Ruth, Sol "The Old Swede" Silverman's nurse, is one of the weirdest calls he's had since the second credit card fiasco at yet another sex resort in Thailand. On that one, the phone rang at home around midnight. Bud was urgently informed that the four escorts staying with him that afternoon in his suite at the resort had just maxed out his credit card at the bar.

"Sir, would you please come down to the beach immediately with American dollars to pay for the ten magnums of Cristal champagne, twenty-six Kobe burgers, and the imported Junior's cheesecakes your girls just ordered as 'lunch on the house' for everybody at the pool?" a heavily accented voice demanded.

"Those girls, whoever they are, may be at your bar on the beach right now," Bud said, "but right now, I happen to be home and in bed in the good old USA watching the 'Jack and the Marijuana Stalk' episode of *Family Guy*."

Nurse Ruth tops that call.

First, she shyly confesses to Bud that she's fallen in love with The Old Swede. This is big news. Even I, with my close connection to the pangs of the human heart, did not foresee this flowering of fervor.

"Watching over him while he was fighting for his life in the hospital after that unfortunate overdose situation, I realized how deeply I felt, how much I cared," Ruth explains softly. "He's always been a complete gentleman to me. Sure, I see him transfixed by my breasts when he should be reading, eating, or watching TV, but he's never made the slightest of moves."

"Love works in strange ways, Ruth. Who can explain it? Who can tell you why?" Bud says.

"He needs to see me in a new way, not as his caretaker but as the exact type of woman he's looking for—a woman even more attractive to him than that damn Nancy Pelosi. He's obsessed with her."

"He is, isn't he?" Bud says. "I wonder if many other men his age think of Nancy like she's the captain of their high school cheerleaders, and not an eighty-three-year-old woman who likely looks remarkably different from her public persona when the alarm goes off every morning?"

"He's obsessed! Obsessed!" she says, raising her voice. "He says he would be a slave to her charms, and he gets wildly jealous when Chuck Schumer stands too close to her at press conferences. He spends hours watching C-SPAN hoping to catch a glimpse. He loved it when she'd put her pandemic mask around her neck and speak wide-eyed into the camera, hardly moving her lips and sounding a bit like an aged Marilyn Monroe. And when she's on the news, it's 'Look, there she is, there she is—that walk of hers, those high-heeled shoes of hers, those big...' well, you-know-whats of hers, right, Bud?"

"Yes, I know the *whats* of which he was speaking, Ruth. Mr. Silverman is a strange man—loveable, sex-crazed, courtly, out of touch with the times. Some say he's a bit like a wedge of iceberg lettuce in a world of—"

"I've been thinking that," she interrupts.

"...and I'm really sorry that his preoccupation with Pelosi has you so upset," Bud concludes.

"Well, that's what I want to talk about, Bud, because I think I can turn the whole Pelosi thing to my advantage."

This, I figure, is likely to be the scheme Lombardo wants Bud to hear.

Spoiler alert: little do I know that her plan will send us all to Washington with Sol "The Old Swede" Silverman, who will be acting as an adult chaperone for a local third-grade class visiting Nancy Pelosi on a school trip.

Interested?

Me, too.

Nurse Ruth explains, "Mr. Silverman read in the paper that some students won a trip to DC and would have a half an hour with Pelosi. So he gave the kids' elementary school a hundred and sixty thousand dollars to hire three more social media trauma counselors. Of course, the donation wasn't due to his sudden interest in helping children confront the perils of PopJam and

Kidzworld; it was a bribe so he could join them and ogle Pelosi in person. He actually thinks she'll leave her husband for him. He's certain he'll make a love connection while he's showing her the children's crayon drawings of her banging the gavel in Congress."

"How do you figure you'll use this to your advantage?" Bud asks, in the clipped professional manner of Erin Andrews grilling Coach Andy Reid about the strategy he'll deploy playing Tom Brady, who's not happy with retirement and now competes with a cast on his throwing arm.

"Mr. Silverman has to see me as a woman, not a nurse, and believe me, I won't be wearing my medical uniform," she says. "Far from it."

Ruth goes on to explain that after hours of complicated research in a darkened corner of the National Archives, she confirmed that she has precisely the same physical measurements as Pelosi and is forty years younger. Ruth then went all out and hired a personal shopper at Target. The shopper put together a form-fitting pantsuit that she reasoned would be similar to the kind of outfit the former Speaker of the House will be wearing when the kids arrive in her office at the Capitol.

"I'm dyeing my hair brunette like hers and getting the same kind of long bob haircut. I'll have a brooch on my lapel and heels a full inch higher than hers. Believe me, I played Ulla in *The Producers*. Mel Brooks wanted a statuesque character who reeked of sexuality for that part, and he said he'd never had a better Ulla than me, except for my Southern accent, which is why I got replaced on the road, 'cause I was supposed to be Swedish. Anyway, Sol's going to see me standing next to her, and suddenly it'll be no contest—compared to me, Pelosi's going to look like Frances McDormand in that burlap sack she always wears to the Oscars."

Lombardo orders Bud to go to DC to shoot this caper as the final episode of The Old Swede's reality show.

"Let's just hope," Lombardo says, "that he'll hobble off into the sunset with Ruth, sell us the station, disconnect that stupid watch, and this will all be over like a bad dream."

The big-bucks donation The Old Swede gave to the school got him a say in the planning of the outing. He'll be one of five chaperones for the thirty kids. He forced the school to contractually guarantee that he'll meet Pelosi personally, or they'll have to fire the media trauma counselors and give him his money back with interest. He'll be the one showing her the kids' drawings.

Because some of the parents—mostly the ones who wouldn't let their kids get vaccinated—didn't want their third grader passing through airport metal detectors, the group has to take a chartered bus to DC. The chaperones also have to promise the same parents that their children will not learn anything about the nation's history on the trip.

It's a five-hour drive. So fearful was he that the small toilet bowl in the bus's tiny bathroom would prove too difficult a target for him, he demanded twenty guaranteed restroom stops. In addition, The Old Swede appointed himself in charge of the entertainment on the journey.

"I may be a little old, but I know what's fun for kids. I vividly recall the games of my youth—marbles, jacks, drop the handkerchief, kick the can. The hours will fly by. I'll lead them singing rounds of 'Ninety-Nine Bottles of Beer on the Wall' all the way through the state of Virginia."

Mack gets Ruth's prep and planning on tape, so all Bud and I have to do is take the train down to DC and join the action.

"The children know you and the Wonder Dog are coming," Mack tells Bud. "That excites them, so get Spike ready for a lot of petting. But they've got no idea who Nancy Pelosi is. Sol 'The Old Swede' Silverman went to their classroom. He showed them pictures of her. The principal was able to cut him off right as he was proclaiming to the kids how he could hardly wait to be with her in person and see her big…well, big you-know-whats."

"I know whats," Bud says. "Bless the principal, but those third graders are never going to be the same after a long day on the bus with him."

"The kids basically think they are going to Washington to meet The Old Swede's grandmother."

Mack tells us that Ruth will board the bus wearing her green nurse's uniform with her hair under a hat. She'll nip into the ladies' room as soon as they're in the Capitol, and emerge in her new outfit.

"I saw her in it," Mack tells us. "We shot her at the Target store, and she looks phenomenal. The Old Swede is going to—"

"I hope that's what he's going to do," Bud says. "But are you certain there are no problems in getting Spike in there, into the House office building?"

"We got a whole list of guidelines from her office. He's in. They know about Spike and you; they even know about Piles and the whole kidnapping thing. They did indicate that Nancy Pelosi is crazy about dogs, and even has a tradition of decorating her dogs at Christmas. She always outfits the poor things with those silly reindeer antlers for dogs. We figured maybe Spike could wear an antler set. The staffer who wrote the memo told me Pelosi would get a big kick out of it. I can get Joe the taxidermist down here to rig up something that'll be really funny-looking on Spike."

"Sure," Bud says, with complete disregard for my self-esteem. I've been figuring I'd walk into Pelosi's congressional office as Spike the Wonder Dog, nonvoting canine citizen of these great United States, not as a sight gag. Ah, but wearing reindeer antlers will be a small price to pay to see the big moment when The Old Swede meets Nancy Pelosi, a romantic encounter rivaled only by when Jeff Bezos dislocated his shoulder trying to hug his new rocket.

Bud and I get to the Capitol before their bus arrives. We sit in a lobby watching slippery politicians and slippery lobbyists walking on slippery marble floors. By the way, we observe that dynamo of the Senate, Chuck Schumer, close up when he stops in front of us and bends way over to tie one of his shiny black shoes. The little glasses that are always perched on his nose don't fall off. Bud tells me some people use glue for everything.

Mack phones from the bus.

"The Old Swede was getting exhausted," he whispers to Bud. "But he popped a couple of pills and was talking a mile a minute. In around ninety seconds, he explained the history of Washington and described in detail all thirty-two of the monuments the class will see tomorrow. His blathering got so annoying, the kids started begging him for more of the Mel Tormé music he played all the way from Fayetteville to Roanoke Rapids."

"Keep us posted," Bud instructs. "We're waiting."

A little later, as we're listening to the velvet tones of three lobbyists convincing a bewildered freshman congresswoman about the urgent need to dig several new coal mines on indigenous people's sacred burial sites, we get a text from Mack.

"We're heading in now. Delay so Ruth can change. Kids excited to see Spike. Sol ate a huge five-layer meat burrito at the Taco Bell stop. Big mistake."

Bud texts back: "All good here. Will do. Re: Burrito—does that mean he's farting again but doesn't realize he is, like in that meeting with Lombardo a couple of weeks ago?"

"Affirmative. Children amused. Adults annoyed. Driver bought Glade at unplanned stop. Ruth says Sol's large intestine can bellow like the foghorn on a tugboat when provoked."

"I know."

"He's coming through the door now," Mack texts.

"And we thought the attack on the Capitol was bad," Bud responds.

Several kids swarm around me. In my enthusiasm, I jump up and greet them but knock over two little girls. Not good.

"Do you want to put these big antlers on Spike so Mrs. Pelosi will laugh?" Sol "The Old Swede" Silverman asks the girls as they're getting up.

About three minutes later, and after much pushing and pulling and nearly being blinded, I've got huge antlers on my head. I look like a bull elk in the full urge of mating season about to search for an available female, which I figure is likely a good metaphor for many of the men here in Congress.

We're a bit surprised to see Senator John Hickenlooper rushing over for a selfie with me.

"We've got the largest elk herd in the world in Colorado," he explains. "This photo's worth a thousand votes. Wow, what a rack!"

"Pelosi!" The Old Swede cries, whirling around to scan the lobby. "Where?"

"Shut up, Sol," Bud tells him.

"Where? Where? Huh?" The Old Swede asks Hickenlooper, passing gas and vibrating with excitement.

"Er, never mind that photo for now," Hickenlooper says, hurrying off.

We head to Pelosi's office. Bud, Nurse Ruth, and me are lagging back so Sol doesn't see how phenomenal Ruth appears. Here's my report.

Nurse Ruth is smashing in a perfectly tailored pink pantsuit. The white angora sweater under the jacket appears way too tight for congressional standards, but would probably be perfect for a receptionist at Imagine Entertainment hoping to be discovered by a casting director. Her new hairstyle screams, "I could be a Speaker of the House or in a 1960s sitcom!" The eyeliner, lashes, makeup, and carefully lined red lips say, "I got this done free at Macy's this morning. Whadda ya think?" She's topped off with a gentle application of alluring Guerlain Shalimar perfume that will render Nurse Ruth highly sniffable to President Biden, if he happens to be stumbling around Congress desperately trying for a deal to get a bridge—any bridge, anywhere— repaired before he leaves office.

An intern from Nancy Pelosi's staff is at the front of our group chatting politely with Sol and a couple of parents. It's a long, slow walk, 'cause Sol

"The Old Swede" Silverman is not exactly an Indy 500 pacesetter on his feet. I'm glad we're goin' slow, 'cause every time we speed up, the damn antlers slip over my eyes and I can't see, and accidentally poke Ruth a little hard from behind. I don't know what The Old Swede is in for if he does hook up with her, but I'll tell you this—she really enjoys being prodded in the ass by antlers.

Just sayin'—but any of you antler fetishists out there, don't write; don't send pictures. I just don't want to know.

You gotta figure this is a big day for all of us, bein' in DC, but how excited can Pelosi be at the prospect of spending part of her busy day trying to hold the attention of a class of eight-year-olds? Particularly on the day it's been announced that one of the rioters who broke into her office on January 6, rummaged through her desk, and left her a threatening note has just signed a seven-figure development deal with the new Patriot Vision streaming service.

There's ample room for all of us in the large foyer that's part of Nancy Pelosi's offices. After the long, slow walk, the kids are happy to finally sit down and get back to their video games. The Old Swede is huffing and puffing and leaning on a chair, and is staring at the big green door to Pelosi's office like Marilyn Chambers is about to emerge and whisper, "OK, cutie, you're next."

Instead, a strained but efficient-looking woman appears from behind the green door. With the enthusiasm of an exhausted Olive Garden hostess welcoming a party of ten to the restaurant five minutes before the kitchen closes, she says, "I'm Mrs. Gardner, Mrs. Pelosi's assistant. She will see you now, and the children should put away their phones and video games, please."

"Shit!" a couple of eight-year-old boys mutter.

We file through a large, desk-lined room and pass through another one. Along the way, staff members are laughing, pointing at the red, white, and blue Christmas tree balls now dangling from my antlers. I don't care. It's all show-biz to me. I got a tiny HD wireless mini camera on the highest horn. Mack's shooting with his handheld 4K cam, and Bud's got our HD minicam.

Sol "The Old Swede" Silverman's limping slowly. He stops, pops a pep pill. I hear him muttering, "Ruth. Where's Ruth? Don't worry, Ruth, that's only my third."

Nancy Pelosi seems lovely. As the Target personal shopper guessed, she's wearing a pantsuit—not peach, like Ruth's, but tan with a white blouse under the jacket. Nurse Ruth's eyes twinkle, and she smiles a confident, knowing smile as soon as she sees Pelosi. The same kind of confident, knowing smile Meryl Streep flashes every time she learns she's nominated for another award.

Pelosi seems warm and genuine when she says, "Welcome, children. I'm so happy to see you today."

I glance at her assistant, Mrs. Gardner, who rolls her eyes at me, suggesting, "'Happy'? Five minutes ago, you were moaning that you had to do this."

Bud's phone pings with a text from Lombardo: "You're gonna love the little surprise I set up there."

Nancy Pelosi starts with an explanation to the class about how her office works and what she does for her job.

The kids are about as interested in what she's saying as they'd be if their fathers were telling them about the intricacies of installing drywall.

Sensing her audience has only slightly more of an attention span that Donald Trump's every time she was forced to talk to him, she pivots to the next item on her agenda—the kids' artwork.

As she's about to go to the big moment of calling The Old Swede forward to show her the drawings, she spots me, antlers and all, standing next to The Old Swede.

Bud made me stand next to him.

"I hate to do this to you, Spike," he told me, "but The Old Swede's flatulence is terrible. If you're close to him, maybe Pelosi will think it's you, and she won't suddenly end the meeting because of Sol's fumes."

That's just great; blame it on the dog—and you know what I mean. Every dog owner in America who's ever cut a big one in front of guests immediately blames it on their dog. I didn't come all the way to Washington to be part of another cover-up. But here I am. TMZ headline: "Spike denies airborne toxic event at Pelosi's office."

"Oh wow!" Nancy Pelosi says, pointing at me. "This is hysterical. I knew Spike the Wonder Dog was coming, but I didn't know he'd have the biggest rack I've ever seen."

"You do!" The Old Swede yells.

I look at Sol and bark to make it seem like he was talking to me.

"Right, sir. Spike, you sure do," Pelosi responds. "Come here, buddy. I've got a treat for you."

Nancy Pelosi smells nice. From my dog's point of view, I'd say she has exceptionally good ankles and terrific shoes. Not too sure about the panty-hose—aren't they kind of out of date? But the rest is terrific.

"I love your balls, Spike," she says, bending over and examining the decorations.

Mrs. Gardner bursts into hysterical laughter.

Pelosi seems annoyed. "What's so funny, Linda?" she asks.

Mrs. Gardner conveys a most complex facial expression and nods in the direction of what's dangling under my tail.

"Ha! OK, cut that line from the video, Bud. If it goes viral, six weeks of working on voting rights will get knocked off the front page.

"Now, let me get you a couple of dog treats, Spike," she says.

She can't find the treats. After a fast minute of rummaging through her desk, she says, "What the…? Wait a minute. Have the interns been eating the dog biscuits again? That's it, Linda; we're going to have to start paying them!"

She feeds me half of a Maryland crab cake sandwich she apparently started eating before we got there. It's good—just a little light on the tartar sauce, but using corn flakes to bind the crabmeat was brilliant. However, I digress.

"I'm told," Nancy Pelosi says, "that one of your chaperones is going to show me some very special drawings you children made for me to decorate my offices. Please come forward, Mr. Sol Silverman."

The Old Swede is momentarily paralyzed. It's as if he's tasered himself with his long-simmering lust for her, and he's thinking of the consequences that might result from his forthcoming inappropriate actions.

He's imagining his trial, the jail time, the possible loss of his toupee to a violent bald cellmate, the weight gain from all that starchy prison food. He's processing the inevitable comparisons to Andrew Cuomo's behavior, or maybe even that creepy Jeffrey Epstein's, but wait—she's eighty-three years old, not fifteen, so no Epstein; but Cuomo, yes, Cuomo. "I'll be compared to Cuomo," he's thinking, "that slobbery-kissing, denying-everything, rubbing-your-back-without-asking Cuomo." He sees the horror of the headlines in the papers back home: "Old Swede Gives Pelosi a Feel on School Trip: Faces Twenty Years but Declares, 'Worth it.'"

"What the hell," he thinks, as he slowly shuffles toward her with his arms outstretched and the fingers on his concupiscent hands twitching. "It's now or never. Here I go," he says to himself.

PART FOUR

HEADED TO EAST HAMPTON

T hat's got to be a misprint there. How do these things happen? Ask Mr. Boggs, not me. Or talk to the publisher. I'm just telling you the story as best I can. Yes, sure we're probably going to East Hampton, and it might even mean big trouble or it might not. But right now, we are still in Pelosi's office and Sol "The Old Swede" Silverman is inching toward her.

He's moving so slowly that Pelosi fills the silence by reading some of her briefing material on him.

"According to our research," she says, "Mr. Silverman is either ninety-three or a hundred and two years old. He regrets not serving in World War Two because of head wounds encountered during botched hair transplant surgery. He's a retired accountant with one daughter. He's healthy today but was recently released from the hospital after…er, well, er…a three-day permanent…ah, never mind, children. He's the owner of WGHP-TV station in High Point, North Carolina, and calls himself The Old Swede because of his bright blond hair."

She looks up. "Nice to see a mullet on Capitol Hill again, sir. And of note, Mr. Silverman holds the distinction of having had himself paged at The Beverly Hills Hotel pool in the 1970s more often than Robert Evans. Thank you for escorting these fine young Americans here, and welcome, Mr. Sol 'The Old Swede' Silverman," she says, smiling.

He's closing in. Both of the widening palms of his gnarled mitts are aimed squarely at her, ready to commence groping.

I'm thinking maybe he's going to pretend to fall and the only thing he'll be able to grab for balance will be her…well, her…her you-know-whats. Maybe he'll lunge at her? He claims he was on the fencing team in prep school. Maybe he'll…

"Mrs. Pelosi," he says shyly, with a tear running down his cheek, "will you please hold my hand?"

"How sweet. I'd love to, Mr. Silverman," she says.

The Old Swede and Pelosi are standing at the front of the group looking like the bride and groom figures on a wedding cake, except the groom's eyes are fixated on the bride's bodice.

Everyone's applauding for The Old Swede. They all know how much he wanted to meet Nancy Pelosi.

She notices he's staring at her. Figuring he's nervous in her presence, 'cause sometimes people are, she seeks to relax him, softly inquiring, "And how are you feeling today, Mr. Silverman? Are you enjoying your visit to Washington?"

"I've been to the mountains!" he proclaims, eyes bolted onto her blouse. "Oh, I've been to the mountains and I've looked over, and I've seen the promised land."

"I know you're of a generation that was always supportive of the great Dr. Martin Luther King," she tells him, unaware that his was a different mountain analogy than in King's famous speech.

Two children appointed by The Old Swede show her the drawings.

Unfortunately, some of the renderings are terrible, because the day the class drew them, the "world leader of the day" picture on their computers was Kim Jong-un. The photograph of Nancy Pelosi that they were supposed to copy was hanging at the front of the class. To make it easier, the kids in the back of the class traced Jong-un's face and filled in Pelosi's hair around the face. The large toy missile Jong-un was holding became the gavel Nancy Pelosi was supposed to be banging.

Pelosi politely applauds the creativity of all the children, and conveys only the slightest grimace each time she comes across one of the conflated drawings of her and Kim Jong-un.

All the while, I'm studying the face of The Old Swede. He's deeply concentrating. Is he wondering what just happened? Why is he being so shy? Once close to her, did his lust evaporate? Is he realizing that foolishly he's let his golden moment pass him by? Or is he just trying to avoid passing gas?

We'll never know, because next is the surprise Lombardo set up.

Still holding hands with The Old Swede, Nancy Pelosi reads, "No group during the pandemic deserved more credit than our front-line medical workers: the doctors, the nurses, the technicians—all of whom saved millions of lives. We have with us today a nurse who gave up a lucrative career working with Mel Brooks to join the medical profession, and to attend to patients and protect them from harm. During his recent hospitalization, she stood by the ailing Mr. Silverman until he was able to…er, ah…let's just say he was able to relax enough to go home."

This is great, I'm thinkin'. Lombardo figured a way to get Ruth to stand next to Pelosi, because…

"So," she continues, "I'm proud to present the COMA—the Congressional Outstanding Medical Award—to…"

Forget that this same award was once given to the Sackler family of Purdue Pharma. It's history now. Forget it.

"...to Nurse Ruth Butler. Please step forward, Nurse Butler, so that I may present you with the medal."

"Thank you for this surprise. I love her; she's been so wonderful to me," The Old Swede whispers to Pelosi.

Nurse Ruth was concealing herself behind a pillar. She steps out and strides confidently toward Pelosi and The Old Swede. You can score this scene with any seductive music you want. Maybe a good choice would be Little Richard singing "The Girl Can't Help It," like he did in his movie with the ultrasexy Jayne Mansfield. Or go for Lou Reed's "Walk on the Wild Side." Or maybe Yung Berg's "Sexy Lady." Pick something provocative, because Nurse Ruth's slow, classic "show it and hide it" walk demands that kind of music.

"What?" The Old Swede gasps. He drops Pelosi's hand.

In that moment, I think Nancy Pelosi is a little disappointed. Watching them, I sense she actually might have been developing an attraction to The Old Swede herself. Maybe it was his deep tan and his courtly country club demeanor, and that little tear on his cheek? Did he somehow remind her of John Boehner and their late afternoons in his cozy office? She'd have a Diet Coke, and he'd blow perfect rows of smoke rings at her over his dry martini.

"Ruth? My Ruth? Oh my word, Ruth, my Ruth, what have you done to yourself? Wow!"

Ruth gives The Old Swede a look that says, "Drink me in with your eyes, Sol. I'm all yours if you want me, Big Daddy," and stands next to Pelosi.

No contest.

I'm not gonna belabor the details. Just a couple of the highlights.

The Old Swede later admitted that the moment he saw Ruth in Pelosi's office, he became sexually aroused without the benefit of drugs for the first time since the end of the Persian Gulf War. Back then The Old Swede celebrated the success of Operation Desert Storm on the Outer Banks of North Carolina with a philosophy major from UNC, who for some reason found old accountants with bad toupees irresistible.

Ruth and Sol left the Capitol building and checked into the honeymoon suite at the Hay-Adams hotel in downtown Washington.

They emerged five days later with plans to move to Florida. Unfortunately, and sadly coincidental to this story, the large property they bought was at the

Silver Singles Hyperactive Community in Boca. It all had looked so wonderful on the internet—impossibly happy seniors everywhere, swimming, playing golf and bridge, engaged in what looked like riveting conversations, and all the while enjoying low-sodium meals.

Omitted was any mention of the infamous cheatin' side of town.

It was there, some years later, under a pickleball court, in a secret subterranean playroom furtively dug by swingers using primitive tools stolen from the cafeteria, that Sol "The Old Swede" Silverman drew his final breath, entangled with three frisky ninety-year-old women who found him irresistible because of his knowledge of Mel Tormé recordings.

The rarely gullible Ruth actually thought her husband was off again playing checkers with the guys.

"Playing checkers" was listed as the cause of The Old Swede's death.

CHAPTER SIXTEEN

TIME AND TIDE WAIT FOR NO MAN

Ike "I Got Money" Piles is sitting on his throne in his mansion in Connecticut. He went to Greenwich when he got out of prison.

"I not ready to go back to Vegas yet," he told reporters, "and Vegas not ready for the all-new and improved Ike 'I Got Money' Piles."

Piles' mansion is on the grounds of the vast estate of his perverted business partner, Scott Blatterman—the guy whose father ran a pest control empire and had trained him at an early age to kill things, the guy who bankrolled Money's dogfight operation, the guy the cops didn't find, the guy who didn't serve time…so, yeah, the guy who owed Ike "I Got Money" big-time.

"Now you gotta be extra good to Ike 'I Got Money' Piles," Money told Blatterman, referring to himself in the third person, which he did so often that strangers usually thought he was talking about somebody else. "You be so extra good 'cause Money Piles got so much proof on you, your fat pink ass'll get worn out in prison first night you inside."

Piles has just been watching a video that his henchman, James One, and his favorite girlfriend, Cartier, and his all-purpose man, Chicago Bob, made to welcome their boss home from prison.

"This sizzle reel be first step we need to get Oscar-winning movie made of your life," James One told him. "Your movie be far more greater than Malcolm X movie."

"Be far more greater movie 'cause Ike 'I Got Money' Piles be far more alive at end. Roll that video again. You do narration, James One; you make James Earl Jones sound like squeaky weather girl on Channel Two."

"OK, watch now," James One says. "Opening shot, you be ziggin' and zaggin' at a hundred and twenty miles an hour down the Strip in SUV you disguise as live-human-organ-tissue-transplant vehicle to get you 'round Vegas traffic fast as possible. Now here Money Piles' man cave in Vegas, and there your WBC, and WBA, and IBF middleweight championship belts, and framed letters from judges and referees thanking Ike 'I Got Money' Piles for all the Cadillacs, cash, and call girls you send their way."

"I so good, I bad," Piles says.

"This the needle," James One continues, "that be used to roofie your rival Carl 'the Kitty' Williams just before start of fight. Here the picture of Kitty collapsing as you throw first jab."

"He woulda gone down anyway if I'd hit him, but I still set record for historic knockout in zero-point-one seconds of first action-packed round."

"Here your Street Hustler of the Month medal from International Association of Street Hustlers, and your Toxic Masculinity trophy that some women's deliberation group sent you. You not even have to pay for them like you pay for them other trophies on shelf. And here Ike 'I Got Money' Piles smiling and happy on opening day of your Build Back Better breast-enhancement spa."

"I happy 'cause Zodikoff, I mean Diller, get Ike 'I Got Money' Piles big government funds to build spa. Fools in Washington FedExed me a million dollars overnight 'cause he fill out request form sayin' we'd be improving infrastructure all over Vegas."

"And special effects in this video make it look like you actually sittin' on couch next to Robin Roberts on TV. We fix your voice so it look like you able to make sense and answer her questions."

"She bad," he says.

"This be your video of groundbreaking ceremony on radioactive land you sold to mayor of Henderson for new children's playground. You be only one wearin' hazmat suit; everybody else in street clothes," James One describes. "How come nobody suspicious that you dressed like researcher in deadly virus lab?"

"When Zodikoff, I mean Diller, make deal with them, they not know land radioactive, so he schedule groundbreaking for Halloween. They think I in costume. Here it come!" Money shouts. "Here it come! Money Piles on *Tonight Show*."

"This video shot by Cartier in green room. There you be tryin' to buy Willie Nelson guitar; now you tryin' buy Spike the Wonder Dog from that guy Bud. You got a wad of money in your mighty Ike 'I Got Money' Piles hand. Bud shake head no, no, no, he not sell Spike. He nuts."

"If that asshole had took the twenty thousand for stupid dog, I have no problems today. I wanna hit that ugly dog over head with tire iron and smash Bud in face, too."

"Calm down, Money. Here you be with Jimmy Fallon promoting your fight. You doin' good job, but now here the problem, Money; here why they cut segment so short."

"Turn up volume," Piles orders.

"Jimmy," Piles says in the video, "Ike 'I Got Money' Piles invite you out to Vegas next week for fight."

"Well, I don't know," Jimmy Fallon says, "er…thanks, thanks, thanks a lot, champ, but maybe with hosting the Emmy Awards show that weekend…I can't come."

"This now reason you get thrown off show and never invited again," James One says.

Back in the video, Money Piles reaches into the inside pocket of his black Bottega Veneta leather jacket. He pulls out a plastic phallus-shaped container.

"You not comin' to my bout?" he says to Jimmy. "Then you miss the after-fight orgy, so I give you free tube of my Money Shot Pleasure Gel now. It turn rough, sandpaper hand of Kentucky coal miner into soft love glove in ten seconds. Work for you. I send you lifetime supply, and I leave this one here for Willie Nelson."

The screen goes dark as the audience screams.

"OK, OK, I seen enough," Money Piles says in real time. "Very important now, 'cause Ike 'I Got Money' Piles got question. Here it be. 'Time and tide wait for no man.' What that mean? What that mean, Chicago Bob? What that mean, Cartier? James One?"

"Take laundry out of washer?" Cartier asks.

"Not 'bout laundry, bimbo," Piles snaps.

"It's simple. I Googled; I got it here," Chicago Bob tells him. "It means that 'human events or concerns cannot stop the passage of time or the movement of the tides.'"

"Oh," Money says, "a course I knew that. Just checkin' to make sure computer be right."

"Just wondering, why are you wonderin' that, Money? You never wonder 'bout anything 'cept how much your money pile is growing." Chicago Bob says, a little sarcastically.

Cartier and James One laugh.

"You keep makin' them laugh at me like that, Chicago Bob, I send you to jail, too. You never got caught when you were going around country makin' money at racetracks workin' as a horse doctor even though you not even a proud third-grade graduate, like Ike 'I Got Money Piles' be."

"But why are you wonderin' bout that?" Cartier asks. "It sounds like something that Judge Judy might say and everybody applauds but nobody understands."

"I saw on TV that Muhammad Ali say that," Piles explains. "He be greatest of all time in ring except for me. He smart, he funny, he never wrong like me, except for that Muslim worship thing he did. Got him in trouble. If he be worshippin' money like me, he not lose so much time outta ring. He woulda fought exhibition matches in Army; they never woulda sent him to Vietnam to shoot at no crooks."

"Very exceptionally brilliant as usual, Money," James One says.

"Before I be tellin' you why what Ali say be most important to Ike 'I Got Money' Piles, I need your opinion. Even though mighty Money Junior down there almost be big enough to be my third leg, I spent offa my money pile to get this," he says, waving his prosthetic leg at them.

"I need new shoe here on foot of artificial leg. Money like it better than plain old normal human leg 'cause Money take off at night so more space in bed for Cartier and my Butter Girls."

"Wow, right," Cartier says, rolling her eyes at Chicago Bob.

"Which shoe you vote for? You got choice. I got shiny black handmade thirteen-thousand-dollar Ambrogio wing-tip lace-up like Blatterman and those fat Greenwich dudes wear with their baggy blue suits, and I got twenty-thousand-dollar blue-and-white Nike Air Force One Playstation sneaker like Dr. Dre might wear to go out and get his mail. They say sneaker more collectible than Mona Lisa painting. Which lucky shoe go on my beautiful new made-by-science carbon foot with custom movable big toe?"

"Sneaker, sneaker!" Cartier squeals.

"I like the shoe. It's more like you're a titan of industry kinda shoe," Chicago Bob suggests.

"OK, and what about you, James One?" he asks.

"Ike 'I Got Money Piles' no ordinary sneaker- or shoe-wearin' human bein'," James One explains. "You a colonic figure. You man who created world's first sex dolls brothel with custom-fitted dolls; you man whose triple-money-sign tattoo logo now seen on gang members everywhere; you man who own chain of solid-cheese-crust pizza parlors who be smart enough to make customers sign legal document so you no get sued when they break teeth on crust; you man who win—"

Piles cuts him off. "I know man who be man I be. I know I be a famous high-colonic figure. But which fuckin' thing best on my foot?"

"You wear one a' both!" James One suggests. "It become part of Ike 'I Got Money' Piles' outta-prison style that you always be wearin' different shoes on your feet. You 'splain it be that way so you able to spend piles a' money on new shoes each week. Woman love you for that."

"So whadda you sayin?" Piles wonders.

"You wear wing-tip on good old reliable original still-human, all-toes-movin' Money Piles left foot, and you sport highly collectible Nike Air Force One on magical new right foot. When you movin' big toe inside sneaker, you fool 'em all, and nobody realize leg made in same factory in China that make shower curtain rods."

"Smart. That why you still James One, James One," Piles says. "I do it."

"OK, business," Piles says. "If Ali say time and tide wait for no man, then my clock sailing away."

"Ah, ha, very good," Cartier says, pretending to understand what he means.

"You doin' it again, Cartier," Piles snaps. "If it be so 'ah, ha, very good' like you jest say, what I mean by that?"

"Er," she stammers, "er, ah, oh, ah, like that time in Jamaica when you jumped off boat and you lost your Rolexes splashin' and thrashin' tryin' to swim, and the lifeguards at Round Hill had to—"

"Shut up!" he barks. "Everybody know I was screamin' for help 'cause Ike 'I Got Money' Piles was pretending to be drownin' to give bored celebrities on beach excitement, 'cause all they doin' was reading James Bond novels under their huts."

"Yeah, right, boss, and you no need those two Rolexes you always wear on same arm, and once they dragged you to shore and give you artificial inspiration, you be so good at coughin' up so much water and comin' back to life, you fool big-name guest on beach Paul McCartney, who watch and say to me, 'He's lucky to be alive,' and Paul be second-smartest Beatle, they say," James One says.

"Alright, since nobody figure out what my time-and-tides problem be—" Chicago Bob interrupts. "Time passin'. You want to settle the scores, you can't wait to—"

"Hooray for Chicago Bob for once," Piles says. "If you knew as much about puttin' shoe on horse as you know about figurin' how Ike 'I Got Money' Piles' mighty brain works, you actually be real vet. Is Diller on my video feed?"

"He's standing by," Chicago Bob says. "He can't hear us, so let me say this about your mighty brain. That mighty brain's takin' a big risk using Diller as fixer. Police always keepin' an eye on him. He'll land you back in—"

"Ike 'I Got Money' Piles not goin' back to jail. Older brother Moses 'I Got Real' Piles is bribing Nevada court judges in case there be trouble for me in future," he explains.

"You right, boss," James One says. "Your brother best briber in world. He give gleamin' new Cadillac Lyriq to referee who be in ring with our boy Chuck 'Big Climax' Clyde when he fighting your old foe Joe 'the Rotten' Apple for title at MGM Grand Saturday. Referee promises he stop fight by fourth round and declare Clyde winner, even if our boy Clyde already beaten to a pulp and lyin' on canvas bleedin', half-dead, and bein' counted out."

"OK, tide goin' out listenin' to you goin' on. Show me Diller," Piles commands.

Appearing on a huge flat-screen TV are the gleaming bald head and slightly pitted face of Kayko Zodikoff, the personal fixer for the entire Ike "I Got Money" Piles operation.

Piles calls Zodikoff "Diller" 'cause he once met mogul Barry Diller at the bar at the Carlyle hotel, where Piles always takes his Butter Girls for a festive orgy when they visit New York. Since Diller was bald, with the same-shape head, he nicknamed Zodikoff "Dirty Work Diller."

Kayko Zodikoff doesn't care what Piles calls him as long as the fifty thousand a week in cash from Piles keeps rolling into his office.

Zodikoff is ruthless, tough—a guy who bats a thousand with a Louisville Slugger in a dark alley. He runs an operation like viewers saw on the *Ray Donovan* show. Dov, one of his top men, is a former Israeli special forces agent. His other lieutenant, Ivan, had a big job handling Putin's personal security. The female at his office, Nikole, was a supposed prostitute, cited by Putin to be among the top twenty-five Russian call girls he'd ever "met."

Actually, Nikole was a secret agent in Russia for French intelligence. The Russians caught on to her when a suspicious KGB agent going through her laundry discovered French nipple cams sewn into her bras.

All it took to secure her safety was an immediate flight from Paris to Rio in a private plane with no number on the tail. Once she was in South America, a hundred thousand dollars of the world's best plastic surgery rendered her face and body totally unrecognizable to anyone who'd ever known her—except, of course, to her faithful Siberian husky, Anna, who found her to be even more beautiful.

Anna, unfortunately, was never able to adjust to the heat of Copacabana Beach, and grew to resent the lifestyle change. "Why couldn't we have simply gone to the rocky coast of Brittany?" Anna wondered.

So, folks, remember: before you make a move that radically changes the thermostat in your hemisphere, please consult your dog.

"Diller!" Piles yells at the screen. "Time and tide wait for no man. You know that, right?"

"Impatience is never wise in my business," Zodikoff says flatly. "What do you need?"

"Complete update on the scores I aimin' to settle, and where we goin' from here."

"Your cousin Franco in South America who sent you Monstro, the dog you provoked into attacking you—"

Piles interrupts, "That dog mangle my leg, now leg gone."

"Yes, so, Franco is now singing 'Angel Eyes.'"

Piles hits the mute button. "What the hell that 'angel eyes' mean, James One, Chicago Bob? Some kind of code?"

"That song, 'Angel Eyes,' ends with the lyrics about how the singer is gonna disappear. Franco's likely disappeared," Chicago Bob explains.

"Good!" Piles yells. "What else?"

"Your former henchman James Four, who ran out on you when the dogfight operation was raided, he's now singing 'Somewhere My Love.'"

"What the fuck do that mean? Chicago Bob? Diller talkin' to us in strange code 'cause we on a video? Right now we on a private five-hundred-dollar-a-minute-plus-tax video feed. This Zoomin' line more secure than my two-hundred-thousand-dollar bet on Clyde's fight Saturday night."

"That song was theme song from movie *Dr. Zhivago*. James Three is now likely shivering in a very snowy, very cold Russian labor camp," Chicago Bob explains.

"And that Julio—that ugly, salsa-slurping, smelly-burping Julio who testify against me—where he be?" Piles asks. "He worst, 'cept for that ugly white dog."

"As of two weeks ago, your problem boy Julio's been crooning 'Bossa Nova Baby.'"

Piles hits mute again and turns to Chicago Bob. "He be buried on beach near girls from Impa—"

"Money, that song is the only hit from meager soundtrack of *Fun in Acapulco* movie. I think Julio might've made an unplanned dive offa the high ledge at La Quebrada cliff in Acapulco," Chicago Bob explains.

"How the fuck you know this shit?" Piles asks.

"Common knowledge if you listened to Sirius while tending to Blatterman's horses all day," Chicago Bob says. "Just give me some a' your favorite topics and I'll make playlists for you, Money."

"I am learning so much about music and geography today," Cartier interjects. "But I gotta leave to get my blonde roots done and get another Taylor-Swift-at-Coachella double-process bleach job on my hair. And it's been almost twelve hours since my last Brazilian wax, and I wanna look good for my Money this weekend in case we go to the Carlyle. So long, Mr. Zodikoff."

"And you spendin' big offa my money pile to look that way," Piles complains.

"Goodbye, honey," Zodikoff says. "Let me know if you hear from Eboney."

"Eboney was track star in high school," Cartier explains. "She was out the back door in Brooklyn the instant she saw police. She gave me her stilettos and took off barefoot. Probably ran to that bossa nova place by now. Bye-bye."

"Fuckin' Eboney. She my number-one Butter Girl; every day she say she love me," Piles mutters. "Too many people run out on Ike 'I Got Money' Piles jest 'cause a' some minor legal problems like police raid."

"You pay me for council," Zodikoff says, "so, Mr. Piles, sharpen your leadership skills. It will help you when times get rough."

"I lead with my pile a' money. That's all it takes," Piles shoots back. "Diller, you not so pretty as Nikole, so let me have a look at Nikole. For fifty thousand you take offa my money pile a week, I gotta be able to see that face and get peek at that body and hear that accent," Piles demands.

"I'm right here," Nikole says, popping onto the screen.

"Ahhh...there you be, Nikole," Piles says. "You so beautiful, and so trim and fit like Chicago Bob now be. Look at Chicago. He go on Eric Adams' Brooklyn Vegan Diet and he lose thirty pounds. Chicago Bob now startin' to look more like Morgan Freeman, not so much like fat old Shaq anymore."

"Can we talk business?" Zodikoff complains. "This startin' to sound like *The View*. You wanted that Wonder Dog and that TV guy Bud taken care of. Nikole has been on it."

"They worst! How soon before they start singing one of Zodikoff's songs?" Piles asks her.

"Not so simple, Money. These are public personalities," she says, "and their links to you are well known and made national headlines. You are dealing with Spike the Wonder Dog, who is enormously popular. He's at the top of his game. He even shot a movie with Jim Carrey. Only thing bothering him is a relationship issue with his girlfriend."

"What else is new in show business?" Zodikoff cracks.

"Ha, yeah, true," she continues. "Anyway, the dog's very smart. I've watched all his videos closely. He's also very funny, very clever, has a well-documented sixth sense of danger. He understands and reacts to human conversations. He is tremendously strong; some say his breed is the supreme athlete of the canine world, and, as you know, when provoked, he can be quite fierce."

"He bite my finger. Finger gone."

James One interjects, "Everybody workin' around Spike at dog ring like Spike. Remember, Money, you had a sizzling-hot brandin' iron in your hand about to sizzle a huge painful triple-money-sign logo on his ass, but first you put other hand in Spike's mouth to admire his gleaming teeth. What you expect?"

"Why stupid dog not want be branded? I bran' all my best dogs; it be honor for them. After burn marks finally heal, they show friends."

"He obviously knew exactly what you were about to do. The other dogs didn't," Nikole says.

"Fuck that Spike the Wonder Dog!" Piles yells.

"Yes," Nikole says, "we understand your sentiments, so may I continue? He and Bud have an otherworldly connection. It's almost telepathic. Bud's a popular guy and a savvy, outstanding athlete—black belt and so forth. Bud's about to break even bigger. He and his boss, Lombardo, appear almost certain to buy a TV station, and they'll go into production on all manner of content, some with Spike at the forefront. The higher their profiles, the greater your risk—our risk."

"What you do so far?" Piles asks her.

"We hit Bud hard financially. Had identity theft working for a while. We spent tens of thousands of his money at sex resorts," she explains. "Docked his bank accounts. Drove him nuts with credit card hacking. We drugged the Wonder Dog at the Colony hotel in Florida; Spike looked like a cowardly fool. *Inside Edition* showed video—people thought he'd lost it."

"OK good, but that dog be fool anyway, and he gonna lose it. What else?" Piles asks.

"It wasn't easy, but we were able to remote-control program a huge mechanical alligator with very sharp teeth to crush him to death, but something went wrong and Spike and the alligator ended up having dinner with Tim Allen and Jim Carrey in Palm Beach."

"Whaaat?" Piles yells. "I hire mean old Zodikoff Associates, not a dogs-and-celebrities matchmaking service! What the fuck else you do?"

"We paid Todd Corker, a guy who had a grudge against Spike and Bud, to go to their house when Bud was away. The guy bought two huge mastiffs and he fed them Angry Man meals—"

"Those meals suck," Piles says. "Besides, all I need to get angry is not get laid in morning—"

"I'll continue," Nikole interrupts. "So Corker took the two dogs over to Spike's yard, figuring they'd maul Spike to death. He opens the gate. The dogs charged toward Spike, but he just stood his ground and stared them down."

"He what?" Piles asks. "Why they not tear him apart like I want?"

"It's like somehow he communicated to them," she says. "He stopped them in their tracks. I've looked at the tape a hundred times; it's like he was saying, 'Hey, what are you doing here? Go home, relax. Why fight?' It's weird. Anyway, that's about it."

"The parrot," Chicago Bob says.

"Right, Bob, thanks. I forgot," she says. "We sent them a parrot that Chicago Bob trained to say—"

"I know what dumb bird say. He say, 'Spike dead dog, Spike goin' down, Spike goin' down,'" Piles says.

"Yeah, you figure a parrot suddenly arriving at your door saying you were goin' to die might just kinda freak you out," Nikole says, "but Spike and the parrot bonded immediately. They loved each other. He told Spike his life story. Bud was crazy about the parrot, too. So we stole the bird to upset them. That worked. Now Chicago Bob's stuck with the parrot again."

"He's a good parrot," Chicago Bob says. "Herbie's a good boy."

"So, Money," she says, "we also had some juicy crap about them planted in the tabloids. Didn't affect their popularity, actually increased it. We sold them fake production insurance and fake completion bond policies on the reality show they were shooting. If something went wrong, they'd have been in deep financial and legal trouble. On the final episode, we hoped that this creep Sol 'The Old Swede' Silverman would grope Nancy Pelosi big-time, and they'd get hit with a massive sexual harassment lawsuit, and all the salacious evidence would be right there on the video they were shooting, but no."

"Nancy Pelosi? This Swedish guy's nuts?" Ike "I Got Money" Piles barks. "She old enough to be a founding father's mother. Why anyone wanna grope her?"

"He appeared to be obsessed with her, with her, well, her, you know…," Nikole says.

"What?" Piles demands.

"Her, er, her you-know-whats."

"Her what-what-whats?" he demands.

"Her, er, never mind, Money. So, here's where we are," Nikole says. "We're going to bribe a woman Bud had a one-night stand with in North Carolina to go public with some made-up gossipy crap we tell her to spiel, like that he can only have sex when he's dressed as Whoopi Goldberg."

"That good, but no Whoopi. She kinda hot. I love to get down and smoke a couple a' blunts with Whoopi and see what under those costumes she wear on TV," Piles says. "I bet she wild woman. I get her to scream 'Whoopi!' five times when she havin' a big splooge."

"Very nice objective there, Mr. Piles, and fine, so no Whoopi. But we say end it with them now. You don't want to be singing one of Mr. Zodikoff's songs about two popular national figures being killed under mysterious circumstances. You run risk; we run risk; we all run risk of getting caught. Let it go, Money. Let it go," Nikole says.

"That's what the firm suggests," Zodikoff adds.

"No way!" Piles yells. "Where they be right now?"

"They are staying at an Andy Gordon's big apartment on Eighth in New York. Bud's got a vacation coming up, and he and the dog are going to East Hampton for a little while. A friend of his wrote a play, and your Bud and Spike are in it," Zodikoff explains.

"What I payin' you big-time offa my money pile for, to give me *Variety* headlines? Jest go to Eighth Avenue and shoot them right now," Piles demands. "A lotta gunplay in New York every hour—they be latest victims."

"We don't shoot people, Mr. Piles," Zodikoff says. "We arrange for them to be in situations that just might cause them problems. Your burping friend Julio somehow ran into our Dov in a seedy bar in Acapulco, and after three hours of free tequila, Dov encouraged him to see the bay from the top of the cliffs. Can we help it if he stumbled off the cliff? But Spike and Bud are different."

"OK, OK, so then listen, you two. No more payin' you if you playin' around with me on this," Piles says quietly. "My patience and my Tide pod runnin' out. Ike 'I Got Money' Piles demand revenge."

"Mr. Piles, a Confucius saying is 'Before you begin a journey of revenge dig two graves,'" Zodikoff warns.

"That is fuckin' confusing saying," Piles blurts. "Why I make James One dig two graves?"

"It means dig one for you and one for your enemy," Nikole explains.

"I want you two get even with ugly Spike and that jerk Bud, not advice on cemetery plots. Take care of it or you fired."

Nikole and Kayko Zodikoff look at each other and nod.

"OK then, Mr. Piles, if we must," Zodikoff says, "we can consider trying this—your friend Mr. Blatterman, we understand, has a secret place in East Hampton. We will deliver Spike and Bud to you at Blatterman's, and you can take it from there."

Ike "I Got Money" Piles makes a slashing gesture over his throat and smiles.

CHAPTER SEVENTEEN

Fast-Breaking Events

"Goddamn it," Lombardo barks over the phone to Bud. "From the heights there is nowhere to go but down."

"That's encouraging, boss," Bud says. "What happened?"

"We're not rid of The Old Swede because…"

(Note to reader: I promise I'll cut this short. We've all had enough of The Old Swede, and when Lombardo gets upset like this, none of us is happy.)

"He'll sell, but he's demanding to be a one-third owner of the station; he's demanding to be our minority partner; he's insufferable; he's…"

(Note to reader: you have my assurance that any subsequent book chronicling my adventures will not be dominated by Sol "The Old Swede" Silverman—maybe six, seven pages at the most. However, please understand that it will be a while before the twice-daily regimen of testosterone shots that his wife, Nurse Ruth, will be giving him, and Apple's adjustment of the four-barrel carburetor on his V Plus watch, will combine to create the aged mattress mechanic he'll become, which will lead to his ultimate demise under the pickleball court as previously stated.)

"Relax, boss," Bud says calmly. "At two to one, we can always outvote him. Don't worry. This is not like you."

"My God," Lombardo says. "Thanks. I was so upset that I didn't even realize that. The guy really gets under my skin."

"You're not the only one. Something about The Old Swede's visit musta gotten under Pelosi's skin. Buffy heard Pelosi called in sick the following day and missed the chance to help corral the votes to finally ram through the next infrastructure package," Bud tells him.

"They'll never repair that fuckin' bridge I drive over every day. I've already blown out two rims on the Maserati," Lombardo complains.

Actually, she didn't miss work because of The Old Swede. Bud learned that Pelosi was so mortified by the way she looked in the kids' drawings that she was compelled to rush to her cosmetic dermatologist in Silver Springs for a forty-eight-hour "refreshing."

Cut to minor show business headline here—no, no, not that Tyra Banks on *Dancing with the Stars* might be a robot; many viewers started questioning that the first season. Bud's made a commitment to costar in a new play, *Pardon My Privet*, at Guild Hall in East Hampton, written by some guy named Bill McCuddy.

Pardon My Privet is described as a "comedy of manners on the eastern end of Long Island." It's slated to open following *The Bride Wore Tattoos*, a three-act noir potboiler written by a Southampton socialite who uses the pen name Sue Z. Essman to boost ticket sales.

Bud met McCuddy at a documentary film festival in New York. They'd both walked out in the middle of a ponderous two-hour film about mutations in reindeer sperm caused by global warming. Bud was standing in the hot lobby, probably worrying about his own sperm count, when this McCuddy guy recognized him from TV and said hello.

In New York, one thing quickly leads to another with new acquaintances, and that's how it all happened. Good news is, the four-night stand at the theater coincides with the vacation Bud had planned for us after The Old Swede's show was wrapped. The better news is that there's a part in the play for me.

The casting's a little on the nose, 'cause I gotta play a dog. Seeing those antlers and all from Pelosi's office, I'm considering branching out (no pun intended) to play a wide variety of horned animals in possible future acting assignments.

The play concerns the Gramm-Bushes, a rich, snooty, out-of-touch, alcohol-addled East Hampton WASP family that lives on Further Lane in a home with a magnificent view of the ocean. Brooke Shields and Matthew Broderick, who live in Amagansett, are set as the Gramm-Bushes.

Bud plays Jerry, a mostly high-all-the-time artist who has made millions creating wildly expensive "interactive" paintings that are nothing more than frames with about a hundred dots of psychedelic colors on large white canvases. The interactive gimmick is that each work includes thirty powerful pot gummies attached to the frame. Each painting comes with the instruction "Look at painting forty minutes after consuming two gummies."

The plot has Jerry moving into the house across from the Gramm-Bushes and planting massive privets to enclose his property. The Gramm-Bushes suffer an immediate onset of privet envy syndrome (quite common in the Hamptons) until they realize the new tall hedges block their ocean view, so they set out to destroy them.

The hilarity ensues in a faux A. R. Gurney–style comedy of manners as the Gramm-Bushes' daughter, played by Elle Fanning, falls for Bud's Jerry, thus ending her engagement to the scion Throckmorton P. Gildersleeve IV.

The Gramm-Bushes begin popping the gummies on Jerry's paintings. They wander the corridors of their mansion stoned all the time. In their new happy but addled state, they miss three charity dinners in a row. That's justifiable grounds for them to be banished from the Hamptons *Social Register*, which still follows the kind of protocols you see on the HBO show *The Gilded Age*. Having nothing to do at night, and far more loose-limbed because of the gummies, the family starts doing the Frug, inspired by a Bob Fosse dance number they saw in a movie on TCM.

As the curtain drops on *Pardon My Privet*, the privet is slowly dying while the family is writhing around in the stiff, lip-biting, "Hey look at what I can do" manner of WASPs hopelessly trying to dance. Thatcher, the Gramm-Bushes' dog (me!), was assigned the task of urinating on the bush nonstop at the beginning of Act One, so all's well that ends well for the Gramm-Bushes.

OK, so it's not *Private Lives*. It's not even *Moose Murders*. But this guy McCuddy is kinda funny, even though his main credit is cranking out a gossip column that disembowels the rich and famous on Long Island's East End in the local *Dan's Papers*.

This means, of course, that Bud has to cut back on anything that could affect his short-term memory (read: bongs full of pot) and learn his part.

For the first rehearsal, he went to East Hampton on something called an Ambassador coach. They advertise the service as being "beyond luxury." Not sure what kind of luxury exists in the great beyond, beyond luxury, but that's what they claim. Sounds swanky, right? It's actually a bus. Sorry, Hamptonites. I know you get a cocktail napkin and a bottle of water, but it's a bus. It's the shape of a bus. The wheels go round and round like the wheels on a bus go round and round. It burns diesel fuel like a bus. It gets crowded like a bus, but it's called an Ambassador coach 'cause you wouldn't feel comfortable texting the hostess at the Southampton dinner party to tell her, "I'll be late for cocktail hour because of engine problems on the bus."

Anyway, I'm not involved in rehearsals at the start, 'cause the script says that I mostly just lie on an Oriental rug (wait, should that be "Asian rug"?) watching the Gramm-Bushes get drunk. My only real acting is that I take my cue and leave the stage each time Mr. Gramm-Bush says, "Thatcher, please go across the street and make a little wee-wee on the big naughty privet."

I'm glad to be staying mostly in town. My father, Rocky, and my brother Billy will be coming up for the Westminster Kennel Club Dog Show at the Garden. I don't want to miss them.

Big news is that Andy spent a ton of money on gear to upgrade Virtual Andy. He bought experimental equipment directly from the top development engineer at Meta headquarters. The new stuff equips Jane and me with collar sensors so Virtual Andy can monitor us up to a mile from the apartment while our new board-certified professional dog walker takes us out.

Yeah, sad to report that our former non-board-certified dog walker, Wanita, ran off in terror one afternoon and dove into the lake in Central Park.

What happened was that Virtual Andy noticed on his monitor that Wanita was only taking us a block from the apartment. She'd plop down on a small bench in an area by a Chipotle, order a burrito, and take a picture of the burrito, which was basically the same picture every day. She'd slowly eat the burrito while scanning her phone for an hour. After all that activity for us, she'd rush Jane and me home, once again having proven herself a true professional in her chosen fields of canine care and burrito photography.

Since the new sensors also enable Virtual Andy to be outside with us in hologram form, he suddenly materialized next to Wanita on the bench and calmly asked, "What are you doing, Wanita?"

She dropped her burrito, which Jane and I pounced on, and ran up Eighth Avenue toward the park screaming, "Voodoo! Voodoo!"

Bad for her, but good that we got a new and more trustworthy, board-certified dog walker. We need her. Bud's away a lot with the *Privet* thing, and Andy's recovering from an injury he sustained on a recent date. He came home howling in pain from what he was calling "dreadlock lash." He'd gotten smashed square across the face by the two-foot-long plastic dreadlock braids attached to his date's head while she was whirling around next to him on the dance floor at Marquee New York.

If you become a victim of dreadlock lash—or God forbid, existential dreadlock lash—don't seek relief with Unguentine ointment. Young Andy loves the stuff. Within a minute, the fumes had temporarily blinded him.

In another fast-breaking development, Bud got a call from Leslie Davis at the animal casting agency. What happened was pure luck. Bud had posted on Facebook about how my mighty father, Rocky, and my genius brother Billy were coming up for the dog show.

Billy'd won a couple of Best in Group trophies, beating out all the other terrier breeds in several dog shows around the country. He was being considered one of the favorites to maybe win the big Best in Show prize this year at Madison Square Garden.

Because of his success, our breeder, Mrs. Erdrick, has been besieged with dozens of requests for Billy to stand at stud. (Remember, we dogs do it standing up, not bouncing up and down like humans—which, by the way, sometimes accidentally changes the sleep setting numbers on your mattress, which is the real reason you wake up with a sore back the morning after a wild night in the sack.)

Sadly, Billy was neutered as a puppy. He suffered terrible phantom balls syndrome for weeks. Billy's smart, he's clever, he's resourceful, but there's no way even he could fake breeding. So, to meet the demand for a sire with Billy's conformity, Mrs. Erdrick is showcasing our proud father, Rocky, as a stud at Westminster.

By the way, this turn of events has not made our dear mother, Apollonia, very happy even though she knows Rocky has to do it. Dad's acting like he's really upset about this new stud service assignment, but Billy and I aren't so sure.

Sharp old Leslie Davis sees the FB post at the same time she's getting a casting notice for two generations of dogs needed to shoot a commercial for the new All in the Family dog food. Apparently the dog-loving great-grandchildren of Norman Lear, the creator of the legendary sitcom, have developed what's being reviewed as the world's best dog food.

Leslie Davis calls Bud. She says, "Spike can take the lead in the commercial, but we'll need his father, brother, mother, and one other female dog who's not an English Bull Terrier to play Bud's girlfriend. The trend in commercials the last few years is to have blended families, so they don't want the entire dog family to be all one breed."

"Oh," Bud says, "interesting. Do you need a special kind of female dog? Spike's living here with a beautiful golden retriever named Jane. I'm sure she can do it—she's very smart and well-mannered. I know she'd be fine; you'll love her."

That's Bud. If the guy has confidence in you, he somehow senses what you'd be able to do well, even if you don't know it yet. Plus, he's pitching Leslie Davis so he can get a complete package deal on the dog talent fees for Andy to negotiate. He knows Mrs. Erdrick could use some cash.

"Great," Leslie Davis says. "Shoot a little video of this retriever taking a couple of commands, like 'Go to your bowl and eat,' and if I think she's right, we'll send someone over there to fit her with the appliance."

"What the hell kind of appliance?" Jane and I are thinkin'.

"Appliance?" Bud asks.

"Yeah," Leslie Davis says, "it would be a big puppy-bump costume we'd fashion for a golden retriever."

Pregnant girlfriend!

This is just great. Now Daisy's going to see me on TV with a bitch expecting a litter and go nuts. Then I remember (phew!): I'm finished with Daisy. I'm a stress-free, happy bachelor. But don't let that give you any ideas about Jane and me; we're just fun-loving friends. But I hafta admit she's very easy to get along with. We enjoy each other.

"Why the pregnancy?" Bud asks her.

"They'll want it to look like Spike's girlfriend is expecting a big litter. Gives them promo for their All in the Puppy Family line and enforces the blended-dog-family angle."

The storyboard for the commercials has Jane and me looking at each other lovingly, and then taking huge bites from the glistening food piled in our "His and Hers" bowls. We chew, which will be seen in slow motion. Our eyes will be glowing with satisfaction. They want the same extremely self-satisfied, artificially happy looks on our faces that the people in the medical commercials display in slow motion while the product's disclaimers at the bottom of the screen list all the ways the medicine could incapacitate them for life.

The commercial ends with all five of us gobbling away in slow motion. The tag for the spot features a woman who resembles the blonde daughter Gloria from the sitcom saying, "And save a can for you; it's perfect in shepherd's pie," followed by a loud sitcom-laugh-track laugh.

I figure the long, fake laugh might make you wonder if she's only joking about the shepherd's pie or maybe figure she's not joking. Some people will make shepherd's pie with it. After one taste, they'll realize dog food's been the principal ingredient in shepherd's pie all along.

Leslie Davis was in the middle of organizing the shoot day for the commercial when Mrs. Erdrick called to ask if my mom would be jumping around a lot in the commercial, because she'd just discovered mom was "expecting." Dad obviously was rehearsing with her to make up for the new stud-duty assignment.

Good for him. All I'm really looking forward to is seeing my family—my loving mom; my brother Billy, whom I idolize 'cause he's way smarter than me; and, of course, my dad, who's one of the most formidable Bull Terriers of his generation. He's solidly in the prime of his life. He's taken some blows on the job, but he's tough and fearless. He's been singled out again and again for his guard work at Mr. Erdrick's small carpet factory in the very rough Kensington neighborhood of Philadelphia.

I haven't seen Mom and Dad since I was eight weeks old and Bud picked me out of the litter box. They know all about my being the so-called Spike the Wonder Dog, but I'm also guessin' that to them, I'll always be their little Elmer, the name Mrs. Erdrick gave me when I was born.

One thing I wonder, though. How have they reacted to some of the crazy things they've seen me get involved in? Dad will love how I smashed the door to save the strippers. Mom will be crazy about my being in a movie with Tim Allen, one of her favorites.

But will they like my latest publicity? I don't know. It's the video on *Entertainment Tonight*, *TMZ*, and Fox News of me at the Capitol, looking ridiculous in those big antlers foolin' around with Nancy Pelosi. Bud heard that Pelosi's people liked the optics of the antler sequence way better than the video of Sol "The Old Swede" Silverman lurching toward Pelosi with arms outstretched looking like he was going to palm her…. Oh my God, how did we get back there again? No more! Bad dog!

Everybody's really busy. Bud's rehearsing and doing Zoom shows. Jane and I are having lots of fun playing with Virtual Andy while Actual Andy's flying around the country making almost as many deals as he turns down.

He nixed a guy who wanted financing for a new sex podcast, *Talking Head*. "I will not dishonor the legacy of the great David Byrne," Andy humphed, "even though I fell sound asleep midway through his recent Broadway show."

Until he got a cease-and-desist order from the Cabbage Patch doll creators, Andy was all in on backing a chain of Cabbage Patch grooming spas to serve the remaining women in America who will not submit to bikini waxing.

"Cabbage Patch dolls were before my time," he complained. "Who knew?"

All of this has been giving Virtual Andy virtual stress.

Keeping up with Actual Andy is overloading his circuits, so Actual Andy called the Meta headquarters in Silicon Valley for help. A voice identifying itself as Virtual Mark Zuckerberg got on the line and adjusted the cyber circuits to cut Virtual Andy's virtual stress level with virtual Ativan. While on the phone, Andy had the brainstorm to make a deal for Mark Zuckerberg's breath for his Celebrity Breath Strips product. He made a pitch to Virtual Mark and got put through to the humans known as brand extension engineers.

After waiting an hour, he was disconnected. "Zuckerberg's breath just missed its big chance," he told Bud. "Andrew Gordon doesn't call back."

And this guy used to be our intern.

"I know that comparison can be the thief of joy, Andy," Bud said to him, "but your career is on fire. Move over, Elon Musk."

Play rehearsals for Bud are not going well.

The original director was the same guy who just staged *The Bride Wore Tattoos* at the theater. Unfortunately, he got fired 'cause he was directing *Pardon My Privet* like it was a grim noir mystery, like the bride play. A new director restaged the show. She found all the laughs in Act One, but *Privet*'s opening night got pushed back so she could finish Act Two. Otherwise, the first act would have been like *Father of the Bride*, and the second like *Nightcrawler*.

Who cares?

In a couple of days, I'll be reunited with my mom, dad, and brother Billy.

It all feels so good, but none of us could have imagined what kind of family reunion it actually turns out to be.

SOMEWHERE IN EAST HAMPTON

Scott Blatterman had just finished three cheesesteaks. Cheesesteaks made with American cheese, Vidalia onions, and horsemeat.

Yeah, unfortunately, horses were the latest animals that Blatterman had decided needed to be taught a lesson—like the lessons he'd taught to those dumb dogs he and that moron Ike "I Got Money" Piles put in the fights, and the lessons taught to those damn beavers who were starting to block that small creek near his Greenwich estate, and the lessons taught to all the squawky parrots he bought at every bird store in Connecticut.

The only parrot he couldn't touch was that fuckin' Herbie. Chicago Bob wouldn't let him have Herbie. And Blatterman wouldn't dare cross Chicago Bob. He was afraid of him. Chicago Bob looked tough, like a guy who'd seen it all.

Scott Blatterman was afraid of a lot of things. Scott Blatterman was a big, fat, trust fund, never-worked-a-day-in-his-life baby, whose unfortunate hobby was killing things. It all started with those ugly little mice his dad made him trap and drown when he was five years old, when he'd go with his father on house calls for the family's extermination business.

"Teach those pests a lesson!" his father would scream at him when at first he seemed reluctant to toss the squirming little mice into the bucket.

The more mice he tossed, the more it seemed his dad loved him.

"I was repulsed by the killing of things as a child," he once lied in an interview with the *Greenwich Sentinel*. "That's why I sold my ownership shares in our family's pest control empire shortly after we went public. Today I'm a lead supporter of PETA."

The PETA part was true. For the hundred thousand a year he forked over to those animal-loving softies, Blatterman figured he got great cover for his "hobby." Plus, he loved looking at all the different animals on the calendars they mailed him each year, so he could imagine…

But now, trouble. That prick who works for Piles, that Chicago Bob prick, didn't like what he was doing with those old racehorses—the crossbow-and-arrow-pistol thing with them. So what? Did Chicago Bob know what happens to old racehorses? "Let them run around the field. Let me try some target practice, maybe even use my new graphite hunting bow," Blatterman thought. "Let me do them a favor. It's just an act of kindness. Dad would like it."

Blatterman lived on a vast estate in Greenwich with his three chunky children and his addicted-to-cosmetic-fillers wife. "Did I just pay ten thousand dollars to put those walnuts in your cheeks?" Blatterman would sometimes scream.

But the dermatologist and his needles made her happy. Good. She could go to lunch in the city with her wide-eyed, plastic-faced, platypus-lipped friends. "The less focus on me," he figured, "the better."

His family had no knowledge of his "hobby." Timber, their dog, had suspicions—because, well, he's a dog and we get suspicions. It's like a scent sense. Ever notice your dog, out of nowhere, start growling at a stranger? That's the scent sense. We smell it. We get information that way. You humans require subpoenas.

Scott Blatterman was happiest at his private retreat. The place deep in the woods on Long Island that he called his "hobby house." A couple hundred years ago, one of his English ancestors had bought hundreds of acres far from New York City in East Hampton. Over the years, chunks of the land had been sold back to the state. Some of that land had become a small airport, but Blatterman never flew his private plane to East Hampton. He drove. Nobody ever knew he was there.

The hobby house, where Blatterman was now wolfing down yet another horsemeat cheesesteak, had been built by his great-grandfather during Prohibition. During World War II, the US Army had acquisitioned it to be a well-hidden interrogation headquarters for captured spies. After the war, it had gone back to his family. Blatterman liked it. It was big, dark, and still mostly camouflaged.

Day or night, you couldn't spot the place from the air.

He was pouring more ketchup on the rest of his cheesesteak while Hilda, his servant, was getting the guest wing ready for Ike "I Got Money" Piles. He'd hired Hilda because she was vision-impaired and hard of hearing. The Helen Keller International foundation had given him a dinner for the good example he was setting.

"The fools," he thought. "I just don't want her to know what's going on."
Blatterman was eating that fourth cheesesteak too fast, because he was annoyed.

Zodikoff, that fixer guy who works for Piles, had just called.

"I know it's unwise for you and Mr. Piles to have direct contact, Mr. Blatterman, so I'm calling to inform you that Mr. Piles needs an accommodation from you, and he needs it right now. He requires a place for us to conduct some East Hampton business for him. Mr. Piles will be coming for a little while. Otherwise, the information about the dogfights we have on you goes to—"

"Wonderful, of course, get him out here right away," Blatterman said, contorting his mouth in disgust.

"Good," Zodikoff replied.

"Really looking forward to his company," Blatterman lied.

"Knowing you, Mr. Blatterman, based on what he has planned, you'll particularly enjoy his company," Zodikoff told him, hanging up abruptly.

CHAPTER EIGHTEEN

A FAMILY REUNION

Our breeder, Mrs. Erdrick, showed up at Andy's at 4:50 a.m. We were all sound asleep.

Mrs. Erdrick really knows dogs, particularly her specialty, English Bull Terriers. She's recognized in the dog world as a bit of a savant as a breeder, but the timing of her arrival is more evidence that she has some problems navigating the world away from her sparkling kennel.

She'd never driven the hundred or so miles to New York from her home outside of Philadelphia in Devon, Pennsylvania, before.

"I wanted to be here by nine, and they say the traffic is always bad with the tunnel and all. I was worried, so I left at three a.m.," she explained.

"Always do a little extra research on what 'they' say," Bud muttered to me later.

She'd let herself in with the key Andy had sent her.

I heard the door. I figured it was Andy sneakin' in early from another date with Gwen, the existential-dreadlocked beauty.

"I'm sorry about what I did to your face," Gwen had told Andy on their last date. "I'll make it up to you."

After I heard Andy whisper to Bud that he'd finally learned why people liked sex so much, I figured Gwen was making it up to him in the sack. So what if the dreadlock bruises on his forehead were deep purple and his cheeks were covered with what looked like pink tire treads? The guy was happy, and smiling through the pain.

As the door closed, I offered a soft, warm bark, thinkin' I was welcoming Andy back from an all-night session with Gwen.

Three seconds later my dad pounced on me.

"Sleeping? Is that what you do all day in show business? I'm at work by this time every day," Dad growls, sorta joking.

From over in the corner of the bedroom, I see my brother Billy's eyes. "Let him assert himself," he's tellin' me. "You have no idea how proud Dad is of you."

Bud raises his head, blinking, waking up.

"What? What's happening? Dogs here? Mrs. Erdrick, is that you? What time is it?" he groans.

Jane, who's a deep sleeper, comes to and starts barking and snarling at my father, thinking he's attacking me. Then she spots Billy, takes a step in his direction, and growls. Dad doesn't like that, so he blasts even louder barks at her.

"What is this?" Bud yells, reaching for the light and knocking over the lamp on the nightstand.

Billy's joined in. He's making a lot of noise, barking away for the sheer pleasure us dogs get from a good gang bark. Then Dad realizes Jane's a friend, not a problem, so he switches to howling out of sheer family-reunion happiness. I'm not being left out. I'm goin' all at it with full-throated hammer howls. Why not? We're dogs. This is what we do.

"Stop, please, Spike! Stop this!" Bud yells.

Mom comes strolling in. She'd been enjoying Andy's vast view as a boat sailed up the Hudson River at dawn's first peeping.

In ten seconds, it's quiet. Mom gives us a big "shut up right now" look. Her arrival is well timed. She ends the barking and howling commotion after only three minutes.

"But, Madame Board Chairwoman, it was only three minutes," Andy will say a month later, when he's called in front of the co-op board for noise complaints.

Virtual Andy will reveal that he recorded the barking. Virtual Andy will then point out to Actual Andy that the building's bylaws protect him from the ten-thousand-dollar noise fine he's facing, since they say, "The fine will be imposed for five minutes or longer of continuous noise that's a disturbance to more than two apartments."

"What would I do without you?" Actual Andy will ask Virtual Andy after his successful defense at the co-op board meeting.

"You'd be alone, confused, and still using Unguentine," Virtual Andy will tell him.

This wacky morning—with its out-of-control barking, with Bud breaking the lamp, and with Mrs. Erdrick getting lost when she goes across the street to purchase flowers as an apology for waking us—this crazy morning is ushering in one of the happiest days of my life.

Pretend for a moment you're an eight-week-old puppy.

OK?

Wait! Pretend also that you've been magically housebroken so you don't have an accident while you're pretending to be an eight-week-old puppy, since puppies are still generally incontinent at that point.

OK?

There you are in the crate with your brothers and sisters. It's another happy day together. Next thing you know, a buyer picks you outta the litter. Sold! A little while later, you're driving away with a total stranger, and you've got the slow-growing realization that you'll never see another member of your family again.

Today, I'm the luckiest dog in the world.

Mom goes off and sits with Jane in the early morning sun. Jane's the kind of dog other female dogs just love. She makes new friends with them all the time.

"Nice girlfriend you've got here, Elmer," she tells me. "Oh, I guess I should call you Spike now. I like Jane. She's wonderful."

I try to tell her that Jane and I are just friends. Yeah, we have a great time together—big fun all the time. Yeah, I like her, but this is not romantic. "We're just friends, Mom."

Mom rolls her eyes.

I stroll back to the bedroom to see Dad and Billy. I'm wondering if Jane thinks maybe we might be becoming more than friends, 'cause we have been cuddling up a couple of these past nights and it feels so natural, not like with Daisy, when I was waiting for the next thing to happen that might displease her. Daisy seems like a million years away.

"My sons," Dad says to Billy and me. "My sons."

He looks proud, but since he's a father, not the president of the international Spike and Billy fan clubs, he feels obligated to go into "I'm still your father" mode.

He praises Billy for his smarts. Billy was the smartest of the litter. He was the leader and kept order among Oswald and our sisters, Lulu and Minnie. Yeah, we all got named after cartoon characters. Fortunately, Bud changed my Elmer to Spike.

Would "Elmer the Wonder Dog" have worked? Probably yes, actually.

You know, I almost told Mr. Boggs to use an exclamation point up there after the "probably yes, actually." But in defiance of every person on Facebook who uses three or even four exclamation points on every post, I chose not to!

"I'm going to Westminster this week," Billy tells Dad.

Dad's disgusted at the mention of dog shows. Even though Billy's got some small trophies, Dad lets us know what he thinks—buncha phonies. Judge a dog by what they look like first thing in a natural state, not after they get washed, and combed, and waxed, and polished by somebody who'd be better off making an honest living using those skills Simonizing cars.

But he lets Billy know he's still proud that Billy has won some Best in Group at shows. He knows that it's Calvin and Bee, Billy's owners, who work with Mrs. Erdrick to put him in the shows.

"Billy, you're so smart, so gifted," he tells him. "I never wanted this for you.... I thought maybe someday you could be...a national obedience champion, a national intelligence champ in the UK, but this...," Dad trails off, looking away from him.

"We'll get there, Pop. We'll get there," Billy lets him know.

Dad asks if I remember what he told me the week before Bud came by and I left the puppy pen with him for our life together.

How could I forget?

He'd picked me out of the little pen and carried me over to the corner of the living room. It was the first time I'd ever been alone with him. His head was about as big as my whole body. He had a fierce energy about him. I coulda been afraid of him, like Oswald was sometimes, but I wasn't. I knew he was my dad and that he loved me.

He looked me straight in the eye. "You got something special, Elmer, a special property your mom and I haven't seen before." He told me that they'd had three litters, fourteen pups so far, and that they both sensed something extra in me. "There's a force with you. You're going to do good things for our breed in your life."

I look at Dad now, feelin' kind of shy recalling this.

"And look at you," Dad conveys to me. "You're Spike the Wonder Dog. I know what you had to do because of that Piles creep, and how you saved those women by busting a door open, and about your movie and the TV show, and now we're in a commercial together. You are special, Elmer. But do you remember the last thing I said to you that day in the living room?"

I let him know I've never forgotten it.

"Just carry this with you forever, Elmer," he'd said. "Remember me, remember Mom, remember your brothers and sisters, and never, ever, ever doubt yourself. You will prevail."

He'd looked at me, and I felt his love covering my body, somehow protecting me and strengthening me with his faith and confidence. Fatherhood at its best.

"But I forgot to tell you one other very important thing that day," he says.

"Oh boy," I'm thinkin'. "This is gonna be big, real big."

"Never let anybody put antlers on your head."

Jane keeps to herself that afternoon, knowing it's best for the four of us to be together.

We want to hear the stories from Dad about work. We know our father has faced some tough circumstances on the job—being the night guard dog at Mr. Erdrick's little factory in a Philadelphia neighborhood that's getting more dangerous by the year.

Dad doesn't share stuff like that. That's the way he is.

Mom tells some stories—the time he got clubbed over the head with a baseball bat and pretended to be unconscious so at just the right time he could sprint off to hit the alarm; the time he took a twenty-two-caliber slug square in the shoulder and kept charging at the robber and tore off the guy's pants as he was escaping through a broken window; the time outside the factory he ran around in circles to block traffic so the robbers couldn't get away. And there's way more.

We're staring at him pie-eyed. "Say something, Dad."

"OK, if ya gotta know, I'll tell you three things I've learned in my life. One, a lot of humans aren't nearly as tough as they look and act. If you're facing them down, you can see what they really got inside them right there in their eyes. Another thing: if you have to be in a fight, never hesitate—charge straight away, then back off and wait. And, oh yeah, in life, always look for the silver lining."

Mom nuzzles Dad's big shoulder with her head. He licks her ear. She licks his face.

Unfortunately, the golden glow of that afternoon was interrupted by Mrs. Erdrick barging in to get Billy ready for the dog show. His prep required only a simple bath, but sometimes washing an English Bull Terrier can be like trying to wrestle a Brahman bull in a bathtub, and Billy doesn't like baths.

She gave herself ample time to get to the show. Fearful that she couldn't get a taxi, she chose to take no chances by walking Billy straight down Eighth Avenue to Madison Square Garden. As they passed through Times Square, a Spider-Man leaped at her. This startled Mrs. Erdrick, who thought, "Oh my God, it's the real Spider-Man!"

As a defense, Billy showed fangs and snarled at the guy in the costume. Suddenly, a man in a cowboy hat and G-string, two Lady Gaga impersonators who appeared to be men, and a guy in a cheap Buzz Lightyear outfit surrounded them, demanding money. Mrs. Erdrick had to give each one twenty bucks before they'd let her go on her way.

It's stuff like this that makes Times Square the cozy, don't-miss, international tourist attraction that it is.

Billy was glad to come home early. He'd lost the group competition to Sedgewick, a beautifully groomed Lakeland terrier who couldn't see because of the thick red hair combed over his eyes—that little trick by the groomer likely won him the trophy. Actually, though, Billy never stood a chance. Mrs. Erdrick had been in such a rush during his bath—fearing crowded sidewalks and possibly street fairs with large groups of slow-walking, mouth-breathing tourists—that she didn't take the time to dry him properly. Billy was damp when he left the apartment, and all the soot and exhaust fumes that settled on him during the hot twenty-block walk to the Garden turned his white coat a light gray.

It's that crisp, clear atmosphere of Midtown Manhattan that makes it a must-experience destination for nature lovers around the world.

On the way to the commercial shoot, Dad is nervous, feeling out of his element. It's odd to see him this way. Mom is cool. Billy is looking forward to experiencing something new. Jane doesn't know what's in store, but she likes the Meathead flavor of the dog food samples they sent us, so she's figuring no problem: "I just eat, right?"

Not so simple.

The script starts out with a voice-over that sounds suspiciously like Rob Reiner: "Spike the Wonder Dog is always hungry. That's why he really likes All in the Family dog food."

The dog food bowl is on the floor, and the camera is set on a level shot with the bowl. I saunter up to the food, glance into the camera, and nod in agreement with the VO. To do this, I employ my usual minimalist acting style that was influenced by my two favorite screen stars, Leonardo DiCaprio and Flipper. Neither ever made a false move on camera.

Gloria, the director, who fancies herself the Jane Campion of dog food commercial directors, says, "No, no, no, Spike. Bigger nod, bigger nod, much bigger nod, please. Bud, tell your dog, bigger nod."

By the time I go as far as she wants, it's about as subtle as Brendan Fraser's binge-eating scene in *The Whale*.

The VO continues: "And Spike's girlfriend enjoys it, too."

Jane has to walk up to the bowl, eat, glance at me, eat some more, and then start to eat out of my bowl. She does this well.

"Perfect, Jane, perfect, but let's do it again," the director says. She makes us do nineteen takes and after each one says, "Perfect, but let's do it again."

At this point, we've consumed about four cans of food apiece, and there's a break while both of us are discreetly taken to the indoor relief area, which also, unfortunately, features the studio's candy-and-cookie-vending machines. Bud gets peanut butter cups.

Meanwhile, my mom's asleep, and Billy and Dad join us in the relief area.

"This is stupid, stupid," Dad barks. "You two got it right the first time. Why didn't she yell, 'Cut and print,' like Clint Eastwood would have? Now you're eating so much you'll get sick. What's up with the over and over crap?"

Billy lets him know it's likely because they feel they have to justify the cost of renting the studio for a full day, 'cause this facility doesn't do half-day shoots, according to a sign he saw on the wall.

"That's showbiz, Dad," I bark.

In the middle of the big family-feasting-together scene, Leslie Davis finally shows up. She interrupts the director midway through the nineteenth take, telling her she's violated animal acting protocols.

"Read the contract, Gloria," Leslie Davis says. "I put in the same clause for the dogs' eating as I do for the Aflac duck's quacking. No more than five Aflac quacks per scene for the duck. You have a three-can consumption limit per dog, Gloria, and I just counted forty-seven empty cans in your trash. And by the way, where can I wash my hands? This All in the Family dog food might be good, but it still smells like dog food."

Thinking that she has to get on Leslie Davis' good side and advance her career from working with dogs all the way to working with ducks, Gloria hurries us through the final shot.

"Great shoot, dogs," she says. "That's a wrap."

She immediately corners Leslie Davis.

Revealing the kind of desperation that's a big no-no in showbiz, she pleads, "I love ducks; I'm famous for loving ducks. Please consider me for Aflac, or anything with a duck or even a goose—I love geese. And I'll be honest, I'd even lower myself to do horses, and I don't mean that in a sexual way," she says. "I've heard you represent Mr. Ed the Sixth, and there are rumors of ED commercials with him. I know all about ED; believe me, I know ED"

"TMI," Leslie Davis says.

We're bored, tired, stuffed, and glad to get the hell out of there.

The next morning, we get two calls that don't make anybody happy.

The ad agency people for All in the Family dog food won't accept the way the commercial ends. Because of the director's rushing, the final shot has Dad yawning, Mrs. Erdrick putting the leash on Mom to drive her back to the kennel that night, Billy burping while trying to read the fine print on the can's label, and Jane and me staring at Gloria waiting for a cue.

"All we need today are Spike and Jane. We're going to end it on a close-up with them," Bud is told. "But we need them immediately."

"Oh, nuts, Spike!" Bud says, hanging up. "I'm pissed. Today was gonna be our day together. You and Jane and Billy and your dad—we were all going to go to the park. Now it's canceled. Making it worse, right before the call about the commercial, I got an urgent text that the play's PR people want us in East Hampton ASAP for a photo shoot and interviews they just set up. It's for you, me, Brooke, Matthew Broderick, Elle Fanning, and McCuddy."

Bud hastily makes arrangements for the dog walker and an assistant to take care of us while he's away for the day.

"So, they're sending a car for you and Jane, but now the magazine story, the TV, and all the press photos will be missing the Wonder Dog. Nuts!" he says.

"Take the father," Virtual Andy suggests, jolting us, 'cause sometimes hours go by without Virtual Andy uttering a word when he's in a virtual funk over problems with his virtual girlfriend in the virtual for-avatars-only hookup site in the metaverse.

All eyes turn to Dad. Yeah, he does look a lot like me, just needs a bigger black spot on his right eye and concealer over the small spot in the middle of his forehead that looks like it's been caused by bumping his head to the ground bowing to Mecca at sundown each night for the past seventy years.

"Hmmm," Bud mutters. "Might be fun to see if we could pass your dad off as you, Spike."

At this point, I'm thinkin', "Come to your senses, Bud. Most attention is gonna be on Matthew, Brooke, and Elle. McCuddy will be lucky if he even gets in the shots, and nobody's gonna notice much else, except 'Hey, there's Bud and Spike.' Do it."

He gets his makeup kit and transforms my father into a reasonable facsimile of me, except his muscles are even bigger.

"I'm takin' the car," Bud says. "We'll make it back tonight for a romp in the park together after dinner."

On his way out the door, Dad turns and looks at me, shooting a glance that says, "Your life is completely nuts."

To handle the scene with Jane and me, the agency people have brought in their top director, Mary "the Tooth" Price, a so-called method commercial director. Gloria, the original director, was assigned the washing, drying, and crushing by hand of several dozen emptied cans of dog food. In no business can you rise or fall faster than show business.

Apparently, this Mary "the Tooth" Price is a method director because she's never shot a commercial without first sampling the product.

Legend has it that she got the Tooth nickname 'cause she once had a perfectly healthy molar extracted and endured a dental implant, to prepare herself for a shoot with a dentist advertising that he could "give anyone a complete mouthful of dental implants, pain-free, in one easy session."

She came to regret the assignment, and resent the nickname, when she was informed by registered mail that the dentist was a shyster and that hundreds of his patients were showing up at police stations carrying handfuls of dislocated implants.

Maybe you saw video of the dentist's trial? If not, it's easy to visualize. Mary was pelted with teeth while she tried to testify.

The morning of the shoot, after she devoured two cans of the Meathead flavor straight from a dog bowl without utensils, the Tooth felt a rumbling in her lower tract. We could have told her. Consumer advisory: if you accidentally feed your dog too much All in the Family dog food, please take care to walk them outdoors during high winds afterward.

I'm with Jane. The camera's in front of us. The makeup artist has covered parts of our faces with dog food. The Tooth wants the shot to begin with each of our faces deep into our dog food bowls. We'll then slowly lift our heads while we frantically lick the bowls. The voiceover is going to be "All in the Family dog food. It's good to the last lick, and lick, and lick…and… lick…and…," with the word "lick" softly trailing off as Jane and I lick each other's faces.

I've never licked Jane's face before, and she's never licked mine. Maybe I'm slightly nervous at the intimacy the shot is introducing. Maybe I'm not? All I'll remember clearly later is that we started to lick each other and couldn't stop.

With each big, long lick, I feel this surge of warm feelings, and I can tell she does as well.

Then, during the licking, there's this completely unexpected moment. We look into each other's eyes, and we both suddenly realize, "Wow, this could be the start of something big."

"Perfect! Perfect! No more takes," the Tooth says. "OK, you can stop licking now."

But we don't stop, because we can't stop. I open my eyes, and everything looks brighter. There seem to be stars in Jane's eyes. I can swear we're hearing Jennifer Hudson singing, "If this isn't love, what is?"

"I've been waiting for that for a long time, you old fool," Jane lets me know on the way home. "If this isn't love, then the whole world is crazy."

CHAPTER NINETEEN

A Body On The Sidewalk

When we got back to Andy's, Jane and I each went to a separate terrace. It wasn't that we were shy, or uncomfortable with the intimacy we'd experienced. We didn't go off alone, like humans might, to "process" what had just happened. We knew what had happened. We retreated for privacy. We'd each just consumed enormous amounts of dog food, and we wanted to be discreetly away from each other.

Time passed. Gas passed. The dog walkers never showed up.

"These New Yorkers, no sense of responsibility," Billy complained when he had no alternative but to "do his business" on a terrace.

Midafternoon, Bud called with a happy message: "Spike, I love you. Andy, I don't think you are, but if you're back from Florida and get this, Rocky and I should be home in a couple of hours. Get ready for some fun."

"Actual Andy's not here, but that's good, Bud. The dogs will be happy," Virtual Andy told him.

Time passed. No Bud.

The apartment got dark. Virtual Andy was able to turn on a couple of lights.

I was scared. Where was Bud? I was thinking the worst—an accident on the Long Island Expressway, maybe? He hated that road. He'd seen people texting and driving at seventy miles an hour. Some rock star had died on the LIE. Some big-shot film director had died on that road. Bud felt safer on the jitney than in the car.

Jane was by my side in a way she'd never been before.

"He'll be here. No concerns, Spike," Jane had been letting me know, but I could tell she was getting as worried about things as Billy and I were.

Virtual Andy turned on the eleven o'clock local news. There was our old friend, the WNBC anchor Chuck Scarborough. I was imagining the worst about Bud, but there was no report of a deadly crash on the LIE, just the typical nightly coverage of senseless shootings, gang murders, smash-and-grab robberies, and videos of the ragged cardboard homeless encampments that are rapidly spreading to every neighborhood in Manhattan. They oughta change the lyrics of that "New York, New York" song to, "I wanna wake up in the city that never sleeps—indoors."

Billy was mostly quiet, pondering the situation.

"Do all you can to connect to Bud, Spike," he told me. "Use our ancient powers. Go off to Bud's room; find what you can feel."

I spent that night in Bud's spot on the bed.

A wonderful thing had happened between Jane and me on the commercial shoot earlier in the day, but she knew to stay away and sleep on her own.

I tuned in on that special connection Bud and I have with each other. Instantly, I felt one certain thing—he wasn't dead. In big trouble, maybe, but not dead. I knew he needed me.

I'd never been so scared during the night, not even when I was alone those creepy nights in my cage in the corner of Money Piles' arena. I'd managed to prevail over what they'd thrown at me then. But now I was helpless. I had no control. I lay in bed thinking that this was how military parents must feel when their son or daughter is thousands of miles away fighting in a dangerous combat zone, and there was no word about their well-being.

Around five in the morning, I got up and walked over to the big window. There was a nearly full moon, and off to its right, a bright, twinkling star. I remembered some song about wishing on a star, and what could happen when you need something and make a wish.

I remembered as much as I could of that wish-on-a-star song, and then I got down with my legs folded under me, and I wished. I wished as hard as I could on that twinkling star. I wished that I could help Bud. Yeah, I admit it was probably magical thinking. But maybe sometimes in life ya gotta believe in magic, just like the man who wrote that song probably believed in magic, and just like those people on their knees in church praying every Sunday believe in magic, whether they want to call it that or not.

The next day, there was a knock on the door. What happened showed me maybe the wish on that star might have worked. I sure hoped so, because before the knock, things had gotten way worse that morning.

Again, no dog walkers had shown up. Weird. They'd been coming on time every day.

We were three hungry dogs alone in an apartment and ill equipped to open any of the three dozen cans of dog food the Tooth had sent over to Bud as a thank-you. The best I could do to get us a little food was to crunch as hard as I could on a can with my vice-like jaws. I was able to puncture the metal (and it was not easy—the All in the Family cans are made in America with decent tin, not like those flimsy Chinese ones that you can penetrate with a fingernail if you work on it).

Anyway, after a massive effort, I'd squeezed out little ribbons of food for us to lick off the can. Jane got some first, then Billy, then me. And then I'd start to grind away on another can.

Billy was sensing there was maybe a link between Bud being gone and no dog walkers. He reasoned that something big was going down and we needed to get ready to face whatever it was. Jane was calm and comforting to me, which is what I needed. The last thing you want during a crisis is to be in a relationship with someone who's panicking, and you gotta deal with calming them the hell down as well as controlling your own anxiety, and of course trying to figure out what to do. And OK, yeah, in case you haven't read enough romance novels to realize it—I will now finally admit that Jane and I are in a relationship.

Andy was still away, somewhere around Key West on a yacht trying to make a deal with his clone people to see if they could grow chickens with six boneless wings to meet the demand by the increasingly health-conscious American public for larger and larger portions of deep-fried wings. To date, the dragonfly DNA the clone people are employing has succeeded only in growing long antennae on the birds—not additional wings.

Which brings us to now. As he does every day, Andy phones to check in and say hi to Bud.

Virtual Andy informs him Bud's missing. Of course, Andy freaks out, 'cause unfortunately, he just happens to be the kind of guy who freaks out easily. When he was playing basketball in high school and had to make a free throw with the game on the line and two seconds remaining, his foul shot would sail over the backboard and hit someone in the face. He's no Steph Curry under pressure.

Andy calls the East Hampton police to report Bud missing.

It takes several tense minutes of waiting for news. Finally the desk officer tells us what happened. A half-naked man was lying unconscious on the sidewalk on Main Street, raising complaints because he was partially blocking the entrance to Gucci. The ever-vigilant East Hampton police decided to see what was going on. The body was Bud's, and he's now in the Southampton hospital.

The officer reports that the door to Bud's car was open. The car reeked of a couple of half-empty bottles of Seagram's 7. They found oxycodone pills scattered all over the floor, and discovered three thongs and some stained silk lingerie tangled on the back seat.

Bud's facing multiple criminal charges, including three counts of driving with soiled thongs. There's an accusation about alleged distribution of illegal drugs, since there was a sign in the car's window: "Hey kids, after-school special—OXY—three for twenty-one dollars."

The officer checks with the hospital, and it's very bad news. Bud's still unconscious.

Andy's upset, panting into the phone. He says he'll get a lawyer. Unfortunately, like he always does when he's nervous, he tries to make light of the situation, and quips, "This is gonna be worse for Bud's career than when Hugh Grant was married to Elizabeth Hurley, but got arrested for getting a blow job in his car on Sunset Boulevard from a trans hooker, and made things worse by going on *The Tonight Show* to explain he did it 'cause he felt like having a blow job."

"Actual Andy, can you please calm the hell down?" Virtual Andy suggests softly.

I'm thinkin', no way! Bud had a cousin killed by a drunk driver. He just recorded a PSA about how buzzed driving is drunk driving. He has never, ever, driven under the influence. He certainly wouldn't have been drinking at all before the three-hour drive back home. The pill thing's ridiculous. We've done multiple shows on the dangers of oxy addiction for high school students. Plus, with the massive supplies of Chinese oxy these days, seven dollars apiece is ridiculously high.

Oh yeah, and where's Dad? The cop said no dog was at the scene. I can hardly imagine my honorable father, an acclaimed guard dog, would decide to go for a carefree romp on the beach while my master Bud's unconscious, sprawled out on his back half-naked on the sidewalk. (Whoops, TMI on Bud, 'cause that's not a pretty picture. Maybe just pretend he was on his stomach, not his back.)

What really happened?

There's one loud, hard knock on our door.

"I gotta come in," a big voice shouts, followed by more hard pounding.

The three of us start barking. (Note to dog owners: you could have the best-trained dog in the world, but if they don't bark when someone's pounding on the door, consider them either deaf or overtrained.)

Virtual Andy's confused. He's momentarily stressed, the same way Actual Andy would be freaking out with three dogs barking frantically and a stranger hammerin' on the door demanding to be let in. In his virtual stress, Virtual Andy briefly turns on the sprinkler system in the living room, which drenches the furniture but feels good to Jane, Billy, and me, 'cause the apartment's way too hot.

"It's Chicago Bob. Whoever's there with those dogs, let me in!"

Chicago Bob? That guy Herbie loved so much? What?

Virtual Andy's still panicking. The refrigerator door flies open, the lights in the apartment are flashing in Andy's new "I'm a swingin' bachelor" disco mode, but the sound system starts blaring Christmas music, which really doesn't go with the strobe lights—especially the annoying sound of those singing chipmunks. Oh yeah, and the garbage disposal's grinding away on a spoon Actual Andy accidentally left in the drain.

More pounding. Then a familiar squawk, "Bud goin' down, Bud dead man, open fuckin' door!"

Herbie!

I walk over and look at Virtual Andy.

In the way dogs are quickly learning to communicate with virtual people, I calm him down. We've been calming real people for thousands of years, so the artificial ones are a snap.

Virtual Andy finally pops open the apartment door.

Herbie flies in, soars to the ceiling, swoops down, and lands on my head. For an instant, he drops his foul-mouthed-tough-guy act and whispers in my ear, "Missed you, Spike, my pal."

Standing in the doorway appears to be not the guy I'd visualized as Herbie's friend, the horse vet, Chicago Bob. No, the man standing there is round, overweight, bald, and has an enormous bushy white beard. He appears to be the alternative-medicine guru, nutritionist, and celebrity doctor who's not nearly as suspect as certain other celebrity doctors, the twinkling Dr. Andrew Weil.

Virtual Andy calls Actual Andy, who we learn is now sailing near the small island of Bimini, a location not known as the number-one destination in the world for good cellular coverage.

He announces that Dr. Andrew Weil is visiting the apartment with a parrot.

Andy's intrigued at the opportunity to get some free holistic guidance on excess acid in his diet, but Herbie yells into the speaker, "Shut the hell up and listen, stupid! Andrew Weil does not make house calls."

Chicago Bob takes over, peels off the fat pads, the white beard, and the bald cap, and blots off the makeup before explaining himself and why he's here. He's a handsome guy, looks a bit like Dave Chappelle—he's got that same kinda ironic half-mocking smile.

We learn a lot very quickly that day. Chicago Bob is wanted by police on a charge of impersonating a veterinarian at racetracks for the last twenty years. Bob's dad served as the veterinary officer in the last branch of the US Cavalry to employ horses in a mounted charge when the US Army fought the Japanese in the Philippines in 1942.

After the war, Chicago Bob's' father, known as "Southside Robert, DVM," worked as a vet for a famed equestrian academy near Washington Heights outside of Chicago. Young Bob loved horses, and by the time he was twelve or so, his father had taught him all he would ever need to know to care for a horse in any condition, especially if the horse had been wounded that day by Japanese gunfire. Unfortunately for Chicago Bob's police record, his mother was an amateur pickpocket who taught her son every trick of her trade, including a couple of the obvious moves that got her arrested.

A while back, using his pickpocketing skills, Bob lifted the jail keys from a corrections officer and was able to escape his small cell, where he'd been for months in a prison outside of Waco, Texas. The only reading material at the jail was every nutrition book written by Dr. Andrew Weil, apparently a distant cousin of the warden.

Once on the outside, Chicago Bob was a wanted man. When he traveled or moved from place to place, he disguised himself in the unique appearance of Dr. Andrew Weil. He'd also made a few bucks in the guise of Dr. Weil by occasionally giving a lecture called "Horse Medicine By a Guy Who's Been Called a 'Horse Doctor'" at small racetracks in the South.

The phone connection with Andy is bad, so Virtual Andy asks, "Most interesting, Mr. Bob, but why are you and that parrot here?"

"I couldn't take what I saw Blatterman doing to those horses when we got to that secret place of his in the East Hampton woods. I couldn't take another day of crazy Money Piles' ego and his demonic quest for revenge," Chicago Bob says. "Plus, I got nothin' against Spike. Any dog that can save a couple of strippers is good with me, and Bud seems like an OK kinda—"

"So you know Bud? It's horrible," Actual Andy yells through static. "Bud's in the hospital. What happened could be as bad for his career as when Hugh Grant—"

"Give yourself a blow job and shut the fuck up," Herbie squawks from his familiar perch on my head.

God, it's good to have Herbie back. So often he says the things I think but can't express with any form of barking—because, like emails, dog barking lacks nuance.

"The guy in the hospital isn't Bud," Bob announces, "and—"

"Look, I just called the hospital," Actual Andy interrupts, "and they've identified him as—"

"Listen to me, please," Chicago Bob implores. "Kayko Zodikoff engineered the whole thing. The guy in the hospital who's still unconscious looks a little like your Bud. He was drugged at a bar and planted on the sidewalk. Zodikoff's seductive operative Nikole had easily distracted Bud. Zodikoff's men Ivan and Dov needled Bud and darted the dog they thought was Spike. They threw them in a van and headed to Blatterman's. Another man dumped the guy from the bar on the pavement with all of Bud's IDs."

The fur on my back slowly rises in a straight line from my neck to my tail as I realize that Ike "I Got Money" Piles' has got Bud and my dad, and thinks my dad's me.

"What the fuck," Actual Andy says. "I thought Spike was there in my apartment now, and who the hell is Kayko Zodikoff?"

"Here's what happened," Virtual Andy says. He goes on to explain why Bud and my father went to East Hampton. He then gives us a thirty-second briefing from the research he's done on Kayko Zodikoff and his crew.

"That thing's good," Chicago Bob says, nodding at Virtual Andy. "Well, for now, Piles thinks the dog they've got is Spike, and what's in store for him and Bud isn't likely to be good. But I've got a plan."

"I'm calling the hospital! I'm calling the police!" Andy screams.

"Hold it!" Chicago Bob yells. "Just hold it."

He explains that Zodikoff has all bases covered. "He's the best in the business. He's almost certain to have someone at the police department out there who's involved in the case in his pocket, and he's using high-quality oxy pills to pay off an addicted nurse at the hospital. She'll keep the fake Bud unconscious until Piles has finished his job on Bud and Spike's dad."

"Call the FBI! File a 'Missing TV Star Dog and TV Star Human' report!" Andy screams.

"Not quite, and calm down," Chicago Bob says sternly, "'cause here's what I figure we're gonna do."

In an hour, Chicago Bob would take me to East Hampton on the jitney, and we'd be part of the operation he's devised to rescue Dad and Bud.

He explains that once we get out there, we'll go directly to an old friend of his who's a rogue kind of sheriff in Suffolk County. "Zodikoff could never get to this guy. I'll tell him face-to-face about Blatterman's horse abuse and Piles' revenge obsession, and he'll immediately set up an animal welfare raid," he says.

"Why not call him now?" Virtual Andy asks.

Bob explains that Zodikoff likely has the lines tapped at the county offices, and it's not worth the risk of tipping him off.

When Billy and Jane hear the plan, they let me know there's no way they aren't going with me.

Chicago Bob feeds us a big meal while telling us that horses love the All in the Family dog food, too. For dessert he offers me something he claims the horses like—a big syringe filled with his brew of dark yellow energy booster serum that would make me capable of running much faster, but also induce a mad desire to mount and breed with the first horse I see. I decline the needle.

"The Biden people wanted this formula from me," he boasts. "They said they'd only give the prez a shot on the days he has to walk all the way up the steps to *Air Force One*. I declined, even though Jill might have enjoyed the side effect."

Time is passin' too slow. I'm watchin' the clock; all I wanna do is just get out there.

Then...

"Mistake! Mistake!" Virtual Andy suddenly yells. "Jitney leaves in six minutes. Mr. Bob took jitney time from weekend schedule, not today's. Wrong time. Go now! Go fast!"

Bob flies into action. He runs in the other room, grabs his vet bag and the Dr. Weil disguise gear. He starts putting it on but has trouble with the fat pads.

"Jitney on corner! Leave now!" Virtual Andy shouts.

Wearin' only the fat pads and with the beard half crooked, and no bald cap or skin makeup, Chicago Bob commands, "Let's go, Spike."

Herbie is attached under me like in the old days back home. Jane and Billy charge out right behind me. Virtual Andy locks the door from the inside.

"Let these dogs back in!" Chicago Bob says, pounding on the door.

"Have a nice trip, everybody, and hurry—two minutes. Over and out; fare-well," Virtual Andy drones.

Jane and Billy run down the hall to the elevator. I let Jane know things are probably gonna get rough. "That's why I'm here," she lets me know.

When the doors open, Bob can't keep them out.

Mercifully, the elevator stops only once on the way down. It's the old lady on the eleventh floor who's always got something stupid to say about what's happening in the elevator each time she hobbles on.

She looks at Chicago Bob. "I've always liked your rice. Where have you been?" she asks.

As the door in the lobby opens, Chicago Bob is explaining for the third time that he's not Uncle Ben.

As soon as we spot the jitney, we relax. The driver's still loading some baggage into the storage hold as a woman and two young teenagers are approaching to board.

"Get on somehow," I signal Billy and Jane.

"We're with you," Jane signals back.

Bob gives the attendant on the sidewalk a ticket for me and one for him. I scamper up the steps with Bob behind me.

Then: "Hold it right there, Chicago Bob. You're under arrest."

"Fuck no!" Herbie squawks as he flies from his perch on my stomach.

I hop up on a seat. Out the window I see three cops manhandling Bob, trying to force handcuffs on him, as he's deftly angling his loose hand to lift a key from the policeman's belt. The few passengers outside and everyone on the jitney are watching the arrest. Of course, they're fidgeting, already upset that this is slightly delaying their departure, but also happy that it will give them something to talk about upon arrival other than their usual chitchat about the LIE traffic, how long it took to make the trip, and how worried they are about how long it will take to get home.

Amidst this sidewalk diversion, Jane and Billy quietly sneak on board.

Herbie's watching this, enraged.

He flies outside and hovers over the cops. He's hurling obscenities at them, using every trick he learned insulting tourists all those years at the bar in Casablanca. He strikes a nerve by repeatedly calling the fattest of the cops a little-dicked, flabby-pig gumshoe.

The cop, who must have skipped his anger management class that morning, takes out his billy club and swings wildly, trying to knock Herbie out of the air. "Shut the fuck up, asshole parrot!" he screams.

Herbie's swooping all around the guy, squawking, "Missed me, fatso!" after each wild air-woosh of a swing.

The driver turns on the ignition for the bus. Bob yells, "Get on, Herbie! You can't help; it's a setup by Zodikoff."

"Fuck him," Herbie squawks. He flies into the bus just as the cop takes one last swing at him, misses, and splinters his club on the jitney's doorframe.

It was good to learn later that the "assault on a parrot" videos some bystanders shot went viral. The police officer was condemned by bird lovers around the world, and also reprimanded by his superior officer for firing his taser gun in anger at the bus as it drove away. He was assigned to work weekends in Central Park as the assistant recording secretary for West Side Bird Watchers Anonymous.

CHAPTER TWENTY

THE TRIP

Toto, where are you now? "Don't take life too seriously," you told me in that dream. "It's all a joke."

Is it? Maybe? OK sure, why not? I'm looking around.

The bus is rumbling along. All twenty-five people on board are completely oblivious to the fact that three dogs and a parrot are traveling with them, unsupervised. It's like we're merrily headed off to the East End of Long Island to our timeshare in Sag Harbor, and we're responsible for dinner. And guess what? Tonight, it's freshly baked African grey parrot. Aren't humans supposed to be a little more connected to their surroundings? If you had a bus with twenty-five dogs and three humans, all the dogs would be keenly aware of the humans.

But now?

I'm next to a gamer guy who's got a phone in each hand, simultaneously playing Fantasian and Inside. I could be a corpse festering in a dog suit, and he still wouldn't notice. Billy's a few rows back sitting with a gray-haired woman, who looks about as excited to be making the long journey to visit her grandkids as she would be if she were getting her kidneys pumped in the front window at Bergdorf's. Jane's with someone of an undetermined sex swilling booze out of a small silver flask and using an eyeliner sharpener to put a point on the tip of a pink crayon for a RuPaul coloring book.

I want to do whatever I can. I want to use all my powers. I'll lay down my life if I have to, to save Bud and my dad, but I gotta face it: our only hope of trying to find our way to Blatterman's lair is a parrot who's in the midst of an ornithological-style nervous breakdown. He's under my seat, lying beak-down, with his wings over his head, peeping and moaning over the arrest of his beloved Chicago Bob.

I can't pretend this is all a big cosmic joke like Toto told me, 'cause I'm scared. I'm afraid for Dad and Bud. Real scared. What was it Mike Tyson said about the power of fear? "Fear can be your friend." If "Iron Mike" is right, I gotta find that friend fast.

I look back at my brother Billy. "Just sleep," he signals me. "We will handle this. For now, sleep."

I'm gonna need all the rest possible. I fall sound asleep, and I start havin' a weird dream. You think maybe at a time like this, I'd be dreamin' I was the sidekick of Liam Neeson in yet another *Taken* movie, as we're tryin' to find his daughter, who seems to have a strange knack for getting kidnapped by Albanian human traffickers every couple of years. But no, in this dream I'm starring as Stanley Kowalski in a revival of *A Streetcar Named Desire* at the Ethel Barrymore Theatre in New York. Jane's playing my wife, Stella, and Daisy's the crazy former Southern belle Blanche DuBois. It's opening night. Herbie has above-the-title billing, starring as the courtly Mitch. They yell, "Places, please!" but Herbie's way too stressed to go on. At the last minute, he's replaced by his understudy, the singer Peter Cincotti.

As I'm dreamin', I'm also somehow aware this is completely nuts, but I can't pull out of the dream. The curtain goes up; I don't know my lines. I'm panicking—the actor's nightmare. Daisy and Jane know all their lines, and they've got just the right Southern accents. Peter Cincotti's very good, considering that instead of speaking English, like Daisy and Jane are doing so well, he's barking. The audience loves it. I'm getting more and more tense. All I can do is wander around the stage, dragging my leash, smoking a big cigar, uncomfortable in my strange costume of a tight white undershirt, waiting to scream the only line I know: "Stella!"

I wake up. Out of my left eye, I see a green road sign that reads, "Twelve Miles to Southampton." I'm breathing hard but relieved—at least this tense dream is over. I take a couple of deep breaths and go back to sleep, but I get pulled back into the goddamn dream. It's now Act Three. I yell, "Stella!" over and over. I instantly feel better about myself, 'cause the critic John Mariani's in the audience shouting, "Better than Brando, Spike!" Peter Cincotti's playing his big scene with Daisy when Herbie flies on. The audience goes wild. Herbie forces Cincotti offstage. On the way out, Cincotti gets tangled in my leash. "I hate these leashes," I'm thinkin'. "Hate 'em." Herbie takes over as Mitch and shows a great command of the part.

The next thing is we're all suddenly at the cast party at Sardi's restaurant. The walls are covered with hundreds of identical caricatures of Herbie, and the partygoers are swiping them as souvenirs. The only non-Herbie drawing is of Streisand, and Babs herself is guarding it, ready to pepper-spray anyone who tries to take it off the wall.

Herbie's surrounded by celebrities, all trying to touch him. "Let Shakira through," he squawks, "and send over Styles; I miss him. Adele, great earrings, love 'em. Is that Drake? Come here, buddy. Let Herbie peck your head."

I wake up. Oh God, weird—too weird.

"Herbie," I think, "are you OK now?" I peer under my seat. He's out cold on his back, with his little beak hanging wide open.

"You're awake," the guy next to me says, apparently eager to launch into a conversation. "Has anyone ever told you that you look like that Spike the Wonder Dog? On YouTube?"

I nod.

"But you're better-looking. That Spike dog sometimes looks a little stupid. Don't you think?"

I nod again, knowing he's just trying to butter me up with a compliment, 'cause he needs to talk, most likely about himself. I listen, hoping this guy's rap maybe will distract me from the anxiety I'm feelin'. Every mile gets us closer to whatever's in store.

"Look what I did," he says, holding up a phone indicating his games are over and that he's earned the second-highest score of the day in the ambidextrous division of the gaming competition. "But here's my goal: I want to win the world title in the quadruped division. Look..."

He shows me a video of a Korean woman using both hands and both feet, gaming on four devices.

"This is the future of my sport. I get physical therapy six days a week to lengthen my toes. Ya gotta have very long toes to play this as well as I want to."

While I suspect we'll be seeing plenty of this new quadrupedal gaming in the next Olympics, I'm done with this strangely coordinated man. I look him straight in the eye while launching a long yawn, and turn my focus to the TV—the international signal to any person trying to engage with you to "leave me the hell alone."

On one of the little televisions above the seats, I see the movie's ending, which must mean we're near our stop. It was yet another installment of that *Sex and the City* franchise—a ninety-minute romp of aging women complaining to each other about how old they are, while trying to be as hip and youthful as possible.

Long Island TV comes on, and there's a story on Bud.

"Disgraced TV star still unconscious, additional unwashed thongs and pills have been found in trunk of his car," LTV's Angela LaGreca announces.

She's got Bill McCuddy cornered for an interview. "Bill, it seems that Bud might have been living a secret life."

"Bud was perfectly fine at the photo shoot and substantial press day for my play, *Pardon My Privet*," McCuddy says. "By the way, the laugh-packed farce is still scheduled to open tomorrow at Guild Hall, and tickets are available. It looks like we'll be going with Joe Smith, a janitor at Guild Hall, as a replacement for Bud, and—"

"Let me ask you this," she interrupts. "Have you—"

"Have I had a run-through yet with Joe Smith? Well—"

"Excuse me, no, please, Bill," LaGreca says. "When they found him, Bud was on the sidewalk, unconscious, with reported blood alcohol of almost thirty percent, which is about the same level as surgical anesthesia, and that was only twenty minutes after he and Spike left the lawn at Guild Hall for the photo shoot for *Dan's Papers*. Our research indicates he would have had to drink almost all of the two bottles of Seagram's Seven they found in his car in those twenty minutes. Bill, that's like an ounce every minute or so. Are you sure he wasn't already somewhat impaired when he was with you?"

"With math skills like that, Angela, you could handle our busy box office," McCuddy says with a laugh. "Because tickets are selling fast, so—"

"But about Bud, please. Bud's condition at the photo shoot?"

"Look, let's be realistic, he was probably very thirsty. It was quite hot on the lawn during the *Pardon My Privet* photo shoot, but wait, I must mention we did have plenty of refreshing Perrier, which is one of the sponsors underwriting my new play, *Pardon My Privet*, which we vow will open, in spite of the protests from those cranky anti-thong activists."

"He seemed perfectly normal?" Angela asks. "Bud really seemed OK? Was anything strange?"

"No, Bud just said he was looking forward to getting back to the city as soon as possible, but, come to think of it, Spike seemed odd. Usually he's quite friendly, but every time someone suddenly came up to Bud, Spike was kind of menacing, growling at them."

"No kidding, Bill," I'm thinking. "My father's a guard dog."

"And Spike also looked a little different, kinda older and even more musclebound than we remembered. Somebody said maybe the Wonder Dog had gone the Jeff Bezos super-jacked body route and got bigger muscles the way Bezos claims he did—by sleeping more."

"Spike the Wonder Dog was not found with Bud, which seems odd. Any thoughts on Spike's disappearance?"

"A discounted balcony ticket to anyone who finds the Wonder Dog and gets him to Guild Hall by opening night. If Spike doesn't show up, his part in my new play, *Pardon My Privet*, will be played by the janitor's dog, Joe Junior."

"Thank you, Mr. McCuddy, and—"

"Trust me on this. Even though the janitor's dog has no stage experience, he has been in several home videos and—"

"Back to you in the studio," Angela LaGreca says.

As we're pulling up to our stop on leafy Main Street in East Hampton, I'm worried. What if someone notices three dogs strolling down the bus aisle toward the door, dragging their leashes, without an owner in sight? What if they call the dogcatcher?

Herbie's still out of it, and he's the only one of us who has a clue as to where Blatterman's place is, because he was there. Ugh, I gotta pick him up and carry him out of here. Would you want a live parrot in your mouth—the body, all those warm feathers, that five-chamber heart pounding away? Eeek.

And what if somebody sees that in addition to dragging my leash, I've got a parrot nestled in my massive jaws? And what if people start screaming 'cause they think I'm eating the parrot? And what if Herbie suddenly comes to and squawks to let him go, and passengers start beating me with their tennis racquets to release him? There's a lot of anger in America today, and probably no better way to release it than by violently attacking a dog who you think's eating a parrot, right?

People start filing off the bus. As I'm reaching under the seat to attempt to pick up Herbie without accidentally biting off his head, Jane stops me. "I got this," she conveys, and in one easy scoop with the soft mouth of the golden retriever she is, Herbie's secure and Jane's discreetly heading offa the bus.

Phew! Thank you, lovely Jane.

"Look, Mom, that's Spike the Wonder Dog," a cute little girl says as she's passing me in the aisle.

"Shouldn't you be on TV?" his mother asks me, which is kinda stupid, 'cause when you're "on television" you actually do get to go out in public now and then. Or maybe she thought what she said was funny—your call. People say ludicrous stuff like that to Bud all the time. You know what? I'm sorry. I'm feeling so tense, scared, and cranky right now that the human foibles I'm experiencing seem way more aggravating than usual. That was a perfectly normal dumb thing for a human to say to a dog.

We make it off the bus. We're standing on the sidewalk on Main Street in East Hampton. Now what?

CHAPTER TWENTY-ONE

BLATTERMAN'S LAIR

Rocky had seen guys like Ike "I Got Money" Piles before. They had others do their dirty work. They cheated. They pumped themselves up. They couldn't take a slight, always needed praise. He'd heard the reporters on ESPN goin' on about how Piles was constantly suspected of bribing judges. The jerk put on a big front, but underneath it, he was a coward. "When the time is right, I can handle this guy," Rocky thinks, tugging on the chain tethering him to the floor. "When the time is right."

The Zodikoff people, though, the ones who snatched them, they were the real deal—tough, solid as bricks. No emotions. Pros. First, a beautiful Russian woman stopped Bud on his way to the car and asked for his autograph. Rocky could usually sense danger, but not with her. She smelled so nice, like Chanel No. 9; maybe that's what threw him off. "I should have figured this out," he thinks. But credit to them, she and the guys with her were good. If you want to take a dog off a scent, either Chanel No. 9 or large amounts of cheese rubbed all over a woman's calves will do the trick, and somehow, they knew that.

A bear of a man had come out of nowhere and jabbed Bud with a needle. If he hadn't been enjoying that perfume, Rocky realized, he might've caught a whiff of him and stopped him. But when he whirled to knock him over, a man with a thick beard fired a dart at him. Right away, Rocky knew it had hit mostly bone. "It might only be partially effective," he hoped to himself, "but I gotta fake like I'm unconscious, so I can try to figure out what's going on."

It was about eleven miles from Main Street near the Guild Hall theater to Blatterman's heavily camouflaged lair deep in the woods, southwest of a small airport.

A vine-covered metal gate swung open. The SUV drove down a narrow strip for about a mile. Once that gate closed, Rocky realized, nobody would be able to get in there unless they walked through thick woods.

Rocky was hanging on, using all of his strength to stay awake, 'cause the dope in that needle was strong stuff. He'd never had a challenge like this, not even those times at Mr. Erdrick's factory when he'd work a triple shift. Then he somehow had been able to stay on guard for over twenty-four hours, but now?

They carried them underground to a big cement room with a dirt floor and one dirty glass window about twenty feet above. Bud was dumped in a corner. Ivan, the big guy with the beard, shackled Rocky to the floor. Each time the hammer hit the spike, Rocky subtly pulled on the chain. "It might not be in the ground as solid as this guy thinks it is," Rocky hoped. He might be able to work it loose enough to get free when the time was right.

"Well, there you are, Mr. Piles," Nikole summarizes. "You've got your Wonder Dog, you've got your Bud, we've got our cash, and we are out of here. Good luck."

"Nikole, you so beautiful. You smell so clean and perfumy. Don't go runnin' back to Zodikoff headquarters," Piles says. "How 'bout you and me tippy-toe upstairs and I play some highly romantic Kool Keith rappin' 'Spasm in the Chasm' that get you in the mood for my spasmin' in your chasmin'?"

Money Piles' girlfriend, Cartier, shoots him a disgusted look.

"As I said, Mr. Piles, we are out of here. Mission accomplished," Nikole says.

"The way your white pants so tight in front on you now, Nikole," he says to her. "I take you upstairs and play dreamy sounds a Lil' Kim tenderly singin' 'How Many Licks,' and you can start countin' them licks till you screamin', 'Stop it now, Ike "I Got Money" Piles! Stop it!'"

Nikole wheels around and heads out.

"Shit, Nikole, you missin' golden pleasure opportunity to have—"

"Shut up, Money," Cartier says. "That ugly dog Spike over there be better at lickin' than you. Your tongue got as much sense of direction as the GPS that made the Japanese tourists drive into the ocean."

Ike "I Got Money" Piles is incredulous, although he wouldn't know what the word means. He can't believe that any woman, particularly one as beautiful as Nikole, would reject him. He looks at Zodikoff's men, Ivan and Dov. "What wrong with her?" he asks.

"Maybe it be that time of the month," James One says to placate him. "Not be your fault, Money. You a temptation to all woman spanning the wide world of earth, 'specially all the womens who you pay, and you payin' her."

"Back in Russia, she was great, Mr. Piles," Ivan says. "Now she's gone American about sex in workplace—won't sleep with us, won't even give us simple hand jobs under the desk after lunch. Not like factories and offices in Moscow; back home, most guys only want to get a job so they can prey on the girls at work."

"America has really fallen behind in so many ways," Dov adds dryly. "Let's go, Ivan."

"Wait a minute!" Piles yells. "What I do with them?" he asks, pointing at Bud and the dog he thinks is Spike. "You stay and help me. Need help. Chicago Bob run away. James One dumb as shit, and he not be brutal as you guys be, plus I pay Zodikoff big chunk offa my money pile eve'y week."

James One looks away, trying to hide his anger at Money Piles for the insult.

"Sorry, Mr. Piles," Dov says. "We're like the Ikea of fixers. We make the delivery; you gotta put pieces together all night."

"With Ikea, you at least get pages of hard-to-read tiny-print directions," James One says. "Maybe you tell Ike 'I Got Money' Piles some directions so he be happy with results a' your delivery."

"That be brilliant for change, James One. Blatterman help me tonight. He turn Spike loose on field and try out new crossbow-and-arrow pistols on him. No matter how fast Spike run, Blatterman will get him good. But Bud, he be actual human, and Blatterman only do animals."

"That why Chicago Bob left—Blatterman shoot at horses runnin' in the field with dat weird crossbow," James One tells them. "It ugly, and Bob sneak off during night, and take parrot."

"Your Mr. Bob has been apprehended," Dov says. "It's been even easier than ever to pay off some police since threats of defunding."

"What I do with him?" Piles asks, pointing at Bud in the corner. "Help me. And don't forget that night after my fight with Carl 'the Kitty' Williams. You owe me."

Ivan and Dov look at each other. Zodikoff has strict rules about this, but they do owe one to Piles for including them in the drug-fueled orgy he promoted as "a Money Piles superspreader event" at his Vegas villa. It was a small, select group—members of the Las Vegas boxing commission, the three boxing judges, the referee, and the ring announcer who'd worked his bout that night at the MGM Grand.

It's the code of manhood, they realize. Anytime a guy goes so far as to fly in top-tier Russian and Israeli prostitutes just for you, you gotta repay the favor.

"We'll be honest," Dov says. "Zodikoff generally charges five hundred dollars a word for advice like we're going to give you, but we do owe you."

"Yeah," Ivan says, "and we're both still in touch with Natasha and Rachel from that night. Our wives think they're our cousins from the old country who always want us to show them around New York. So, all right, Mr. Piles, here's one way to approach this. To start, you could…"

"This is brutal," Rocky thinks as he listens to Ivan and Dov. Rocky knows that his will is his best weapon, and he thinks that Piles has no strong will of his own, just the big bucks to pay people for the dirty work. But maybe, for once, this time he's on his own—this sycophant James One's not capable of doing the ugly stuff they're suggesting. What about this Blatterman character? When will he take the measure of this guy, he wonders?

Upstairs, in the aboveground part of his hideaway, trying to take a nap, curled up in his white silk pajamas in his big, soft bed with its custom-made gray duvet, under his huge black canopy, Blatterman is having his usual trouble trying to fall asleep.

"Damn diet pills, fuckin' pills," he thinks. "Can't sleep. It's their fault. Everything's their fault. Pills give me nightmares, then I wake up, I want to exterminate something. The goddamn wife goes on about me weighing over three hundred. She gets pissed that I have trouble standing up and walking after I eat a lot of pies. Wants me to lose fifty. Does she know what a daunting task that is?

"Gotta blow off some steam—have some fun with that new arrow pistol on that ugly Wonder Dog. Yeah, he's only a dog, not like those old thoroughbreds. Those horses were probably headed to a dog food factory anyway. Fuck Chicago Bob. I didn't do anything wrong. Let them do what they gotta do to that asshole from TV so I can get Piles the hell outta here. He's a one-legged sex-addict blowhard, but he was a good front man for the dogfights…but the stupid jerk never should've been caught. But it was the fuckin' Wonder Dog. I'll deal with him tonight."

Blatterman presses a button next to the bed. "Hilda!" he screams into a special device so she can hear him. "Bring me some pie and vanilla; I can't sleep. I want the cold cherry pie—the whole thing—and bring my special spoon, and make it fast. I gotta rest up."

CHAPTER TWENTY-TWO

A SEMI-INCREDIBLE JOURNEY

The Hamptons jitney pulls away, continuing east toward Montauk.

We stand on the sidewalk, shaking our heads to get our bearings. My brother Billy is thinking hard, pointing out we're likely to draw attention immediately—a golden retriever with a parrot in her mouth, and me, a semi-recognizable TV personality who's supposed to have disappeared with his sidekick, Bud.

Our first interaction with humans is a mother and a daughter carrying several blue shopping bags from Ralph Lauren who stop to look at us.

"Hi there, you three. Now aren't you all cute. Waiting here for your masters?" the mother asks.

"Mom—I mean, birthing person—please, no, no, no. You're embarrassing me in front of dogs again. Never, ever again use the term 'master.' You can't define the relationship of canines that way anymore," her daughter instructs. "It's terrible. You could be attacked on social media and maybe have to stay indoors till it blows over."

"OK then, owners."

"No, wake up, Mom—also bad. That relegates them to being property. You should simply ask, 'Where are your persons?' Or maybe use 'Mom and Dad,' or better still, ask them, 'Where are the guardians for you three?'"

"Ugh! Guardians, that's stupid," the mother blurts. "I'm so sick of violating you and your new college friends with my non-PC terms."

"Oh my God," her daughter says, doubled over, clutching her stomach. "Please, never let me hear you say the word 'violating' again."

As the daughter starts explaining to the mother why she's been violated by the word "violated," Billy sees I'm impatient to get moving. For security reasons, he signals me to hold back. He shoots a glance suggesting something to Jane, and she gets the message.

Jane moves closer and looks up at them.

"Oh hi, sweetheart," the mother says to her.

As the daughter starts to correct her mother about "sweetheart," Jane opens her mouth as wide as she can, and there's Herbie.

The loaded Ralph Lauren bags bounce off their knees as they run down the street shrieking, "A dog's eating a parrot!"

Billy signals that we need to get away from pedestrians and move to the middle of the lawn of the inn near the jitney stop. I'm dependin' on Billy maybe to be the brains of the operation, and as usual, he doesn't disappoint me. He opens his mouth, lifts his tongue, and reveals a little black-and-white thing that he's been carrying during the trip.

"Good move, Billy," I'm thinkin'. At first, I thought he was about to show me an old cough drop, but even better, he lets me know it's one of Andy's new, advanced Apple AirTag trackers.

"Might help," he tells us.

Jane gives me a look that says, "He's quite the guy."

"I also swallowed a twenty-dollar bill just before we left," Billy tells us. "Never hurts to have some cash, but to get it I'll have to…"

We let him know that it's kind of obvious what he'll have to do to retrieve the twenty.

Jane has lived out here. I forgot that. She knows the general direction of the East Hampton airport. But that's it. According to Chicago Bob, Bud and my dad are stashed miles behind the airport somewhere in dense woods. To find the way, we need Herbie. And we need him now.

"OK then, we'll take a chance," Jane indicates. "I'm gonna do something. He won't like it, but let's see if this might work."

She raises her head and emits a low growl that swells into several loud "wake up" barks.

"Stopppppp! Stopppppp!" Herbie squawks, launching into full flight, swirling above us. "Here I come to save the day! Sergeant Herbie's on the way!"

Billy says we gotta stay calm and have a meeting to hatch a plan, but it's hard to contain Herbie. He's squawkin' for us to get moving; he's nuts over what happened to Chicago Bob. He wants to have at it with Money Piles and Blatterman. He's flyin' around squawkin', "Troops, grab your cocks and drop your socks, every swingin' dick double time. Move your dumb ass, Wonder Puppy."

"It might've been better when he was passed out," Billy indicates with a sigh.

True, but we have a bigger problem—we gotta get there as fast as possible. According to Chicago Bob, by midnight tonight, Piles will have done whatever he's goin' to do, and he'll be driving back to his Greenwich mansion with James One and Cartier. He's got a wholesome evening planned—a couple of Money's Butter Girls will be stripping while he watches live dogfights beamed from Thailand on Blatterman's closed-circuit network.

Billy thinks it's probably gonna take more than six hours to walk there— way too long. He says that dragging the leashes will slow us much more. We start to chew through each other's leashes. (Leashes have very little taste, by the way.) Billy orders Herbie to fly a reconnaissance mission. "See what's going on around here. Spot a way we could get a ride—something we could jump on that would get us closer."

My stomach is in a knot. The only way to make this work is to get a ride.

I notice a taxi stopping for a couple of people. My talking dog collar's being repaired, so I can't bark out, "Blatterman's lair, please, and step on it," with the deep authority of my Adam Driver voice setting.

We need a ride.

But how?

CHICAGO BOB IN THE SADDLE

Chicago Bob was sitting calmly in a big police facility. Bob had been through this crap before—arrested, put in a cell, yanked around in the court system— but never in New York. He was trying to figure how to get out fast. He'd lifted a set of keys that he was hoping to use when he was ready to make his move.

They'd taken him to a big facility but not yet to a cell. That was a good sign, and as soon as he walked in, he could smell horses. Police horses. He had a lot of respect for all horses, and particularly police horses.

Because of the horses, he got lucky.

Two cops in the corner of the room were talking about Valiant, a beloved old police horse that had fallen ill in his stall. They were complaining how all their vets were dealing with injured police dogs in the Bronx, so no one was around to treat Valiant. Bob couldn't hear the cop's conversation, but once again, he thanked his dear old mother for training him to read lips.

"Bob," she'd told him, "this skill will always help you if you decide on the righteous path of being a professional pickpocket, like your loving mama."

"I can help Valiant. I know what to do," Bob called to the cops, who were shocked that he had "heard" them.

The policemen didn't know what this Chicago Bob guy was all about. They simply had directions to hold him for a week and then let him go. Kayko Zodikoff had personally arranged the short stay because he liked Bob. Why get a perfectly decent guy like Chicago Bob thrown in jail for years just 'cause he'd run out on Piles in a rage because that fatso Blatterman was abusing horses? Zodikoff liked horses, and besides, Bob was the only guy around that egomaniac Piles who had any wit and intelligence. Plus, Bob knew music. Zodikoff loved American music, especially the old-time stuff. He'd never been able to stump Bob on a music question, not even one about the repertoire of niche performer Spats White.

"Hold him for a week and let him go," was the arrangement Zodikoff had engineered through his inside men.

Chicago Bob didn't know this. He figured he was goin' to be put away for a long time. He had to find a way to get out of this holding room before any cell door slammed on him.

"I'll help that horse. Look, look at this," he called to the cops.

Chicago Bob pulled a small folder of pictures out of his pocket. There he was in his vet outfit with racehorses. There were shots of him at the Kentucky Derby and Belmont and Gulfstream racetracks with jockeys.

"I'm a vet. Let me see him," Chicago Bob said.

The cops were a little dubious, but then he showed them a picture of himself holding his huge horse syringe, standing next to a famous white-haired thoroughbred trainer whose name they couldn't remember. Behind them was a racehorse with a demonic gleam in his eyes. The photo was signed, "I think he liked your brew. Thanks again, BB."

The cops had seen a lot of needles in their line of work, but none nearly as massively impressive as the syringe in the photo. "With equipment like that, this Bob fellow has gotta be the real deal," they figured; so they took Bob with his black vet kit to see Valiant. The horse was lying in the straw in his stall, gasping.

"Hmm...looks like a sudden attack of plutonomotinitis, Chicago Bob said, making up the word. "Possibly plutonomotinitis in his lungs, but he's lucky—this should do it."

He took out an enormous hypodermic and slowly filled it with dark yellow fluid.

The horse snorted as Chicago Bob slowly injected the medicine into his dark brown flank. Within two minutes, Valiant was on his feet, bristling with confidence, showing signs of a slight erection, and pawing the floor to get into action.

"Now I want to show you something specific about handling this particular horse in the future," Bob said. He pulled over a mounting block, grabbed Valiant's mane, and swung onto the horse's bare back.

"When riding an older horse, you gotta be careful not to do this," Bob said softly, sounding a bit like Kevin Costner in *Yellowstone*. He clicked his tongue three times and jammed his heels hard into the horse's ribs. Valiant reared up, whinnied mightily, and leaped from his stall.

The cops were screaming, "Wait, stop, no, stop!" as Chicago Bob bounded out of the facility. He made a sharp right turn on West Fifty-Third Street and galloped through the traffic, showing the finesse of the equestrian skills he'd learned on bareback as a small boy.

He charged over to Eighth Avenue, made a right, and deftly weaved around the oncoming honking and swerving vehicles, giving the finger to livid, profanity-spewing drivers all the way to Forty-Second Street. He handed Valiant's reins to a guy dressed as Woody, the cowboy character in *Toy Story*. As Chicago Bob disappeared into the subway, Woody and Valiant were posing for pictures at twenty a pop for a group of wide-eyed Japanese tourists, most of whom had never seen a horse with a full erection before.

ON THE WINGS OF A PARROT

Herbie reports back in ten minutes. He spotted a taxi stand with waiting cabs and saw an art event going on at Guild Hall. Two clergywomen were smoking pot behind an Episcopal church. He would've been back sooner, but he stopped to hover out of the sight of the two women and squawk, "God sees you, God sees you."

I'm leery to go anywhere near Guild Hall, where we rehearsed *Pardon My Privet*—seems like weeks ago, and it was only a couple of days. Tomorrow is the opening night. What if McCuddy, or any of the other people from the show, spot me? These aren't normal empathetic human beings; these are theater people. When they see me, they'll think only one thing: "On with the show." Right?

McCuddy will probably use my sudden return to sell more tickets, and then they'd drag me into Guild Hall, keep me locked up, and force me to go on tomorrow. I'd have to work with that janitor playing Bud's part who hasn't learned his first line yet. Of further comfort, the entire cast would show no remorse that as far as they know, their costar Bud is in trouble with the police and lying unconscious in a hospital bed. All of this would be heaped on me because, of course, "the show must go on."

Billy suggests that maybe I'm being a touch paranoid, and perhaps if they spotted me, it could lead to something good. Oh really, Billy? What about this? Maybe I won't go on. Maybe they'll grab my collar, drag me inside, and call the cops, who'd charge me with distributing the pills in the car to my five-year-old fans. It could happen. No, wait, there I go again—imagined outcomes. I'm not thinking straight. I'm tense, paranoid, and doubting myself because the stakes couldn't be higher. I'm loaded with dread that this caper is not going to end well.

Jane comes over and nuzzles me. She helps me breathe and relax, and reminds me of the important words from that song Andy plays all the time. To paraphrase, they're: "What do you do through it all when there is doubt? You eat it up. You spit it out." She puts her head on my shoulder.

"What kind of a love scene you two playing over there?" Herbie squawks at me. "Wake up, Wonder Puppy. Snap to it. Active duty now."

I take a deep, deep breath. Out of nowhere, I begin to twirl in a tight little circle—round and round. Faster and faster. English Bull Terriers do this sometimes when we play. It looks funny. Check it out on YouTube—people are always recording us spinning around. What we're doing is a remnant from our long-ago fighting days in nineteenth-century England. We'd suddenly gyrate to confuse an adversary. I'm twirling wildly now, in the grasp of my ancestors' power.

Billy looks at Jane. They nod to each other, "He's unleashed!"

That's the highest mental state a dog can reach—unleashed. Sometimes we can reach it running with wild abandon across a wide-open field, or charging into a burning building to rescue a child, or, like my fabled ancestor Brick, while fighting to save his owner. Please don't boo "owner." I can't get used to saying, "To protect his person," but of course I'm just the dog in the equation, not a twenty-year-old Mao-leaning college student at Oberlin.

But anyway, I don't care what you think of my word selection. I've got a taxi stand to check out, and I'm handling this operation my way.

PILES VS. THE PIPE

Ike "I Got Money" Piles had never been a druggie. But of course, there were...those very...er, ah...challenging situations when he'd smoke because he couldn't handle the reality of his responsibilities—that dreaded feeling of being afraid. He remembered some of the other times he'd turned to his custom-made gold, silver, and diamond dragon pipe for help. There was that time he'd been afraid of having a colonoscopy. They were goin' to shove a camera up his ass. Money had been freaked; he'd figured it would be big—long and wide with an IMAX lens. He smoked some primo crack before the procedure. By the time he got to the doctor, he didn't care if they rammed the Hubble telescope up his ass.

"The Dragon" helped oh so much.

When he held the Dragon, it was like shaking hands with his best friend. He'd fire up some rock today, hoping it would give him the chest-thumping courage he needed to do what had to be done.

Ivan and Dov had outlined a plan for handling the guy and the dog, which he didn't want to hear, let alone carry out on his own. They gave him a new made-in-China cattle prod, a replica of the infamous ones used at the Urumqi No. 3 Detention Center to electrocute prisoners. It featured settings ranging from number one ("Wake up, asshole") to number five ("Time for your daily torture") all the way up to ten ("If I touch your big toe now, you'll explode").

"It's a very simple device," Ivan explained, "but remember, once it's plugged in, be as dry as possible and always wear these special gloves. To operate, we recommend you yell at your victim for about a minute to get them relaxed, then gently apply for five seconds on the number-eight setting to any bony extremity. Next, pour yourself a chilled Stoli, sit back, and savor the results of your effort—the convulsions, the foaming at the mouth, the eyes turning black, and voilà, it's over. Later, very easy: drag him naked about a half-mile into the dense woods out there, coat him with this quart of untraceable organic Russian honey, a favorite of bears everywhere, and enjoy your weekend—you've earned it."

"What about that ugly dog?" Piles asked them nervously.

"We are not certified to do dogs, cats, or any household pets, sorry," Ivan said, "but I'm sure the fat guy upstairs won't disappoint you with some of his ideas. Otherwise, you've always got your prod, but not on the eight setting for the dog—you'd have quite a mess on the walls and ceiling."

Dov and Ivan wished Piles luck and departed.

Ike "I Got Money" Piles was scared, which of course he would never admit. He hated the feeling of being alone and responsible. It had all started when he was five and his parents left him and drove to Coachella for the day. Their goddamn friends had tricked them into thinking that the afternoon's music would be a gangster rap extravaganza, not a celebration of '70s pop hits.

Little Ike's mother, Lucille, and his father, Leon "I Got the Biggest" Piles, somehow got trapped in a mosh pit during a Barry Manilow show. They fell asleep during "Mandy," only to be trampled awake by gyrating boomers during "Can't Smile Without You." They fled Palm Springs for Vegas for a couple of nights at the Excalibur, to recover by stuffing themselves on the eighteen different preparations of ribs and wings at the Roundtable Buffet and hopefully finding some gangster rap.

Little Ike Piles was home alone. He ate peanut butter for three days and was quivering with fear when his parents returned. Leon and Lucille offered Little Ike no sympathy. They barged through the front door enraged—in no mood to deal with a wailing toddler. A few years later he learned exactly why his parents had rushed by him that night and run into the kitchen and started drinking Johnnie Walker Red straight from the bottle. Just before his mom and dad were set to make the ninety-minute drive home, the concierge at the hotel had convinced them to see someone named Celine Dion. "The rap on this is that the Vegas gangsters think it's the greatest show in town," she'd told them.

This piqued their interest.

"…and the seats I have for you are the best in the house, right there in the center in the middle of the longest row in the theater," she'd boasted.

After ten minutes of Celine belting out songs they'd never heard, Leon and Lucille tried to leave; but so transfixed were the sobbing Dion fans as she sang "My Heart Will Go On," none would move their legs even slightly to let them pass. When Leon and Lucille finally did make it all the way to the aisle during the standing ovation for "O Holy Night," they found the exit doors chained and heavily guarded.

"No one leaves while Miss Dion is singing," a security guard yelled at them over the applause.

Leon slipped the guard a fifty, begging to get out, but they were forced to stay for two more blood-curdling hours. All they could do was claw helplessly at the sealed exit door trying to escape. Once released, they drove home screaming obscenities, even though Lucille had to admit that she kinda liked that song about the beauty and the beast.

In all the years that he'd been fighting and running his sex businesses in Vegas, Ike "I Got Money" Piles had one ironclad rule for his employees: "Mention Celine Dion, and you fired." Whoever this Celine was, she was the root of all his insecurity, he knew.

Now he was alone again, and afraid. He knew James One wouldn't do the electric prod and would not even help with the dragging into the woods.

"Money," James One had told him, "even if you give me extra offa your money pile, if you ever do get around to payin' me again, I not be doin' no killin', and my DNA and me doin' no body draggin'. When I was twelve, my mama and my daddy made me promise I'd never drag no dead body into the woods."

Money knew Cartier was useless, worrying too much about ruining her fuckin' two-inch nail extensions to help him. Blatterman was so fat, he could barely walk into the woods, let alone lift a body.

"What I do?" he wondered, as he took a first big hit from the Dragon.

Whoosh! He felt it.

"I love smokin' crack," he thought, "'cept sometimes it make me want to clean my teeth for hours with Tide sticks. By time I finished, my mouth look like it full of gleaming elephant tusks."

He sat and hit the pipe for almost an hour.

"Why that damn Bud and ugly Spike still be sleepin'?" he wondered, looking over at them, not knowing they were both awake now and faking it.

"Ah, ah, ah, smoke finally makin' me think clear, way more clear," he recognized. "Why go to all the time and trouble of draggin' that jerk Bud into the woods? Maybe I can get Cartier so high that she be gleeful to touch Bud's toe with the prod. All we do then is stuff the body in that big triple-thick smell-proof plastic garment bag that my floor-length Mongolian snow leopard coat came in. We lock bag in a basement closet. James One can shove him in the bag and zip the zipper. Cartier and James One carry bag to closet, and maybe I give James One another used car as reward."

Money Piles wasn't worried that someday someone might pry the closet door open and discover the bag. To ship the illegal endangered-species coat through customs, the Mongolian Mafia had put a huge Men's Wearhouse outlet store logo on the bag to fool the customs agents. "Someday maybe somebody break open closet door, take one look at bag, and think it only filled with cheap clothes from some guy's warehouse," he figured.

"OK, it all worked out by me," Piles said with a smile, clutching the Dragon, "so now we all fire up and have some fun first."

"Cartier, James One, get down here and smoke some nuggets wit me. No excuses. Let's party, 'cause we got a big night ahead."

THE L'ARF AND A LUCKY DRUNK

Gliding by on Main Street is a golf cart–like tram with a pink canvas roof. Billy figures it's a service to ride people around the streets of East Hampton for free.

It doesn't exactly have a blinking "Airport Shuttle, Our Specialty: Dogs" sign on it, but we'll give it a shot, 'cause a taxi's gonna be tough. If somehow we do get into one, and somehow little Herbie can tell the driver to head to the airport, and somehow the guy's crazy enough to actually want to take us, he's gonna want to see money upfront. Unfortunately, in spite of eating spicy turkey chili he found in the trash can on the lawn, Billy hasn't been able to "produce" the twenty he swallowed back at Andy's.

We run across the street and wait for the next little trolley. The only person sitting at the stop is a white-haired, deeply tanned, middle-aged man who's wearing yellow shorts and reading a thick book. He has two bags loaded with groceries from Citarella, and I smell gazpacho. If Billy could just down a heaping container of it right now, we'd soon have all the cash we need to make it to the airport.

We pile into the rear seats of the thing, which is like a stretched golf cart. Herbie's perched in his favorite spot on top of my head, enjoying the ride. At the next stop, three teenage girls get on. Interestingly, the girls aren't giggling and taking pictures of each other from different angles for Snapchat posts; they're simply bouncing yellow tennis balls up and down.

"Hey, if you're headed off to play tennis, where are your racquets?" the gazpacho guy asks, giving off a slightly pervy vibe, 'cause the question has given him an excuse to ogle their smooth young legs.

Note: I don't think the guy's actually a perv. He was reading an autobiography of Thurgood Marshall. Would a perv be reading that? Doubtful. But I digress.

The girls giggle. "Oh, it's such a nice warm day. We're just going to the park to have a catch. It's good practice; we're on the tenth-grade softball team."

Billy and I look at each other. Are we in *Back to the Future*? Is it suddenly 1955?

We're witnessing young teenagers without phones clutched in their hands, unescorted by overprotective parents, venturing outdoors to play on a sunny afternoon? How rare is this? we wonder. I nudge Jane, but she's oblivious, mesmerized by the bouncing yellow tennis balls. Billy and I start following the bouncing balls ourselves. "Oh boy," I'm thinkin'. "They're having a catch."

"Don't do it, Spike!" Herbie squawks.

I know, dear reader, there's a certain amount of tension at this point in the story for you. I know you know we're in a race-against-time situation to somehow get to Blatterman's lair. I know you know about that cattle prod, and my beloved dad and my master, Bud, and their plight. So knowing this as you do, I'm not particularly proud of what happens next, but we get off the trolley to run around and play with the girls.

Bounce tennis balls in front of dogs for five minutes, and what do you expect?

But, as so often happens in life—like when, by accident, Mr. Boggs somehow ended up wandering around Caesars Palace at four in the morning, met Frank Sinatra, and after chatting together, the singer volunteered to appear on his talk show—the folly of our stopping to play ball with the girls ends up working out for the best.

The lawn where we have the catch with the girls is next to the beautiful East Hampton Library, where Bud did a couple of the early readings for *Pardon My Privet*. The library is having some kind of fundraiser today, with a silent auction, sponsor product promotions, and authors signing their books.

Herbie is so pissed off at us for stopping to play that he takes off on another reconnaissance flight, and it's a good thing he does. He comes back and reports that on the far side of the library grounds, he spotted an exhibit of the new super-advanced electric automobile, the L'ARF. For the past two months, all manner of media have been flooded with advertising for the L'ARF as the world's first vocally driven car.

The L'ARF acronym stands for "Lamborghini. Apple. Rivian. Ford."

Lamborghini, Apple, and Rivian each contributed millions of dollars of research on secret new autonomous systems, voice controls, and predictive GPS technology. Ford was only needed to contribute an "F" to make it "ARF." Why ARF? Because some branding genius who'd watched *Mad Men* as a little girl came up with the slogan "So simple, your dog can drive!" The car's media campaign features Sofia Vergara, Leonardo DiCaprio, Vin Diesel, Serena Williams, Lady Gaga, and of course Tom Hanks, with their dogs showcasing all of the L'ARF's advanced features.

At the end of each spot, the star's dog is sitting confidently behind the wheel. The celebrity says, "So simple, your dog can drive," and they roar off.

OK, if this all sounds a little too good to be true for us...well, here you go.

I'm completely familiar with the car from seeing the commercials millions of times. All I have to do is get in and turn it on by pushing the button that says "Function." At that point, the word "airport" needs to be spoken into the large molded ear that's replaced the traditional steering wheel.

The three of us, plus a wildly excited Herbie, pile into the bright red L'ARF. I turn the system on by jamming my nose into the function button—so far, so good. The car immediately speaks to us, employing the voice of Brian

Cox, playing a *Downton Abbey*-style butler. L'ARF comes with many inter-active celebrity voice options; Brian Cox, Dr. Dre, and, incomprehensively, Debbie Boone, rank as the three most popular.

"Yes, my lord or lady, where dost thou wish to go?"

Deepening his squawk to a low G note, Herbie commands, "Airport."

Cox intones, "Of course, sire, but there are approximately five thousand two hundred and seventeen airports in the United States, not including John Travolta's private landing strip behind his home. Might you please be a touch more specific in your request?"

"The East Hampton airport, you asshole," Herbie squawks.

"Regrettably, my system has noted abusive language. To assure that you're not giving impaired drunken commands that would lead us to drive you into the ocean, like that cheap GPS you mentioned earlier in the story did to the Japanese tourists," Cox says—how the car knew we mentioned that GPS, we have no idea—"might you please breathe ever so gently into the small open-mouth portal that's flashing by the large ear?"

Billy exhales a long breath into the thing.

"Lovely," Cox says, "and surprising how many of our privileged clients are also enjoying the healthy benefits of All in the Family dog chow these days, and nice to know your day has included some spicy turkey chili from the trash can near The Palm as well. Your journey is about to begin; cheerio for now."

The 395-horse-power electric engine purrs. Lights flash, doors lock, and the car fills with the scent of Dior Sauvage cologne. Cox asks if we'd like some crafted cocktails with the amuse-bouche quickly being prepared by the tiny, very angry Gordon Ramsay robot in the back.

Billy, Jane, and I are so excited that we've pulled this off, we're "high-paw-ing" each other.

Eleven feet into our quest, the high-pawing stops as we're slammed to a halt several feet before clearing the library grounds.

"Start this junk heap," Herbie squawks.

"Dreadfully sorry, old chums," the Brian Cox voice announces. "Our gyronomic passenger measurement system indicates a vector-five reading, meaning that your voyage has, regrettably, been canceled for the following four reasons.

"One, no humans on board. Car must have one human over the age of five or the cyber equivalent to operate."

"Cox," Herbie demands, "what the hell is vector five?"

"Two, a parrot must be caged to protect the plant-based imitation fine Corinthian leather on the vehicle's seats, which, by the way, are hand-stitched by children in Bangladesh."

"Shut the fuck up and just drive, Cox," Herbie squawks. "No cage. Drive, and drive now! I hope you die at the end of *Succession*."

"Three, further chemical analysis of the breath submitted showed no presence of alcohol," Cox continues, "but did, unfortunately, reveal to our dismay that due to excessive chili consumption, the passenger who submitted it is currently filling with more gas than the Keystone Pipeline."

"Airport, airport, airport, airport," Herbie screeches. "Are you deaf?"

"If I may continue, and most importantly, four: the guy at the shop forgot to charge your vehicle this morning."

"Clients' ejections are under way. Protect your head, take your valuables, and tell your friends about L'ARF. Tallyho," Cox says merrily. The doors fly up, the seats rise to a ninety-degree angle, and we tumble onto the lawn.

"Fuck you, Cox," Herbie yawps while carpet-bombing the L'ARF with parrot poo. "You're washed up, Brian. If you're lucky, you'll end up with glued-on ten-inch whiskers touring North Korea in *Cats*."

Jane and Billy nod at me, conveying, "That's our boy Herbie, but now what?"

The "now what" is the accidental good fortune of being at this spot exactly at this time because we stopped to play.

Slurred speech calls to us, "That was...was fuckin'-A great. I luv you guys...hey, Spikie, I'm your biggest fan, goddammit."

We spot a grizzly-looking young man splayed out on the lawn. We don't need to be downwind to smell that he reeks of booze.

"Whadda ya need? I'm here for you," he says, crawling our way. "That car treated you like shit. Cars can...be so goddamn mean. I hate mean cars. Good for the parrot. I got a car, I love it, I love my car, let's go forra ride." He stops, rolls on his back, and takes a gulp from a small bottle of Jack Daniel's. "Airport, is it? I love airports."

Billy looks at me—with this guy at the wheel, we'd be arrested or dead before we could make it through the first light, but let's see what we can do.

"I love golden retrievers. I love all animals plus monkeys. But I love you most, Spikie," he says as he reaches me. "Let me hug you, huh? Please. Oh, you smell good, Spikie…real good. They call me 'the Wonder Nose.' I'm da best. You smell real good."

I've never understood my vast appeal to the non-sober market, 'cause this surely isn't the first time something like this has happened. I enjoy letting them pet me, while trying to prevent the occasional river of saliva from landing on my head. This drunk, I like. He's about forty, with a three-day growth, wearin' a flannel shirt on a hot day. He's got bloodshot brown eyes and beautiful-smelling whiskey breath, with no trace of tobacco, not like the last bombed bum who cornered me. There's something about this fellow that screams "analog" in a digital world—at least that's my first impression. He seems like the kinda man who still carries a penknife, uses paper maps, and always needs change for a pay phone, if he could only still find one.

"C'monna my car over there. Let's go. I'll crawl along wit ya."

We make it over to his blue Mazda hatchback, which he forgot to turn off. He grabs the door handle and hoists himself up off the ground. He swings the door open.

"OK, Wonder Dog and his pussy…I mean…posse…posse…I mean… here we go.…Just call me Winston.…Get in while Winston has a little picker-upper from his friend Jack."

He pours the rest of the small bottle of Daniel's in his mouth, swishes it around, and swallows with a big, "Goooood!" He lights a thick blunt, takes two long, deep hits, and snuffs it out on the car door.

"Ahhh…oh boy, good now, feel good. I ready to roll to beautiful East Hampton airport with my pals.… Let's get in."

I look at Jane and Billy, indicating, "We can't let this guy drive."

"I got it covered," Jane tells me. "He's not driving. We are."

She leaps onto the driver's seat and puts her paws on the spokes of the steering wheel.

"Oh m'God, howda you know I luvit when dogs drive? Take it away, honey." He clambers into the back seat and twists open another bottle of Jack. "Get back here wit me, Spike; you're my paaaal," he says with his head on his chest and mouth hanging open.

Using my mighty jaws, I shift the transmission lever on the console between his two ketchup-stained car seats to Drive, and hop in the back. Billy's on the floor, set to work both the gas and the brake with his brick-like head. Herbie takes his spot as navigator in the center of the dashboard under the filthy rearview mirror.

"Airport, please, and step on it, baby," he hoots.

Getting anyone's undivided attention these days is challenging, so you shouldn't be surprised at how little notice is taken of a golden retriever driving a filthy 2010 Mazda hatchback along the two-lane Montauk Highway. The couple of times we stop at lights, people in the other cars are texting frantically.

A big police car heads our way. Driving toward us is the infamous hard-nosed veteran Suffolk County sheriff, Brent Beatty. He smiles and waves as he passes, probably figuring we're making one of the many movies being shot in the Hamptons this week. Sheriff Beatty has no idea that he'll turn out to be the only witness to what we're doing, or that his nephew Winston is passed out in the back seat cradling Spike the Wonder Dog's head in his lap.

Jane is barely able to manage the sharp right turn off Route Twenty-Seven onto Daniels Hole Road, which leads to the airport. Ya gotta wonder how Daniel himself feels about a road being named after him that way.

We pull into the airport's mostly empty parking lot—limo drivers pick up the celebrities, the ultrarich, and the well-dressed coastal elite directly from their private jets on the runway, thus saving their clientele from enduring boring encounters with regular people who might be in the terminal. We all agree that if we are able to rescue Bud and Dad, as a thank-you, Bud's gotta lend us his car so we can plan a road trip together.

Winston is sound asleep, so Jane deftly parks the car in a cool, shady spot, and we leave the AC running. Far be it from us to be the first dogs to leave a human locked in a car on a hot day.

OPERATION MILK-BONE

We need a code name for this military-like thing we're attempting. After a couple of contentious minutes with Herbie demanding it be "Herbie's Finest Hour," we vote for "Operation Milk-Bone"—figuring if we save Bud, he'll likely reward us with Milk-Bones.

We had some seriously good intelligence. My brother Billy was paying strict attention when Chicago Bob was explaining to Actual Andy and Virtual Andy that Blatterman's lair was hidden somewhere deep in the woods southwest of the airport.

Virtual Andy had uncovered some highly classified World War II reconnaissance maps using the newly installed programming that gives him complete access to everything in the National Archives, except for the secret files on the Kennedy assassination, autographed eight-by-ten color headshots of creatures from outer space, and the illegal wiretaps of Hunter Biden secretly ordering paint-by-number kits from an art supply house in Wilmington, Delaware.

Based on what Billy's steel-trap mind has retained from studying those charts, he indicates that the most direct route to the place is straight across the airport's tarmac into the woods. To get there, we spend a solid thirty minutes taking turns digging under the chain-link fence guarding the landing strip. (Note to the mayor of East Hampton: if three dogs can do it, so can any crazed, dynamite-carrying town resident who's been pissed off about the roar of private planes over his hot tub for the last ten years.)

Our next move is to wait for a clear moment to race across the airstrip and dig our way out under the fence on the other side.

Herbie, with a maximum speed of forty-five miles per hour, takes the lead across the runway.

I feel a shudder when I hear the static of the loudspeaker system turning on. A voice announces, "Attention, attention, security, on the runway now, two white pigs or possibly two large white rabbits and a yellow coyote are chasing a green seagull across the landing path."

If these are the keen observations of the air traffic controller in the tower, I understand why two planes accidentally touched down on the beach last week.

After about a half hour of winding our way through what's way more like a forest than your basic patch of woods, I'm slowly getting nervous. My only experience in the wild like this was searching for lookalikes on our reality show, and that location was relatively close to a parking lot. I'm feeling kinda spooked and tryin' not to show it.

Billy's doing his best to keep us on course, but he's got even less cred in the woods than me. Smart as he is, he's scared and I can tell it. He keeps saying he thinks he smells bears. "Do you smell bears?" he asks. "I think I smell a bear." I hafta let him know I have no idea what bears smell like and neither does he.

Can we really find our way? What if we don't locate Blatterman's lair, and what if Bud's not OK? And my dad? Is he alive? Has Piles shipped Dad to Thailand to fight? Are we gonna screw up this mission? There again—imagined outcomes, my imagined outcomes. "Stop it," I tell myself. I think of Dad—"Never doubt that you can prevail, Spike."

Not helping our quest is normally unflappable Herbie (no pun intended), who's lost control of himself.

Why?

Owls.

He's terrified of being attacked by an owl. Apparently, somewhere in his lineage, maybe six generations ago, one of his ancestors, in a playful, offhand moment of teasing, planted the idea in his offspring's minds that the biggest danger they'd ever face in life would be owls in the woods.

Take note here, parents: you never know what large or small thing you might say or do that will change the course of your gene pool. Herbie says the instant he was born, he started looking around for owls. Right now, he's attached under me with his eyes closed, hoping to get out of the woods intact.

As leader, I got a responsibility for the team. It's going to be dark soon, and we're all hungry. We're in the woods. Does this mean we'll have to eat grubs? What if it's off-season for grubs? And anyway, what the hell are grubs? How do you spot a grub? Are they in the thickets? If so, where are the thickets? I don't know, but you always hear how someone survived in the wilderness by eating grubs.

This is when I'm shocked to see that my brother Billy has stopped and is actually digging for grubs. He urges us to join in, and tells us that even though they're a bit of an acquired taste, he's been eating them on a daily basis for a couple of years. He explains that when he was about five months old, his owners, Bee and Calvin, entertained a noted nutritional scientist for dinner. The evening was a bit of a disaster because Calvin, who fancied himself a fine gourmet cook, served chicken tenders fried in coconut oil.

While the scientist was stealthily feeding overcooked chicken tenders to Billy under the table, he explained to Calvin and Bee that grubs were the only organism known to contain PQQ, pyrroloquinoline quinone, which was discovered by a NASA probe on Mars. NASA immediately classified the revelation "top secret" and sent the data to the national records.

From this, you gotta deduct that the US government, in its infinite wisdom, doesn't want us to know that Mars is teeming with grubs. The scientist further explained that the PQQ stuff has been proven to dramatically increase the number of cells in your brain, which leads to vast enhancement in intelligence.

"Within a month of my daily grub routine," Billy announces somewhat sheepishly, "I was doing long division in my head."

As far as I'm concerned, they're slimy, dirty little bugs with thousands of squirming, highly weird, hairy little legs. Starving to death is a better option than surviving on these things. (Google "grubs" and take a look.)

While devouring the grubs, Billy has a massive coughing fit. His eyes are crossed, and his thick pink tongue's hanging out. He's choking. No one's ever invented a Heimlich procedure for dogs, so all we can do is stand by watching helplessly. I figure one of those creatures reversed course and is using those tiny legs to crawl out of his throat to escape. Not so. We don't notice it at the time, but the thing that eventually flies out of his mouth isn't a grub getting a second chance at life, but the Apple AirTag he's been carrying under his

310

tongue. We don't know it yet, but we've lost the one chance we had of maybe being traced by Virtual Andy.

CHICAGO BOB

Chicago Bob hadn't really had a good ride on a horse in a while. That dash down Eighth Avenue had been great. He smiled as he recalled jumping over a guy in a wheelchair crossing against the light.

The doors to the uptown subway car closed behind him. "Gotta find a way to keep riding horses," he thought. Short of the fountain of youth he believed frequent sex provided him, Bob figured an hour a day on a horse would be the next best thing to keep him youthful.

His last mount had been Winnie, one of the old racehorses Blatterman acquired to serve his dirty deeds. Winnie'd given him a fair ride, but the horse wanted Bob to drop the reins so she could go. Even though there were a pretty clear twenty acres on all the land behind Blatterman's place, those little fixtures in the ground for the fat creep's laser alarm system could really foul up a hoof. He was tempted to take the risk, but didn't commit to the galloping both he and the horse had been yearning for. The two of them should have blown it out anyway, because ten hours later Winnie was dead at the hands of Blatterman and his sinister bow. Chicago Bob had left, vowing to find a way to stop Blatterman.

He'd had enough experience listening to Zodikoff and his team plotting things with Piles over the last couple of months to know that Zodikoff would track him down now that he'd escaped. Piles would want him found, and Zodikoff would soon be indicating a song to fit the circumstances of the unfortunate disappearance of Chicago Bob. He'd just beaten the cops, so he figured Zodikoff's crew was already on his trail.

He ripped out the inner sole of his left shoe and found the tracking device the police planted for Zodikoff. At Ninety-Sixth Street, he got off the subway car and went into a store and bought a fifty-dollar Whole Foods gift card. Next, he needed to find a hungry-looking homeless person on a downtown train. He went to the platform and waited for the train. There were plenty of desperate-looking people to choose from. He wanted someone who'd be able to get off the subway and walk several blocks, so he picked a disheveled woman who wasn't burdened by hauling around all of her worldly possessions in large plastic bags like most of the others.

A minute after he struck up a conversation, she was asking for a handout. He gave her the card and said it was only good at the Whole Foods way downtown on East Houston Street. He attached the tracking device to her dusty jacket while giving her a warm pat on the back. He wished her good luck and suggested she try the mangoes.

He got off the train at Times Square and headed back uptown on foot. "I'll get my cash, get my guns, and try not to be too spooked by that overfriendly Virtual Andy thing," he told himself.

BUD, ROCKY, AND BLATTERMAN

Ike "I Got Money" Piles, flying high from burnin' rock, commands James One to wake up Bud and Rocky, who are still feigning sleep. "Maybe we get that dog to smoke some; we see what happen. And that jerk Bud, let's tease him. They both be sleepin' way too long," Bud hears Piles say.

"Well, here we go," Rocky thinks.

"Use that cold-water hose on that dumb Wonder Dog, James One. He need a wake-up shock. Squirt him in the face, then squirt that jerk Bud in his nuts, then squirt Cartier, and aim that freezin'-cold blast a' water at her more-than-ample frontage."

"Shut up, Money," she says. "I'm high and dry and happy. Why don't you let these two go, throw that pipe away, and we go back to Vegas and have some fun again? You're too serious these days. Prison make you angry and turn you from rich dumb man into a not-so-rich but still just-as-dumb man. I like it when you were plain rich and dumb."

"I more richer than ever. Blatterman just tell me my cut of bet collections from dogfights. Those crazy dogs around the world makin' my money pile more bigger and piled with money than ever."

"You bad," James One says.

"Squirt her now, James One. I rig finals of Vegas International Big Blonde Babes Wet T-Shirt Tournament for her to win. What she do? Stay and have lively group grope with me that night? No, still in her drippin' wet clothes, she fly home to show her good Catholic mother trophy. Hose Cartier, so I can gaze wide-eyed at my number-one Butter Girl."

"Money, you flyin' on crack and gettin' horny as usual, but you smoked so much, your 'Mighty Little Ike' is now more fast asleep than that dog," Cartier says. "And the big bad cold water from that hose would only make Mighty Little Ike into Really Tiny Ike. I wanna go home."

Rocky appreciates the blast of water to his face. Feels great. He opens his mouth and takes a couple of big swallows. He shakes his massive head, flaps his ears, starts licking the water pooling under him.

"Nothing like being hit with a torrent of cold water from a hose on a warm evening while shackled to a dirty floor, surrounded by a meth-crazed lowlife plotting to kill you," he thinks.

James One stoops over and peers at Rocky's face.

"This guy's breath smells worse than Lionel Messi's jock strap after an overtime match on a hundred-and-four-degree day in Argentina," Rocky thinks.

"Ike Piles," James One says, "I now be lookin' here an' doin' some serious Wonder Dog wonderin'. Spike might be trans dog; he look like he be usin' Maybelline mascara to make spot on eye bigger. Cold water makin' black lines from spot run down his face. With streaks on face, he now be as strange-lookin' as that Rudy guy with face streaks they still show eve'y chance they get on CNN."

"What you mean?" Piles asks.

"You look, Money. You look at him with your powerful money-vision eyes. Spike been usin' makeup to make eye patch more patchier."

"That's not Spike," Bud says.

Money Piles twitches in a paranoid spasm. "Who dat? Where dat voice come from?"

"It's that guy Bud," Cartier says.

"He be awake?"

"I'm not talking in my sleep, Money. Your hit team got the wrong dog. That's Spike's father, Rocky," Bud says.

Piles thinks, "What the fuck?" then takes a breath, steadies himself, and sneers angrily at Bud. "When I meet you at Jimmy Fallon show couple years back, I say I buy Wonder Dog for twenty thousand plus I give you a free night with my Butter Girls. You say no deal. If you sold me that day, your money pile be higher and I still have leg and finger, and best for you, then you see why they be called my Butter Girls."

"Looks like you're a poor loser, Money," Bud says.

"I may lose then, but I beat you now. You goin' down."

"I wondered if that dog might not be Spike," Blatterman says, descending the stairs from his trophy room. He's wearing a red velvet robe and carrying the hammer he just used to nail a set of three mounted, stuffed squirrel heads on the wall next to his prized black rhino trophy. Putting the little heads next to the big one was his idea of a most creative and hilarious sight gag. "The guys from our Poaching Pride Club are gonna love it," he thinks.

Piles jumps and screams, "Where voice comin' from now?"

Blatterman looks at Piles. "For God's sake, calm down, Money. Take a look at this dog. Spike had a face scar from his fight with Monstro, and he lost a little piece of his left ear in the match you made for him against Little Nipper," he explains. "And this dog is older, more mature, and slightly bigger in the chest than Spike. I bet he'd be one hell of an attraction on our circuit."

"Spike's father wearin' makeup? What the fuck?" Piles says. "By the way, you got cherry pie on your chin again, Blatterman."

"They say Liza Minnelli's father and one of her husbands wore makeup," Cartier chimes in. "I read about it on the cover of a magazine at ShopRite."

"Wow! Show business so weird," James One says.

"You both so weird!" Piles yells. "How I get my revenge on Spike now? Do Blatterman have to kill that dog instead?"

"Anything for a friend, Money," Blatterman answers. "I was thinkin'—"

"Now hold on, Mr. Blatterman, you look like a reasonable man," Bud interrupts while observing that in that robe, Blatterman actually looks more like a maniacal, three-hundred-pound version of Hugh Hefner. "I know you're an esteemed deacon in your church and a teacher of Bible studies at Sunday school in Greenwich. Why not convince your friend Mr. Piles here to forgive? Follow the Christian way. Ask him to turn the other cheek."

"The only person around here turnin' any cheeks is Cartier," Piles quips, thinking he'd score a laugh, but his lame sex joke falls flat.

"Sorry, Bud," Blatterman says, "this is pure business between Mr. Piles and me, plus I never hit a fast-moving dog with the bow yet. Not simple, but he's white and at night, with the lasers and all, it'll make him a pretty easy target. Getting rid of Spike, and now probably his father, too, well, it's simply what my partner Mr. Piles wants."

Bud looks at Ike "I Got Money" Piles, feigning awe. "Money, you're a hero to so many people. What you did in your early years in the boxing ring won you that Wheaties endorsement. You made Mike Tyson jealous that he was never on a cereal box like you. Only other person in history to make Mike Tyson jealous was Robin Givens. Think of that, Money: you and the highly acclaimed dramatic actress Robin Givens alone at the top of that unique category."

Piles nods in appreciation of himself. He briefly recalls that he once thought Robin Givens was one smokin'-hot chick. "Now that Meghan Markle remind me of Givens, but why she not seem so smokin' hot like Robin?" he wonders.

"Before jail," Bud continues, "you were about to be hailed as Business-man of the Year in Vegas for the way you built your sexual services empire, which all began with your brilliant idea to take a generic Vegas tour bus, paint 'See Sin City and Sin' on the sides, and convert it into a cathouse on wheels with a naked former Miss Las Vegas as tour guide and driver."

"You shade, Money, you bad shade," James One says, watching his boss beam with pride.

"I first met Money when I auditioned to be one of the...oh, what were we called? Oh yeah, 'attendants' on the original bus," Cartier proudly tells Bud, "and it was love at first...er, well, anyway, he called me his 'Lady Gag Gag.'"

Bud interrupts, "And it was you, you, Ike 'I Got Money' Piles, no one else, who, in spite of strenuous objections from the trustees of the beloved Broadway musical, created The Guys and Dolls Club, the world's first sex-dolls-only brothel. Now it's a franchise opportunity like Subway."

"He right, that me!" Piles boasts, completely besotted with himself.

Bud continues with paeans to Piles' self-perceived perfection. "HBO produced that brilliant documentary on your career and the example you set for young people by using steroids instead of rigorous training to build your chiseled physique, and your generosity to fans with that three percent discount on Money Piles gear one day a year, and your unique relationship with hard-nosed Vegas boxing judges. They showed the video of how you, like no other fighter in history, were knocked out cold, flat on your face, but still won that championship bout, and think of all..."

As Bud is laying on all the *This Is Your Life*-style praise, Rocky sees what he's up to. "He's buttering up this guy like a piece of burnt toast in a bad diner," he thinks. Piles' formerly meth-dimmed eyes are now gleaming with satisfaction. What was that saying Mrs. Erdrick quoted so much? "Let us be grateful to people who make us happy—they are the charming gardeners of our souls." Bud is making this jerk happy.

Rocky strains his shackle to make it just far enough over toward Blatterman to lick his hand.

"Oh, wow, what's that?" Blatterman asks himself. He glances down and sees Rocky's tongue on his fingers. "My, that feels good...so, so, good—don't stop," he says, vaguely recalling that the last time anyone licked him was twenty-nine years ago on his honeymoon.

"This isn't really too bad; he tastes good," Rocky realizes. "I'm lucky this slob eats the pie crust with his hands." He keeps licking until Blatterman lumbers back upstairs to get more pie and put on his bow-shooting costume for his evening's activity.

Rocky listens as Bud keeps lauding Ike "I Got Money" Piles. "And your lone foray into porno movies, *She Stoops to Conquer*, yielded praise as 'a neo-classic of the dildoian genre' from the most highly respected pundits of that school of filmmaking. Your idea to cast it with two unknown San Fernando Valley X-rated actors who you claimed were the industry's only Native American porno stars, Johnny Bear Balls and Mary Squirting Water, was a promotional stroke of genius even though you were forced to settle several six-figure lawsuits from California tribal councils for misrepresentation."

"This Bud good," Money is thinking. "He good. Maybe 'stead of gettin' rid of him, I hire him to be a fresh, new yes-man. Maybe I get Zodikoff mess up his face a little so he be not so pretty on TV, and then he need job. I pay him fifty dollars a day plus continental breakfast. He be by my side fourteen hours on duty sayin' stuff like he doin' now, then he spend time off thinkin' up new ways of praisin' me and agreein' with me all day."

"And, Ike 'I Got Money' Piles," Bud continues dramatically, "when at one of your massage parlors you discovered a large storage unit filled with boxes of unused ribbed condoms, each with an unfortunate tiny pinhole flaw in it, what did you do?"

Money struts around the cement floor, recalling his genius.

"Money, I ask you, did you do what so many great captains of industry like yourself would have done—ship them COD back to the manufacturer, threatening to leak the story of leaking condoms to the media and bring the company to its knees while you were suing them for refunds, damages, outrageous storage charges, and, of course, for millions of dollars in child support because of fictional claims you'd concocted about hundreds of unwanted pregnancies at the massage parlors that had occurred because of them?"

"No, no, he not do dat! He too dope to do dat," James One chimes in urgently, realizing Bud's stealing his thunder with all this great stuff he's saying about the boss.

"Right, James One," Bud says. "Money Piles, what you did next was show great largesse and civic responsibility..."

Bud looks at Piles and sees he's got him in the palm of his hand.

"He just might be getting us out of this," Rocky thinks.

"The Boys and Girls Clubs of America. That's right, you opened up your heart to the fabled Boys and Girls Clubs of America with your generous donation of thousands of colorful ribbed condoms to healthy, active young lads and lassies across our great nation who had never even known ribbed condoms existed. And this generosity yielded you a hefty tax donation, I might add. And that's not all—"

Cartier interrupts. "But he did send a dozen of the rainbow color to his gay ten-year-old nephew at boarding school."

"Any good uncle do that," Money says. "Plus, remember, Cartier, I take one out of that box, and at night we try it in hot tub."

"Yes, yes," Cartier squeals. "Oh my God, I remember! Ahhhhh!"

"And it doesn't end there, Ike 'I Got Money' Piles, does it?" Bud asks, delighting in the party-like atmosphere he's succeeded in creating.

"The award, the award," James One barks.

"Yes, Ike Piles, you gave yourself a well-deserved award—a large plaque made with endangered tropical woods, embossed in twenty-four-karat gold, citing you as the Boys and Girls Clubs' Man of the Year.

"Oh, oh, I love the last part...next, next," Cartier squeals, while James One steams with rage at all the attention Bud's getting.

"Right, Cartier," Bud continues, "the best, the very best, was yet to come. Ike Piles, you successfully bribed the now-disgraced former features editor of the *Las Vegas Sun* to print a large above-the-fold color photograph, ingeniously Photoshopped to show you with several wide-eyed young boys and girls dangling condoms from their little hands right there on the front page of the paper. And it was the lead story in the well-circulated Sunday edition."

"I the man," Piles boasts. "Headline say, 'Boxer's Gift of Balloons Makes Children Smile'!"

"Ridiculous bullshit," Zodikoff's hit man Ivan yells, stunning everyone as he barrels down the stairs.

Bud and Rocky exchange a "What the fuck?" look.

"You're so bad, you're fuckin' stupid, Piles. Don't you know that this asshole you said you hated is trying to make you love him by jerking your chain and feeding your always hungry ego? He's angling to get on your good side, so he can get the hell out of here alive."

"Right, Ivan, right!" James One yells. "It my job to jerk your chain, Money, not him."

Ivan stands there smirking at Piles, his hands on his hips, striking the most macho pose he can muster. He looks like the kind of thick-necked, red-faced, unshaven Russian grifter who'd be trying to sell you a fake fur coat ten seconds after you got off your cruise ship in Saint Petersburg.

After demanding that his presence be top secret, and getting assurances that his boss Zodikoff would never know he's been here, Ivan explains why he's returned.

He makes up a story. He says that he doesn't trust Piles himself to "do what is necessary to safely eliminate Bud and the dog." To have a clear conscience, he feels compelled to come back to help out, "'cause," he says, "Ivan afraid you get in trouble." Of course, this is a bigger crock than anything Bud has just said; the only reason Ivan is there is for Money's money.

We all will find out later that Ivan was in a race against time to get his clammy hands on every dollar possible because he was trying to buy a yacht. "Where I come from," he says, "to keep your marriages intact, to have infinite string of willing bimbos and party with fine drugs and Almas caviar, you need a yacht."

For most of his life, Ivan had never thought much about yachts. His hands were full working for Putin as a member of the elite Federal Protective Services, the group charged with guarding Putin's body night and day, except when Putin's bedroom door is closed. Like all the agents, when Ivan reached age thirty-five, he was forced to retire.

He was sad to leave Putin, whom he admired greatly for having the manly courage to be an irrational, soulless fiend. He was grateful for Putin. Under his boss' tutelage, Ivan realized, he was able to become the well-paid, unsentimental, amoral murderer he is today.

For the last two years of his service, he held the most prestigious job of all the agents in the protective unit—he served as Putin's anabolic-steroid tester. Every day before Putin got a single jab by his nurse, Ivan would be injected twice. If Ivan didn't foam at the mouth or jump out a window trying to fly, Putin felt safe enough to get his shot.

"Steroids make Ivan's balls like size of grapes," he says, pointing at his crotch, "and Ivan's biceps like party balloons, but Ivan knew he was serving homeland."

Like most members of Putin's elite presidential protection group, at retirement he was qualified to have a choice of three great jobs:

1. He could work for a foreign government that was seriously committed to violent regime change as their specialist in grab-and-go assassinations.

2. He could teach Mental Health, The George Santos Way, at any kindergarten in Russia, where it was a mandatory credit to graduate to first grade.

3. He could be the director of security and crowd control for hookers on an oligarch's yacht.

He took an assignment on the *Nymphiana*, a vast superyacht rumored to be owned by the very oligarch who was rumored to have introduced Putin to his rumored mistress, with whom Putin was rumored to have rumored numbers of rumored children, all of whom were rumored to be far off in Switzerland, so Putin could do what he was rumored to be doing when you couldn't guard him 'cause his bedroom door was rumored to be closed.

"Yacht life so good, Ivan say 'wow' when he see the way call girls swim a half-mile out from shore hoping to get on board. Forget about invading innocent countries," he boasts, "that's real power. I knew Ivan have to make fortune and one day have yacht of his own. Can Ivan do that in Russia when Ivan in a simple security job? No."

He explains that during the Ukraine War, moments before the *Nymphiana* was about to be seized by Italian officials in Positano, he cracked open the oligarch's flimsy made-in-China safe with a ballpoint pen, took out several thousand in cash, and escaped on the *Nymphiana*'s tiny submarine to Naples. He set out for the US and found his way to Zodikoff, where he's been pulling in big bucks as a fixer's fixer, but not enough money for a yacht, hence his many secret freelance assignments.

"There's a fire sale next month in Fort Lauderdale of seized oligarchs' yachts," he explains. "Steven Colbert guy on TV announce that owning an oligarch yacht is more politically incorrect than watching recent YouTube videos of Bill Cosby wandering around a funeral home after dark.

"Nobody wants to buy the yachts, but Ivan make bids, so a hundred thousand from you, Ike 'I Got Money' Piles, help Ivan get exactly what he need."

"I want a yacht, too," Piles says. "I never seen swimmin' hookers. Who knew hookers can swim? You ever see swimmin' hookers, James One?"

"No, Money, but bet they not be as good swimmin' as you," James One says, disregarding that his boss not only can't swim but had to be rescued twice from his huge hot tub back at the Vegas mansion.

After captivating Piles and James One with a story of the time they'd been sailing almost a mile from shore and hoisted writhing, nearly drowned hookers from the sea with large nets and dumped them on the deck, and how the ship's drunken captain, squinting into the sun with a massive hangover, thought they'd hauled in bluefin tuna and set sail for the fish market in Naples, Ivan gets around to outlining his plan.

He brings out the knives and saws he needs, and instructs James One to find a long table to serve as his carving station. "My dumb Russian wife lend my carving table to her friend for massage," he complains. He outlines the grizzly details of what he'll do on the table, and the plan for the "guaranteed untraceable" body disposal.

"Ivan uses highest-quality Siberian sulfuric acid with easy-pour spout—same acid that accidentally made that red spot on Gorbachev's head. Ivan has Prime monthly acid delivery subscription service; everything come in limited-edition souvenir canisters, handsomely embossed with dissolved victim's name—highly collectible in the best circles in Moscow. Here's what it does…"

Cartier listens and throws up. Ike "I Got Money" Piles pretends not to be afraid of the sounds he knows he'll be hearing. James One puts on gloves so his fingerprints can't be traceable on the table he has to find. Upstairs, Blatterman hears it all and thinks, "This guy's good. Maybe I could hire him as a consultant."

CHAPTER TWENTY-THREE

It Was A Dark And Stormy Night

Actually, it only felt like a dark and stormy night. The silvery moon cast shadows as we crept to the outer edge of a vast field and caught sight of Blatterman's lair, the former World War II interrogation center. It's like we were in that classic movie *Where Eagles Dare*, where a commando team has to make a very difficult assault on a Nazi fortress on a mountaintop. I'm the star, Richard Burton, the officer in charge, except I'm not stumbling around with a massive hangover trying to remember my lines on the first day of filming, like Burton was.

We're filthy. Billy and I are light brown. Herbie looks like a crow. Jane could be a giant squirrel; she's brownish gray, and her tail's three times its normal size, matted with spores, mud, leaves, sap, and all the other crap that washed off of the trees when it poured rain for about an hour. We had to slog through mudholes and cross a couple of deceptively deep streams. I thought my brother Billy was a competent swimmer but, well, anyway, Jane helped get him across. Every once in a while, Jane and I look at each other and realize we kind of became a couple earlier today, and now, somehow, we're on a nightmare first date.

We're hungry again. It turns out grubs are like the Chinese food of insects. Plus, we stink—we really stink. For years, I've heard humans ask, "Does a bear [you-know-what] in the woods?" The answer unfortunately is yes. And it's very easy to step into massive piles of you-know-what, particularly after it rains. I don't think the director of *DC League of Super-Pets* would have put his cast through stuff we've had to endure.

Herbie flies reconnaissance.

He reports spotting a couple of drones sprinkling food pellets over the field. Blatterman was on the porch, standing next to a pile of archery equipment, decked out in a weird costume. A big rabbit ran out of a hole to get some of the food, and Blatterman shot at him; both arrows missed. All the windows in the place are blacked out except one in the back, which gave Herbie a chance to peek down into a big chamber, which had likely been the interrogation space. Bud and my dad are chained there. He spotted Ike "I Got Money" Piles, James One, Piles' blonde girlfriend, and a Russian guy who'd been around once or twice.

I bark the family bark. It's a distinct sound—a single bark that Dad taught me the day before Bud was coming to pick me up when I was a puppy. I've never needed to use it. Most dog families have a special bark to employ as a signal in times of unwanted separation. If Dad hears it, he'll know I'm here.

Dad barks back immediately, but the sound's not coming from the basement. I hear him from across the field.

Staying low in the grass, we creep forward. My heart's pounding. Herbie flies out again.

We inch closer but set off a green laser that somehow signals a small search-light on the roof to scan the area to locate us. We're lucky it doesn't spot us.

"This is his killing field," Billy says. "He wants easy targets."

"Rocky on front porch," Herbie reports, "in cage, looks like—"

A wild array of lasers and lights goes off, triggered by Blatterman releasing my dad, who's running in serpentine movements to try to avoid being hit by arrows. A thin rope attached to his collar unspools as he runs. Blatterman is shooting at him with some kind of a bow gun that fires eight-inch arrows in rapid succession. If he doesn't hit my father this time, he'll use a winch to haul him back by the rope hooked to his collar, and try again.

I leap to go to Dad, to stop Blatterman, to do something, create chaos, anything. Billy grabs my tail in his jaws. "*Stop!*"

I snarl at Billy, but he won't let go. I'm growling, showing fangs to my own brother.

"Listen to him," Jane calmly signals.

Billy's figured how to avoid setting off the lasers and lights. "This way now, and fast," he indicates.

In one tense minute, we're with our dad. He's crouched in high grass. He's been hit with one arrow but only grazed. There's blood oozing outta his left shoulder. To fool Blatterman so he's not hauled back immediately, Dad's howling like he's fatally wounded and possibly barking the big one.

"Billy, Elmer, my sons," he says. "My sons."

Jane, Billy, and me start gnawing through the rope to free him.

"Aren't you the big sissy?" Blatterman yells from the porch. "I hear you. Looks like I got you on the first try. You're not the tough guy I thought you were, and I bet your son Spike's even more of a fairy."

Billy and Jane wrap the chewed rope around a small log to create a decoy. Billy figures Blatterman won't immediately know Dad's not attached if he tries to reel him back.

So far, so good, but then things go out of control in an instant.

Dad's enraged; he's vibrating with anger, licking the blood that's oozing from his shoulder. I only knew him when I was an innocent puppy. I never saw anything like this in him.

"Sons and Jane, follow me," he commands. "We charge now, straight away!"

He bounds over the high grass before we can try to stop him.

Billy's shaking his head, "No, Dad, no, no."

Arrows sail. Blatterman's in full attack mode.

Even though this seems like a suicide blitz, I'm with him. I won't spend the rest of my life thinking that this day I was a coward.

I move forward, staying as low as I can. When I reach Dad, I shudder. Blatterman's already hit him three times. There's an arrow in his chest, one in his shoulder, and a loose one in his left flank. Two arrows are in pretty deep, but Dad's not howling or even moaning, just lying there stoically, breathing heavily.

Billy and Jane crawl up behind us.

Are we watching him die?

Blatterman leaves the long porch and shuffles toward us through the high grass. There are automatic arrow guns in both hands and a longbow over his shoulder. He's wearing the official John Rambo Halloween costume, available only online by searching "Do they still make that stupid John Rambo costume with the mask that doesn't quite look like Stallone because of copyright issues?"

"I don't hear you now, Rocky. I wonder why? I wonder why?" Blatterman mocks.

"Get out of here," Dad commands. No need for you…"

We slip far enough away to avoid detection.

"Ahhh," Blatterman mocks, hovering over our father, "there you are, mighty Rocky—all bloodied up and goin' to doggie heaven, 'cause I think that arrow in your chest might've punctured a lung. Hmmmm, what should I do? Maybe call a vet? Oh, sorry, Rocky, I don't have my phone. Guess you'll have to stay here overnight. It's always fun for me to see how much work the scavengers can do by morning. Nighty-night, you pansy."

This guy is going down. Billy takes a deep breath, pauses to control himself, and then explains the strategy he's devised for our assault.

Herbie will be the first wave.

"Roger, read you. Piece of cake, Commander Billy," Herbie squawks.

The second part of the plan is organized around what Billy learned hanging out with Virtual Andy and Chicago Bob earlier in the day, which now seems like several chapters ago. Virtual Andy had used his access to the digital National Archives files, which I mentioned earlier, and found the original floor plans from 1943, when the place was an army interrogation center. Billy figured rather than chase a ball around the apartment like Jane and I were doing at the time, it would be better if he memorized the layout of the place.

Jane originally was set to be in the operation, but now the top priority for her is to stay with Dad, to use her soft golden retriever mouth to try to delicately work the arrow out of his chest. Billy or me can't risk doing it because our heavy, brick-like heads would likely make it impossible.

"Why does the female always have to be the nurse?" Jane asks, half joking.

If the shaft hasn't penetrated the lung, he might survive, but he's losing blood.

My brother and I set out together to get to Bud.

BUD'S VODKA GAMBIT

In the bottom of the old house, Ivan hears Rocky's howling and starts howling himself, because he's gotten, as you humans say, "howling drunk." In a desperate improvisation to play for more time, Bud managed to lure Ivan into a vodka-drinking contest.

"I don't know if I just jab you with fifty milligrams of fentanyl," Ivan said earlier, "or, to get it over with faster, maybe use the souped-up cattle prod on the Make Him Explode setting."

"Eww! Sounds messy," Cartier said. "And don't waste fentanyl. Money has a big supply in his safe, but he forgot the combination again."

"She right, but my mighty brain remember the three numbers soon," Piles said. "But I warning you, Ivan, for all the money Money Piles payin' you, Ike 'I Got Money' Piles not doin' any cleanin' up of head parts offa the floor if you use that prod."

"Whatever," Bud said. "But at least I think I should get the chance to have a final drink—one final drink."

"He right," James One chimes in. "Big Joe, friend of mine on death row in Alabama prison, he be served a microwave-fresh Hungry Condemned Man meal the morning before they make five attempts to execute him. All fail. They say, 'OK, Big Joe, no luck today. We sharpen needle with this penknife and try again tomorrow. Big Joe even get free dinner next day. Give the guy a drink, Ivan.'"

"You Americans all so soft, you think—"

"Excuse me, Ivan," Bud interrupts, "Blatterman's got a full bar setup over there. How about pouring me a big glass of Tito's? It's the world's best vodka, made right here in the USA."

"Tito's taste like camel piss," Ivan howled, sounding like Bob Dylan on a bad day. "The best vodka in world is Stolichnaya. Comes from Russia, where we drink more vodka in a day than you ever drank in a year."

"Well, Ivan, I won the Pennsylvania State Vodka Drinking Contest in the Cub Scout division when I was only twelve years old," Bud fabricated, "and I won drinking Tito's. I drank the other kids who were chugging your watery Stoli under the table by the third bottle."

"My mother was drunk on Stoli every time she breastfeed Ivan. Stoli in my blood. Stoli vodka just another example of Russian superiority over soft, flabby, inferior Americans."

"Ha, you're crazy," Bud said. "America's the best. Give me a Tito's. You have a Stoli, and let's see who can down it the fastest."

Fortunately, Bud had been able to survive forced drinking during fraternity hazing in college by employing a stage technique he'd learned in drama class. He was able to empty a glass while swallowing only a tiny portion.

"My God," Bud asked Ivan, "how did you do that? I've never seen a full glass disappear so fast. I'll beat you on the next round. Set 'em up."

"I wonder if he can snort coke that fast?" Cartier whispered to Money and James One.

"He bad; he beat Bud for sure. This fun," Piles whispered. "Fill an empty Stoli bottle with water, James One, so I chug whole thing and be winner like I always be."

Now, with the vodka flowing and Ivan howling with Rocky's howling, Bud takes it further: "Ivan, how can you possibly think Russia is superior to America? Let's have a cold shot for every single thing you think is superior in your homeland."

"Line 'em up, James One. Pour 'em...out," Ivan croaks.

"Russia has best call girls!" he yells. "That's why US always wants to invade Russia—to capture our call girls."

"OK, I'll give you that. You're off to a good start," Bud says.

"Russia has best…what, what, what you call them? Oh, conspiracy theories. Kremlin disinformation make QAnon shit of yours seem like certified scientific discoveries."

"You win again. Let's drink to that," Bud says, reaching for a glass.

Russia has world's fattest action hero movie star, Steven Seagal. He weigh more than three Chuck Norrises."

"Drink up. You got us there."

"No country have better paranoia than Russia. Average Russian general fifty times more paranoid than your General Michael Flynn."

Bud's hoping he can keep this thing going as long as possible.

Outside, on the porch, Herbie's hidden in the eave of the roof directly above Blatterman, who's gleefully shooting arrows at anything that moves. He's bagged a deer and a rabbit, but boredom is setting in and he's contemplating letting out one of the old racehorses.

A fox sets off the spotlight. The arrow flies. It misses.

"Shit," he says.

"Jesus hears you," Herbie whispers.

"Sorry," Blatterman answers.

"God loves you," Herbie yaks a little louder.

"Amen, amen," Blatterman mutters to himself as he strings another arrow.

"Whoever is righteous has regard for the life of his beast," Herbie squawks.

"Proverbs twelve, verse ten, from the Bible. Ah, church," Blatterman thinks, and immediately remembers how pissed he is that his wife just spent five thousand dollars for a pair of authenticated Tammy Faye false eyelashes now displayed under a magnifying glass on the altar at their church back in Greenwich.

"Fuck her," he mutters, as he shoots an arrow at one of the cows sleeping in the high grass.

"For every beast of the forest is mine, the cattle of a thousand hills."

Blatterman thinks, "Ah, that's Psalms fifty, verse ten…. Wait…wait a goddamn minute. What the hell is going on?" He looks up and spots Herbie peering down at him.

"I am Jesus, the Lord incarnate, your only hope for salvation, making a rare guest appearance here tonight in the shape of a lowly crow," Herbie says softly.

"What the fuck! Is this—"

"The evil man will not go unpunished…. Woe to the wicked…for what he deserves will be done to him," Herbie continues.

"Forgive me, Jesus, forgive me," Blatterman pleads. "I'll never stuff tissues in an offering envelope instead of putting in money again."

"Jesus loves all creatures great and small, but *not* you, Prescott Blatterman. May fire, brimstone, and burning winds blow up the leg of your Rambo costume and singe your saggy scrotum."

"I repent, I repent."

"May your pie turn to sand—"

"No! No!"

"Verily I say, as Jesus turned the water into wine, I shall turn thy ice cream to frozen balls of cow dung."

Blatterman throws down his bow and runs into the house screaming.

"May the ox of your field move into your guesthouse, may your wife finally do it with the pool boy, may you spend all of eternity watching Peppa Pig cartoons, may you—"

The door slams.

"So long, cocksucker," Herbie squawks. "Mission accomplished."

I'm at the back window looking down into the basement. The Russian guy is woozy. He's flailing his arms, saying, "Russians have best steroids, our female athletes twice the size of your garage doors, we have—"

"I've heard the voice of Jesus! I've heard Jesus!" Blatterman yells, stampeding down the stairs.

"This not time for you to be born again, again, Blatterman," Ike "I Got Money" Piles sneers. "Ivan 'bout to spring into action."

"I heard Jesus; he spoke to me. He appeared as a crow."

"Shut your fat face, Blatterman," Ivan says. "Ivan just got text from client. I now got two early-bird executions tomorrow morning at a diner in Manhasset. Ivan need a drink to clear head, and then he hurry to get work done."

Herbie flies into the room, screeching, "Rejoice, I have risen! I have risen!" He perches on top of a tall lamp.

This is not good. It's not part of Billy's plan, but Herbie can't resist doing more of his Jesus routine.

"When I say to the wicked," Herbie Squawks solemnly, "you will surely die—"

"He's among us!" Blatterman shrieks. "Forgive us!"

"...all of these will pay the penalty of eternal destruction..."

"That not sound like no Jesus to me," James One says. "Jesus gotta have deep voice, like Denzel. Why this Jesus sound like squeaky Katie Couric?"

"Jesus loves you, but doubt me and ye will burn forever in hell, and—"

"What the fuck you Americans talking 'bout? That's not a crow; that's Chicago Bob's big-mouthed parrot," Ivan says. "Wash the ugly thing down, hose the parrot to shut him up, and Cartier, plug in that fuckin' cord; the prod has to warm up."

James One chases Herbie around, battering him with water.

"He *is* a parrot!" Blatterman screams, grabbing a small net to snare Herbie. "No parrot will make a fool of me!"

Herbie flees up the stairwell, squawking, "Grey Goose best vodka. Amen."

Ivan's poking around Bud's body trying to figure out the best point of contact for the cattle prod.

"Instructions say wear gloves," he says. "Hand me those latex gloves, James One. Ivan never had the privilege to use one of these, but saw them in action watching the autographed boxed set of execution DVDs that China's president gave Putin as a welcome gift at dinner during their first summit conference."

Bud's breathing deeply and inconspicuously tugging at the chain on his wrist, trying to loosen the stake in the dirt floor.

I bark softly. It's the bark I always used to get his attention when there's something I think he needs to notice.

To Piles, Ivan, James One, Blatterman, and Cartier, the bark is just another sound in the night, but Bud looks up immediately. His eyes widen as he spots me at the window.

Ivan's got the gloves on. He's squinting, trying to read the tiny print on the instructions to make sure the prod's completely operational.

Bud and I are locked in on each other.

"OK, directions say all of you should shield your eyes and move back ten feet from the victim, unless you're a relative; then you should be forced to watch," Ivan explains. "And make certain you are not standing in a puddle, do not need to urinate, and have not swallowed any large metal objects since breakfast. OK?"

Money Piles says, "The only large object Cartier swallow since then was my—"

"Shut your mouth the hell up, Money!" Cartier yells. "Have a little respect for this Bud guy. You want the last thing he hears in his life to be you exaggeratin' like your manhood's the size of that garden hose, when what you're really packin' is the little spigot it's attached to?"

"Shut up, Cartier, shut up," Money snaps. "I be payin' you extra money every week to be spreadin' the word internationally that I got BDE 'cause I be hung like a rhinoceros, so you—"

"Enough with the dick talk. I need complete quiet," Ivan demands. "This goddamn thing has a Bluetooth setting. I have to waste time now linking it to my phone. Whatever happened to goddamn on-off switches?"

As soon as Bud signals me, I'm gonna back far enough away to be able to build up the right speed so I can crash through the window, sail down around twenty feet, and hopefully crash-land on this ugly Russian. I'm scared. It'll be like a dock dive toward a cement floor. I'll have glass in my head. If I miss and hit the cement floor, I could break legs, or Ivan could cattle-prod me before I can get to him. I don't know if I can do this, but I'm hearing Dad's voice from that long-ago day: "Never doubt yourself, Spike. You can prevail."

Ivan picks up the prod. He paces slowly, pointing the prod at Bud's naked foot. "Ivan just want you to relax, Mr. Bud, and when Ivan scream '*now!*' you imagine you're sticking your big toe in the socket that controls the lights on top of the Empire State Building."

"One more drink," Bud pleads as he signals me.

"You already had two full bottles of my Tito's premium vodka," Blatterman complains. "I'm not wasting another drop on you. And Ivan, if I like the way this thing works on Bud, I might order one to tickle the racehorses."

My brick-like head shatters the glass. I plunge to the floor. Blood's streaming into my beady little eyes. Ivan whirls around, looks up, and sees me but can't get out of my way. I knock him over, and he rolls into a puddle of vodka that's accumulated under the table where Bud's splayed out. He shrivels into a ball, screams, and stops breathing.

The electric prod in his hand must've made contact with the vodka Bud dribbled down there when he was faking some of the drinking.

On top of the table, Bud's shaking, yelling, "*Oh my god! Oh my god!*"

When I hear those words, I know something's seriously wrong, 'cause Bud's not one of those people who typically react with "Oh my God" to practically every event in their life. Originally, "Oh my God" was a phrase women created for themselves to scream during multiple orgasms. But now it's morphed into a shallow expression of delight or surprise, and it's everywhere: "*Oh my god, cheesecake!*" "*Oh my god, what great socks!*"

An electric jolt from the puddle has traveled up the metal table legs and shocked Bud. His eyes are crossed like mine were after he accidentally hit me in the nuts with his Big Bertha golf club during a practice swing. He's drooling like—well forget about that—but he's alive.

Bud smiles weekly at me and gestures toward Ike "I Got Money" Piles. "Get him," he says in a weak whisper. "Get him."

I turn to face Ike "I Got Money" Piles.

"Shoot him, James One. He gonna bite me! Shoot the fuckin' Wonder Dog—he's comin' at me!" Piles yells.

I head-butt Piles and knock him over. With the artificial leg, he won't be able to get up too fast.

With roaring barks, Billy springs through a trap door in the corner of the floor. The compound plans he memorized indicated a secret tunnel with an entry point hidden behind rocks twenty yards from the house.

"What dat dog?" Money Piles blurts. "What happen? Another Spike magically appear?"

As James One's fumbling to get a small pistol out of his overalls, Billy clamps on his wrist and forces him to the floor. He gives James One a look that says, "Don't want to harm you, pal, but make a move, and the hand with the gun will be dangling from your wrist like a bunch of overcooked asparagus."

"This phantom Spike got me, Money. Can't move my arm. Cartier, take the gun."

"Forget the gun," Blatterman says. "I'll club both these dogs to death with my custom-made baby seal club."

Blatterman lunges at me and swings wildly—probably the same kind of swing that's enabled him to consistently score rounds of golf over two hundred at the Greenwich Country Club. Blatterman may be fat and slow, but if he smacks me with that club, he's gonna do damage.

I bark for Herbie. He comes sailing down the stairwell straight at Blatterman.

"Behold, I will spread refuse on your faces, and you will be taken away with it," Herbie yaks with delight.

"My God, that's very obscure—Malachi two, verse three," Blatterman thinks an instant before shrieking like a child, "Help, wet wipes! A parrot made caca on me. Wet wipes!"

Herbie sinks his talons into Blatterman's cheeks.

"Verily I say unto you, turn your big fat cheeks," he caws.

Piles struggles with his artificial leg, trying to get up. "Cartier, the gun, shoot them."

"Wet wipes! Wet wipes first, Cartier. I can't see. Get all this parrot poo offa my face, eeeeewww!"

"No, Cartier!" James One yells. "This other Spike dog hurtin' my wrist big-time. No man who work for Money Piles want to have injured right wrist, 'cause he have so many pleasurable opportunities to use wrist at work."

Piles is still struggling to get up. "He right, Cartier. So shoot that other Spike first, then shoot original Spike, then carefully shoot parrot off Blatterman's face without wounding Blatterman nose—I got no nose insurance. Then shoot Bud, who easy target."

"Money, what the...?" Cartier protests.

"Do it now, Cartier," Piles says. "Four quick shots—*bam, bam, bam, bam*—and we get fentanyl to celebrate. I finally remember secret code to drug safe; it be one, two, three."

"Who you think I am, fuckin' Annie Oakley? You do your own shooting!" Cartier screeches. "Spike saved those strippers from that burning club. Strippers are loyal to each other. We're isolated from society, like topless Amish. Spike's our hero. You want me to go down in our history as the pole dancer who shot the Wonder Dog?"

While I'm considering if "the pole dancer who shot the Wonder Dog" might make a good pitch for a movie, what with the seedy locations, naked women, oily dances, rich and horny men, burning buildings, and bows and arrows and stuff, I move to stop Cartier from reaching Money Piles.

"Now you're even makin' Spike growl at me, Money. Fuck this. You're on your own. You never shoulda got involved in fighting dogs in the first place," Cartier yells. "I'm goin' upstairs, opening the safe, and relaxing with some of your precious lab-fresh fentanyl."

"You're finished, Cartier!" Piles shouts. "Blatterman, get rid of that parrot now. Hose that ugly bird off your face, hose him, then go club that other dog and give me gun and I shoot Spike, and we throw that parrot out the window. And somebody prod Bud, 'cause Ivan's lookin' more dead than he usually look. Then we all relax and have normal pleasant evening bein' high and watchin' TV and shit."

"Now your mighty brain workin' like you directing Bay of Pigs invasion, Money," James One says.

With a thick stream of cold hose water, Blatterman knocks Herbie to the floor. He flails helplessly as Blatterman sprays him in the face with Raid Flying Insect Killer.

"Well, flapping Jesus, the arrows of the Almighty are within me, and my poison your spirit now drinks. Job six, verse four," Blatterman recites. "Ha!" He sneers as little Herbie squawks and squirms helplessly on the floor.

"OK, Money, I've had enough of these ugly animals. Extermination time is upon us," Blatterman says joyfully. He grabs his club and starts toward Billy, who's still got James One's wrist clamped in his jaws.

He raises the short, heavy, monogrammed black club over his head. The instant we see his elbow move to slam it down, I spring at Blatterman and Billy leaps out of the way. He misses Billy but smashes me in my right side. Rib's cracked—instant bad pain. I limp away. Blatterman follows me, slowly chanting, "I've got you now, Wonder Dog. I got you now."

James One tosses the small revolver at Piles, who grabs it as it hits his chest. He aims at Billy. As fast as I can, I head for Piles, but Blatterman swings at me again. This time he misses my head but smacks me really hard in my left shoulder. I'm hobbled.

Piles fires at Billy but only nips the corner of his tail. The sound of the pistol in the cement basement is colossal. Piles shakes his head violently, trying to stop the ringing in his ears before he shoots again.

"Don't do it, Blatterman!" Bud yells.

Blatterman corners me. He's caressing his baby seal club.

"No, Blatterman, no," Bud says, pulling frantically on his shackle.

"Shut up, it's only a dog."

I'm barking at Blatterman, hoping the noise will hurt his ears after the gunshots clogged them.

"The more you bark, Spike, the more I'm gonna club you," he yells in the extra-loud voice of someone whose ears are not working.

My shoulder and rib are killing me. I try to leap at Blatterman but barely leave the ground.

"Now, Spike, let's pretend you're an adorable baby seal!" he screams. "And it's just you and me on a rapidly melting ice floe somewhere. Imagine how happy you'd be to donate your hide for part of a coat that'll be sold for a massive amount of cash to rich tourists in some back room in Riyadh."

Billy's partially shielded from Piles under a small workbench behind a thick wooden leg. He darts out to help me. Ike "I Got Money" Piles fires at him and misses. Blatterman screams, "No gun! You'll make us deaf. I got this." But Piles shoots anyway. He stops Billy, plugging him in the back leg with one of the little bullets. Billy rolls over. He's hurt, maybe bad. Can't tell.

"No, Piles, stop it," Bud says.

"Good shot," James One screams at the top of his lungs, 'cause his ears are blocked, too. "Money, you better aim than Clint Eastwood in every movie he in 'cept *Bridges of Madison County*, where he didn't shoot Meryl Streep but shoulda shot her 'cause of her weird accent."

"Fuckin' loud gunshots," Blatterman complains to me, as if I'd offer sympathy to a guy who's getting set to club me to death. He's hovering over me. All I see is his fat face blocking the bright light from the ceiling.

"Blatterman, no, don't do it," Bud calls from the table. "How 'bout I give you a weekly segment on my TV show devoted to hunting? We'll call it 'The Joy of Poaching with Prescott Blatterman.' It'll be a TV first."

"Sounds too much like a cooking show," Blatterman says, but I notice a familiar glint in his eye. I've seen it many times in the expressions of people contemplating the fame they think they'll achieve if they could only appear on Bud's show.

Billy and I notice a familiar bark. Jane?

"Blatterman!" Piles yells. "No TV show for you. Club away on them, I give you a thousand dollars a swing, plus set you up with that hooker you met in Vegas at the counter in Marie Callender's restaurant. The one I fired 'cause she got too fat from eating pies."

"Leave the hooker, take the pies," Blatterman says with a laugh. "This'll be too much fun for me."

Blatterman shakes his head and stretches his big mouth open, trying to unclog his ears. As he does, he moves just enough for me to spot Jane staring down from the window. She's panting. Must have just gotten here.

This is great. Could anything better happen on a first date than having your new girlfriend save you from a sadistic animal killer? Well, actually, yes, maybe wild sex after dinner and drinks, but a close second would be if she were to save your life.

Jane, the first runner-up in the *Dan's Papers* Hampton Dogs Dock Dive for Charity, sails gracefully though the air at Blatterman.

"Watch out, everybody! It's that giant man-eating squirrel that lives in the woods. We're all finished!" Bud yells.

Blatterman turns just as Jane smashes onto his chest and flattens him to the floor. She yanks the club outta his hand and tosses it across the room.

"What the fuck is this now, James One?" Piles asks. "First, parrot thinks he's Jesus, then Spike twin pops outta floor like Penn and Teller trick, now world's largest squirrel flyin' in here. What up?"

"Like we be in a scary *Cabin in the Woods* movie, Money," he says. "*Cabin in the Woods.*"

"Shut up about movies, One!" Blatterman screams. "Please, Money, for God's sake shoot this big squirrel on top of me. I mean, I mean, shoot whatever this flying thing is, and somebody get me my club."

Ike "I Got Money" Piles takes an unsteady shot and misses Jane, but grazes Blatterman's shoulder.

"Aaaaagh! Money, you moron, you just shot me. Goddamn it."

"Good shot, Money," Bud says.

"I no moron, Blatterman," Piles says defensively. "I not bad shot, considerin' it be unfamiliar weapon and also 'cause I never fired no gun before. My people do that for me."

"Fuck you and your people, Money. I'm bleeding, and this squirrel thing's gonna kill me. Cattle-prod it—prod it right now, put Neosporin on this shoulder, or maybe get me a tourniquet or EMS, or..." Blatterman looks at the bright red blood oozing from his shoulder. "Help, help, Mommy, help! Your little Blabby got shot!"

Jane fixes on his throat. Blatterman trembles. "OK, OK, good squirrel, good squirrel. Don't bite me, don't bite me. I'm your friend. Let's go eat peanut butter pie." Jane snarls as Billy somehow is able to limp over and sink his teeth into James One's thigh and drag him to the floor.

"James One, that other Spike got you down again," Money says. "You got one of them little MGM Grand souvenir penknives I give as your Christmas gift each year? Use it and stab that dog. I got one bullet left here, so I'm takin' careful aim and killin' Wonder Dog right now."

"Get outta there, Spike!" Bud yells.

"No, I got this one, Bud," I signal him.

"No, get outta there now!"

"Bud, your stupid old Spike not listen to you; he comin' at me real close. He fool enough to think some bullet from this little pistol not sink into his big ugly head? You dead, Spike, now you be dead," Piles says, sitting up and pointing the gun straight at me.

He steadies his arm. As he's about to put his finger on the little trigger, I release a warm torrent of urine directly onto his crotch.

"B-brilliant move, Spike," Bud stammers.

The bullet hits the ceiling, and I pin Money Piles down by his throat.

"Aaaagh, no way. Spike, you bitch, you soak my new Gucci jeans and my three-hundred-dollar Bottega Venetta boxers with dog piss!"

I hear a shuffling sound across the floor upstairs. I glance at Billy. His ears perk up, and so do Jane's.

A noise at the top of the stairs—someone's coming down. Cartier? Has she taken that old Thompson submachine gun off the wall to finish us all off to get back on Piles' good side?

I stretch to see what I can, and spot a pair of tan cowboy boots on the stairs.

"Oh my," Chicago Bob says with a big smile. "Ike 'I Got Money' Piles, you're so scared of Spike that it looks like you wet your pants big-time."

"Dat not true. Dry me off, Bob, bein' careful not to touch my mighty Little Ike," Piles instructs.

"And nice to see you again, too, Money," he says.

"Fuck yeah, it always nice to see me," Piles boasts, "and you, you bastard, Chicago Bob, Ike Piles thought you run away, but now he see you so loyal and faithful and devoted and obedient to your Ike 'I Got Money' Piles that you come to help him in his hour of neediness."

"Of course, Money," Chicago Bob says.

"I knew you'd be back. Now do me a favor. First, get me a towel to dry off this dog piss, then kill everybody, OK?"

"Well, the towel will have to wait, Money, 'cause I'm here to make a deal. I can't help noticing that you three are pinned down with dogs at your throats."

"This bad, Chicago Bob. I be breathin' dog breath so long, I gettin' hungry for Purina," James One gasps. "Get this dog offa me."

"Like I just said, One, I'm here to make a deal with your man Piles and his partner, Blatterman. You all know my connection with animals—a word from me and they'll be happy to finish you. Cartier's asleep upstairs with a lit pipe in her hand, so she's no help. It's just me. I got my two Colt revolvers. I can clean up all of this for you just like you want. The dogs and Bud won't know what hit them."

"Chicago Bob, Chicago Bob, help!" Herbie squawks. "Bug spray in eyes."

"Just wait, Herbie, just wait a sec," Chicago Bob says calmly.

"What deal you want, Bob?" Piles asks. "Anything for you. Anything. You know I love you. How about this? You run away two days ago, so I take you offa payroll then. How 'bout I generously pay you for two days off even though you not be workin'? Good deal, huh?"

"I guess I'll take my parrot and leave, then. I want a little more."

I don't know where this is really going. Bob's obviously playing Money, so I tighten my grip on Piles, figurin' it might help somehow.

"Aaagh!" Piles yells. "Spike be hurtin' me."

"Oh, I think it could get way worse for you than that," Chicago Bob says. "Spike looks quite angry. He can't be happy you were going to have his man Bud killed."

"Umm…accurate statement, there, Mr. Bob," Bud says through his electrocution stupor. "He was payin' Ivan there under this table to electrocute us."

I tighten my grip a little more on Piles.

"Aaagh! OK, Chicago Bob, I give in. I pay you for full week and—"

"You cheap son of a bitch, Money. OK then, so how about you, Blatterman? Wanna make a deal with old Chicago Bob, so I can get that dog offa your throat, patch up your shoulder, and maybe even bring you down some pie?"

"Name it, Bob," Blatterman says. "Name the deal. Tell us."

Chicago Bob stuns us. He wants in on their operation. He demands 30 percent on worldwide dogfighting revenues, and then explains that he's found a lucrative black market for videos of Blatterman's archery work on the old horses.

"You're in for thirty gross of the dogfighting," Blatterman instantly agrees.

"I want Albania and Japan, too," Chicago Bob demands. "I heard you and Piles talking last week about your big new outlets there."

"OK, we'll cut you thirty on revenue from the two new private cable contracts."

"Good, but what about Piles?" Chicago Bob asks.

"So, Money, we got a new partner, OK?" Blatterman tells him. "It's gonna cost us, but Bob will clean up all this mess you started in the first place by kidnapping Bud, and Bob'll do it all nice and neat for us. You agree here, Money? Is Chicago Bob in?"

"Goddamn it, yes, I OK the dogfight part of deal; always plenty of cash from dogfight betting to go round. That's how I bought six pair a' these Gucci jeans like Spike ruin. But, Chicago Bob, now I no pay you the hundred and eighty-seven dollars and forty-three cents for two days' back pay I said I would."

"As far as your offer to me on the racehorses," Blatterman says, "I've just paused in a Godly-good manner to pray for guidance on this question, and the Lord told me that as long as my face isn't shown in the videos, and my wife or my Sunday school class never finds out what I'm doing, I can bow-hunt as many horses as I can get, and you can make as many videos of my archery work on them as you can sell, so it's a new, heavenly blessed venture for us, fifty-fifty, you and me."

"Very good, and let me ask you, for a thousand a horse, what if I'm also your man to supply you with the old racehorses? You'll need a fresh string every month. I can get you way more of them than you've been getting from Joey 'Three Thumbs,' the Kentucky mob guy," Chicago Bob proposes.

"No, Chicago Bob, no!" little Herbie squawks. "You love horses, Chicago Bob."

Right, Herbie, this is sad, 'cause it's all about humans and the perverted lure of cash. Here's this horse-loving hypocrite, Chicago Bob. This morning he was telling us how repulsed he was by the dogfight syndicate, and worse, by Blatterman's killing old racehorses, and now he's their partner in crime. I just want Bud and Jane and me to move to an island populated only with friendly animals—no humans, just friendly animals. I'd be happy, but unfortunately, I got reason to think Bud might get bored.

"When I'm not teaching Bible studies or rehearsing the choir back home, I get out here and use the bows on a couple of horses each week, but the sky's the limit on what I can do in that field. We've got the stable space, so yeah, Chicago Bob, that's a good price. You have my word," Blatterman agrees.

"OK, settled," Bob says. He unholsters his guns and twirls them three times.

"Chicago Bob, let the dogs go," Bud pleads.

"You actin' nuts, Chicago Bob," Herbie squawks.

If this is death, I'm way more calm than I oughta be. Maybe it's fatalism or denial, but looking him in the eye right now, I can't believe this guy's gonna knock off Bud and murder three dogs in cold dog blood. But his guns are aimed at me.

"Spike'll be first," Bob says. "The Wonder Dog deserves top billing."

"I finally got you, Spike," Piles boasts.

"But wait a sec, Money, wait a sec," Bob says. "Spike's a big star in your world. Maybe instead of eliminating him, you might wanna consider sendin' Spike and his brother as touring attractions at your dogfight rings. We all could make some money doin' that. Or, hold it, maybe even better, I heard the Chinese guy Chang Ho has a substantially larger fight operation than you guys do. Maybe we send 'em both to Mr. Ho and take a cut of Ho's revenue? Whatta you think?"

"You crazy, Bob? Me and Blatterman got a way bigger business than that sick ho Ho do. Chang Ho brag, but he only stage twenty fights a week; we do hundreds worldwide," Piles boasts.

"Ike, think of the cash we can all rake in on a series of farewell tours for Spike the Wonder Dog," Blatterman suggests. "We put Spike in super-easy bouts. He'd be on a farewell tour—like, say, Elton John's tour—but we'd keep bringing him back on comeback tours like the Who's been doing for forty years. Big bucks there; let's do it."

"That's it then," Chicago Bob says in an oddly different tone. "Confirming?" he asks.

"Confirming," Piles says. "Now get these dogs offa me. And right after I go upstairs, put on dry pants, and have a couple of hits to stop my ears from ringing, shoot Bud."

"Shoot Bud. That's the last piece we needed—that statement, right?" Chicago Bob asks in the same odd, detached tone. "So come on down."

"Yeah, we just make a deal to shoot Bud like we comin' on down on *Let's Make a Deal*, so shoot him," Piles demands.

Chicago Bob cocks both of his revolvers. I get in position to leap to stop him.

"No, Spike, relax. Not for Bud," he says, shifting his body and aiming his guns at Ike "I Got Money" Piles and Blatterman.

"Bad news for you guys, but good news for the dogs and horses of the world: you're both finished. You're under arrest," Chicago Bob says with a big smile. "Come on down," he orders into the wire he's wearing under his cowboy shirt.

Animal enforcement officers and pistol-wielding FBI agents stampede into the basement. They're holding their guns with two hands and scanning the room with them. An old-timer later told Bud that they didn't wield guns like that when he started as a cop. "It was one-handed then," he said, "but now we gotta do the two-handed thing like on TV. People demand to see it like that when we're rescuing them."

Before Ike "I Got Money" Piles can yell, "What the fuck now?" for the third time, he's in handcuffs.

"I pay all my taxes! I pay almost eighty-four dollars last year! Let me go!" he yells.

Suffolk County sheriff Brent Beatty steps forward. "OK, guys," he says, "I'm taking it from here."

The lead of the FBI team objects: "Federal case."

Beatty jabs him softly in the chest, and in a very low voice says very slowly, "I called you, and as I just said, I'm taking it from here."

"What about him?" the agent asks Piles, pointing to Bud lying on a table and shackled to the floor.

"Shut up, agent Mulrooney," Brent Beatty commands. "I'm asking the questions."

"Oh dat, dat guy," Piles says. "Dat nothing. He lyin' there 'cause he be one of those weird show business people who into S and M," he tries to explain. "He beg us to do that."

"The recording has you ordering Mr. Chicago Bob to kill him," Beatty rebuts.

"No, no," Piles says, "kill him with comedy. Chicago Bob so funny. He tell jokes and this crazy Bud so perverted, he get off on it while chained up."

"You're full of shit, Piles," Beatty snaps.

"Have a good time in prison, Money," Bud says. "You'll get off plenty there, but you won't be laughing."

"Piles," Beatty snarls, "my wife founded the local dog shelter. We're dog lovers and Spike fans, so we've had a special interest in this case. I've been tracking you since we had word you might be in the East Hampton vicinity, and—"

"You do this to all Hamptons tourists here on harmless vacation?" Piles interrupts.

"Shut up, Piles. You're as bad a criminal as you were a fighter. You left a trail here as wide as Blatterman's ass. I'm handing you over to the Feds. Our old friend Chicago Bob just got everything we need for a clear conviction. You and that slob Blatterman, who's curled up praying and babbling like a baby, are going away for a long time. Take him upstairs," Beatty bellows at the agents.

The Feds, not accustomed to taking orders like this from a local man, hesitate.

"I said move. That means you guys move now—move!" he commands.

As they're carrying him away, Ike "I Got Money" Piles tries one last ploy—selling out James One and his long-suffering girlfriend Cartier as Blatterman's real partners in the dogfight operation.

"He's lying; I innocent," James One says, trembling.

"You're only a person of interest, Mr. One," Beatty tells him. "And the rap on you appears not to be criminal."

"Agents," he orders, "hold it. Put Mr. Piles down. He needs to hear part of this report on his number-one man. I think he'll find it most interesting: 'James Barton, labeled James One by Ike Piles, appears to be a professional sycophant to Mr. Piles. He's a simple, kindly man who genuinely seems impressed by Ike Piles, but is not above extracting revenge for the verbal abuse he absorbs from Mr. Piles every day by—'"

Ike "I Got Money" Piles interrupts, "That no abuse—all them insults, all them put-downs, like when I tell James One he be most stupid person on earth so I not gonna pay him that week, that all be joking to make James One feel good."

"Then why you no pay me that week every time you say it?" James One asks.

"Cause you be most stupid person in world.... Oh, see there, I did it again. Just got to be a bad habit with me last several years," Piles tries to explain, "plus also good way to avoid payin' him sometimes."

"If I may finish reading, Piles," Beatty snaps, "you will particularly enjoy this excerpt: 'It appears Mr. Barton, aka James One, takes his revenge on Piles by bedding Piles' willing girlfriend Cartier...'"

"What da fuck?" Money Piles yells.

"Shut up, Piles, or we'll get Spike to piss on your stupid unmatched shoes. Our report also states that each week, Piles pays Cartier to post phony photos of his private parts on PornoGram. But the shots, which boast of the size of

Piles' manhood, are not photographs of penises from the anatomy section in the book of world medical records, like she tells Mr. Piles they are, but shots Cartier takes of James One's private parts each week."

"Ha, ha, that's it, Money—that true," James One boasts. "That why you no ever see your James One in shower near you in locker room at your gym—not want you to recognize what you convinced your tiny self you thought you were."

"Cartier, it over with you!" Piles screams. "Over, and I want money back I paid for that world record book I bought you."

"Damn right it's over," she says. "If they don't throw James One and me in jail just for being your paid friends, then my 'Big Pickle' and me are gonna live in Hollywood, 'cause James One applying for job as much-needed new yes-man for Will Smith."

"You nickname James One 'Big Pickle,'" Piles yells at her, "and how sometimes you be callin' me your 'Little Gherkin'?'"

"Figure it out for yourself, Piles," Sheriff Beatty snarls. "OK, guys, get him the hell outta here," he instructs. Carry the sucker all the way to the van, throw him in, and put on the Celine Dion music."

As I'm enjoying watching my nemesis Ike "I Got Money" Piles get carried away kicking and screaming, FBI agent Mulrooney tries to score a point with the sheriff: "Beatty, that dead man under the table in the vodka puddle holding the Chinese cattle prod is a Zodikoff operative, one of his heavy-duty fixers."

"Mulrooney, you think I didn't know that? By the way, he's not dead," Beatty tells him.

Chicago Bob is treating Billy's gunshot wound. I limp over to Jane to find out about Dad. She couldn't get the arrow out. He was still bleeding when she left him, and we'd better prepare ourselves that he might be "gone" when we find him.

"OK, you, Blatterman, unlock yourself from that fetal position and stand up," Sherriff Beatty orders. "Stop the crying, and put your lord and savior on pause after you let him know you'll need all the help he can give you to ward off the romantic pervs up there in your cell block in Dannemora."

"My wife can't know about this," he pleads. "Don't call her."

Sheriff Beatty tells us that the first thing they saw in the field when they were approaching was an English Bull Terrier with small arrows lodged in him. Chicago Bob treated the dog, who looked to be dying, and the fingerprints on the arrows matched Blatterman's fingerprints in a national file.

"By the way, that was fast work on the fingerprints, Mulrooney. Thanks to your team for that," the sheriff says. "Now, Blatterman," he continues, "the best thing you can do is plead guilty and try to cop a plea and reveal all the information on the international dog ring you have. Otherwise, Humane Society International has a powerful reach, and they can work with lawyers to get you and Piles convicted in multiple countries."

Blatterman is blabbering names, numbers, email addresses, and every location he can remember as they escort him up the stairs.

Herbie watches Blatterman go, saying, "The Lord will render unto every man as according to his deeds."

"No, no, no," Blatterman sobs.

"So long, you freak. May the IRS give you IBS," Herbie squawks.

Agent Beatty pulls the stake loose, and Bud slowly tries to sit up.

"Phew, thank you, sheriff. I'm really out of it. I literally drank that Russian guy Ivan under the table. Thank you, thank you," he says. "The vodka-drinking contest probably saved my life. I faked as much as I could, but I'm probably headed for the worst hangover in human history."

"I've got some pills we confiscated from an oxy lab in Stoneybrook that might help with that, Bud," Sheriff Beatty tells him. "And by the way, nice to meet you. We've enjoyed your work with Spike on TV and YouTube."

"That all seems like a lifetime ago," Bud says.

"Well, you'd better consider clearing your head," Beatty continues. "My wife was happy to hear I was coming to get you; she says you're appearing in the opening-day matinee of *Pardon My Privet* tomorrow. Her friend Bill McCuddy asked her to let him know as soon as we found you. He wants to set a rehearsal for you and Spike first thing in the morning."

"Oh shit, Spike," Bud says, glancing at me.

Bud, don't look to me for support. Sure you're drunk, but with these rib and shoulder injuries, I'm near a ten on the pain chart. A performance tomorrow? Let's start with the fact that I can hardly walk. Plus there's been a minor emotional toll, like that we both almost got murdered. And uh, yeah, my father's hovering near death, my brother's been shot, my girlfriend's the color of a squirrel, Herbie's crankier than ever, and now this McCuddy guy's gonna show up with his big smile and try to convince us that we're such true show business pros that we just gotta make the curtain for his play tomorrow afternoon because "the show must go on"?

Why the hell must the show go on? Who came up with that stupid rule?

CHAPTER TWENTY-FOUR

A COUPLE OF WEEKS LATER

I'm back in my beloved orange doghouse in the big yard behind our house in Thomasville.

I'm with Bud, but otherwise alone.

Billy is back with his owners, Calvin and Bee. His wounds are healing, but the scars finished him on the show circuit. He plans to enter the Genius Dog Challenge competitions, like Dad wanted him to do.

I almost cried when my little pal Herbie left. Chicago Bob took him on the road. Bob's working again, at small racetracks in the South. Every once in a while, he'll speak at a Rotary luncheon disguised as Dr. Andrew Weil. Herbie warms up the audiences with insults about how unhealthy they look before the fake Weil takes to the podium.

Andy relocated full time to Beverly Hills and took my girlfriend, Jane, with him. We were upset to part, but we've got no illusions about having a long-distance relationship. Andy offered me a virtual Jane as a girlfriend, but I'm really not ready for virtual sex, and you shouldn't be either.

I'll wrap things up.

You probably figured, yes, we went on in *Pardon My Privet*. Wondering why? McCuddy convinced Bud that it was a fabulous career move, because he'd lured CBS News' *Sunday Morning* team to come out from New York to tape the opening matinee and interview Bud about the big story of Piles and Blatterman getting hauled off to jail. They didn't show—the CBS crew was diverted to Washington, where it was rumored "the Rock" would be making a major announcement, likely declaring his candidacy for president.

Unfortunately, the Rock was only introducing his new Rock for President bobblehead. By the way, the bobblehead's gotten thirty-one electoral votes so far, and the election's still months away, with no clear candidates. Those new voting reforms are really doing their job.

At *Pardon My Privet*'s debut, Bud and I had enough painkillers and speed in us to be pain-free during the show. Unfortunately, Bud was so addled with the vodka-hangover-oxy combo that he was mostly line-free, too. He did quite a bit of supremely relaxed and funny improvisation to cover himself. Bud figured his friend McCuddy would be furious at the changes, but the play got a standing ovation, so McCuddy was happy. It's good that McCuddy isn't aware that these days, 98 percent of all plays in America—no matter how bad—get standing ovations, probably because people are relieved the thing is finally over and they can get the hell out of that boring theater, and get back to—what else?—aimlessly scrolling their screens.

Let's get to the serious stuff.

Right now my dad's in a coma at the Hamptons Animal Hospital. This is something Billy and me are living with night and day. We gotta have hope. Hope that one day he'll wake up and be OK. What else can we do?

Andy was still sailing near Bimini when Virtual Andy conveyed the entire story of what went down at Blatterman's. It was initially reported that my dad, Rocky, was dead, so Andy, Mr. Excitable, immediately called the Sherman Oaks cloning institute, where he's a partner. He'd taken DNA samples of all of us back in his apartment the day we showed up. As I write this, scientists are attempting to clone my dad. OK, great, right? But the thing is, Bud is saying he wants to adopt my dad. This means I could end up raising my father.

What's next is a touch personal. Daisy had our puppy.

Before I left our house in Thomasville for the stay at Andy's, I'd had a last encounter with her. It was supposed to be an "OK, let's just say goodbye" meeting. One thing led to another, and somehow Daisy and I had an anger screw. I don't know what you humans call these things when people who're tormenting each other somehow rise to a level of passion in the midst of it all and do "the deed." I'm calling what happened an anger screw. We both take responsibility.

When Bud heard this news from Buffy, he immediately asked if we could have it. Buffy said yes, she'd love for us to have little Tippy. She named our puppy Tippy 'cause he's got black tips at the ends of both ears. Let me tell you right now, no son of mine's going to be named Tippy.

I don't know how this is gonna actually play out for me. Everything you introduce to your life adds a layer of complexity. It appears I'm facing a future where I could be simultaneously raising both my father and my son, with all of us crammed into my orange doghouse. Maybe I shoulda gotten that junior one-bedroom doghouse that Daisy always wanted.

Like all hardworking humans with families, I'm wondering how I'll handle work-life balance. Dr. Judy Kahill's given up sex therapy for family counseling. If it wasn't for that perfume of hers, I'd make an appointment.

Bud and Lombardo are closer than ever to finally buyin' the station from Sol "The Old Swede" Silverman. Sol's loving wife, Ruth, is urging him to cash out so that they can travel and more fully enjoy their life in the Silver Singles Hyperactive Community in Florida.

The Old Swede's happy. His daughter Shoshana's finally settled down for a domestic life when she's not workin' in Vegas. She and the Man of a Thousand Paychecks bought a house in Malibu. My brother Oswald's spending most days gleefully playing with their neighbor. Funny how things work out sometimes, isn't it? Their condo is right next to Gary Busey's beach house.

If Bud ends up half-owning the station, it'll mean a lot more work for me. On top of that, I might be getting a film offer that would mean travel and major distractions from the important duties of fatherhood and family. Leslie Davis wants to cast me in a movie, and there's a good part for Bud, too. It's a big Hollywood production. We'd get to stay in a bungalow at The Beverly Hills Hotel. But somehow, I can't see Bud trying to housebreak his new puppies on the hotel's lawn with thirty people in the valet line cheering him on.

Anyway, career-wise, I got a good feeling about this possible movie. It's a sci-fi thriller set way in the future. I'd be playing the leader of a pack of dogs that somehow have survived the nuclear devastation of Earth. The story pits us dogs against the descendants of the only Americans who've survived—they're alive because before starting World War III, Putin ordered the installation of an anti-radiation laser shield to protect the posh Florida resort where the only Americans he wanted to save were living. The film is set on a bleak planet Earth many centuries later.

The title?

Planet of the Trumps.

There's no end to this stuff, folks.

Will you ever hear from me again? Don't know. Mr. Boggs and I just might have another book in us. It depends on how things go for Bud and me. Maybe I'll be back; maybe not. Who knows where time and tide will take us?

The main thing is, thanks for reading my story. We hope you've had a few laughs.

Let's pause there...

Your pal,

SPIKE

"You will be remembered by the tracks you leave."

Acknowledgments

Spike and I give special thanks to Trevor Boggs, Jane Rothchild, Barry Dougherty, and Jeff Leibowitz for their help, support, and dog bones.

About the Author

Bill Boggs is an Emmy Award–winning TV talk show host, producer, and author who began his career in comedy. His books include the comic novel, *The Adventures of Spike the Wonder Dog*, a self-help book, *Got What It Takes?*, and *At First Sight*, a love story optioned by Hollywood.

Photo by Brent Scheneman

His TV credits include the long-running *Midday Live* out of New York City and programs on Food Network, PBS, CBS, NBC, ABC, ESPN, Travel Channel, and Showtime. He served as the executive producer of the groundbreaking *The Morton Downey Jr. Show* and was the co-creator and host of the syndicated series *Comedy Tonight*.

BillBoggsTV on YouTube features hundreds of Bill's interviews with some of the most notable personalities of our time. He lives on the tranquil island of Manhattan in East Hampton and Palm Beach with longtime girlfriend, "Lady Jane."

His website: BillBoggs.com

Follow him on Instagram @RealBillBoggs